Dear Readers:

When GOD DON'T LIKE UGLY was published in October 2000, I prayed that it would be a success. Thanks to you, my prayers have been answered many times over. I hope you all enjoyed reading it as much as I enjoyed writing it.

I wish that I could thank each and every one of the book clubs personally for their contributions to the success of this book. However, the list is too long (thank God).

I am especially grateful for the tons of e-mail messages that so many of you took the time to send. Your feedback was extremely important. It was because of your questions, suggestions, comments, and even your criticisms that I decided to write a sequel. Annette Goode, Rhoda Nelson, Scary Mary, and Pee Wee are characters that stayed with me long after their story ended.

The sequel that so many of you demanded, GOD STILL DON'T LIKE UGLY, will be available September 2003.

I sincerely appreciate your support.

Mary Monroe

Mary Monroe

GOD DON'T LIKE UGLY

MARY MONROE

KENSINGTON PUBLISHING CORP.
http://www.kensingtonbooks.com

KENSINGTON BOOKS are published by

Kensington Publishing Corp.
850 Third Avenue
New York, NY 10022

ISBN 1-57566-607-3

First Kensington Trade Paperback Printing: October, 2000
40 39 38 37 36 35 34 33 32 31

Printed in the United States of America

Dedicated to Ocie and G.W. Bonner

ACKNOWLEDGMENTS

Thanks to the following:

Robin Givens, whose interest in this story, when it was a screenplay for her called *Girlfriend,* kept me from tossing it onto that *huge* pile of rejected manuscripts I now use as a weight-lifting device.

Sheila Cunningham Sims, Heather King, and David Akamine—dinner and drinks are on me!

I greatly appreciate the help and advice I received from my former agents, Charlotte Sheedy and Joseph Vallely.

I am very grateful that this novel fell into the hands of my super agent, Andrew Stuart, whose encouraging telephone calls and letters always came at the right time.

Special thanks to my editor, Karen Thomas, whose expertise and patience finally gave this book the chance it deserves.

To the crew at the New Century Theater in San Francisco, don't forget Pretty Black.

CHAPTER 1

To this day I don't know exactly where Mr. Boatwright came from. He slid into my life one dark miserable day in October 1956, when I was six years old. I arrived home from school and there he was, decked out in a fleecy white suit and a lopsided fedora. He was grinning all over the place as he removed his musty things from a large military bag and placed them on our already cluttered living-room floor. His pointed-toed shoes lined up in our hallway looked like a row of little missiles.

"Who are you?" I asked, eyeing him suspiciously.

He looked about a hundred years old. I stayed close to the door and kept my hand on the doorknob, ready to run if I had to. First, he looked me up and down, bobbing his head like a rooster. A lot of people did that the first time they saw me. I was probably the only first grader in Ohio who weighed almost as much as an adult. Suddenly, and for a brief moment, I suspected and hoped that he was the grandfather I had never met. He was a heavyset man with copper-colored skin and sparkling brown eyes that looked out of place on his wide, flat, heavily lined face. His lips were thin for a Black man. I looked around for Mama. She appeared within seconds with a smile on her face that stretched from one side to the other. She stopped in the middle of the floor and started wiping her flour-covered hands on her crisp white apron. Standing close to the man, I could see that he was not much taller than Mama and she was only five-foot-two.

"Annette, this here is Brother Boatwright. He fixin' to move in with us," Mama informed me.

Stunned, I looked from her to him then back to her. "Is this my granddaddy?" I asked. My heart was beating about a mile a minute.

"No." Mama chuckled. "You ain't got no grandfolks no more. Brother Boatwright is just another brother in need of a place to live."

"He's just a strange man?" I gasped, disappointed. I was the only kid I knew who didn't have grandparents to visit and expect gifts and money from. I tightened my grip on the doorknob.

"No, he ain't no strange man!" I could tell that Mama was getting frustrated with me by the way she narrowed her eyes and jerked her head from side to side when she talked. "Him and Reverend Snipes go waaaaaay back," she told me, waving her hand dramatically. I did not want some strange old man, especially one that might start bossing me around, invading the space I shared with Mama.

"Oh," I mumbled. I let go of the doorknob and moved closer to Mama. "Is he going to sleep with you like a husband, Mama?" I asked anxiously. I had been praying for Mama to get married again and have a baby sister or brother for me to boss around. I rolled my eyes at the man. The mean look I gave him upset him, and I was glad. A puppy-dog expression replaced his annoying grin, but I didn't care.

"Don't you never disrespect Brother Boatwright like that again, Bride of Satan," Mama hissed. There was a look of embarrassment on her face as she pulled me into a corner. "Sleep with me? Brother Boatwright is a man of God." Mama turned to the old man with another smile, and continued, "Brother Boatwright, you arrived right on time. I know you know your Bible. You see the mess I got on my hands? This young'n is out of control. We don't keep a eye on her, next time we look up, she'll be robbin' banks or tryin' to shoot President Eisenhower."

I returned to Mr. Boatwright and apologized. He smiled and tickled all three of my chins. His smile seemed empty and false. There was sweat all over his face, and it wasn't even hot in our house. He removed a flat box of Anacin pills from his shirt pocket and rapidly gobbled up a handful.

"Ain't it the truth, Sister Goode. I'm gwine to keep both my eyes on this girl! Praise the Lord!" he shrieked, nodding for emphasis. I jumped almost a foot off the floor. The old man and Mama laughed.

"Mama . . ." I started.

"He walks with Jesus so he say that sometime when he get excited,"

Mama explained. I didn't care how holy he was. The way he was looking at me, making me feel like I was something good to eat, I should have known he was up to something nasty even then. "Like I said, Brother Boatwright and the Reverend Snipes, they go waaaaaay back. He get a disability check every month from the white folks so he goin' to he'p us pay our bills. And he just loves to dust and mop and sweep and cook."

"You got any kids I can play with, Mr. Boatwright?" I had to force myself, but I managed a smile.

"I sure ain't. But if I did, I declare, I'd want me a little gal just like you. You just as thick and fine as you wanna be. I bet you can pull a plow by yourself. I bet you can tear down a house by yourself!" he exclaimed, squeezing my arm.

His statements frightened me, as they would have any other lazy child. I went out of my way to get out of doing housework and any other chores, let alone something as strenuous as pulling plows and tearing down houses. He'd be the type to boss me around like I was a slave, I thought. He'd have me washing dishes, mopping, dusting— things Mama had always done while I lounged on the couch watching television and nibbling on snacks. I sensed a future filled with doom and despair.

Mama turned to me, and a serious look appeared on her face. When she folded her arms and started tapping her toe, I took a few steps back. "God led Brother Boatwright to us for a reason. In addition to providin' you some spiritual guidance, you just now heard him agree to keep both his eyes on you while I am at work. You better mind him and do *everythin'* he tell you to do. Do you hear me?" Mama snarled, stabbing me in the chest with her finger.

"Yes, Ma'am." I sighed with defeat.

Mama then turned to the old man, and continued, "Brother Boatwright, you got my permission rightcheer and now to coldcock this numskull whenever you feel she need it."

"OK, Sister Goode," he said eagerly. I could smell his sour breath from a foot away. Looking into his terrible eyes, I was certain he was insane. I knew then that my life would never be the same again.

CHAPTER 2

Other than Mama, I didn't have any other relatives in Richland, Ohio. According to her, my grandparents on both sides were dead. I had just a few other distant relatives scattered throughout the South that I had never met. The only one Mama still communicated with was her older sister Berneice, who lived in Florida, near Miami, where we had come from. When both of her parents died within weeks of one another when she was sixteen, Mama married my daddy out of desperation. After six miscarriages, she gave birth to me at thirty-four.

Mama and I looked a lot alike, but she was called pretty, I was not. We had the same high cheekbones and heart-shaped face with small nose, bow-shaped lips, lashes so long and black they belonged on a doll, and beauty mark on the right side, just above our lip. People called her beauty mark a mole. They called mine a wart. Not only was Mama light-skinned, she was slim. Just being light was enough by Black standards for her to be considered attractive. Being slim was icing on the cake. No matter how pretty I actually was, people made it clear I was too dark and too fat. My short kinky hair was a crown of thorns. Black people with dark skin were usually looked down upon by light-skinned Black people. I was certainly no exception. When a light-skinned, pretty little girl from our church died, I overheard one of the church ushers say, "too bad it wasn't that gnome Annette." A knife in my heart couldn't have hurt me more.

Because of the things I'd already experienced, I could remember back to when I was three. Daddy was still around then. Like a lot of Black folks in south Florida, we didn't have much. We lived in shacks, wore secondhand clothes, and moved often enough that we always managed to stay a few steps ahead of our bill collectors and the Klan. We bought a lot of stuff on credit that we couldn't always pay for, like food, medicine, and every now and then a luxury item like a Christmas gift or something for one of our birthdays.

Daddy was an outspoken man who stood up in church and at political rallies and cursed the way white folks were treating us. "With God's help, we ain't goin' to put up with Jim Crow the rest of our lives!" he used to shout, standing on a podium waving our shabby Bible. News about his arrogance always reached the Klan, and he received veiled threats too often for his comfort. That's the main reason we roamed around like gypsies. I remember a very close call one night. While we were attending a revival somebody threw a firebomb in the front window of our house. We got home just in time to grab the shopping bags and battered suitcases we kept our belongings in. That same night we hid in a church member's barn until Daddy arranged for somebody to drive us to a safer part of town, where we stayed in another shack until we had to flee again.

Daddy was a migrant laborer and worked in the nearby fields six days a week. Mama cleaned and cooked for rich white folks in Miami two days a week. The year was 1954, and segregation was a way of life. "I ain't about to set in the back of nobody's bus," Mama often said. Mama didn't even bother trying to ride in cabs, so we usually walked or hitched a ride on somebody's mule-wagon to her jobs and everywhere else we went. She would prepare us a few sandwiches, usually sweet potato or baloney, and we would leave the house early in the morning right after Daddy did. Those walks were long and hard, and even though the Florida sand was soft, my feet developed calluses that remained with me for years.

I liked going to work with Mama. It made me feel grown-up and important. Rather than stand around all day waiting for Mama to finish her duties, I earned a few cents for myself doing odd jobs, like walking and bathing a dog or baby-sitting some old person. My favorite responsibility was sitting on the front porch of a large red house with an elderly Italian woman. Her name was Rosa Piaz and she was more than a hundred years old. Her daddy had owned slaves, and her mind was so far gone she thought I was one. "Go get me some goobers,

Spooky," she used to tell me. I'd sneak into the house for goobers and whatever else I could find to nibble on. My job was to fan her and empty her spittoon. She dipped a lot of snuff, so I was forever running around emptying spit. When nobody was looking, the old woman and I threw rocks at moving cars. When I made her mad, like the time I couldn't find any more rocks for us to throw, she threatened, "You lazy heifer! I ought to sell you to one of them cane jockeys—make a field hand outta you!" When she made me mad I waited until she went to sleep, then I pinched her flabby neck. I knew the woman was senile, so I just hid my face and laughed every time she threatened to have me sold. A minute later, we'd be friends again, chasing some of the kids in the fancy white neighborhood where Miss Rosa lived with switches. One time Mama caught us. She grabbed my arm and shook me so hard my whole body ached. "Girl, Miss Rosa can do whatever she want. She white. But *you* can't be messin' with no *white* kids!" Mama and Daddy had me believing we were as good as anybody else, so it confused me when I got scolded for sassing or upsetting somebody white.

Every time I got comfortable in a particular situation, we moved and I had to start all over again. Our rootless existence was the only life I had ever known. I was used to it, but I didn't like it. It made me feel like I was different from other kids in a way I didn't understand, and it made me feel like I didn't belong anywhere.

My favorite time during that period was when we lived at the bottom of a hill off of a dirt road in a rural section of Miami called Hanley. Our house had a living room, a kitchen, and one bedroom. I liked it because we were so close to the woods that squirrels and other creatures wandered into our backyard to eat out of my hand.

The only furniture we had was a stove with no legs and an icebox that shook so much we kept it unplugged most of the time. We had a table in the kitchen but just one chair. Mama and Daddy took turns sitting on the chair. There were two tree stumps at the table that we used in place of chairs. I always had to sit on the smaller one. In the living room we had a couch with a floral design. It was clean and comfortable, but both arms were about to fall off. Things like coffee tables and lamps were not only luxury items but cumbersome. When we left a place it was usually in such a hurry we only left with what we could carry.

We slept on the bedroom floor in our clothes until a preacher gave us a stained mattress, a ripped sheet, and a blanket that was so old and worn you could see through it. We ate off of cracked plates or out of cans most of the time and drank water from a spring a few yards from the house. We had one forty-watt lightbulb that we carried from room to room and hung naked from an extension cord. When it died, Mama brought home a coal-oil lamp she had found along the side of the road. "God sure is good," she swooned, shaking the rusty, cracked lamp in my face.

On the days that Mama didn't work, she was busy sewing, cooking, and washing our clothes by hand with homemade soap. There were no kids my age close enough for me to play with, so I spent most of my time running around with squirrels. One with a white paw got so friendly with me he was bold enough to climb up on our back porch and scratch the door. Mama would chase him away with a whisk broom. Daddy always petted the squirrel, and yelled, "Annette, you got company!"

Mama and all the other Black women I knew made soup and stew out of most of the wild creatures that inhabited the woods, even snakes. When Mama suddenly started getting too friendly with my squirrel, petting and feeding it, commenting on how plump he was, I got scared. The week before at a church dinner, one of the sisters brought a big bowl of some type of mysterious meat floating in fiery red sauce. It was delicious. I had two helpings. "Your girl sure is lappin' up that squirrel soup," the sister commented. I ducked out of the church, ran behind a tree in the back, and vomited, praying that I had not eaten the squirrel I had become so attached to. When we got home, it was too dark for me to look for my squirrel. But the next morning he came to the back door. Mama and Daddy were still eating breakfast. I took the squirrel deep into the woods and turned him loose. I never saw him again, and when other squirrels ended up in a bowl on our dinner table, I refused to eat any, afraid it might be my former pet.

Daddy returned from the fields around the same time every evening, just before it got dark, no matter where we lived. Every evening I would sit on the front porch and wait for him like a spider. He brought home fruit for me, and sometimes discarded toys he found along the road. My eyes would light up when I spotted him struggling to make it the rest of the way home from the main road. I would jump up from my spot and run and leap into his arms, almost knocking him down. "Girl, can't you see how tired I am," he used to scold, all the while helping me climb onto his back. Then he would carry me back to the house. The first thing he would do was check with Mama to see if it was time for us to move again. I was glad every time Mama said, "Not yet, Frank. Not yet."

We didn't have a radio or a television. They were two of the many luxuries we didn't allow ourselves to think about owning. That's why we didn't know about the tornado coming one Sunday after we had come home from church. The day had started out like any other summer day in Florida—hot, dusty and humid. We got up, peeped out the windows, and later that evening we walked two miles to a Baptist church across the main highway. It was during the sermon when the wind started whistling, and it didn't seem as hot as before. "Mama, it's going to rain," I whispered, sitting between her and Daddy on a wobbly bench near the back of the crowded little country church. "Shhhhh!" was all she said, then she went back to shouting, "Amen," like everybody else. I just hoped that we would get home before the rain started. We didn't have anything to protect us from it and rain—unless you had naturally straight hair—was considered one of a Black females worst enemies. I hated when Mama had to straighten my hair with a hot comb, what little bit I had.

After we arrived home from church, Mama started cooking, and I followed Daddy to a nearby lake, where he fished for part of our supper. The lake contained fish, crawdaddies, crabs, and things I couldn't identify. Everything in the lake was free, and often it was all we had to eat. We just had to catch it.

"Don't you get too close to that water, girl," Daddy advised. "You know I ain't got the strength to jump in there after you."

"All right, Daddy." I smiled. By then, not only was the wind howling, it was darker than usual for early evening. I guess that's why I was not doing what I usually did when I was at the lake, running up and down the bank beating bushes with a stick and throwing rocks in the water. Instead, I sat down on the ground next to Daddy and placed my head against his chest. I liked being so close to him. I could feel the heat his body generated, and I could even hear and feel his heart beating like a drum.

When he was not looking, I stared at the side of his face. Compared to most of the other men I knew, he was good-looking. He had big black slanted eyes, but there was sadness in them. I had the same eyes. There were noticeable lines on his face and around his mouth. His nose reminded me of the noses I saw on some of the Indians in the area, big and hawklike, but still attractive. He had said something about having Indian blood. One of Daddy's front teeth was missing. A white policeman had knocked it out with a billy club when Daddy sassed him. You hardly noticed the missing tooth when he talked or smiled because he had a thick mustache. He was tall and powerfully built, and dark brown like me. I didn't know how old he was, but his hair was thin and starting to turn gray.

The fish were not biting much, so Daddy and I left the lake after he had caught only two catfish. Mama cleaned them, fried them, and we feasted on the fish, some pork, and yams and greens from a garden Mama had around the side of our house. It had started raining, and the wind was stronger. Our little house was shaking and rattling so much our table wouldn't stay still.

"It's a good thing I didn't hang out them clothes like I had planned." Mama sighed, looking toward the kitchen window. Mama frowned at me and let out her breath. "Annette, stop chewin' so loud." She paused for a moment, then turned to Daddy. He seemed to be worried about something. He was eating real slow and staring at the wall. I just figured he was concerned about the storm. When it rained too much, he couldn't work in the fields. And when he didn't work, he didn't get paid. Less money meant less of everything, and we were already on the poverty level. "What's wrong with you, Mr. Goode?" Mama asked. Daddy's first name was Frank, but I only heard her use it when she was mad at him or when she was serious. Daddy didn't answer right away, he just kept staring at that wall.

"Maybe the cat got his tongue," I suggested. Not only did I get a cold, hard stare from both of them but Mama shoved a pig foot into my mouth. That's what they usually did when they wanted to silence me. It was no wonder food became my "drug" of choice.

Before Daddy could respond, Mama felt his forehead. "You want a dose of cod liver oil or some homebrew?" she asked.

Daddy just shook his head, and said, "No, I'm all right. We'll talk after the storm." He was talking to Mama but looking at me. My first thought was Daddy was going to talk to Mama about another move.

He pushed his plate away, then got up from the table and went to sit on a footstool in the living room and started looking out the window.

"What's the matter with him?" I wanted to know.

Daddy was a strong man. Not just physically, but he had a strong personality. Unlike some of the Black men I knew, Daddy didn't back down from white folks. I used to see men bigger than he was cowering nervously and keeping their eyes on the ground when talking to white folks. Daddy looked white folks straight in the eye when he talked to them, and when white folks called him "uncle" or "boy" he corrected them, and said firmly, "My name is Mr. Goode."

"Hush up," Mama said to me. Like an afterthought, she grabbed another pig foot and aimed it at my mouth. When she saw I was still gnawing on the first one, she pressed her lips together, shrugged, and put the pig foot back in the bowl in the middle of the table.

The rain was really coming down by then, and it was dark enough for Mama to light the lamp so she could sit in the living room and sew. She occupied the couch, and I sat on the floor next to Daddy on his footstool. Just a few minutes later, the tornado came roaring at us like a runaway train.

Nobody said anything, but we all knew what to do. Mama blew out the lamp, grabbed me by the arm, and we followed Daddy into the bedroom, where we all crawled under the blanket on the mattress and waited. The hardest part was not knowing if we were waiting to live or waiting to die. Tornadoes were tricky. One could destroy everything in its path including people's lives and dreams, it could tease then move on to another area or it could suddenly cease. This storm was a teaser. Our house shook violently one moment, then was still the next. The window on the side of the bed exploded, and most of the glass ended up on the mattress with us. Mama prayed, Daddy cussed. I didn't do anything but lie there and cling to my daddy. He had one arm around me and one around Mama. The storm gave the house a real hard jolt, so hard Daddy stopped cussing and started praying along with Mama. God must have been listening because not long after that the storm ceased. By then it was morning.

The next morning we cleaned up the glass, then checked to see how much damage we had to deal with. Miraculously, our house was still intact. But our backyard outhouse was gone. We found out later that a shack occupied by an old Seminole Indian man had been relocated to a field in the next county with the old man still in it, dead.

Somebody's frantic and confused hog ended up in our backyard, but ran into the woods as soon as it saw our faces.

Daddy put on his work clothes, and Mama fixed breakfast like it was just another day. But it was not just another day. He said he didn't have time to eat. Instead he started walking around the living room like he was nervous and glancing out the window every few minutes.

He looked at me a long time standing in the middle of the floor watching him. Suddenly Daddy left the room and returned a few minutes later holding one of our shopping bags in one hand and a lunch bag bulging with baloney sandwiches in the other. "Annette, you better be good," he said in a low voice. He started walking toward the door but turned around and ran over and kissed me on the forehead.

"Daddy, what's the matter?" I wanted to know. I was puzzled and afraid when Daddy didn't answer me. Mama followed him out the door, and I heard them arguing on the front porch. I couldn't tell what they were talking about, but both of them were cussing.

I ducked back into the kitchen, grabbed a biscuit, then ran to the living-room door in time to see a white woman in a dusty green car drive down the hill toward our house. Daddy jumped in the car while it was still moving. I stood on the front porch next to Mama, watching the car turn around and shoot back up the hill.

"Mama, who was that white woman? Is she giving Daddy a ride to work today?" I asked with my mouth full.

"Finish your biscuit, girl," Mama said tiredly. Then she went to the kitchen and started sweeping and crying. We spent most of the day cleaning up the mess the tornado had left behind. She kept sweeping, wiping, and cleaning the same spots over and over, and yelling at me every time I tried to get her to tell me why she was crying. "You ain't nothin' but a child! You don't know nothin' about nothin'!" she insisted. "Get that broom yonder and get busy."

I did so much sweeping that day my arms got sore. Later, Mama started sewing on a quilt she was making for a lady at church. When she ran out of things to do, she went to the mattress and fell facedown and cried some more.

The days seemed so long when Mama and I didn't go to her work. With no friends and hardly any toys, there was not much for me to do but eat. I left the bedroom and went to the kitchen to finish off a blackberry pie. After I felt good and stuffed, I went back to the bedroom.

"Mama, what's the matter?" I asked again. I sat on the edge of the mattress and patted Mama's trembling leg. The only other times I had seen her cry was when we were running from the Klan. "The Kluxes coming again?"

"Go to the yard and see if the storm messed up my garden," she ordered. Her eyes were red and so swollen she looked like she had been beaten. "Lickety-split!" She dismissed me with a wave toward the door. I ran to check on the garden and returned to the bedroom within minutes.

"It's got a bunch of nasty old water in it, and the onions popped up out of the ground. The greens and everything else look all right though," I reported.

"Good. We'll still have somethin' to nibble. Least 'til I can figure out what to do," she sniffed, smoothing her hair back with her hand. She had cried so much there was a spot on the bed that was soaked with her tears.

"Mama, what's the matter? We moving again?" I attempted to re-join her on the mattress, but she pushed me away with her ashy bare foot.

"Go in the room yonder and find somethin' to do, girl."

"Ma'am?"

"Read the Bible," Mama growled.

I didn't know how to read yet, but I still fished out our old Bible with no covers from one of the shopping bags in a corner in our living room. The pictures were interesting enough to keep me occupied for a while. When I went back to the bedroom Mama had closed the door. I put my ear to it and could hear her crying again.

At my usual time of the day, when the sun began to disappear, I went to sit on the front-porch steps to wait for Daddy to come drag-ging down the hill. To pass time, I got up every few minutes to stir a stick around in some of the puddles still in our front yard.

When he didn't come home at the time he should have, I went in to eat with Mama. It was the first time we'd eaten dinner without Daddy. I didn't even bother trying to pry any information out of Mama anymore. Her eyes were even redder by then. She was not eat-ing. She just kept staring at the wall and pushing beans and neck-bones around on her plate.

I took my plate with what was left on it and went back to the porch steps to finish eating. When it got dark enough for the lamp, Mama came to the door and poked her head out. "Annette, carry that plate in the kitchen and get ready for bed," she told me.

"But I have to wait for Daddy—"

"Your daddy gone!" she snapped, waving both arms. She already had on her nightgown. "Now, go get in your sleepers and get to bed like I told you. And wash that nasty plate."

"Daddy gone where?" I whimpered. My voice trembled as I stumbled into the house. I didn't believe what I was hearing. My daddy would not just run off and leave us! "Where he go and didn't take us? When he gonna come back to get us?" I choked.

"Your daddy's a good man in a whole lot of ways. But like all of us, he ain't perfect. He had weaknesses of the flesh. One was white women. Before you was born I was hearin' about him and this white woman and her money. He just got fed up and tired of stressin' over havin' such a hard life and rilin' them Kluxes. When this hussy was ready to take him, he was ready to be took," Mama said sadly. "Things like this happen every day." She let out a long sigh and shook her head. There were tears in her eyes, but she managed a weak smile. "We'll be fine. Colored women stronger than colored men anyway, you'll see. Now—like I said, get ready for bed before I get my switch." Mama hugged me and kissed me on the cheek but she still thumped the back of my head with her fingers.

I washed my plate, dried it with the tail of my flour-sack smock, and put it on top of the ones Mama had already washed and set on the counter. My head felt like it was going to explode I had so many questions in it that needed to be answered. The only thing I knew was that my daddy was gone, and he had left us with a white woman in a green car.

After we went to bed Mama cried in her sleep. With no glass in the window, bugs, mosquitoes, and moths flew in and out of our bedroom. There was just enough moonlight for me to see a hoot owl fly up and perch on the sill. I kept my eyes on the owl until I finally fell asleep. When I got up the next morning, the owl was gone and Mama was still asleep. I got dressed and went to sit on the front-porch steps, hoping to see Daddy walking down the hill. After what seemed like an eternity, Mama came out on the porch holding a gray-and-brown clay jug Daddy used to drink from. It was where he kept moonshine he got from a man who lived on the other side of the lake. "We ain't never goin' to see Frank no more," Mama told me again. I let out a long painful sigh. This time I really believed her.

Immediately, our lives changed dramatically. Mama started working five days a week instead of two, and we had to hide from even more bill collectors. One day, about two weeks after Daddy's departure, Mama was in the kitchen rolling out some dough to make dumplings. I was sitting on the footstool looking out the living-room window when another car pulled up in the yard. It was a green car. For a minute I thought it was the white woman bringing my daddy home. I gasped and leaned my head out the window, already grinning and waving. Before I could get too excited, a scowling white man in a black suit leaped out and rushed toward the house carrying a briefcase.

"Mama, here come that old mean Raleigh man walking real fast!" I yelled over my shoulder. Raleigh men were individuals, usually white men, who patrolled the rural areas in cars loaded down with various items that they sold to people like us on credit. A month earlier, Mama had purchased a straightening comb and a mirror, some work shoes for Daddy, and two pairs of pedal pushers and some peanut brittle for me. The first time the man came to collect, she told him, "Come back Tuesday." On Tuesday she told him, "I meant *next* Tuesday." That Tuesday it was, "Come back on Friday." This was his sixth visit, and we still had not paid him.

"Oh shit!" Mama wailed. I heard her run across the floor. "Tell him I'm at the store in town, and you don't know when I'll be back!" Then she fell down to the floor behind the living-room couch.

"Where is Gussie Mae?" The man started talking before he even got in the house. Before I could get off the footstool, he had snatched open the screen door and marched in.

"She gone to the store in town to get some buttermilk," I said nervously, rising.

"Store, huh?" The man started looking around the room, twitching his eyes and screwing up his lips. I got even more nervous when he started tapping his foot. "Well the next time she go to the store, tell her to carry her feet with her." Then he left, slamming the screen door so hard the footstool fell over. I turned around just in time to see Mama's feet sticking out from behind the couch before she leaped up and started brushing off her sleeveless gray-cotton dress.

Mama made some baloney sandwiches, we packed our clothes that night, and left behind our broken-down furniture and that lumpy mattress. We spent the next few days eating baloney sandwiches and sleeping on a couch in the house of a lady from our church. We lived like that for three weeks, roaming from one church member's house to another until we ran out of people willing to put us up. I felt more adrift than ever. Mama and I got on our knees and prayed harder than we usually did. By the end of the month we had found a place to live. "God done come through again," Mama sobbed. We moved into a dank room in a run-down boardinghouse in one of Miami's worst neighborhoods. The windows had plastic curtains you could see through, and there was a sink in a corner with a faucet that never stopped dripping. There was nothing else in the room. It reminded me of a prison cell I'd seen in a movie on television at one of the white women's houses. Mama got us a hot plate, a pan, and a blanket from a secondhand store. We couldn't buy any food that needed to be refrigerated. When we did, we had to eat it all up the same day.

We ate our best meals behind the backs of the white women Mama worked for. One afternoon, peeping out of one of those women's kitchen windows and talking with her mouth full, Mama told me, "Annette, hurry and finish that filet mignon steak before old lady Brooks come home! Wipe that grease off your mouth! Wrap up a few chunks of that good meat and slip 'em into our shoppin' bag! Grab a loaf of French bread from the pantry! Grab them chicken wings yonder!" Whatever I managed to hide in our shopping bag, I usually ate behind Mama's back. Every time I did that, she thumped the side of my head with her fingers and yelled at me all the way home. "You greedy little pig! For bein' so *hardheaded,* God's goin' to chastise you and make you spend your life trapped in a body big as a moose." Because of my hard head, our meals at the boardinghouse were usually baloney and stale bread, grits, some greasy meat, and greens.

The boardinghouse had just one bathroom for the two floors of tenants. It was always either occupied, too filthy and smelly (people would use the toilet and not flush it), or out of order. We used an empty lard bucket that I had to empty every morning for a toilet. We heated water in the pan on the hot plate and bathed in the sink in the corner.

"Mama, we poor?" I asked, several weeks after we'd left the house we shared with Daddy.

"Not in the eyes of the Lord," Mama replied.

We were walking home after cleaning and cooking for Mrs. Jacobs, an unpredictable old woman with hair on her chin and breath as foul as cow dung. Of all the white women Mama worked for, the Jacobs woman was the only one I disliked because we never knew what to expect from her. Some days she was nice and would send us home early with extra pay and leftover food. When she was in a real good mood, she'd have her chauffeur ride us home. When she was not in a good mood, usually when she was mad at her husband or one of her children, she treated us like trash. She would throw away good food rather than give it to us, but we'd always fish it out when she wasn't looking. She suffered with severe flatulence and would pass gas right in front of us and not say excuse me. As soon as she entered a room, Mama stopped whatever she was doing and opened a window. One particular day, right after her husband had slapped her, she marched into the kitchen where Mama was sitting at the table shelling some crowder peas. I was glad all the windows in the kitchen were already open because the old woman started farting right away. I was standing next to Mama with both my hands full of peas. Mrs. Jacobs raised her cane and shook it at Mama, and roared, "Gussie Mae, you get back in that bathroom and shine that commode like I told you! Put some elbow grease on it!" Mama looked up at her, and said, "I just finished shinin' the commode, Mrs. Jacobs." Still farting, the old woman whacked my mama across her back so hard Mama fell out of her chair. I was horrified. "You leave my mama alone—you old heifer!" I screamed. I ran around the table and bit Mrs. Jacobs on the leg so hard she bled. That was the only job Mama ever got fired from. I expected Mama to yell and scream at me all the way back to the boardinghouse, then whup me once we got there. "I was sick of slavin' for that fartin' old witch anyway," was all she said on the subject. "God'll take care of us."

Mama bought a newspaper on the way home that day. There was a whole column of domestic jobs advertised. She started working for another white woman two days later, a sweet-smelling woman who hugged me and encouraged me to play with her kids on a swing set in her huge backyard. Mrs. Myers, a woman with eyes like blue marbles and hair the color of carrots, was always nice to us. "Annette, you lookin' mighty spiffy in those blue pedal pushers," she told me one day, handing me a glass of ice-cold orange NeHi pop. "You should have seen me yesterday! I got some green ones just like these!" I exclaimed, grinning so hard my mouth hurt.

Every day after work Mama and I went through trash cans behind restaurants and stores on our way back to the boardinghouse. We often found food that looked like it had not been touched and a few items for our room. I'd even found a pair of shoes, clodhoppers with cleats. They were boys' shoes that were too big and so heavy I dragged my feet. People started looking at me the same way they looked at Mr. James, a man at our church they hauled around in a child's red wagon because he had been born without arms or legs. I hated those damn shoes, but they were better than the ones I'd been wearing, brown moccasins with pins holding them together. With what help we could get from church and God, we survived.

One day I asked my mama, "We happy?"

Mama smiled for the first time in weeks and squeezed my cheek. She wasn't even mad about me eating up some lamb chops Mrs. Myers had given to us. "We got more than the Lord ever had him, and He was happy," she answered.

CHAPTER 3

About a month after we had moved to the Miami boardinghouse, Mama took me to a prayer meeting at a church across town on a dead-end street. A well-known visiting preacher from Jacksonville who promised miracles was the guest speaker. "It's goin' to take a miracle to get us on our feet," Mama muttered to me, as we squeezed onto a bench near the back of the room.

"Could a miracle bring Daddy back to us?" I asked excitedly.

"Only miracle he care about these days got yella hair and blue eyes!" Mama snapped, rolling her eyes at me.

"You mean that white lady? Can't we just go to her house and tell him to come home?"

"Girl . . . you so young." Mama sighed.

The small church, lighted by coal-oil lamps, was packed with people needing the Lord's special attention. There were people in wheelchairs, people walking with canes, a blind man, and people slobbering and babbling. I got restless and ran to the bathroom every few minutes. I ignored the spry little Reverend Mason skipping all over the stage with his eyes closed, his head and hands shaking, ordering people to "Lay down that cane! Get your rump out that wheelchair!" Two hours into the revival, the only miracle performed so far was a man spitting out a cancer (it looked like a piece of raw liver) after Reverend Mason massaged his shoulders, and hollered, "Heal yourself, brother!"

As far as Mama was concerned we received our miracle that night, too. The preacher had massaged our shoulders so hard mine were throbbing. Our miracle came in the guise of a woman. I had seen her staring at me, shaking her head as I dragged myself up and down the aisle. When the meeting ended, this curious woman, several years older than Mama, who at the time was thirty-eight, came up to us and placed her hand on Mama's shoulder, and said, "Sister, I'm gwine to pray for your girl. How long she been had polio?"

Mama draped her arms around my shoulder, and told the woman, "Oh she ain't got no polio. She just clumsy. It's them brogans on her feet. And you can see she eat like a workin' man," Mama said apologetically.

The woman looked at the dusty clodhoppers on my feet, then made a sucking noise with her teeth. "Oh. Well I'm gwine to pray for her anyway. I came to the meetin' this evenin' to pray for my girl Mott. She mentally limited, and I got her in a home for now."

Mama touched the woman's arm, and told her, "I'll pray for your girl, too."

The woman started visiting us at the boardinghouse, bringing us food and clothes. I kissed her on the neck when she brought me a pair of black patent leather shoes to wear to church and a pair of red tennis shoes to play in. This mysterious woman quickly became Mama's best friend. Her name was Mary. Everybody called her Scary Mary, a nickname a frightened boyfriend she had battered had given to her.

Within a week we moved in with her and the two nice ladies who lived with her. She lived in a big redbrick house behind the church that had sponsored the prayer meeting.

Her house was as grand as any of the white women's houses we'd cleaned. Upstairs and down, the rooms had wallpaper with swans, some floating on a pond, some flying. Her furry brown-and-white furniture not only matched, it was so clean it looked new. She had a fireplace in her living room and great big beige lamps on her cream-colored coffee tables.

Tears appeared in her eyes when Mama showed her the coal-oil lamp we had been using. Mama and I shared Scary Mary's spare bedroom off to the side of the kitchen.

"Is Scary Mary rich?" I asked Mama when she was putting me to bed that first night. She had bathed me in a bathtub for the first time in my life with store-bought soap. I put on some brand-new pink-flannel pajamas with ducks on them that Scary Mary had run out to buy earlier that day. The goose-down pillows on the bed were as big as I was.

"Yep. She rich. She blessed. The good Lord sent her a rich husband with a bad heart," Mama said proudly, with a longing look in her eye, punching the pillows. She rebraided two of my braids that had come undone and kissed me long and hard on the cheek.

"There is rich colored men?" I gasped.

Mama laughed and tapped my head. "There ain't no such a thing. One of her husbands was a rich white man from Ohio, a old banker she met when he was on vacation in Miami."

Scary Mary made me wash dishes and sweep and dust a lot, but there were trees in her backyard that I could climb and hide behind and eat the food that I removed from the refrigerator behind her and Mama's backs.

Scary Mary had gone through all the husbands she would ever have by the time we met her. "After my third husband I got so sick of changing my last name, I got me a lawyer to change it to 'X' nice and legal," she told us, adding, "I kept it that way even after a few more." She told us that the day before we met her she had just run off her last husband, a man she had described as a rogue, who was stingy and dull and who only bathed when she made him. She bragged about how easy it was to control a man just by bouncing a rolling pin off his head whenever it was necessary.

The only one she spoke fondly of was the rich white one from Ohio. "My poor beloved old Mr. Blake. It was a cryin' shame he had such a bad heart and dropped dead on me within a year. But, I don't question God," she told us, shaking and staring hungrily at a shot glass full of bourbon.

Scary Mary called herself a Christian. But during those days, with the exception of the Jewish women Mama worked for, I didn't know anybody, Black or white, who was not Christian. Even the Klansmen who had come after us did it in the name of the Lord. Even though Scary Mary was involved in all kinds of shady activities, like any good Southern woman, she knew her Bible. She only missed church when she was in jail. From one of her jealous, busybody female neighbors, we had heard that when Scary Mary was young, she'd supervised a chain gang. After that, she got a job in some kind of underground factory making bombs. Age and a cruel scar that ran from beneath her left eye to beneath her chin had slowed her down.

One day the police raided Scary Mary's house. They charged her with running a whorehouse and selling alcohol without a liquor license and took her off to jail. Mama and I ended up back at the boardinghouse in the same room we had rented before! Scary Mary had to pay a big fine, and they put her on probation. A week later, she moved to Richland, Ohio.

A few days after she got there, she wrote Mama this long convoluted letter in her spidery handwriting telling her how blessed she was because the Lord had led her to such a wonderful place and that we would be better off up there.

"How would you like to move up North?" Mama asked me after reading the letter to me three times.

"Why?" I wanted to know. I didn't know a thing about the state of Ohio, but I loved Florida and didn't want to leave. I had gotten used to the boardinghouse and a girl my age next door named Poochie.

"So we can have a better life. The South is such a savage place for colored folks," Mama explained.

I was tired of relocating, tired of having to get used to new surroundings and new friends. "I'm sick of packing up and moving all over the place, Mama," I protested.

When Mama saw how unhappy the thought of moving again made me, she stopped talking about it for a while even though Scary Mary kept writing letters to Mama bragging about her good life in Ohio. When she started sending us money and pictures of her posing with prosperous-looking men, Mama gave in.

One night she left me alone at the boardinghouse to go use a pay phone across the street. I was in bed when she returned. "Get up and start packin', girl. There's a train at midnight," she informed me.

"Where are we going?" I yawned.

"Scary Mary's goin' to put us up 'til we find a place." Her eyes were wide, and there was such a big smile on her face I knew it would do no good for me to put up a fight.

Three months after Daddy had left us, we slipped off during the night, tiptoeing and whispering because we owed the boardinghouse woman a month's back rent. I cried all the way to the train station.

"What's wrong with you, girl?" Mama snapped, bumping me with her knee.

"I didn't get a chance to say good-bye to Poochie," I sobbed.

"We'll write her a letter soon as we get to Ohio. I ain't goin' to stay in Florida like Mama and Pa and the rest of 'em done and rot workin' for no white folks. I'd rather be buried alive. Colored folks is so un-ambitious," Mama told me, as we approached the train station.

During the fifties, just moving north meant having ambition to a lot of Black people, even though most of them left the fields in Florida to work in the ones in Ohio. Mama considered herself a step above the field workers. She cleaned white folks' houses and cooked and took care of their kids in Florida, and that's what she would end up doing in Ohio. "I praise the Lord every day. Look what He done for me." Mama said things like that a lot. She was so proud of her work.

But I hated the fact that she had to work so much. As soon as she finished cleaning one woman's house, she ran off to clean for an-other or to tend to somebody's spoiled kids.

I used to wonder what white women were good for. Most of the women Mama worked for told her a lot of their business. They all seemed to be having an affair or seeing a therapist. They couldn't clean their own houses or take care of their own kids or even cook. They sounded pretty useless to me. But I had to admit, white women had it made. They had the world at their feet. Oddly enough, I never wanted to be white. Besides, Mama told me white women didn't age as well as Black women.

I slept during most of the long ride north on the segregated train, dreaming about the "white only" water fountains and restaurants we had never been able to enjoy in Florida. Mama had promised me we'd be able to drink and eat wherever we wanted to in Ohio. I woke up off and on just long enough to eat and stare through tear-filled eyes out the train window at the world going by me.

After we had arrived in Richland, Ohio, which was about a hun-dred miles south of Cleveland, we had to walk from the train station to Scary Mary's house because we couldn't get a cab driver who was brave enough to go into that part of town. It took us more than an hour to get there. By then I was so tired and weak I was dizzy. It was the middle of November and so cold I shivered for the first time in my life. When the urge to pee came over me, I had no choice but to run behind a building and do it there. I got hungry again, and Mama stuffed a baloney sandwich in my mouth.

An ominous feeling came over me as soon as me and Mama, hug-ging our tattered suitcases, walked up onto the porch of Scary Mary's shabby old house, a house very much unlike her nice redbrick house in Florida. There was a bullet hole in one of her front-room windows! On the front door next to a wallet-sized, black-and-white picture of

Jesus was a crude sign that said: NO CREDIT, NO PERSONAL CHECKS, NO WEAPONS ALLOWED. Stray dogs, cats, and people were roaming all over the run-down neighborhood. A policeman was sitting in his patrol car on the street sound asleep. We knocked on Scary Mary's door for five minutes before a man leading a drunk woman down the street told us that Scary Mary was in jail.

"But we ain't got nowhere to stay," Mama told the man, dabbing at her eyes with a dingy handkerchief.

I could see that the man was sympathetic. He looked at us and shook his head. Old and shabbily dressed, he didn't look like somebody in a position to help two homeless strangers; he could barely hold up the woman who was falling-down drunk. All he could do was give us the address to the welfare department, but since Mama refused to accept handouts from Uncle Sam, we didn't go there. Instead, we returned to the train station, where I sat alone on a bench in the waiting area for four hours while Mama went to look for work.

"Don't you say nothin' to no strangers," was all she said before she hurried away.

I ran to the window and watched her drag her weary feet down that cold, mean street. A large tear rolled down the side of my face. The tail of her tattered old coat had started to unravel, and her shoes were so old, the heels were completely gone.

Not long after I returned to my seat, a heavily made-up white woman wearing a floppy hat came up to me. First she let out this long low whistle, and then she said, "I just got to touch those pigtails. Can I?"

"Yes, ma'am," I replied. The woman laughed, patted my rough braids, and slapped a penny in my hand.

"What a little nigger frog you are," she said as she turned to leave.

I didn't know if she had complimented or insulted me. I couldn't think of anything uglier than a frog. But on the other hand, some people thought frogs were cute. The woman's comment troubled me. Even at my young age, I knew that there was nothing complimentary about being called a nigger. So there I was, homeless, helpless, and a nigger frog.

Finally, Mama returned to the train station. I was shocked when I saw her crawl out of a big black car with a middle-aged, moon-faced white man behind the wheel. This was her new employer and we had a new home: his basement. I was glad when we moved into our own house a month later.

CHAPTER 4

We didn't spend much time in our first house in Ohio, just four months. It was this lopsided pile of bricks on a dark rural road. Behind it were some train tracks and in front across the road was a cemetery. Every time a train roared by, the house shook. On both sides were deserted, boarded-up houses with CONDEMNED signs all over the place. Tramps that traveled on the passing freight trains hopped off now and then to sleep in one of the deserted houses and peep in our windows and go through our garbage cans. We had these great big rats that were so brazen they marched across the room right in front of us. They would even climb all over our bed with us in it. We never went into the kitchen without a baseball bat. That was the rats' favorite room.

The house was falling apart, too. One night while Mama was sleeping, some plaster fell off the ceiling and almost crippled her. Another time, she slid through a hole in the kitchen floor that had been hidden under a thin rug. She was lucky she didn't break both legs. The landlord was too cheap to repair anything. Lucky for us, most of the people Mama worked for, especially the men, wanted her there days and some nights. We became live-in help. I slept in so many basements, I developed a phobia, and to this day, I won't enter one unless I'm good and drunk. One employer let us occupy his garage, where Mama slept in a big old easy chair with me on her lap. Our toilet was a big rusty bucket with no handle. We used old newspaper and brown paper bags for toilet paper. We bathed at the Rescue Mission facilities every other day.

At one house, when the weather was warm, Mama's boss let me sleep in a large doghouse with some puppies. When the weather changed, I was transferred to his basement. I don't know where Mama slept. But one night I slipped into the main house and headed for the kitchen. While I was standing there with my head in the refrigerator, I heard Mama's voice coming from a back room. She said, "Hurry up, Mr. Cursey. My jaws is gettin' tired."

I followed her voice, which led me to the man's bedroom. Mama was on her knees with her head between Mr. Cursey's legs. He was butt naked. "Shet up, woman. You know you need this job, and you and your monkey need a place to stay," he told her. I didn't know what I was seeing, so I never told Mama.

A few days later, Mama made me pack again. Scary Mary was out of jail and we were moving in with her. She was now running a cheap boardinghouse for cheap women, and Mama was going to cook and clean for her.

I was told that I would be sharing a bedroom with Scary Mary's daughter, Mott. I was happy about that until I saw Mott. She was fifteen and severely retarded. Though she looked normal, she had the mind of a three-year-old. At four, I was baby-sitting a teenage idiot who called everybody Mama, including me and the many men who came to the house, most of them white.

My life was far from normal. I was so unhappy it showed. Mama promised me that when the time was right, she would find us a decent home of our own, and I'd be able to be just like other little kids. Mama's promise was the only thing that kept me from going off the deep end.

I liked Scary Mary. She was nice and generous, but she bullied people, so like everybody else I was afraid of her. The way she looked was enough to frighten anybody. She was so tall she towered over most people. Her voice was deep and throaty, almost a growl. She was a grim woman, aged hard in every way. Her brutal face was round and heavily lined with wrinkles and a continent of black freckles sprinkled all over her honey-colored nose. She wore a matted red wig and a lot of makeup. She was real heavy-handed with her lipstick; some days she spread on so much some of it ended up on her teeth. The wig didn't cover her Elvis-like sideburns, but she did dye them so that they matched the wig.

One day, marching like a soldier, she entered her cluttered kitchen, where Mama and I were sitting at the table eating greens and corn bread. "Gussie Mae, get up off your rump and come he'p us out. Lorene got the cramps, and everybody else tied up," she barked.

Mama gave me a strange look. Scary Mary looked from Mama to me, then back to Mama. It seemed like they were talking without using words.

I had no idea what was going on until years later. Mama's friend was running a whorehouse, and she often pressured Mama to work for her. "Annette, you go round up Mott and y'all go to the store to get me some chawin' tobacco and a jar of Noxzema face cream. Take your time," Scary Mary told me, caressing her chin.

"Can I get me some candy?" I asked with a pleading look.

"You can get you *one* jaw breaker. One," Scary Mary croaked. She slapped a five-dollar bill into my palm. I stood there looking at the money in my sweaty hand. "One more thing, you can keep the change. Just take your time gettin' back . . ."

I took my time getting back from the store, but it wasn't enough time away for me to miss what Mama was up to. I was sitting in the living room, gnawing on candy bars with Mott, when Mama stumbled from upstairs with two fat white men. Both of them were hugging her. She looked at me, then looked away real quick.

"I thought you was at the store, girl." She shooed the men toward a back room and rushed up to me. "There is things here you don't need to see!"

"I didn't see anything, Mama," I told her. Even if I had seen "something," I would not have known what I was seeing.

It wasn't long before Scary Mary ended up in trouble with the police again. Something about her batting a man's head with a frying pan over some money he owed her. "A slight misunderstandin'. Them kissy-poo po'lice ain't goin' to hold Scary Mary for too long," Mama insisted with a shrug.

We packed again and left Scary Mary's house the next day. A family from our church took Mott in, and Mama and I moved in with one of the nervous white men I'd seen at Scary Mary's house. I dreaded the thought of another basement, but there I was once again, sleeping on a pallet between a furnace and a washing machine.

Mama was always tired at the end of her workdays, but she always had time for me. She would read the Bible to me or sit around with her friends and brag about me. "My girl, she so smart. She read books and can speak proper as any white girl. Oh, she goin' to go real far. She goin' to be a big success. Just like me."

I was smart. Smart enough to know that I was not about to be somebody's slavish maid like my mama. I didn't have to be. I wasn't going to work myself into premature old age or an early grave like Mama seemed to be doing. At least not cleaning up behind a bunch of lazy white folks.

One evening, when we were in the kitchen of the next house we lived in preparing dinner, Mama said tiredly, "I want you to stay like you are forever; smart and good. It'll keep you on the right track, and you'll always be happy."

Her voice seemed so weak and sad, I wanted to cry. It hurt me deeply to see her suffer so much just so we could continue living in such an ugly world. But what choice did we have?

"Yes, Ma'am." Out of the corner of my eye, I saw Mama staring at me with pity.

"I pray no man don't make a fool out of you." It saddened me further when she shook her head.

She started washing collard greens in the sink. I was standing next to her, picking bugs off the greens.

"When I get grown we won't have to eat greens every day. I'm going to get a good job *in an office* making lots of money," I chirped. We had some type of greens almost every day. Greens and some creature like a coon or a rabbit that some man from our church had caught.

"Office job? You? Go read your Bible," Mama ordered. Her threatening look told me I had a whupping on the way. She moved from the sink to the counter, where she started to cut up a yam to lay on the pan around the coon she was going to bake.

I was still standing at the sink rolling my eyes at that dead coon that still had his head on in a roasting pan on the counter.

"You know how many little colored girls would love to be in your shoes?"

"No, Ma'am," I muttered.

"I slave every day so we don't have to go on welfare. I'm realistic. We colored. I know ain't nothin' else I can do but cook and clean and raise white women's kids. I don't like it. It ain't somethin' I dreamed about doin' when I was a young'n. All I ever really wanted was my own restaurant, where I would be the head cook. The kind of dream you talkin' about—you might as well be talkin' about gettin' elected president of the U.S.A. It ain't goin' to happen. Except in your dreams.

You ain't got the moxy Scary Mary got. She didn't get where she at that easy."

"They put her in the jail—again," I gasped.

Mama mauled the side of my head with her fist.

"Fix your lips! Anyway, you got to be . . . a certain type to get one of them uptown office jobs. Folks runnin' offices, they don't set *girls like you* at no desk to answer phones and greet folks. You . . ."

"I know I'm ugly, Mama," I said seriously. "I hear people saying so all the time. And, I'm fat." Somehow I managed a smile. "I see ugly people all the time, and they get good jobs. Like Miss Garra, that dog-face lady you worked for. You told me she work with the mayor now in his office."

"She white."

"Well, Reverend Snipes say beauty is only skin-deep. Real beauty come from the inside."

Mama chuckled and shook her head. Then she moved across the floor and snatched a bowl from the table and started mixing some corn bread on the counter. "Oh, child, that's just somethin' plain people say to make them feel better." She sighed, waving the bowl at me. "There ain't a handsome person alive would trade places with no ugly person."

"You think I'm ugly, too, Mama? People say . . . God don't like ugly." I left the sink and slid into a chair at the table and folded my arms.

Mama stirred the corn-bread mix with a long-handled spoon so hard she started sweating. She glanced at me for a moment with an exasperated look on her face. "You beautiful inside and out to me. It's ugly *ways* God don't like. Worry 'bout bein' good, not ugly." She paused long enough to pour the corn-bread mix into a greased skillet and slid it into the oven. "If you goin' to fantasize, fantasize about somethin' practical. A husband with a good job, good friends, a nice home full of young'ns that mind you and know the Lord." Mama's voice got real low, and she kept her eyes on the floor while she talked. "I only got one fantasy," she revealed. "And it's as big a fantasy as yours about workin' in a big fancy office. It'll never come true. At least not for me . . ."

"What is it?" I left the table and went to stand in front of Mama next to the hot stove. She sighed, then went to the sink and started cutting up the greens.

She shrugged. "Oh . . . it ain't nothin'. Just a pipe dream that ain't got no chance of comin' true. I don't care about no minks and furs and mansions like all them white folks I work for got. Compared to the white folks, I want so little out of life and seem like it's goin' to take me my whole life to get it, if at all. Just a whiff of luxury. Luxury all the white folks I work for knowed all their born days. Me, I'd be happy livin' just two or three days of the good life, praise the Lord."

Mama left the room and returned moments later with her hands full of travel brochures. Very shyly and without looking in my eyes, she said, "Other than runnin' my own restaurant, the only other thing in life I want is to see the Bahamas before I die."

"The Bahamas?"

"All them white women I worked for in Florida went there all the time. And for days after they got home, that's all they talked about. Remember?"

"I remember that time Mrs. Jacobs brought me some seashells back from the Bahamas," I replied.

"It ain't just the money. I know I could scrape up enough to go . . . if I let a few bills slide for a few months or . . . uh . . . be nice to Scary Mary and do her a few favors. It's just that I can't afford to take the time off from work. White folks is so fickle and helpless. I was to leave for a day or two, and I'm liable not to have no job to return to. I can't take that chance."

"But, Mama, you can always find maid work. And even the meanest white folks would probably let you take a few days off if you asked." Mama went to work even when she was sick. Sunday was the only day she had off, and she sometimes worked up to twelve hours a day. "Just wait until I get a good job. You won't have to work so much. You can spend as much time in the Bahamas as you want, stretched out on a beach with somebody fanning you for a change." Mama smiled and hugged me so hard it hurt.

CHAPTER 5

After two years, I still didn't like Ohio, but I liked Franklin Elementary School. There were a lot of other kids in my first grade class who had come from down South. Because of our Southern accents, almost every time one of us spoke, the Ohio kids made fun of us. My accent was not nearly as thick as some of the other kids because right after moving north, I had started imitating the way the Northern kids pronounced certain words.

I had a nice teacher, who encouraged me to learn as much as I could. "Education is the key to success," Miss Nipp told me. Mama worked for her three days a week, so Miss Nipp was nicer to me than to the other kids. Sometimes she gave me a ride home in her shiny blue Buick.

We were living in a gloomy, three-bedroom house on Mahoning Street in a run-down part of Richland, the neighborhood where most of the people on welfare and the criminals lived, when Mr. Boatwright moved in. Right across from us was the city dump. Day and night you could smell fried food and marijuana fumes coming from the houses and foul odors from the dump.

One evening when Miss Nipp drove me home, she stopped at a hot-dog stand and bought me a foot-long hot dog. "I hope you have a pleasant evening, Annette," she said when the car stopped in front of our house. The people in our neighborhood were not used to seeing fancy cars driven by white women on our street. I frowned at the nosy faces staring out of the windows in the house next door.

"I will, Miss Nipp," I said, smacking on the last piece of the hot dog. She was a small gray-haired woman so dainty, the smell of my neighborhood overwhelmed her. She patted my forehead and coughed. "It doesn't smell bad around here all the time," I lied, opening the car door.

"I'm sure it doesn't, Annette. Now you be sure and tell your mother I said hello and that I appreciate her handling my dinner party last night." Miss Nipp smiled. She had given Mama the day off, which meant Mama had some unexpected time to spend with me.

I hated coming home to an empty house and having to wait so late to eat dinner. Knowing that Mama was home and dinner was ready or close to it, I ran up on our porch with eager anticipation until I entered our living room and saw that strange old man unpacking his things.

I didn't sleep much that first night with Mr. Boatwright in our house. When I woke up the next morning I thought I had dreamed him. But within seconds I knew he was real. Before I could get my clothes on I heard his voice downstairs. "Sister Goode, what kind of greens you want me to cook today, collards, mustards, or turnips?" he asked. I cussed out loud to myself, so I didn't even hear Mama's response.

By the time I got downstairs to the kitchen, Mama had her coat on and was about to leave for work. "Annette, you come straight home from school to start gettin' acquainted with Brother Boatwright." She smiled, smoothing my hair down.

I glared at him. "Yes . . . Ma'am," I mumbled, hardly moving my lips.

"And you better mind him," Mama added.

"Oh, me and Annette gwine to get along real good in no time," he said, hands on his hips, smile on his face. He had on a gray-flannel housecoat that touched the floor.

I didn't even eat breakfast that morning. I just sat at the kitchen table staring from one wall to the other while he sat in the living room watching TV. I left to go to school without saying a word to him.

Miss Nipp knew something was wrong the minute I entered the classroom ten minutes ahead of all the other kids. "Annette, are you all right? You look rather down this morning. Is there a problem?"

I had to take a deep breath before I could speak. "This old man moved in with us yesterday, and I don't like him," I admitted.

"A Mr. Boatwright? Your mother mentioned him to me the other day. And why don't you like him?" Miss Nipp asked. She put her hand on my shoulder and started rubbing it.

"Uh . . . I don't know," I admitted. "He's old, and I think he's going to be . . . bossy."

Miss Nipp patted my head and laughed. "Don't be too hasty with your judgments. Your mother is not a fool. She knows what's best for you. Give Mr. Boatwright a chance," she advised.

The first few days living with a man in the same house were rough on me. Miss Nipp came to meet him and liked him, but I resented his presence. Mama made me stop roaming around the house in just my panties, and I couldn't turn on the TV in the morning until he got up. When he shaved he left nappy gray hair on the bathroom sink and pee all over the toilet seat and floor that he took his time cleaning up. But by the time he got settled in, my feelings started changing. He had brought a smell with him that reminded me of Daddy. A musty, pleasant odor I had only smelled on certain men. Every time he entered the same room I was in, I thought about my daddy, and in some ways it was like I had my daddy back. Mr. Boatwright won me over when he started giving me candy and doing all the housecleaning I should have been doing.

He hugged me a lot and rubbed me in various places on my body, and it felt good. He had the same sadness in his eyes my daddy and I had. Once, after he had given me my Bible lesson, he leaned over and said, "Gimme some sugar!" I closed my eyes and smiled, expecting him to brush his lips across my cheek or forehead. My eyes flew open when I felt his dry lips on mine.

"Will you be my daddy, Mr. Boatwright?" I pleaded, licking my burning lips.

"Girl . . . I'm gwine to be more than a daddy," he informed me, kissing me the same way again. He patted my behind, and I laid my head against his lumpy bosom.

Mr. Boatwright quickly made friends with Mama's friends in the neighborhood, and he joined our church. Reverend Snipes sometimes let him sing a solo on Sunday. "And now Brother Boatwright is gwine to honor us with one of his favorite hymns," Reverend Snipes announced proudly. Reverend Snipes was a little, reddish brown man around Mr. Boatwright's age who reminded me of a sad dog. He had a long, narrow face with droopy eyes, a nose that turned up at the end, and shaggy gray hair that stood up around his head like Methuselah's.

During the church services some people fell asleep, and unruly young kids, myself included, had to be restrained frequently. But when Mr. Boatwright sang, nobody could sleep through it. Some of the rowdy kids were so taken aback that they sat ramrod straight from the time he started until he stopped to keep from laughing. Mr. Boatwright would sweat and rock back and forth and from side to side. I stared and listened in horror and disbelief. Mr. Boatwright's yip yip sounded like somebody was stepping on a cat's tail. Every time he sang, I turned around every few seconds to look at the door, expecting a dog to start howling and scratching.

After Mr. Boatwright's solo people started shouting and clapping. Weeping sisters ran up to him with wet towels and wiped his face. Then we walked the two blocks back to our house, where he sometimes sang another solo just for me and Mama. Every time he did Mama got so overwhelmed she cried.

On top of being a respected church member, the man cooked like a veteran chef. He made pies and cakes, which I helped him carry to the church for the bake sales, from scratch. For me he baked tea cakes with smiling faces using chocolate drops for eyes and lips.

I didn't know how much his disability check was each month, but he bought a lot of nice things for the house that Mama had never been able to afford. He even bought us a new television and me a brand-new tricycle.

"Oh, Mr. Boatwright—you just like Santa Claus!" I said, hugging him for buying me the tricycle. "You more than a daddy!"

"See . . . I told you I would be." He tickled my armpit and looked at me long and hard with his mouth hanging open. It was a look that made me so uneasy I suddenly had to pee.

"You want me to run to the store to get you some more Anacin or a bottle of pop or something, Mr. Boatwright? *What you want me to do for you?*"

"Uh . . . just gimme another hug for now," he said, almost out of breath. He leaned down and I hugged him around his neck as hard as I could. He slapped my butt, then squeezed it. That's when I excused myself to go to the bathroom.

He was fifty-three when the nightmare started. I had just turned seven. One evening in August, while Mama was still at work, he ambushed me in my room. I was shocked at the way he kicked open my door and just stood there in the doorway with his hands on his hips staring at me like I was something good to eat. I was lying across my bed minding my own business with a coloring book and some crayons I had found among a box of goodies donated by a woman Mama worked for. A mountain of candy-bar wrappers lay next to me. I had stolen the candy from Mr. Boatwright's room, and I assumed that was why he had entered my room like a bat out of hell—either to scold me for stealing the candy or to give me the rest of it.

"Uh . . . what's the matter? Did I strap your leg on too tight?" I asked, smiling. He had never told me why his left leg was fake, but I thought it was one of the most fascinating things about him. I overheard him one day tell our preacher something about losing the leg in a world war. "What's the matter?" I asked again. Even though he was a grown man, I could talk to him like he was my own age. He had taken me trick-or-treating the year before, and we had collected two big bags of candy that he let me eat all by myself. I liked helping him remove his fake leg and strapping it back on. It didn't look like a leg. It just looked like a piece of brown wood. It was darker than the rest of him and thicker than his real one. It looked like wood but felt like plastic. I could tell that it was old because there was a lot of dents and scratches on it at the knee, where he strapped it on.

I didn't have the time or interest in playing with the other kids in our neighborhood anymore. They couldn't compete with this old man. Mr. Boatwright had become my best friend.

"Mr. Boatwright, why come you looking at me like that?"

"I seen the way you been lookin' at me," he growled. "In India, a girl get married by the time she your age. To men like me." There was a look on his face I could not comprehend. Spit appeared in one corner of his mouth. I was scared and amused at the same time. I didn't know whether to scream or laugh.

"Huh?" was all I could say at the time. Right after I said that, I giggled.

"Don't you laugh at me, girl." Dragging his fake leg, he started to move toward me, taking short, quick steps. There was now a glazed expression on his face. "Let's make out like we in India."

"What in the world—" I sat up so fast that my coloring book and the candy-bar wrappers fell to the floor.

"You want it bad as I do," he told me. "It's written all over your face. You been beggin' for it, *Buckwheat.*"

Everybody I knew felt that Buckwheat was the ugliest Black child on TV. Being called that truly hurt my feelings but I refused to show it.

"Want what?" I said levelly, tempted to roll my eyes.

He was now standing over my bed with his shirt unbuttoned and this suspicious grin on his face. There were beads of sweat on his hairy chest. His nipples reminded me of raisins, and his hands looked like paws. "You want it," he insisted. "You want it more than I do. Oo weee."

"I—what?" I was horrified. I looked in his dark, bitter eyes, and he looked in mine. His did not blink as he seemed to look straight through me. I couldn't stop myself from laughing. "What are you talking about?" Grown folks never ceased to amaze me. If they were not drinking or starting a world war, they were talking a bunch of gobbledygook.

"I could hop on the Greyhound bus tonight to Hollywood and be with Marilyn Monroe, but I choose to be rightcheer with you," he confessed.

Now I was truly confused. He had passed up a movie star for me. Was I that special? Things were happening too fast. To baffle me further, he leaned over my bed and squeezed one of my thighs. Then, he grabbed my other thigh and gently pulled both of them open. Since I was totally clueless as far as sex was concerned and had only seen dogs in action, I had no idea what he was up to. I just did what he told me to do.

"Take off all them clothes," he ordered.

"For what? Am I about to get a bath?" A bath was the only thing I had ever undressed for—but never in front of anybody other than Mama. I started unbuttoning my blouse. "What—why come you feeling me all up and down like that?"

"I'm fixin' to turn you into a woman." He slid my panties off and dropped them on the floor, grinning all the while.

"Huh? What?" I gasped. I had no idea why he was unzipping his pants.

"Raise your rump. Like I said, you want this as bad as I do, and you know it." He slapped my naked behind and made smacking noises with his tongue and lips.

"Want what—?" I didn't like what he was doing. Mama was the only person in the whole world who had ever seen or touched my private parts.

"Shet up," he snapped. Then, without another word, he pushed me down on the bed on my back and climbed on top of me. That was the beginning of a decade of horrors for me.

After he was done with me, I just remained on my back stunned, naked, and sore. I didn't sit up until after he left my room. And when I did, you could have knocked me over with a feather. I almost fell when I stood up. I managed to locate my robe at the foot of my bed. As soon as I had it on, I ran to the bathroom.

Blood was dripping from between my thighs. Mr. Boatwright was coming out of the bathroom, smiling and humming.

"I'm bleeding," I gasped. He led me to the bathroom and stuck a wad of toilet paper between my thighs, then he ran me a tub of bathwater.

CHAPTER 6

The next couple of days, I walked around the house in a trance. Mr. Boatwright acted like he normally did, whistling and yipping his spirituals, quoting Scripture from the Bible and cooking up a storm. During my next Bible lesson, he leaned over and kissed me on the mouth, forcing my lips open with his tongue and patting my crotch at the same time.

"Stop," I whimpered, wiped my lips, leaned back in my chair, and squeezed my thighs together, forcing him to remove his hand.

"What? You done already forgot what I *just* told you about what happened to Lot's wife in Sodom and Gomorrah?"

I sat in silence, with my eyes glued to the floor.

"Huh? You think it's fun's turnin' into a pillar of salt, girl?"

"No sir . . ." I mumbled.

He finished my Bible lesson, we ate dinner, then he sent me to bed. This was one of Mama's late nights. I was not surprised when he steamrolled into my room just minutes after I had turned in for the night. Without a word he wrestled my flannel gown and panties off me. I stared in horror and disbelief as he removed his clothes.

This was the second time, and it was worse than the first. I say that because the first time I was a virgin and I didn't know what was coming. He talked during the whole rape. Two hellish minutes. And to my seven-year-old body, two minutes was a very long time.

"You clumsy heifer!" He was mad because my legs were all over the bed. But I could not help it; the pain was unbearable. I could not understand how anything that felt so bad to me, felt so good to him. "Tetch me. That's the least you can do." He guided my hand to his crotch and forced me to squeeze.

"Ow, ow, ow," I sobbed. Suddenly, I froze, and that made him even angrier.

"Use your imagine now, girl. Don't just lay there like a rug and let me do all the work! All this trouble for a little poontang," he complained between gasps. His foul breath and slimy sweat on my face made the nightmare even worse.

To me the man was unspeakable, but Mama and everybody else held him in the highest regard. Miss Nipp and Reverend Snipes considered him a blessing. On the streets, high-class white people who didn't even know him greeted him with a smile and called him uncle. He even had the nerve to get his picture on the front page of our newspaper, the *Richland Review,* with our white mayor. This was after he had written a long, convoluted letter to the city newspaper editor praising the mayor for supporting some welfare program to build more low-income houses. I promised myself that when and if I reached adulthood, I would never involve myself with men. I would surround myself with women and pets.

I couldn't believe that this man was on top of me. "Yes sir," I managed, lying under his flabby body, stiff as a plank. I didn't know what to do with my legs, arms, or any other part of my body. And he didn't bother to tell me. "I don't like this," I told him. "It feels bad."

"It bees that way sometime," he said seriously. He paused and moaned with his head thrown back and his eyes closed. I couldn't believe that there was a smile on his face. He shuddered and opened his eyes and gave me a hard look. "Let's get this thing over with lickety-split. *Lassie* is fixin' to come on the TV."

"Yes . . . sir, Mr. Boatwright." I barely recognized my own voice.

It was raining and thundering and lightning like mad. We usually had a lot of snow this time of year, but not this time. It had snowed a little, but then it quickly turned to slush. Now it was hail. I just lay there crying and listening to the hailstones tapping against my bedroom windows, all the while hating that sweaty, evil man on top of me talking and grunting like a hog. "Rar back," he instructed.

"Yes, sir," I managed. Confusion and disgust consumed me. I had to hold my breath to keep from vomiting.

"How that feel?" he asked.

"Bad, I told you," I said, sobbing.

"Oh don't you worry about a thing, possum. After we done, go set in a tub of hot water yonder in that bathroom. You can use some of my bubbly bath and sleep under my eiderdown quilt again. And you better not pee on it this time."

"I did all that the other time, and I still hurt," I reminded.

"Hush up. At least there ain't no messy blood this time. Eh?" he said casually.

After he was done with me and I had put my clothes back on, he paid me a nickel and made me promise not to ever tell anybody. He threatened that if I ever told anybody, I would suffer.

"Why you doing this to me?" I wanted to know. "You know I don't like it," I sobbed. We were sitting on the side of my bed. He had put his shirt back on, but his pants were still at the foot of my bed.

He patted his wooden leg, then shrugged and looked away from me. After he thought about it for a few moments he turned back to me and shook his head like he really was sorry. But then he suddenly turned mean again. "Don't you be questionin' grown folks, Jezebel!"

"Mr. Boatwright, I don't like what we do," I whimpered after our latest encounter. He cussed and stopped long enough to chew two Anacin tablets. He swallowed the pills off and on all day, every day, for one thing or another whether he was sick or not. He was nervous because we didn't know what time Mama was coming home. His clumsy, fake leg had slipped and ended up turned halfway around.

He had greasy, foul-smelling pomade on his hair that had dripped on my face. I helped him adjust his leg straps without him telling me to. I continued talking with my face turned away from his. "I don't like this, Mr. Boatwright."

"You ain't supposed to, possum. Women have too much fun as it is. Shoppin' all the time. Gossipin'. Cookin' up some scheme to get one of us to marry y'all."

"I don't do none of that," I informed him. "I don't like the way *this* feels."

"Don't be such a crybaby. Folks do this all the time, and it ain't supposed to feel good to no gal. God cursed y'all so it wouldn't feel good on account of Eve bitin' a plug out that apple in the Garden of Eden. If you gals was meant to have a good time, God would have gave y'all dicks, too. Shit."

"God didn't—" I cried. He interrupted me with a ferocious outburst.

"GOD INVENTED CURSES!" His face became an ugly black mask. He gasped, then he reared back and roared, "That's why they made him God!"

He stood up from my bed, yawning and stretching his arms high above his head. "Well now. I guess that'll have to do . . ." he sighed. He reached over and patted the top of my head. Then he slid into his pants. "Why you so quiet?" he asked casually, hands on his hips. I turned to look at his face, not knowing what I was to say, but he spoke before I could. "You made me do this," he informed me.

"What?" I gasped. My mouth remained open, and I rubbed my ears. "How did I make you do this, Mr. Boatwright?"

"I seen you struttin' around in here naked like a peacock one night. Tryin' to be cute. Showin' off."

"How do you know I was in here naked?" I yelled. I attempted to stand, but the glare on his face scared me enough to make me sit back on the bed and lower my voice. "My door was closed."

Incredibly he said, "What you think they make keyholes for, girl?"

CHAPTER 7

I was now thirteen, and the only person I had ever had any sexual contact with was Mr. Boatwright. Things had not changed much since our first encounter. Every now and then I got up enough nerve to threaten to tell Mama, and he'd usually say something like, "Ahhhh . . . and who do you think would believe you with your ugly self? What do you think your mama will say when I tell her how you throwed yourself at me for a nickel?"

One night, a week before I turned twelve, I threatened to tell Mama again. I held my breath as he hobbled out of my room and returned within minutes, waving a gun I had never seen before. "See this here?" He walked right up to me and placed the barrel against my forehead. "Bang."

My heart was beating so hard I could barely breathe. I was too scared to move. He smiled and took a few steps back. "Don't think I won't use it."

Richland's population remained around thirty-two thousand with approximately a twenty percent Black population. There were two steel mills, a brickyard, and a few other factories that provided decent employment for a lot of the Black men who couldn't get good-paying jobs anyplace else in town. There were a lot of farms on the outskirts of town where migrant workers from Florida and the Carolinas worked picking mostly beans, strawberries, apples, potatoes and peaches, from May to November. A lot of the local people, mostly Black, worked on those farms, too.

Downtown Richland was nothing to write home about. There were two five-and-dime stores, Pluto's and Bailey's, where most of the Black folks did their shopping. There were a few clothing stores, one wig and hat shop, two furniture stores, two shoe stores, a few businesses, and the police station. The more upscale stores were located in Sheldon Village, a large shopping center right off the freeway.

There was only one Black doctor in town and one Black undertaker. Other than Black churches, the only thing there was an abundance of for Black folks were bars. Mama called bars beer gardens. "Them beer gardens cultivate a alcoholic quicker than fertilizer," she warned me one day when we passed the Red Rose Tavern on the way home from church.

"Amen." Mr. Boatwright nodded. I figured he had forgotten about the time he had left me standing outside for twenty minutes while he ran into the Red Rose for a highball one afternoon on the way home from the market.

The people with money lived on the south side of town, near a set of railroad tracks. Most of the low-income people lived in the northern part of Richland. The people with money bought their groceries at Kroger's and the A&P. We bought ours at a shabby disorganized discount market called the Food Bucket, where the quality of almost everything they sold was enough to make you sick. A few times they had even tried to sell me and Mr. Boatwright spoiled meat. I hated when Mama sent me and Mr. Boatwright there to get groceries. Some of the clerks were rude and no matter which checkout line you got in, most of the people in front of you had welfare orders, coupons, and checks that needed to be verified. It took longer to check out than it took to collect a cartful of groceries.

In addition to the Sampson River there were several lakes in the Richland area where people went to fish and swim. The rich people went swimming at a fancy pool called Sun Tan Acres, with all kinds of concession stands and other services and lifeguards who looked like Troy Donahue and Elvis. The Black folks and the other poor people went to the lakes and Sampson River to swim or to Jason Pool about a mile from the city dump. At Jason Pool they even let dogs jump in the water. The two dumpy lifeguards were not handsome, but they were nice and really looked out for all the swimmers.

I liked Jason Pool, but I'd only gone there to swim a few times. Weighing close to two hundred pounds, I didn't feel comfortable even though there were a lot of other overweight people flopping around in the water like seals. No matter how hard I tried, I could never find an attractive bathing suit I could afford. I couldn't figure out what made designers think fat people liked swimwear with big flowers, tutus around the waist, and zippers that got stuck or pinched. Whoever was in charge did not clean the pool regularly, like the people did at Sun Tan Acres. People peed in the water and threw things in it like beer and pop cans that floated around for days.

We had two movie theaters, both on the south side of town. The rich people saw first-run movies at the Mt. Pilot Theater. The Strand, just four blocks from the Mt. Pilot, didn't get movies until months after they had been released. The ushers at the Strand did nothing when people got loud or brought in their own refreshments and alcohol. Fights often broke out when somebody stepped on somebody's foot, somebody stole somebody's seat, or somebody had the nerve to stroll in with somebody else's lover. People smoked weed, and the ushers ignored them. I loved going to the movies so much, I tolerated all that. Every first of the month, when Mr. Boatwright received his disability check, he treated me to a movie at the Mt. Pilot Theater, where we could eat fresh popcorn and hot dogs and enjoy a recently released movie in peace. I treasured those outings. No matter what movie was showing I enjoyed the experience, even with Mr. Boatwright next to me sometimes snoring so loud the ushers came over to wake him up.

I still didn't like having sex with Mr. Boatwright and avoided it every chance I got, but now the sex itself didn't bother me as much. And I knew him well enough by now to manipulate him to my advantage. I offered to pick up beer for him from Scary Mary, which he would drink right away, get drunk, and give me extra money that I used to go to the movies by myself or buy magazines and paperback books. I had him convinced that my periods lasted ten days when they only lasted four. He was superstitious about touching a female on her period.

"Woman's curse could ruin a man iffen he got too close," he told me once with a grimace on his face.

"Oh yes I know. I read all about it," I agreed, nodding.

He was getting so forgetful he would wake up with a hangover, come to my room, and I'd convince him that we had already had sex. "Did I pay you?" he asked seriously on one occasion.

"Um . . . no, but that's OK this time," I lied. With the exception of the food Mama and I had stolen from her white employers in Florida, I didn't feel right taking something for nothing too often.

Mama often told me, "What goes around comes around." Her example was us skipping out owing all those creditors and landlords in Florida. Because of that, Mama couldn't get credit anywhere in Richland. Our phone bill and our utility bill were in Scary Mary's name, and Reverend Snipes cosigned for every house we rented in Richland. "You be good, and God'll be good to you," Mama assured me, and I believed her.

CHAPTER 8

Over the years, Mama worked for a lot of rich white people in Richland I never got to meet. Then I met the employer she gave up all her other commitments to work for exclusively; a retired judge name Bill Lawson. Judge Lawson was one of Scary Mary's most frequent visitors and one of her closest friends. I had overheard her tell Mama that the judge was the main reason she always got out of trouble with just a "talking-to" every time her house got raided.

The judge was a tall, gray-haired, barrel-chested white man with a narrow face and bushy mustache. He reminded me of Jed Clampett on my favorite program at the time, *The Beverly Hillbillies*. He had the bluest eyes I'd ever seen and thin lips that were always smiling. He lived in a big blue house on a hill with an enclosed swimming pool, and he owned houses all over town. Every time I saw him he had on an expensive-looking suit.

"How do you like school, Annette? Your mama tells me you get straight A's," he said to me one night when he dropped Mama off.

I broke into a grin when he slapped a one-dollar bill into my anxious hand. "Oh I have some real good teachers, and I like to learn," I told him proudly, walking behind him as he strode like a cowboy across our living-room floor.

Mama and Judge Lawson sat down on our living-room couch and popped open cans of beer. I sat on a chair across from them, caressing my dollar. Mr. Boatwright was in bed.

"Hmmm. Ever consider going into the teaching profession when the time comes?" Judge Lawson asked, taking a long swig from his can.

"Oh no, Judge Lawson. I hope I can get a good secretarial job after I graduate," I replied excitedly.

"Well if there's anything I can do to help, all you got to do is let me know and I'll fix it," he said firmly. Then he put his hand on Mama's knee and started rubbing it.

Judge Lawson's offer impressed and stunned me, but I didn't take him seriously. I knew he was rich, didn't have any kids, and was not on good terms with his family. But he had a lot of friends. Mama told me that he entertained a lot. He often had lavish poker parties. Every time he did, Mama had to stay late cooking and running around serving his guests.

Something happened shortly after Judge Lawson's offer, and Mama was forced to call on him for a favor. An inspector came snooping around our neighborhood, and our house was one of the ones he condemned because the place had extremely bad and dangerous wiring, termites and roaches sliding up and down the walls, plaster falling from the ceiling, and holes everywhere he looked. We had thirty days to find a new place to live.

Mama couldn't afford to take time off from work, so Mr. Boatwright and I went out looking for a new house. We took buses when we could, but we did most of our searching on foot. With Mr. Boatwright's leg situation it was a long, exasperating experience. Because of him I couldn't walk as fast as I normally did. And every ten or fifteen minutes we had to find a bench for him to rest.

The next day we looked at three more places. The ones we could afford looked worse than the one we were in and were located in neighborhoods even rougher and more run-down.

"I don't know what to do," Mama moaned one evening. She had just come in from work and still had her coat on. Her eyes appeared to be in pain. They were red and swollen from all the crying she had done over our knotty problem. "We ain't got but ten more days to vacate these premises."

"What happens if we don't move by then?" I asked. I was on the living room couch with Mr. Boatwright. An hour earlier he and I had prayed out loud on our knees asking God to help us find the right house.

With a worried look on his face, Mr. Boatwright replied, "The sheriff will come out with a crew, set our stuff on the ground, and put a lock on the door."

Time was running out, and we still had not found a suitable house to move to.

"What are we going to do, Mama?" I was getting scared. I was not that crazy about our house, but it was all we had.

"Well, Scary Mary done already told me, I can stretch out on a pallet on her livin'-room floor, you can sleep with Mott, Brother Boatwright can pile up on her livin'-room couch 'til we find a place."

It was never discussed, but I knew that Mama was tired of having to fall back on Scary Mary so often. I sure was. Scary Mary was the type of person who would eventually call her favors in. Whenever she wanted Mama to come and help entertain her male friends, Mama got kicking and screaming mad, but she went. "Blackmail. Scary Mary blackmailin' me," Mama said under her breath to herself one day after getting off the phone with Scary Mary.

"What did you say, Mama?" I had entered the kitchen just in time to hear her.

"Nothin'!" She then sucked in her breath, and told me, "Go lay me out some clean step-ins that ain't got no holes or ravels, go to my bureau and dig out my black brassiere, and iron my red dress."

"That red dress you said was too short and tight?" I gasped, worried about what I had heard her say about Scary Mary blackmailing her.

Mama looked away from me as she spoke. "Uh . . . it ain't that short and tight," she said, her voice cracking.

Scary Mary now lived across the tracks in a huge green-shingled house in a neighborhood with nothing but nice houses. With all the women working for her, and the money the rich dead husband had left her, she could afford to. She had moved there several years earlier. It was the same neighborhood where our only Black undertaker, our only Black doctor, and one of the only two Black barbers lived. The rest of the neighborhood was white. I liked Scary Mary's house, but I didn't want to stay there even for a few days. I didn't want to live in that big nice comfortable place, then have to give it up and go back to living in another falling-down shack like the ones we always rented.

With just five days left for us to vacate, Mama came rushing into the house after Judge Lawson had dropped her off. "Annette, Brother Boatwright, y'all come quick!" I ran from the kitchen to the living room where Mama was, wringing her hands and hopping around like she had to pee.

"What's wrong, Mama?" I gasped. Her hair was askew, her lipstick was smeared, and her dress was buttoned wrong. It looked like she had just been mauled.

"What's gwine on?" Mr. Boatwright yelled, hobbling into the room from upstairs.

"Y'all know that big house with the white aluminum sidin' on Reed Street direct across from that colored undertaker, one block over from Scary Mary?" Mama shouted.

"Yeah. The house with the buckeye tree settin' in the front yard." Mr. Boatwright, arms folded, nodded. "What about it?"

"The tenants moved out a few days ago, and it's up for rent!" Mama said, waving her arms like she was directing a 747. I had never seen Mama this excited before. There was a big smile on her face, and she was sweating.

"The rent must be three or four times what we pay here, Mama," I said evenly. "We can't afford to live in a place like that."

"Oh yes we can afford it! I just found out it's one of Judge Lawson's properties! *My* Judge Lawson. I told him about our predicament and right off he said he wouldn't stand by and let us get set out on the ground long as he livin'." Mama paused and scratched her head, then continued. "After all these years, the judge decided he didn't like the people livin' there. They was too hard to get along with and was always complainin' about one thing or another. He say we can move in right away with no deposit, and we can rent it for the same rent we pay here."

"Praise the Lord!" Mr. Boatwright was so overwhelmed he started shaking and sweating so hard he had to sit down and compose himself. He snatched a handkerchief from his pocket and started fanning and wiping his face.

"Judge Lawson's got one foot in the grave, Mama. What if he dies next month?" I asked.

"Well, Miss Smarty, that's already been considered. The judge promised me first thing in the mornin' he would have his lawyer revise his will sayin' me and mine can live in the Reed Street house, rent to *never* increase, for as long as we want!" Mama yelled. She dropped her tattered coat to the floor and started dancing like a tribeswoman around a ceremonial fire.

"Oh," was all I could say as I rolled this information around in my head. I sat on the couch and started smiling. It sounded too good to be true. "Why would Judge Lawson do all that for us? What's in it for him?" I wanted to know.

Mama stopped dancing her jig, and a strange, faraway look appeared on her face. "God told him to do it I bet." She sighed. "It ain't no wonder with the way we all been prayin'."

Mr. Boatwright and I agreed with her, but I knew there was more to it than that. I'd seen Judge Lawson look at Mama the same way Mr. Boatwright often looked at me, like he'd just bought me by the pound.

In June of that year, 1963, we moved across town to the house on Reed Street. It was a bigger place and much nicer than any we had ever lived in. The front porch had a glider that came with the house. Not only was there a big buckeye tree in the spacious front yard, but there was also a gigantic weeping willow directly across the cobblestone walkway opposite the buckeye tree. I felt like we'd just moved to Norman Rockwell's neighborhood. The floors in our new house had nice dark brown shaggy carpets. In the bright yellow kitchen there was a stove we could turn on without using pliers like we had to do with our old one, a refrigerator that defrosted itself, and linoleum that shone like new money on the floor. Our old neighborhood had lots of bars, and I saw drunk people staggering about and peeing on the ground in broad daylight. Our new neighborhood had only one bar, and my new school was only a ten-minute walk from our house.

Scary Mary's house was right behind ours on the next street over. Our backyards connected. She had a cherry tree, an apple tree, and a buckeye tree in her part of the yard. From my back bedroom window, I counted dozens of grinning, well-dressed (most of them white) men in and out of her back door. Just like when we lived with her.

Our new house had four bedrooms. Mama took the largest one, which was the one downstairs. Mr. Boatwright took the one upstairs across from mine. And the fourth bedroom, right at the end of a long hallway, was to be used to store things, Mama said, like the brand-new sewing machine Judge Lawson had ordered from Sears and Roebuck. I felt warm and secure in my new room even though all I had in it was my lumpy bed, a big old, chipped chifforobe, and a nightstand with a goosenecked lamp on it leaning over my bed like a sentinel.

I livened up my room with colored pictures of stars from my movie magazines and dandelions I picked from our front yard.

It didn't take me long to get used to our new neighborhood. It was cleaner, quieter, and safer than the one we had just moved from. For weeks, Mr. Boatwright didn't bother me for sex. I thought that he had gotten tired of me or, because of his age, his sex drive had run its course. I was wrong.

For the upcoming Fourth of July, we planned a trip to a slaughterhouse to get some ribs, pork links, and chicken parts for him to barbecue. Before going to the meat market, he took me to the Mt. Pilot movie theater to see a new Steve McQueen movie. After the movie, we ate at a Kentucky Fried Chicken restaurant.

"Hurry up and finish eatin' so we can get to the market and back home before *Perry Mason* come on the TV," Mr. Boatwright urged, chewing so hard he bit his tongue. There was grease on his lips and chin, and bits of chicken were lodged between his front teeth.

"OK. After we watch *Perry Mason,* I'll help you marinate the ribs," I told him. I was halfway through my second three-piece dinner meal. Every time I put on a pound, I recalled Mama's prediction when I was four about how God was going to curse me with a body the size of a moose. At 210 pounds I didn't have too far to go. Though he seemed to enjoy it, Mr. Boatwright told me all the time how much he hated my bloated body. I made myself believe that eventually I'd be so fat he wouldn't touch me anymore. "Mr. Boatwright, can I get some more chicken?"

The slaughterhouse was a big brooding gray building across the road from a truck stop. On a normal day it was a madhouse. With a holiday coming up, one that was close to the first part of the month when all the low-income people got their checks and still had money to spend on meat, the place resembled a crime scene. A mob of boisterous people wearing Bermuda shorts and sandals, who had already completed their shopping, stood in front of the market waiting for a bus to take them back home. The parking lot was completely full, and some of the vehicles belonged to the police.

The men who worked inside were running around with bloodstains on their white smocks. Sweaty, impatient customers were standing at the counters five deep trying to bargain, trying to get credit, or trying to get an extra pound of something for free.

Because of all the chaos and the fact that it took Mr. Boatwright so long to walk from one counter to another, (he had to lean against the wall and rest for ten minutes between each counter we went to) it took us longer than we expected to get our orders filled. By the time we walked out of the market, there were so many people ahead of us boarding the departing bus we had to wait for the next one. It took us another hour to get back to where we had to transfer to the bus that would take us back to our neighborhood. By then it was too late. The last bus for the day on that route had come and gone.

"I guess we'll have to take a cab from here," Mr. Boatwright said angrily.

"Let's walk the rest of the way home," I suggested. Our house was fifteen blocks away, but I didn't mind.

"What's wrong with you, girl? I'm lucky to be alive after all the walkin' I done did today," Mr. Boatwright snapped. There were times I forgot about his fake leg and the fact that he was an old man. "All these packages we totin' too. Let's get to that pay phone yonder and call a cab." The nearby pay phone at the corner in front of Thurman's Pharmacy was out of order. "Maybe that drugstore there got one. Start steppin', girl."

I followed Mr. Boatwright inside the drugstore. While he went to the back to use the phone, I waited on a stool at the soda counter with our packages, enjoying the air conditioning and a strawberry milk shake.

A well-dressed Black man in his mid-forties entered. With his head held high and his shoulders back, he strutted like a king, greeting some of the other customers with a nod and a smile. He was tall like my daddy, but much more handsome. He looked a lot like Mama's favorite entertainer, Harry Belafonte. He had dark brown skin, full lips, wavy black hair, and, of all things, green eyes. He nodded and smiled at me, revealing a set of dazzling white teeth. I smiled back and watched him stop at the counter in back of the drugstore where they filled prescriptions. Mr. Boatwright returned with a tortured look on his face.

"What's the matter?" I asked.

"We ain't got enough to cover no cab from here to the house. Damn that bus!" he hissed. "I guess—" he stopped and shaded his eyes. He was looking at the Black man with the movie-star looks. "Ain't that Brother Nelson yonder there?"

"Who?"

"The undertaker that own that big white house directly across the street from us. He come up to me when I was in the yard the other day and introduced hisself," Mr. Boatwright explained. We watched the man walk toward us, still smiling. He reached out and shook Mr. Boatwright's hand so hard I thought Mr. Boatwright was going to fall.

"How're you feelin', Boatwright?" the man drawled in a deep, husky, slightly Southern accent. "It's good to see you again."

I pushed my milk shake aside and leaped up off my seat, smoothing the sides of my cheap corduroy jumper.

"Oh I'm fair to middlin'. The Lord's good to me, Brother Nelson." Mr. Boatwright nodded in my direction. "This the young'n live in the same house with me and her mama. I know you done seen her up and down that tree shuckin' it for them buckeye nuts. Annette, this Brother Nelson."

"Hi, Mr. Nelson," I said shyly.

He shook my trembling hand. "I got a girl around your age. She's spendin' her summer vacation with her aunt down South," Mr. Nelson told me. "Uh . . . look like you folks got a lot of shoppin' done there."

"Yep. We been to the slaughterhouse out on Highway 80. We can't afford them high-and-mighty prices at Kroger's and the A&P like you. Me and this girl here go to the slaughterhouse two, three times a month. Even Kroger's can't beat them screamin', meaty pork ribs the slaughterhouse sell, praise the Lord." Mr. Boatwright laughed, shaking his head.

"Well I wouldn't know. We don't eat pork," Mr. Nelson informed us with a serious look on his face. "You know, Black folks would be a whole lot healthier if they'd give up certain things, especially pork."

I bobbed my head up and down in agreement. "I read about it in that Black Muslim newspaper they go around selling. They say too much pork can kill you," I offered.

Mr. Boatwright rolled his eyes at me and sighed with exasperation. "Well mighty funny you wanted to stand in that long line just to get them *pork* link sausages," he teased. "That's why we missed the last bus, and now we ain't got no way to get home lest we call the po'lice," Mr. Boatwright complained. He immediately turned to Mr. Nelson and looked at him with pleading eyes.

"I'm goin' in your direction. Y'all welcome to ride along with me," Mr. Nelson told us, opening his arms like he was going to hug somebody.

Mr. Boatwright couldn't gather our packages fast enough. There was a shiny black Cadillac parked in front of the drugstore. The same car I'd seen in front of the undertaker's house. Mr. Boatwright jumped in the front, all the while complaining about his leg, and I got in the back.

"How your family doin'? Scary Mary tells me you got your hands full," Mr. Boatwright boomed, drowning out Miles Davis coming from the tape deck.

"Well, that woman of mine is goin' to force me into the poorhouse. That hardheaded boy of mine is drivin' me crazy. He and his sister fight like a cat and dog. That's why we shipped her to her auntie this summer."

"How your mama? I hear she's havin' some health difficulties," Mr. Boatwright grunted, looking with envy at the undertaker's well-groomed hair.

"Well, Alzheimer's is pretty serious, but we manage to live with it. She's a handful though. We can't keep a nurse more than a few weeks. That's why I let that crazy half brother of mine move in, so he can help look after her. And, as you probably heard, my wife is not well, or at least she doesn't think she is. Every other day I drop off a new prescription."

"Well, I be seein' your wife in the yard wrestlin' with them rosebushes y'all got, and comin' and goin' with shoppin' bags from every store in town every day. She look mighty healthy to me," Mr. Boatwright said seriously, still staring at the undertaker's hair, blinking fast and hard.

"She cut her finger on a steak knife the other day and took to her bed, certain she was goin' to get infected. Today it's a cramp in her foot." Mr. Nelson laughed.

I sat in silence while Mr. Boatwright and Mr. Nelson talked. As soon as we got home, Mr. Boatwright started bad-mouthing Mr. Nelson.

"We don't eat pork," he mimicked. "Hmmmph! I bet he'd eat pork iffen he didn't have nothin' else to eat. And what he need with a car that big? Iffen I had a wife like his'n, always whinin' about a cut or a scratch or cramps, I'd slap her!"

"Mr. Nelson seems like a real nice man," I said casually. We were putting the meat away. I kept the pork links out so that I could eat a snack before dinner. "He doesn't look like an undertaker," I added thoughtfully.

"And just what is a undertaker supposed to look like?" Mr. Boatwright sniffed, shaking a pack of chicken wings in my direction, his other hand on his hip.

"Well . . . you know . . . grim, heavyset, spooky. The way you—" I covered my mouth with my hand. Mr. Boatwright looked at me like he wanted to slap me, but he didn't.

"I bet he ain't half the man I am, *iffen you know what I mean.* Scary

Mary say he got a balled-up sock stuffed in his crotch." Mr. Boatwright laughed.

"And she should know," I said sarcastically.

He lifted one of the links, shook it at me, and grinned. "You won't find no balled-up sock in my shorts." I pretended not to hear him. "Hurry up and eat your links. Then I'll give you the real thing."

"Mama'll be home soon!" I snapped, slamming the refrigerator door so hard it shook.

"Not tonight. The judge givin' his poker party tonight. We got plenty of time to have a good time."

"You mean *you* have a good time. I thought—" Before I could finish my sentence, Mr. Boatwright slid his knuckles along the side of my face.

"You sassin' me over a little poontang?"

"I'm not sassing you. I'm sick of doing . . . what we do. You know it's not right. Why can't you get a girlfriend your own age? Somebody who *wants* to do it with you."

Mr. Boatwright looked confused. He leaned back on his legs and put his hands on his hips. "Like I said, I could get any woman I want."

"Then why don't you?" I had lost my appetite. I wrapped the links back up and put the package in the refrigerator.

A long uncomfortable moment of silence passed. "You know I could make your life a livin' hell, girl."

"You already have," I assured him.

Mr. Boatwright gave me one of his meanest looks. One that took so much effort, his nostrils started flaring. "I'll remember that the next time you need money for the movies or books or somethin'." With that, he hobbled out of the kitchen and went to the living room.

I went to my room and lay down on my bed, proud that I had stood up to him. I just had to do it more often. Minutes later, he entered my room. "What do you want?" I barked.

"You can't tease me like you been doin' all day and get away with it," he said hoarsely. He rushed over to the bed and grabbed my arms and pinned them behind me. "Come on now, girl. This ain't gwine to take but a minute. Look on the bright side." That was the bright side. It took only a minute to satisfy him. As long as he was happy, he was good to me, and being alone with him so much, that was important.

On one side of our house was an empty lot. On the other side lived a widower named Caleb Davis and his thirteen-year-old son, Jerry. Caleb was a barber, and he had his shop in his house.

He and Scary Mary came to the house almost every day. Sometimes three to five times all in the same day, even when Mama was not at home. They would sit and drink beer with Mr. Boatwright and complain about almost everything. Mostly, they trashed other people, and it seemed like every time they got together one of them had some mind-boggling physical ailment that they liked to discuss in great detail. They tried to outdo one another. Scary Mary had high blood pressure and various female problems. Caleb complained about high blood pressure and ulcers, but the thing Caleb had, which ranked him way up there with Mr. Boatwright's fake leg, was a bullet lodged in his head from a war injury.

Caleb was nice, but I didn't trust him or feel comfortable around him. In fact, I didn't trust or feel comfortable around any male. Not even a preacher or an undertaker. I was convinced that they were all boogiemen. All because of what Mr. Boatwright had done to me.

Yet, I liked Caleb as much as I could like any male. He brought me candy and rib sandwiches and other tasty stuff and always said something nice to me. "That's a mighty pretty frock you got on, possum. Them some nice T-strap shoes you wore to church today."

Caleb was much taller and thinner than Mr. Boatwright, but they looked enough alike to be brothers. They were almost the same shade of brown, and each had a wide flat face.

I didn't let Caleb in when I was home alone. I didn't want to find out if he was a rapist, too.

Caleb's son Jerry was called Pee Wee because he was short and puny. With no encouragement from me, this boy eased himself into my life and became in many ways my shadow. Mr. Boatwright and a lot of people were convinced that he liked boys. He was what we called "funny," and it was no wonder. He was swishy, and he didn't play sports. He cooked, made most of his own clothes, and hung around with girls and old folks.

Even though Mr. Boatwright thought that Pee Wee was funny, he liked him, as did Mama. Pee Wee was a major gossip and never ran out of scandalous things to tell them.

He wandered into our house without knocking almost every day. "You seen my cat?" he asked one evening.

I had just come home from returning some books to the library and had left the front door unlocked. I didn't hear him come in. I was in the kitchen when I whirled around and saw him standing in the kitchen doorway. I gave him one of my meanest looks. Down South people entered a house without knocking. It was not just a Black thing—even the white folks did it. It was a country thing. I didn't like it there, and I didn't like it in Ohio. To me, it was the height of arrogance. What if I had been naked?

"You look here, boy. From now on, you knock before you come in this house. You don't live here." Funny or not, and even though we had a vague relationship, he was a male, and I didn't trust him.

"Girl, what's wrong with you?" he exclaimed. He snatched open our refrigerator and drank from a carton of milk. Pee Wee was not bad-looking for a boy. He was medium brown, with more than a few zits on his square face screaming to be popped. His eyes were too small and too close together, but his pleasant smile made up for it. Like so many Black boys in the early sixties, he wore his hair cut close to the head. One reason I tolerated him was that he baked cookies for me.

"You can't just walk in this house without knocking. Burglars do that," I told him.

He gave me an incredulous look. Then he let out a short, sharp laugh. "Girl, what burglar would risk goin' to jail to bust in here with all this junk y'all got?" He made a long, low, sweeping gesture with his hand. "Ain't nothin' in here nobody would want, specially me. Now, y'all got any more of that cake bread from yesterday? Hi, Brother Boatwright." Pee Wee rushed across the room to pat Mr. Boatwright's shoulder.

I didn't even know Mr. Boatwright was in. A lot of days I came home to an empty house. Mr. Boatwright spent a lot of time at Scary Mary's claiming to give Bible lessons to the prostitutes. A minute didn't pass before Caleb and Scary Mary marched in and planted themselves at the kitchen table with Pee Wee and Mr. Boatwright. I was pleasantly surprised when Mama walked in shortly after they did. She dropped a bag that was full of beer onto the table. Her faded, ripped scarf was tied in such a messy knot, she had to struggle to get it loose.

"You off mighty early today, Sister Goode," Caleb said. He rubbed his head on the spot where the bullet was lodged.

Mama dropped her scarf and coat on the kitchen counter and let out a long sigh. Her cheap, ill-fitting stockings had rolled almost all the way down her legs. "Judge Lawson is goin' to visit some ex-colleagues in Cleveland. He wanted to get a early start, so he sent me home early with pay, bless his heart," Mama explained. I stood back against the wall as she dragged a chair from the dining room into the kitchen and sat near the rest of the crowd. When Mama crossed her legs, I noticed quarter-sized holes in her secondhand shoes. Everybody's hands were spread out on the table like at a séance.

"Anybody got any juicy news today?" Mr. Boatwright began. He looked directly at Pee Wee. By then everybody had a beer on the table. All the adults that is. I could see Pee Wee's mouth watering for one of the beers. But he knew better than to drink in front of that many grown folks that included his own daddy.

"Well, that uppity undertaker's brother done finally outdone hisself," Pee Wee started. All eyes turned to him.

"Let *me* tell this one here," Caleb interrupted, holding up his thick hand in his son's face. I never noticed before, but Caleb had two gold-plated teeth.

"But Daddy—" Pee Wee pouted.

"Young'n, don't you sass your daddy," Mama advised Pee Wee. She turned to Caleb with a large smile. "Go on, Brother Davis."

Caleb sucked in his breath first, took a long swallow of his beer, then folded his arms, but not before rubbing his head again. "That uppity undertaker, Brother Nelson, from across the street, had me trim his hair last night. Hmph! I bet Nelson ain't even his real last name. He took it on tryin' to put hisself up there on that same pedestal with Ozzie Nelson on the TV and he sure tries to behave like the *real* Nelsons. They is classic white folks. Since when is Nelson a colored name."

"You think he uppity, that woman of his'n call herself *Michelle Jacquelyn!*" Mr. Boatwright roared.

"Go on, Brother Davis," Mama said to Caleb.

Caleb frowned and squirmed around in his chair. With the exception of a shiny black suit he wore to church every Sunday, the only clothes I ever saw him wear were stiff overalls and cheap plaid shirts with patches on his elbows. "I know he conks his hair like all the rest of us, but he won't admit it . . . all them naps along the side of his neck."

Caleb paused just long enough to take another long swallow from his beer. Then he rolled up his sleeves. "We all know the undertaker's white half brother Johnny, is a Bluebeard. I heard he had somethin' to do with them two wives of his'n dyin' early. I bet he done away with 'em to collect insurance. Huh, y'all?"

Everybody nodded and urged Caleb to continue. "He told me once upon a time he wanted to preach. But white folks don't know the

Bible like we do." Caleb paused and waved his hand angrily. "Two things white folks need to leave to us is the gospel and cookin'. Anyway, one of Scary Mary's gals got herself stabbed to death the other night comin' out of that Red Rose beer garden on Canal Street. Ain't that right?" He nodded at Scary Mary, and she nodded back. She reached over to help him massage his head.

"I had told that heifer to stay away from them beer gardens with all them hot-natured, just-released parolee men runnin' amok," Scary Mary said sadly.

"So the undertaker is settin' in my chair and tellin' me all this. In secret now, so don't none of y'all go around town and blab this news. He got the body before it was even cold. And had her stretched out on a slab in his dead room like he was supposed to. That lustin', white half brother of his'n snuck in that dead room after everybody was in the bed and . . . ravaged that dead woman. Pestered her right there in Brother Nelson's dead room." Nobody said a word for several moments, but they all gasped.

Scary Mary waved her hands and shook her head, "Poor Rosalee," she sobbed. "One of my best girls."

"This here white man, when he tried to get up from his dirty deed . . . he couldn't," Caleb announced. His thick fist hit the top of the table so hard, the beer bottles rattled. Now the story really had my attention. "Rigor mortis had set in. Y'all, Brother Nelson was fit to be tied! He had a mess on his hands. Anyway, this nasty dog Johnny's instrument was locked up inside the woman's female area! What a mess, what a mess. It took the undertaker and that big old strappin' teenage boy of his quite a while to pull him aloose."

Again, Mr. Boatwright amazed me with another comment. "That nasty buzzard. I swear to God, white folks is so unnatural. Ravagin' a dead woman. I seen a white man ravage a sheep one day when I was a young'n!" he roared. I glared at him so hard, he flinched.

"I bet a man would ravage a snake if he could find the—" I blurted. A long, threatening look from Mama shut me up.

"Go mop that bathroom floor, girl," she ordered.

Out of the corner of my eye, I could see Mr. Boatwright giving me a threatening look. "And you better not miss a spot!" he yelled.

CHAPTER 9

It wasn't long before I began to use gossip to my advantage. As soon as I heard something juicy I told Mama and Mr. Boatwright.

Some of the news I brought into the house was so good, Mr. Boatwright kept me in the kitchen repeating things over and over so long that he canceled trips to my bedroom. Good gossip always mellowed Mama. What I couldn't pick up from eavesdropping at church or peeping in one of Scary Mary's windows, I got from Pee Wee. Even though he was my so-called companion, he got on my nerves from time to time.

One Sunday when Mama was home, Pee Wee wandered in and made himself comfortable at the kitchen table with Mama and me. Mr. Boatwright had gone to visit his foot doctor. Mama and I had the house to ourselves for a few hours before Pee Wee's invasion.

"Sister Goode, I just stopped by to see if Annette's goin' to pick beans in the mornin'. Brother Jones is pickin' me up at 8 A.M.," Pee Wee said.

I gave him a look as severe as the ones I gave to Mr. Boatwright. Pee Wee wouldn't look at me. I hated working on the farms, and he knew it! I preferred earning my spending money by running errands for Scary Mary and her women.

"I made a whole dollar yesterday," Pee Wee added. I was mad enough to slap him.

"Well now." Mama turned to me. Her look said it all. The next morning I went to pick beans. That was my first and last day in the bean fields, thanks to Mr. Boatwright. A lot of mannish boys worked in the bean fields. Some of them had already fathered a baby or two.

When old Mr. Jones stopped in front of our house to let me out at the end of the day, one of those boys slapped me on the butt as I was getting out of the car. Mr. Boatwright was on our front-porch glider sitting straight-backed and stone-faced, with his hands on his knees like a sphinx. He saw what that boy did to me and hopped in the house before I could get up on the front porch.

Before I could get in the door, Mr. Boatwright had grabbed me by my arm and snatched me the rest of the way in. He was filled with rage. I honestly thought that he was going to kill me or at least make me wish I was dead.

"You fat horny pig!" he roared. He shoved me so hard I stumbled all the way across the room and hit the wall so hard a picture of Jesus fell to the floor.

"What?" I cried.

"You heifer! You wench! I seen what was goin' on in that car!" He waved his finger in my face. "Get a switch!"

"For what?" I had done nothing that warranted a whupping.

"For what? What you mean for what? I seen what just happened. Like you ain't got no shame atall!"

"I didn't do anything. Robert felt on my butt—"

"Get a switch!"

While Mr. Boatwright was whupping me, we fell to the living-room floor with him landing on top of me. Suddenly, he stopped swinging the switch. He gave me a thoughtful look, forced my legs open, snatched my panties down far enough, and satisfied himself with just one violent thrust.

When Mama got home, Mr. Boatwright told her how I'd flirted with a boy from the bean-picking crew who had already made two other girls pregnant.

"You ain't goin' to pick beans no more, girl," Mama informed me. "There is too many boys in them fields. The fields is where I got myself ruined by that bean-pickin' daddy of yours, and look what he done to us! Make friends with some of them girls at the church or when you start your new school. Forget about boys."

"Yes, Ma'am," I promised. I attempted to make friends with a couple of girls my age at church but failed.

Mona Mack, who was thin and considered plain, kept reminding me I was overweight. "You should always wear dark colors, girl, and stay away from stripes and plaids," she told me. I stored away all of my bright-colored clothes and gave my striped and plaid outfits to a secondhand store.

"Ash Hat Shoppe got some new wigs, and you sure ought to get one to cover your head," Mona told me on another occasion.

She enjoyed putting me down, especially in front of other kids. When I realized that, I dropped her.

Being friends with another girl, Francine Bryant, a plump, dark-skinned girl who was already wearing wigs, didn't work out either. She borrowed money from me that she never paid back.

Mama gave me a dollar every week, and I earned a lot by running errands for Scary Mary. But most of my spending money came from Mr. Boatwright. Almost every time after sex, he'd toss me a few dollars. Though I resisted and avoided him as much as I possibly could, sadly I approached him from time to time when I needed money. Once I even went to his room and sat on his bed. "Um . . . Mr. Boatwright, I want to go to the movies with Francine, but we need money for the bus and popcorn and stuff." I trembled.

Mr. Boatwright was lying on his side looking at me with a straight face. He didn't react until I stroked his arm. "I see," he growled. He pulled ten dollars out of his pants pocket and handed it to me, then he reached for me.

"Um . . . the movie starts real soon," I said, rising from his bed. He sighed with exasperation, then waved me away with his hand.

Once Francine and I got to the movies, she left me to go sit with some of her other friends. While I was in a bathroom stall I overheard her tell another girl, "Annette, so stupid! Watch me get a camera out of her for my birthday next month."

Francine's words crushed me. I never told her what I overheard, but I broke off the "friendship" immediately.

"You'll meet other girls when school starts this September," Mama told me when I told her about Mona and Francine.

"I hope so, Mama," I replied.

I still spoke to Mona and Francine when I saw them at church, but turned down their invitations to go swimming or the movies. When Francine sent me an invitation to attend her birthday party, I declined immediately. I was lonely and had low self-esteem but I did have some pride. I didn't need friends bad enough to put up with those two.

* * *

The first time I saw Rhoda Nelson, the uppity undertaker's only daughter, my heart almost stopped beating.

A week before school started, Pee Wee and I were sitting on my front-porch steps when this long black airport limousine crawled around the corner and stopped in front of the undertaker's house. The driver got out and ran to open one of the back doors.

"Oh oh," Pee Wee started. I knew this was going to be something good from his reaction. He stood up and placed his hands on his hips. Rhoda slid out and stretched. "Where you been, Miss Hollywood? Europe again, I bet!" Pee Wee hollered in his sweetest voice.

The girl smiled and waved. "Just the Bahamas," she replied casually.

I stood up and shaded my eyes to see her better. "Pee Wee, who is that girl?" I mouthed. Before he could answer, the girl beckoned for us to join her. I followed Pee Wee across the street as she tipped the driver. I couldn't believe my eyes. She was the prettiest *Black* girl I had ever seen in my life. She was dark like me. She was regally slim and had a rope of thick black hair that almost reached her waist. Lord, let that hair be a wig, I said under my breath. The most striking thing about her was her eyes. They were huge and bright green. She had a heart-shaped face, a small nose, full pouty lips, and teeth that looked too perfect to be real, though I knew they were.

"I thought you was down South for the summer visitin' your white aunt," Pee Wee said to the girl.

"I was. But about two weeks ago, Aunt Lola got mad at her boyfriend and wanted to teach him a lesson. While he was at work we sneaked to the Bahamas and stayed until it was time for me to come back home," Rhoda replied.

Pee Wee looked at me, and said, "Miss Thing here went to Paris last summer."

"Paris, France?" I gasped. The girl was so intimidating I could feel knots forming in my stomach.

"*Oui, oui.*" Pee Wee laughed, snapping his fingers.

"I'm Rhoda," Miss Thing said warmly. She smiled at me and extended her small hand. She had long slender fingers with neatly polished and manicured nails. Compared to hers, mine looked like the Monkey's Paw.

"I'm Annette. We moved to this street in June," I croaked. Rhoda had on a blue-silk dress, matching pumps, and was carrying a baby blue leather shoulder bag. The dull brown, thrift-shop flannel smock I had on had taken on a life of its own. No matter how hard I cleaned and pressed it, it curled up at the hem and changed colors every time I washed it.

"Where did you live before?" she asked me.

"Over by the city dump," Pee Wee told her, wiggling his nose.

"Oh," Rhoda said, moving back a step. "Well, I hope you'll like it over here." She smiled. "What grade are you in?" She tossed her hair back off her face.

"Oh we all in the same grade. Eighth," Pee Wee volunteered.

"Good. After school starts, maybe the three of us can get together and study sometime," she suggested. "Listen, I'm a little tired . . ."

"Girl, as soon as you get settled in, I'll come over and give you all the lowdown on what's been happenin'. I got all kinds of news. Startin' with that loutish white uncle of yours," Pee Wee cried, snapping his neck.

Rhoda rolled her eyes and shook her head. "I heard about poor Uncle Johnny and that dead woman. I'm sure he was drunk . . ." I could tell that she was embarrassed. This white man I kept hearing about was her favorite relative, Pee Wee had told me.

"Well, I got a lot of other juicy stuff to tell you," Pee Wee continued.

"I figured that." Rhoda grinned. I was just standing there, glued to my spot. She then gave me a serious look. "It was nice meetin' you, Nannette."

"Annette," I corrected. She excused herself and started walking toward her house. Mr. Nelson came out on the front porch with his arms stretched out to greet Rhoda. He noticed Pee Wee and me and waved to us.

Pee Wee and I returned to my porch steps, where he spent the next two hours giving me all the details on Rhoda. That gorgeous mane on her head was her real hair. Other than Pee Wee, she had no close friends. She and her family belonged to the same church Mama, Mr. Boatwright, and I had joined since our move. We still attended Reverend Snipes's church occasionally so Mr. Boatwright could continue singing his solos, but we were now members of the Second Baptist Church. Only because it was so much closer Mama told Reverend Snipes. I was convinced it was a prestige thing. All the Black folks with money attended Second Baptist Church on Patterson Street.

Other than Pee Wee, she had very little to do with the rest of the kids.

I had never seen anybody as fascinating as Rhoda Nelson. Not even on TV. She was so intriguing I found myself thinking about her the next day while Mr. Boatwright was on top of me. Pretending that I was her made it a little easier for me to tolerate this beast without going crazy.

I couldn't understand why any man would want to take advantage of me with beauties like Rhoda roaming around. I believed that part of a pretty girl's burden was to have to put up with a lot of unwanted attention. All my life I'd watch men smile and wink at my pretty mother. Judge Lawson was spending more time than ever with Mama in our living room, with his hand rubbing her knee, saying things like, "The house all right, Gussie Mae? You need anything? I'll send my man over to cut the grass. Anything else you need done, let me know and I'll fix it." I couldn't tell if Mama really liked spending so much of her free time entertaining the judge. But she never discussed her actions with me, and I didn't ask.

School started a week after Rhoda's return. I had not talked to her since we had met, but I'd seen her climbing out of cabs with big shopping bags almost every day. I spied on her from the largest window in my bedroom, my front window. When I could avoid that irritating Pee Wee, I waited until I saw Rhoda leave for school so that I could trail behind her. Her beauty was so overwhelming, I actually felt beautiful just being near her.

"Oink, oink. Mornin', Pig Face," Mr. Boatwright greeted me one schoolday morning as I passed him on my way out the door.

"Same to you, butt breath," I yelled back. I sassed him from time to time when Mama or no other grown person was around. It usually got me a whupping from him, but it was worth it. He ran after me and grabbed me by my coat collar.

"Who you sassin'?" He released me, then stood up straight and looked me over critically, long and hard. He screwed up his face like he was in pain. "Get on out my sight!" he said tiredly. "You more trouble than you worth." He dismissed me with a wave of his hand.

I had started wearing ribbons in my hair like Rhoda and a little makeup. This particular day I had even put on some pierced earrings that one of Scary Mary's women had given to me. Mr. Boatwright looked at my hair, my face, and my ears, and shook his head with pity.

"What?" I groaned.

"According to the Scriptures—oh never mind." I thought he was done talking, so I started to walk away. "Makeup, earbobs, and all them hair frills. Don't you know by now, you can't make a silk purse out of a sow's ear, let alone the whole sow. I don't know what I see in you." He sighed. "You look so much better without that makeup and them ribbons," he said seriously.

"You think so?" I said sadly, crushed and confused.

"I know so. You go to that schoolhouse tryin' to be somethin' you ain't, them kids *really* goin' to let you have it. You follow the Scriptures, you'll be all right. You know the Bible almost well as I do by now, so I know you ain't forgot that lesson on Lot's wife." He gave me an affectionate pat on my head and turned and walked away.

I dragged myself back to my room and snatched the ribbons from my hair and kicked them halfway across the room. Before I could remove the makeup, Mr. Boatwright was in my room with a familiar look on his face.

"That's much better." He grinned, as he unzipped his pants.

"Mr. Boatwright, I'm on my period," I lied.

He rushed out of the room, cussing under his breath.

It took me a while to get my hair under control again. Rhoda was long gone by then, and it ruined my day. I was late for class and had to do detention after school. When I got home, Mr. Boatwright gave me a whupping for getting detention.

Once my whupping wore off, I went to sit on the front porch. Rhoda was on hers reading. She looked up and waved, then returned her attention to her reading material. Pee Wee had told me that she was one of the smartest girls in the whole school. She had taught herself how to speak Spanish. She played the piano and knew a lot of grown-up card games that her aunt Lola had taught her. Pee Wee told me that a lot of the kids were afraid of Rhoda, as petite as she was. There were several reasons. She had a ferocious big brother named Jock, who was the leader of a street gang. Terrorizing other kids was a way of life for him. He had even beaten up Pee Wee a few times.

Another reason a lot of kids feared Rhoda was because she had a crazy grandmother living in the house. A white woman. I hadn't seen her yet, but I had heard that she chased cars up and down the street and threw rocks at people and called Black folks niggers. Still another reason kids were afraid of Rhoda was, a policeman had shot and killed her other brother while Rhoda was in his bedroom one night when she was six, and she had never gotten over it. Everybody said it made her act crazy sometimes. And finally, her daddy was an undertaker. To a lot of kids, undertakers and boogiemen were interchangeable. Nobody wanted the boogieman's daughter as a friend.

CHAPTER 10

History was my worst subject. But it was the only class I had with Rhoda, so I didn't mind going to it. Since she was everything I wanted to be and more, I even looked forward to it each day. I flunked most of the tests and arrived late two or three times a week because this was my first class after lunch. I was always one of the last ones to leave the cafeteria because I usually went back in line to get additional helpings of whatever was on the menu.

I had been in the new school for several days before I got up enough nerve to approach Rhoda without her inviting me. The cafeteria was crowded for lunch that day. Sadly, it was divided by race. Our local news covered all the racial problems Black people were having down South, especially the violence. There was an occasional fight in our school between somebody Black and somebody white. Sometimes it was over something as innocent as a comment made about somebody's mother. The words "nigger" and "honky" eventually came up during the confrontation, and that made it a race incident. I think all that had a lot to do with people making such a big deal out of somebody's color even in Ohio. It wasn't a rule like down South, but we still had to deal with segregation. Property managers found ways not to rent to Blacks, jobs advertised in the paper were suddenly "filled" when a Black person attempted to apply, and the service Black folks received in some restaurants was so bad, it was better not to go there in the first place. Most of the time when I attempted to sit with white kids in the cafeteria, they gave me dirty looks and sometimes said something mean about my mama or just moved to another table. It seemed like everything was based on Black or white and a few colors in between, even lunch in a junior high school. The only Asian girl in our school was sitting with the school's only four Hispanic kids at a table in the back of the cafeteria. Near the Black kids, Rhoda was sitting at a front table alone reading *Ebony* magazine. I was sitting at another table halfway between the white kids and us across the room by myself.

I don't know how I got up enough nerve, but I decided to take my tray and go over to her. Most of the food on her tray had not even been touched! I didn't know what to say to her. I took a deep breath, walked across the room to the table by the exit where she was sitting, and said, "Can I have your French fries?" I sat down across from her.

"Sure." She smiled. She sighed and pushed her tray toward me, then returned her attention to the magazine. "Annette, right?" she asked, not looking up.

"Yep! Just like the white girl from the *Mickey Mouse Club* on TV," I told her. She didn't look at me again until I let out a belch that could be heard halfway across the room. "Excuse me," I mumbled, my face burning with embarrassment. Black kids and white kids snickered and glared at me. I had eaten the French fries in record time. I was horrified at my behavior.

"Are you still hungry? If you are, I'll go get you some more," she told me.

"Yeah," I mumbled. "With ketchup."

"Can I watch you eat them?" she asked softly. Our eyes met for a moment. She seemed to be studying me. Suddenly, I felt like the main attraction in a circus sideshow.

"What? Why do you want to *watch* me eat some French fries?" I wanted to know.

"I've never seen anybody enjoy food like you," she said, an incredulous look on her face. "You finished those fries in less than a minute."

"Um . . . did I? Uh . . . don't you eat fries?" I asked.

"Every once in a while. I have to watch my weight. Besides, the fries here are sometimes so greasy I wouldn't feed them to a hog I don't like."

The fries suddenly lost their appeal, as did everything else edible.

"Yeah. They are greasy. And I am kind of full," I muttered. "But, you can go get me some candy bars, if you don't mind."

"Oh, you like candy too?"

"Uh-huh."

"Ooh. I know how to make this real good candy with molasses and peanuts. One day I'll make you some, huh?"

"Yeah!" I tried to conceal my excitement. I was liking this girl more and more.

"I'll go get you some M&Ms for now. You like them?"

"Oh yes. I like them a whole lot," I admitted. "Hurry up," I urged. To my surprise, she seemed as excited as I was! She gave me that smile again, then excused herself.

The next day I attempted to copy Rhoda's answers on a history test. I sat one desk behind her in the next row. She saw me and rolled her eyes at me in such an evil way I shuddered. I hadn't seen anybody roll their eyes that hard since I left Florida. I lowered my head and started tapping my pencil on my desk.

I felt pretty low by the time I arrived home that evening. Mama had left a note saying that she wouldn't be home until after 10 P.M. and that I'd better do anything Mr. Boatwright told me to do. Pee Wee was already in our living room with Mr. Boatwright, gossiping away.

Minutes after Pee Wee left, Mr. Boatwright was on top of me on the living-room floor. All the while I lay under him, I was thinking about Rhoda. I wondered what she was really like. The next moment, a strange feeling consumed me. I had developed my first crush: I was in love with Rhoda.

"How come you so flexible this time?" Mr. Boatwright wanted to know, grinning proudly. "Seem like you finally gettin' the hang of things, praise the Lord."

We had dressed, and I was helping him back to the couch.

"I had somebody on my mind," I told him. My boldness surprised me. "Somebody who likes me . . ."

"Well." He paused, and tilted his head, beaming proudly. "I guess I still got it, huh?" He let out his breath and slapped his hands on his hips.

I sat down on the arm of the couch and stared at him in disbelief. "Uh . . . no, not you. The pretty girl across the street. The undertaker's daughter." I wondered what it would be like to hug her and kiss her the way Mr. Boatwright hugged and kissed me.

"Rhoda?" A sad look appeared on his face. He was clearly disappointed.

"Uh-huh. She's real nice to me. One time she gave me her French fries at lunch and went and bought me some M&Ms. She said me and her and Pee Wee can study sometime."

Mr. Boatwright gasped. "What—now why would a gal like that want to hang around with a booger like you? That little heifer think she white anyway!" His comments hurt me severely.

"She's a nice girl, and I think she likes me," I told him. "I think she wants to be my friend." I smiled; he frowned. "My first real girlfriend," I added, still smiling.

The scowl on his face became so profound, his mouth looked like it had been turned upside down and his eyebrows seemed to protrude. "That whole uppity Nelson family ain't nothin' but a generation of vipers, girl. With they no-pork-eatin' selves! When they shit it stink just as pooty as ours—probably worse!"

"I don't care what you say—"

"You sassin' me?" It was hard to believe, but the scowl on his face got even worse. He drew back to slap me.

"No sir," I whimpered, with my head bowed submissively.

"Now. Let's find the *TV Guide*," he said, almost cheerfully. His scowl suddenly disappeared, and he looked like his old self, which was still bad, but not nearly as threatening.

Later that night, just before Mama got home, Mr. Boatwright came to my room and dropped his evil body onto my bed right next to me and started rocking and humming, "Hush Little Baby."

"Mr. Boatwright," I began.

He turned to face me, still rocking my bed and humming.

"Mr. Boatwright, why do you keep doing what you do to me after all these years?" I asked. I had caught him off guard.

"What you mean?" He gasped and stood, his narrowed eyes darting from side to side.

"You know I read a lot of books."

"And that's another thing, you and all them books. Gibberish! Worldly! I can smell the brimstone. Everything you need to know in the Bible, girl."

"I've learned a lot from books other than the Bible. Things I really need to know. I know that what you do to me is wrong," I said calmly. I think the fact that I didn't raise my voice or seem mad made him even angrier. If looks could kill, I'd have dropped dead on the spot right then and there. I had never seen him look at me in such a mean way.

"You mean what *we* do."

"But I don't want to, and you know I don't want to," I wailed. "You know I don't like it. Why do you still do it?"

Suddenly, he looked at the floor and let out his breath. Then he looked at me with a straight face, and whined, "After all I do for you, how come you so mean to me, possum?" His words made me gasp. When I didn't respond, he lowered his head and shuffled out of my room, gently closing the door.

CHAPTER 11

O f all my classes, the one I dreaded most was P.E. I was always one of the last to be picked for any of the teams, and most of the girls I couldn't stand, because they bullied us unpopular kids, were in this class.

Stege Junior High was only one of two junior high schools in Richland. Taking up almost a whole city block, Stege was filled with mostly upscale white kids, but there were a lot of rowdy, low-income kids from the north side of town enrolled as well. It was bad enough the kids in our school had racial problems, but there were also clashes based on economic levels. Surprisingly, how much money your family had carried more weight than race. It was more common to see rich kids, white and Black, associating with each other than with poor kids of their own race.

Being Black *and* poor, I knew better than to attempt to be part of any of the popular crowds. I hung out with a few other girls who came to school mainly to learn like I did. There were a couple of girls I often ate lunch with, but I'd never been to their homes or invited them to mine.

Now, on my way to P.E., I could not imagine what lay in store for me. I didn't know if the girls were going to ignore me or attack me. My thoughts were interrupted when somebody tapped me on the back. I closed my eyes and expected the worst. When nothing happened after a few moments, I stopped and turned around. It was

Rhoda, dressed in all white. A white ribbon hung from the side of her hair. She was dazzling.

"Hi." She smiled. I had never been this close to her before.

"Hi," I mumbled. Within seconds, sweat started to form on my forehead, and I started trembling. My thoughts were running amok. What could she want from me? My lunch money? My new secondhand scarf. "I'll give you a nickel," I told her, bowing my head submissively.

"A nickel? What would *I* do with *a nickel?* My daddy gives me a whole dollar every mornin'," she informed me. "I just wanted to apologize to you for rollin' my eyes at you in history class. I was havin' a bad day."

I breathed a sigh of relief. "I'm the one who should be apologizing. If I had studied, I would not have had to copy your answers. You always get A's." I surprised myself. It felt so natural talking to her. But I could barely stand to look into those stunning green eyes. I didn't know if I was going to like being a lesbian and was beginning to have second thoughts about it already. What good-looking lesbian would want me? Did I really want to kiss this girl? I wasn't even sure now.

"I study real hard, and I earn all those good grades I get," Rhoda claimed. I knew that Rhoda was originally from down South, too, because she had a moderate Southern accent. I had worked hard over the years trying to get rid of mine, but it was still noticeable. I was proud of the fact that I had never dropped my g's from ing words, something I'd picked up from TV and radio when we still lived in Florida. "Readin' is my first love," she gushed.

"Oh? Mine too. Reading and movies." I swallowed so hard, my throat hurt. She was making me nervous, but I was glad to be talking with her. "I don't have any brothers or sisters or friends, so I have to do something so I won't be lonely."

She followed as I walked on. I didn't want to be late to this class.

"What about Pee Wee?" she asked.

"Well, he's . . . um . . . not really a friend. He's just the boy next door. His daddy comes to our house a lot, so Pee Wee comes, too."

"Yeah, he comes to visit me a lot, too, but I don't consider him a friend. He's just . . . just . . . there." We both laughed. "Hey! You like comic books? *Superman, Archie.*"

"Uh-huh. I read them a lot," I replied, bobbing my head up and down.

"I got a pile up to my knee if you want to borrow the ones you haven't read yet."

"Ooh wee. But . . . why? You don't know me," I said shyly, narrowing my eyes to see her better.

"Well," she shrugged and cocked her head to the side, "since we live so close, my daddy said you're a nice girl and I should be neighborly to you. He thinks I'm too grown for my age. He's always tryin' to get me to make friends at school with other girls." Rhoda paused and her eyes got wide. "I know—maybe we can go to the library or the bookstore or the movies together sometime," she said excitedly.

"Huh?" I gasped. "Me and you?"

"Sure. Don't you want to?"

"Well . . . I didn't think . . . you . . . um." I didn't know what I was saying.

"You don't like me either, Annette?" she asked sadly. We stopped. Our eyes met, and I saw something that frightened me. I saw the same emptiness I felt sometimes.

I shrugged, and said, "I like you. But you . . . you mean you *like* me? Some of the kids don't like me, but I don't really care," I said firmly.

"Well, you're not like any of those other kids. You wouldn't want to be like them."

"What do you mean?"

"I mean, do you want to be an imitation of somebody else, or do you want to be yourself? I don't know you that well, but from what I do know, you're worth five of some of those other girls."

"I am?"

"You're smart, and you've got a complexion I couldn't beat with a stick."

My hand went up to my face. I widened my eyes and looked at Rhoda with great suspicion. "What about my complexion? Everybody says I'm too dark."

"Too dark for what?"

"I really don't know," I said thoughtfully, scratching the back of my neck.

"We're the same shade, and I'm sure as hell not too dark for anything. God didn't think so, or He wouldn't have made us this color." Rhoda paused and smiled. "Your skin reminds me of a milk chocolate candy bar. All smooth and silky and not nary a pimple, a freckle, nothin'. And look at that beauty mark!"

This was the first time the wart above my lip had been referred to as a beauty mark. "But you've got nice skin, too," I stammered.

"Yeah but mine's from the drugstore. If I didn't do facials and didn't wear makeup, my face would look like peanut brittle."

"Thanks, Rhoda. No other girl has ever told me that before," I said shyly. I inspected my ashy hands, turning them over twice.

"Oh, they are probably jealous," Rhoda snarled. "Most of these kids are too stupid for their own good. Who needs 'em?"

"I know what you mean. I just wish they would let me go on about my business. I just want to graduate so I can go on with my life. Sometimes I get so angry I feel like dropping out of school. But I am not going to let them break me," I said levelly.

"I see you sittin' on your porch lookin' by yourself all the time. Then I see you in the cafeteria, alone like me. I sit on my porch alone a lot, and I sit in the cafeteria every day alone. I don't have any close friends either."

"But you're so pretty—"

"So?"

"You could probably have any boyfriend you want. I hear all the girls talking about how they wish they had your shape or your hair or your looks. Even some of the white girls," I blurted.

"But that doesn't mean they like me. A lot of them don't like me on account of they are jealous because my daddy's got a lot of money and everything and my mama's good-lookin'. Madeline Brewster invited every girl but me in Home Ec. class to her slumber party this weekend. I've never been to a slumber party . . ." There were tears in her eyes. I was so taken aback I almost fainted.

"You want to sit on my porch with me this evening?" A lump had formed in my throat. I had a hard time getting my words out without it hurting. She was the first person I had ever invited home since Mona and Francine, the girls from my church I'd tried to be friends with. She smiled and nodded vigorously.

"You know, other than that Pee Wee and my family, my dolls are my only companions. Isn't it odd? The kids probably hate me as much as they hate you. And you and I are as different as night and day," Rhoda told me excitedly.

"I don't have much of a family. Just me and Mama and this aunt in Florida. I don't know exactly where my other folks are. Most of them are still down South somewhere. I know my daddy's somewhere with a white woman."

"Speakin' of white folks, wait until you meet my uncle Johnny.

Before he got religion, he robbed a bank one time with a butcher knife." Rhoda laughed. We heard the bell ring. "We better run."

"You're in this class now?" I howled.

"I transferred today. Today is dodgeball. Nobody's goin' to pick me to be on their team," she said sadly.

"Me neither. I hope the teacher makes the same team take us both." I giggled.

Rhoda and I entered the locker room together. She was chattering away about having to rush home after school to help her mother take care of her grandmother and to clean her room.

Most of the girls had already dressed for class and were standing around chewing gum real loud and cussing up a storm. The ring leader was a tall, good-looking Black girl with red hair named Lena Cundiff. Her daddy was a doctor *and* a preacher, but she was one mean bitch. Lena and her gang glared at Rhoda and me.

"I gotta change my tampon. Watch my stuff," Rhoda told me. She handed me her book bag and strutted past the girls on to the bathroom stalls. Lena snarled something under her breath, and Rhoda turned around and stopped. "Did you say somethin', Cundiff?" Rhoda hissed. Her voice carried so much authority it didn't surprise me when Lena bowed and shook her head. "I didn't think you did," Rhoda added.

As soon as Rhoda disappeared, Lena gave me another mean look. I just let out my breath and sat down on one of the benches and started to remove my shoes. I already had my gym clothes on under my street clothes. Not only did it save time, I didn't have to get my gym basket from the cage. One of Lena's friends was in charge of the cage. In the last gym class when I had retrieved my gym clothes, somebody had stuck a big wad of purple chewing gum in the crotch of my shorts. Before I could get my blouse off, Lena strode over and stood in front of me and folded her arms and gave me a threatening look.

"Girl, you look like somethin' I seen swingin' from a tree in a Tarzan movie. What you lookin' at, Cheetah?" she shouted at me with her nostrils flaring.

"Nothing," I muttered. My eyes were on the floor.

"I'm surprised they make shorts big enough to fit a cow like you," she said seriously. The other girls roared.

"They do," I mumbled. Somehow, I managed a smile.

"And where did you get that book bag? I know for a fact your funky old mama ain't nothin' but a maid cleanin' funky Judge Lawson's toilets and shit. She ain't got no money to afford nothin' that nice. I bet you stole it." Then, without warning and for no apparent reason, other than the fact that she just didn't like me, Lena stomped on my bare foot.

"I don't steal," I told her in a weak, barely audible voice as I massaged my foot. It hurt like hell. I was sure I'd be limping for a few hours, but since I wasn't going to be picked for any of the ball teams anyway, it didn't matter.

"I bet you do. That's a nylon book bag. Lemme feel it." Lena ran her mean hand along the side of Rhoda's book bag. Before I knew what was happening, she dug a big bugger from her nose and stuck it on Rhoda's beautiful new book bag. I was horrified. The other girls roared even louder and harder. It sounded like thunder, but what happened next happened so fast, I don't remember all the details. Rhoda shot across the locker-room floor, grabbed Lena by her arm, and pulled her back to the bathroom stalls. The other girls and I ran behind them. Inside the bathroom, Rhoda forced Lena's head into an out-of-service toilet and held it there for a full minute, then she flushed it. There was sweat all over Rhoda's pretty face. Her eyes darkened, and her face became a mask of absolute rage. Her teeth were clenched, her lips trembled. For a moment I thought that I was looking at the devil. The water from the toilet spilled out onto the floor as Lena tried desperately to get away from Rhoda.

The other girls got so quiet you could hear a pin drop. I actually found myself feeling sorry for Lena. Then Rhoda snatched Lena's head back, pulled her up, and slammed her against the wall with so much force the lockers rattled.

"If you ever touch any of my stuff again, I am goin' to *kill* you, Lena," Rhoda said seriously. "Do I make myself clear?" Her voice was cold and hard, almost like a deep growl. Rhoda didn't seem like herself anymore. I don't know how, but I knew she meant business.

Lena was coughing and spitting up all kinds of filth from the toilet. She wiped her face with both hands, then turned to face Rhoda. "Is that a threat, Nelson?" I could not believe that Lena was brave enough to say anything that might possibly provoke Rhoda again. But most bullies I knew were not smart people anyway. She didn't know any better.

"That's not a threat," Rhoda said, letting out her breath. She was so cool and calm that it was scary. By now, her voice had returned to normal. "That's a promise."

CHAPTER 12

Kids talked about the incident in the locker room for days. What amazed me was the fact that Rhoda did not get in trouble. Pee Wee had told me that even some of the teachers were afraid of her, but I didn't know whether or not to believe him. But the more I thought about it, they must have been. Other kids got sent to the principal's office left and right. Rhoda almost never did.

"Yeah, some of the teachers are scared of me," Rhoda confirmed on our way to school a few days later. We were walking arm in arm like I saw a lot of best girlfriends do. Pee Wee was stumbling along behind us, mumbling something every now and then. It was like it was just Rhoda and me. We had a world of our own.

"Why?" I asked her. We had some pretty scary teachers at our school.

"Oh they think she crazy," Pee Wee offered. "And, cause her daddy's best, best friend, Mr. Antonosanti—richest man in town—is a mean-lookin' Italian with a scar on his jaw."

Rhoda rolled her eyes at Pee Wee. "Everybody thinks I'm crazy." She said it like it was something to be proud of.

"I don't think you're crazy. I just think that you're different," I said gently. "I wanted to be friends with you the first time I saw you because I'm different, too. I've never had a real girlfriend," I admitted.

"Me neither. Not since we moved up here from Alabama." Rhoda squeezed my arm and smiled. "French fries are on the menu today for lunch. You can have mine."

"OK. And you can watch me eat them."

"If anybody gives you any shit today, let me know. I'll take care of them, or I'll have my big brother beat them up real bad."

"Anybody?" Life had taken on a whole new meaning. I never thought I would have my own personal bodyguard.

"Anybody. Jock can beat up every kid in our school. He might be a prizefighter one day, and he needs to practice beatin' people," Rhoda bragged.

"Well, since y'all too busy to pay any attention to me, I'm goin' to the rec room and hang out," Pee Wee informed us. We both ignored him, and he rushed off with a scowl on his face.

Once we were in front of the school, I asked Rhoda in a weak voice, "When you say anybody, you mean grown people, too?"

"Grown people?" Rhoda gasped. She gave me a hard look and glanced around before continuing. "We can't sass grown people, let alone beat one up. I sassed a flight attendant on the plane from the Bahamas, and Aunt Lola whupped me with her shoe right in front of all those people on the plane."

"OK," I muttered. "But I bet your mean big brother Jock would, wouldn't he?"

"Yeah, he would. He even sassed Reverend Upshaw last week. One time he beat up a thirty-year-old pimp for tryin' to put one of his girl-friends on the street."

I felt a sense of security for the first time since Mr. Boatwright had started abusing me.

"What would Jock do to somebody that was taking advantage of some girl? Like raping her and, you know, stuff like that."

"I don't know," Rhoda said quietly. She gave me a suspicious look. "I guess it would depend on who the girl was. If it was one of his girl-friends or me, I am sure that Jock would kill the rapist."

"What if it wasn't one of his girlfriends or you?" I asked. It was hard for me to hide my excitement.

She looked at me for a long time before she responded. Teachers were looking at their watches and giving us mean looks, and I knew it was time for us to get to our first period class or face the wrath of our principal.

"Jock's not stupid. Why would he kill a rapist for rapin' some girl he didn't care anythin' about? Who is this girl? I thought you didn't have any friends."

"Oh nobody. I was just wondering."

I left Rhoda standing in front of the school. Once I got inside, I peeped out the window, and she was just standing there with this puzzled look on her face. I expected to meet her in the cafeteria for lunch, but Wanda Jones told me Rhoda had left school during third period study hall to go home because she had cramps.

When I got home that evening, I had the house to myself for a few hours. Around seven Mama stumbled in the front door with Judge Lawson close behind. They greeted me, ordered me to get them beer from the kitchen, then they made themselves comfortable on the living-room couch.

"Where's Mr. Boatwright? I'm sure he'll want to join us," Judge Lawson said, looking around the room. He turned his beer bottle up and drained it, then let out a long loud belch.

"He wasn't home when I got in," I revealed. Just then I heard the back door open and slam shut and Mr. Boatwright's voice yipping a spiritual.

"Well now!" he exclaimed, rolling into the living room with his arms raised like somebody had pulled a gun on him. "Judge Lawson, you lookin' well!"

"Aahh, Boatwright. I can say the same about you."

"Brother Boatwright, set down here with us. Annette, run get Brother Boatwright a beer," Mama squealed.

By the time I returned from the kitchen with his beer, Mr. Boatwright had manipulated an invitation for himself to attend some of the judge's poker parties.

"Oh, you welcome to attend anytime you'd like. But I must warn you, the stakes are pretty high," the judge informed him.

"I can handle it, I can handle it." Mr. Boatwright grinned.

"Brother Boatwright need more of a social life," Mama said gently. "I feel so bad he spend so much time cooped up in the house keepin' Annette in line when he ought to be out sowin' his wild oats like other men." Mama paused and sucked in her breath, then turned around to face me. "You a big girl now. You can't continue to have Brother Boatwright all to yourself. Turn him aloose. I know you hopeless attached to him, done replaced your daddy with him, but he got to have some fun, too. You ought to be responsible enough to spend time by yourself and not burn the house down."

"Yes, Ma'am. I can take care of myself now," I replied. I turned my head toward the wall so they wouldn't see me smiling.

"How was your day, Brother Boatwright? You go anywhere special today?" Mama asked.

Mr. Boatwright nodded and took a drink from his beer before speaking. "Sister Goode, I picked up some Royal Crown hair grease from the store like you asked me to for when you straighten Annette's hair."

Judge Lawson looked amused. I hated when Black people talked about Black things white people didn't know about. Once when Mama and I were shopping at Pluto's five-and-dime, she asked a young clerk, "Where the straightenin' combs at?" Puzzled, the clerk laughed, and asked, *"The what?"* The clerk was confused, amused, and red-faced by the time Mama finished explaining. "You people have to do all that to your hair?" the clerk questioned, looking at the knotty mess on my head. I wanted to crawl into a hole. We had to find a Black clerk to help us find the straightening combs.

Judge Lawson cleared his throat and shuffled around in his seat. "Mr. Boatwright, you might want to try a sip of this Chianti here," he asked, removing a bag from inside his coat pocket.

"It's real nice and potent," Mama said. Mama was not a sophisticated woman. But she had worked for and "socialized" with enough sophisticated people to have some degree of class. She knew fine wine. From the look on his face, I knew that Mr. Boatwright didn't have a clue as to what Chianti was.

"I read in *Hush Hush* magazine that Chianti is Frank Sinatra's favorite drink," I offered.

Mr. Boatwright snapped around to look at me. "I like Chianti," he mumbled, clearing his throat. I'd seen his Ripple, Thunderbird, and muscatel bottles in the trash, but never any Chianti bottles.

"Go get some glasses, young'n," Mama ordered. Mama kept talking without looking at me. "They serve only the most expensive Chianti at Antonosanti's restaurant and with him already rich and still chargin' folks high prices for everythin' in there."

"Well that suspicious Dago wouldn't have the money he got now or be walkin' around a free man if it wasn't for Judge Lawson here. He was lucky Judge Lawson was still on the bench all them times he had tax problems and liquor-license problems. Runnin' wild with that flashy undertaker across the street. Unspeakable. How many times that undertaker wound up in your courtroom, Judge?" Mr. Boatwright croaked, winking at Judge Lawson.

"I've known Nelson for years, and he's never been in trouble with the law as far as I know. His reputation is flawless," Judge Lawson said with a thoughtful look on his face. I couldn't imagine what he must have thought about Mr. Boatwright.

At times, I couldn't help but feel sorry for Mr. Boatwright. There were so many things about him I didn't know, like his family background and how he had been raised. But it was obvious he had not had much of a life. I had not had much of a life yet either, and I resented rich people up to a point, but my bitterness was nothing compared to his. I assumed it was because of the difference in our ages. His jealousy and resentment toward rich people stunned me because the same people he trashed treated him with nothing but respect and kindness. Judge Lawson didn't bat an eye when Mr. Boatwright drank three glasses of the Chianti. By the time all the alcohol was gone, Mr. Boatwright was so drunk Mama and the judge had to help him to bed.

I slept well that night and the next night. Mainly because the next night Mr. Boatwright attended the judge's poker party and didn't get home until way past midnight. When I got home from school the next day, he still had a hangover and was stretched out on the couch with an ice pack on his forehead. I didn't like to admit it, but I was glad he felt so bad. I didn't have to worry about him harassing me. I turned on the television and curled up on the floor.

"I can cook if you want me to," I offered. "You don't look too good."

"There's the rest of that neckbone casserole from Sunday in the kitchen you can heat up," he moaned with a grimace on his face. I did feel a little sorry for him, but it was his own fault. A man his age had no business drinking so much.

Marilyn Monroe had been dead almost a year, and some of the television stations were still doing specials about her. One we had seen before was being run again. Mr. Boatwright gasped when they showed the scene from *The Seven Year Itch* when Marilyn's dress flies up. I was lying on my stomach. I froze when I felt his toes rubbing my behind.

"I thought you were sick," I snarled, whirling around to face him. I leaped up from the floor and started to back away.

"I ain't *that* sick. You know how Marilyn Monroe make my nature rise." He stood up grinning, "Ooh wee, girl." Before I could respond, somebody knocked on the front door. Mr. Boatwright crept over to the front window and cracked the curtain open just enough to see out. "It's the undertaker! That uppity spook—Brother Nelson!" he hissed, running behind the couch. "Go tell him I'm sick and in the bed with a fever."

My mouth dropped open, and I almost laughed. "I can't fix my lips to say all that with a straight face. A smart man like Mr. Nelson would see through that lie with his eyes closed." Mr. Nelson knocked some more. This time longer and harder.

"Well—just tell him I ain't home." Without another word, Mr. Boatwright dropped to the floor with a loud thud. Remembering the time Mama had hidden behind a couch from a bill collector in Florida I checked to make sure his feet were not sticking out. I rushed across the floor and snatched open the door.

"Hi, Mr. Nelson." I smiled nervously. He looked more handsome than ever. He had on a beige suit, a black tie, and a black hat.

"Hi, Annette," he said, tipping his hat. He was not smiling. "Is Boatwright available?"

I was nervous and frightened, but I lied for Mr. Boatwright. "Um . . . nope."

"Are you sure? I saw him on the front porch not too long ago."

"He went to a prayer meeting, I think. He left out the back door, I think. He won't be home 'til real late, I think. Do you want me to tell him something?" I had a hard time lying to certain people. Mr. Nelson was one of them.

"Well yes." He hesitated. "Tell him I came to see him concernin' a financial matter." He started to back off the porch. I opened the door wider and leaned my head out onto the porch. It was getting cold, and the night air stung my face and ears.

"A financial matter?" I asked, puzzled.

"He'll know." Mr. Nelson smiled mysteriously, tipped his hat again, then left. I waited until I saw him go inside his house. I shut and locked the door and ran to the couch, where Mr. Boatwright was still crouched on the floor with his face covered in sweat.

"He gone?" he whispered, rising. He pulled out his pills and a handkerchief.

"Yeah. He said something about a financial matter," I said levelly, helping him to the couch. Mr. Boatwright shook his head and sighed with exasperation, wiping his face so hard he looked like he was in pain. The Marilyn Monroe special was still on, so I didn't sit too close to him. I sat on the chair facing the couch.

He took his time replying.

"In the first place, with all them simoleons he got stashed away in the bank, he got some nerve comin' over here to pester me about a measly five hundred dollars this time of night," Mr. Boatwright informed me. There was a look of total amazement on his face. "If I'd knowed Brother Nelson was such a shylock, I'd have borrowed from that Eye-talian buddy of his'n in the first place like his brother Johnny done."

"You borrowed five hundred dollars from Mr. Nelson? What for?" I mouthed.

"For the poker game I got dragged into last night at the judge's house."

"Why would he lend that kind of money to you when he knows your only income is a monthly disability check?" I was thoroughly stunned.

" 'Cause I thought I could borrow against my life insurance policy. Them dawgs down at the insurance company say there's a thirty-day waitin' period. Iffen they don't have my money ready in exactly thirty days, I'm gwine to sue 'em."

I had to bite my lip to keep from laughing.

"Why don't you tell Mr. Nelson that? Otherwise, you're going to have to hide from him for thirty days," I pointed out. Mr. Boatwright looked frightened. His eyes shifted from left to right like he was trying to come up with a plan.

"Scary Mary gwine to let me borrow it from her tomorrow after she go to the bank." He sighed with uncertainty. "But I ain't countin' on that unpredictable heifer. She full of surprises. Told me she was savin' up so she could buy her some reliable transportation. The broomstick she probably gwine to buy can't cost that much." He laughed, then suddenly gave me a thoughtful look.

"Then Scary Mary will have to wait for your insurance to pay off?"

"Well, I figured I'd pay off the undertaker and wait a few days. Borrow the money back and pay Scary Mary. I'd let it set in her pocket for a day or so, borrow it again, pay back Brother Nelson again and so on . . ." Mr. Boatwright was still talking, but I had stopped listening. He finally stopped babbling, but I tried to get him started again. Anything to distract him. It wouldn't be long before Mama got home, and he wouldn't have time to bother me if I kept him talking long enough.

"All rich people think about is money," I insisted, nodding for emphasis. I was totally on Mr. Nelson's side, but Mr. Boatwright didn't need to know that.

"That's how they got rich," Mr. Boatwright snapped. He babbled on about the evils of rich people until Muh'Dear got home, an hour later.

CHAPTER 13

Days would go by and there would be no sexual contact between Mr. Boatwright and me. The older I got, the more schemes I came up with to get out of it, such as leaving for school before he woke up. It meant getting up a lot earlier, rushing around a lot, and missing breakfast, but it was worth it. The only thing I didn't like was having to sit on a park bench around the corner while waiting for my usual time to pick up Rhoda.

Richland had only one library, and I spent a lot of time there. But when that time doubled, the librarians started giving me suspicious looks. I didn't care. I had made up my mind that I'd spend as many hours there as it took to avoid Mr. Boatwright.

Then what I expected to happen, did. After about two weeks, Mr. Boatwright complained to Mama that I was spending a lot of time "runnin' the streets."

"Annette, Brother Boatwright is concerned you may get in trouble out there in them streets. And you done missed your last five Bible lessons. From now on, you come straight home from school. And don't you be runnin' out in the mornin' without breakfast."

"I have to go to the library to study—" I attempted to protest.

"How come you can't study in the house like you been doin'?" Mama asked. I didn't like arguing with Mama. I didn't like upsetting her. "You get home and do whatever Brother Boatwright tell you to do. Do you hear me?"

"Yes, Ma'am," I muttered, almost in tears. I always did what Mama told me to do, and Mr. Boatwright knew that.

"Gimme back my dollar!" Mr. Boatwright always made me return his money when I didn't satisfy him in bed. This was the first time in over a week that he had come into my room before I got up for school. I had argued with him, and I had even tried to push him away. But his threats and strength were against me.

He rolled off me and sat up on the bed and gobbled some pills, then gave me one of his meanest looks. The whites of his eyes were so red he looked like he was on fire.

Like me, he had gained a lot of weight over the years. He was not really all that fat, but he was flabby, and his stomach protruded. Having sex with me was the most strenuous exercise he got. I reached under my pillow and slid the dollar out and handed it back to him. "Now you get your nasty self to the bathroom yonder and wash up for school," he ordered.

"Why don't you use those rubber things?" I asked before I left for school that morning. He had started "pulling out" of me before he came after I got my first period, a year earlier.

"Rubbers?" he roared. "Why—what's wrong with you, girl? How would it look for a man like me to be seen by some blabbermouth in a drugstore buyin' somethin' like that? Eeyow! Anyway, them things cost money. *I know you don't expect me to spend even more money on you for a little poontang!*"

"Why don't you get some rubbers from Scary Mary, Mr. Boatwright? I saw a bunch in her kitchen." I sighed. He walked along with me in his housecoat, with a cup of coffee in his hand, as I moved toward the door. I couldn't wait to get to school to get away from him.

He gave me a thoughtful look as he rolled this information around in his head. "Say what?" he gulped.

"In a bowl on top of her refrigerator. I saw them the other day when I went to get you that beer."

"*How you know about rubbers?*" The words shot out of his mouth like spit. He tilted his head to the side and glared at me out of the corners of his mean eyes.

"One of Scary Mary's ladies told me," I lied. A couple of fast girls at school talked about them and brought them to school all the time.

"Which one?" he mouthed, giving me a suspicious look. He folded his arms and blocked the front door.

"Um . . . the one that got killed."

"Rosalee. Poor thing wasn't even saved," he said hoarsely, shaking his head. Sweat was sliding down the sides of his face.

"I could sneak a few rubbers from Scary Mary every time I go over there. Nobody would have to know," I offered.

"Mercy!" he said, grinning as he opened the door for me.

The very next day I grabbed a handful of condoms from Scary Mary's bowl and delivered them to Mr. Boatwright.

"Umph," was all he said.

Even with the money from his disability check that Mr. Boatwright contributed, Mama still worked six days a week for Judge Lawson and up to ten hours a day.

Some mornings she would be gone by the time I got up, and sometimes I would be in bed when she got home. Not a week went by when she did not remind me, "You better do everythin' Brother Boatwright tell you, do you hear me?" And I did even if it meant fighting with him first. Now that I had a powerful friend, I felt a whole lot better. I knew that it was just a matter of time before I told Rhoda what was happening. Somehow, I knew that eventually, Rhoda would be the one to rescue me.

"Did a grown person ever do something real bad to you and tell you not to tell?" I asked her at lunch a few days later. I put my fork down and prayed she wouldn't see my hands shaking.

"Yep. Uncle Johnny slipped some whiskey into my Pepsi one time so he could see me stumblin' around the house."

"Did you tell on him?" My hands were shaking harder now, so I put them on my lap.

"Nope. It was fun bein' drunk. He lets me drink from his beer all the time now. Don't you dare tell that Pee Wee. He would blab to my daddy, and I would get a whuppin'.."

"I won't tell him something like that. I don't think getting drunk is that bad. I was talking about something real bad. You know like . . . um . . . rape."

Rhoda put her fork down and looked around the room for a few moments, making me more nervous. "Will you tell me who is botherin' you, Annette?" Rhoda whispered, her eyes scanning my face.

"I didn't say it was me—" My hands were still shaking, but I picked up my fork again and continued eating.

"I *know* it's you, girl. Just look at the way your hands are shakin'!"

She wiped her mouth and pushed her tray away. A thoughtful look appeared on her lovely face. "Well?"

"Well what?"

"Are you goin' to tell me who it is?"

"*I can't.* I can't tell you that right now."

"Why not? Is it a preacher? Is it Judge Lawson?" she gasped.

"No!"

"Then who is it?"

"I'll tell you, but not now. I have to think it through some more."

She put her hand on my face and caressed it. I needed a hug more than ever. And just like she was reading my mind, she leaned over and put her arms around me and gave me the biggest hug I ever received.

CHAPTER 14

Two weeks before Thanksgiving, Mama learned that she had to work on Thanksgiving Day and because of that, she expected me to help Mr. Boatwright prepare our holiday dinner. A few days later, I went to Rhoda's house for the first time.

Her parents socialized a lot with white people, and it made Mr. Boatwright and Caleb jealous. Mr. Boatwright was convinced that Rhoda's daddy was doing something shady other than processing dead people. He just didn't know what. When I asked him why he was so sure Mr. Nelson was a criminal, he told me that that was the only reason white people would waste their time with spooks.

The Nelsons lived in the biggest, most ornate house I had ever seen Black people live in. It was a huge, two-storied, white-paneled structure. There was a flagpole on the left side of the front yard with a large American flag fluttering proudly. A life-size statue of a woman naked from the waist up pouring water into a birdbath sat near the flagpole. There was a big black sign with white letters hanging from wrought-iron hooks on the front porch that read: NELSON'S FUNERAL HOME. A white garage, where the undertaker kept his big black hearse along with his Cadillac, was on one side of the house. You couldn't see it from the street, but if you walked around the side of the Nelsons' house, you could see the mortuary. It was connected to the back of the house, but it was only one level, with high, dark windows you couldn't see through. Pee Wee had dared me to go with him to look at it one Sunday while the Nelsons were still in church. There were rosebushes on both sides of the mortuary, but just knowing what it was for almost made me sick. It was the last place I wanted to be.

The front yard of the Nelsons' house was flanked by rosebushes, and several fruit trees inhabited the backyard. There was even a life-size dollhouse in the backyard, beyond the mortuary section, that Rhoda's daddy, her brother Jock, and her uncle Johnny had built for her. Before going to Rhoda's room, we ran around the side of the main house, rather than pass through the mortuary, to get to Rhoda's dollhouse.

"You have a million dolls!" I exclaimed. In addition to dolls of various sizes and colors, there was a bike, some skates, and an assortment of other toys. I looked at Rhoda, and she had this proud look on her face, and her chest kind of stuck out. "I wish I were you," I said. She laughed at me, but I meant every word I said *literally*.

"Wait'll you see my bedroom!"

"Does your bedroom door have a keyhole?" I asked nervously. I had even filled my keyhole with gum one night to keep Mr. Boatwright from peeping at me, and he had pushed the gum out with a toothpick.

"Of course my bedroom door has a keyhole, silly. Why?"

"Well, maybe some nasty man might peep in and see you naked one day." I didn't realize what I was saying until I had said it. I immediately wished that I could take back my words.

"Why would some man do a nasty thing like that?"

"Because they are nasty, I guess." I shrugged. She knew I lived with just Mama and Mr. Boatwright. I was surprised that she had not asked me if he was the one who was tormenting me. I couldn't imagine what she was thinking.

"There are no men in my house who would do such a crazy thin' as peep in my keyhole," she assured me. "Not even Uncle Johnny. Well, maybe he would. But then he's the family fool. Remember that time he raped that dead woman?"

"Yeah."

"Look, girl. You've been tellin' me all kinds of weird shit about rapists. Now you talkin' about men peepin' in keyholes. Why don't you just come on out and tell me who is botherin' you so I can help you out of this mess. I bet it's one of those Italian men from down the street. You know those types always like Black girls. They are always sneakin' into Scary Mary's house. I've seen them."

"Oh I know all those nasty Italian men go to Scary Mary's to pester those prostitutes. But none of them have ever bothered me," I admitted.

"Then who is botherin' you? Tell me and tell me now, dammit."

"What could you do, Rhoda? If I tell you—" I moved back a few steps and turned away from her. "Can I go see the rest of your house now? I can't stay over here too long. I'll get another whupping."

I thought that she was going to continue badgering me about my rapist, but she didn't. She just gave me an exasperated look, then motioned for me to follow her.

"Wanna see a dead man?" Rhoda asked me.

"I don't know," I mumbled, slowing down as we got closer to the mortuary. "Do we have to go through there?" I said quickly.

"There's nothin' to be scared of. The room's real pretty, with lavender walls and carpets. It has to look nice for the wakes my daddy handles."

"Dead people make me nervous, Rhoda," I said firmly. "I'll be one soon enough . . ."

"OK." She shrugged, motioning me to follow her back the way we had come around the side the house. "You ever seen a dead person?"

"Oh yeah. Real real dead. This old lady in Florida that used to baby-sit me died in the bed next to me when I was a little girl," I answered. "And a white girl I used to play with and another old lady my mama used to work for."

"There's a man in there they just embalmed and dressed. He's got a bullet hole in his face, so they won't open the coffin at the wake this evenin' or at the funeral. But if you want to see him, I'll open the—"

"Somebody shot him in the head? Who did it?" I shuddered as we walked up on her front porch.

"Some woman. He was a pimp who was always beatin' up on his girls. Well, he beat up the wrong one, one time too many. She pulled out a pistol and went BANG! His brains went all over the place!"

"Shut up!" I stopped in my tracks. Mr. Boatwright had put his gun up to my head and yelled bang more times than I cared to think about.

Rhoda sucked in her breath and narrowed her eyes to look at me before she spoke again. "What's wrong with you, girl?"

"I don't like hearing about guns." I could hardly breathe. "I should go home and . . ." I started to shift my weight from one foot to the other like I had to pee. Rhoda stomped her foot and pulled me on by my arm.

We tiptoed to the main part of the house. The inside of the Nelsons' house was just like them: awesome. The halls were wide and decorated with fancy paintings of Jesus and dead presidents. Our house always seemed to smell like cabbage greens; Rhoda's smelled like the fresh flowers. Our furniture was used, shabby, garish, and none of it matched. Almost all of the furniture in the Nelsons' house was either black, red, white, or gold. They had leather couches, thick shaggy carpets, and drapes that belonged in the White House.

In a room Rhoda called their parlor, sat Mr. Nelson on a white couch. He had on a blue suit and a black tie. Sitting on a white love seat across from Mr. Nelson, wearing a black suit and a black tie, was a white man about the same age and size as Mr. Nelson. The men were smoking cigars and drinking glasses of red wine.

"Hi, Daddy. Hi, Uncle Carmine." Rhoda waved. She dashed across the floor, hugged and kissed her daddy and then hugged and kissed the white man. One thing about attractive people, they hung out together. Mr. Nelson's friend was as handsome as he was. He had a square face and lips as thick as any Black person's. His long, thick salt-and-pepper hair was combed back like a duck. His deep-set, piercing black eyes looked me up and down. I noticed rings on four of his fingers.

"Young ladies." The white man smiled, saluting with his wineglass. Rhoda sat on his knee and started stroking his hair, and he kissed her on her cheek.

"Annette, this is my 'uncle' Carmine Antonosanti," Rhoda said, with her back to me. She had her arms around Mr. Antonosanti's neck.

I smiled; the man smiled and nodded in my direction.

"How's Mr. Boatwright these days, Annette?" Mr. Nelson asked, waving his wineglass.

"He's about the same," I said quickly. For a moment it looked like Mr. Nelson was going to laugh. Mr. Boatwright's insurance money had come through, and he had paid off Mr. Nelson and Scary Mary after boomeranging the money back and forth for thirty days like he said he would.

"Annette is my friend now," Rhoda announced proudly. "She reads a lot, too, and she's smart."

The men complimented Rhoda excessively for the next minute or so. I was glad when she jumped up from Mr. Antonosanti's lap and led me out of the room. As soon as we got back out into the hallway, another white man appeared from a side doorway. He was older than Rhoda's daddy and not as handsome. He was tall and too thin for his height. Limp, thin gray hair hung around his long, chalky face. He stopped, narrowed his beady green eyes, and looked from me to Rhoda. Instead of a nice suit, he had on a plaid cotton shirt and brown-corduroy pants too short for his legs. He was clutching a wineglass, too.

"Uncle Johnny, this is Annette," Rhoda introduced.

"Boatwright's girl?" Johnny slurred, extending his hand.

"Not exactly. He just lives with us," I explained, shaking his cold dry hand.

"You done your homework yet, girl?" Johnny asked Rhoda, glaring at her, wobbling so hard he had to lean against the wall.

"I just got home, Uncle Johnny," Rhoda whined, pulling me away by the arm.

We reached the living room, where a scowling, muscle-bound teenage boy, who looked almost exactly like Rhoda, glanced up from where he was on the floor, angrily leafing through a textbook. I had seen enough on TV to know that some boys didn't think that a sissified thing like homework was a cool thing to do. It made them evil. That's why they had to have so much sex and beer. This boy's frustration was written all over his handsome face.

"Daddy said for you to have your homework done before you park your butt in front of the TV!" the boy snapped at Rhoda. He was fifteen. I had heard about him, and I'd seen him around the neighborhood with his gang drinking beer straight out the can and making obscene gestures to girls. Not me, of course, but the pretty girls that dared go around the bad boys. This brooding pit bull had beaten up a lot of kids, Black and white. As one would expect, he had a skull-and-crossbones tattoo on his right arm. There was a tattoo of a hula girl on his other arm. He was so brazen he even smoked in the church parking lot and sassed some of the old church sisters when they tried to chastise him.

"Nyah, nyah, nyah," Rhoda replied, showing her brother her tongue and flipping him the finger. "I already finished my homework in my last period class." For a minute I thought the boy was going to leap up and attack Rhoda. Instead, he just rolled his green eyes and returned his attention to his book. "Jock-o, this is Annette from across the street. My best friend. She goes to my school now," Rhoda told him.

"Hi, Jock," I said firmly, moving toward him, expecting him to shake my hand the way Rhoda did when I met her.

"GET OUTTA MY LIGHT!" he roared at me, not even looking up from his schoolwork. I almost jumped out of my skin, but, surprisingly, I didn't back down. I did get out of his light though.

"Um," I continued nervously. "I've heard a lot about you," I told the boy, forcing a smile.

"LIES! ALL LIES!" Jock wasted no time dismissing me with a wave of his callused hand.

"I told you he was mean," Rhoda whispered proudly. She grabbed me by the arm and led me back to the hallway. "He's just mad cause Daddy makes him help turn over the dead people on the slabs and stuff when all he really wants to do is fight and drink beer and feel girls' butts up and down. The boy's nasty."

"The boy's a boy." I sighed with disgust. "He can't help it."

"I know," Rhoda agreed with a nod. "I just hope he didn't upset you too much. You'll like him once you get to know him. He's really not that bad. Not since Daddy made him get baptized. Boy did that get his goat."

"I don't want to get to know him. I don't like boys," I said real fast. "I just like girls—and animals."

"Oh I love animals, too. Especially cats. But I'm allergic to them, and that's why I don't have any," Rhoda informed me.

"Rhoda . . . uh . . . what about girls?"

"What about them?"

"Do you like them?" I asked shyly.

"I guess." She shrugged. "I'm a girl. You're a girl. My mom. My aunt Lola, they used to be girls."

"I meant . . ." My crush on her had intensified.

"You meant what?"

"Nothing," I muttered. I cleared my throat before continuing. "How did your daddy get to be friends with Mr. Antonosanti?" I wanted to know. We stopped in the same wide hallway where I had met Uncle Johnny.

"Oh, they go way back. Daddy saved Uncle Carmine's life when they were in the war in Germany a long time ago and Daddy told us Uncle Carmine promised he would make it up to him one day before he died." Rhoda paused and let out a long sigh, smoothing her hair back out of her face. "After they got out of the army, Daddy returned to Alabama and Uncle Carmine returned to Ohio and he and Daddy kept in close touch. Uncle Carmine's family has old money. Tons and tons of it," Rhoda said.

"From bootlegging and hiding money from the IRS?"

"Who in the world told you that?" Rhoda laughed.

"Mr. Boatwright and Caleb. They talk about Mr. Antonosanti and your daddy all the time," I told her.

Rhoda gasped and looked at me thoughtfully. She was no longer laughing. The information I had just shared with her made her angry. "You tell Mr. Boatwright and Caleb to stop sittin' around talkin' trash about everybody! My daddy and Mr. Antonosanti don't sit around gossipin' like women in a beauty parlor like they do! My daddy and Uncle Carmine discuss politics and business, like men are expected to!" Rhoda paused and sucked in her breath. "Anyway, to make a long story short, my play Italian uncle put up the money for Daddy's mortician trainin' and everythin'. Everythin' Daddy needed to get him started came from Uncle Carmine. We moved here from Alabama, and they are still the best of friends. It pays to have powerful friends," Rhoda told me, and winked.

"I know," I agreed, giving her a pensive look. "Uh . . . you ever seen or touched any of your daddy's dead bodies, Rhoda?"

She nodded first, then told me, "My other brother, David, was the first dead body I ever touched. He . . . died in my arms." Her voice cracked.

"Oh." I had been warned by Pee Wee that Rhoda's dead brother was something to avoid discussing in front of her. I urged her to take me to her room.

Rhoda's bedroom was just what I expected. All pink and white. The only thing missing was a canopied bed. But she had her own TV and record player, and her closet was full of beautiful and expensive clothes. She motioned with her hand for me to sit on her bed while she stood in front of a wall mirror to check her hair. The bed felt like a soft cloud.

Suddenly, a slim, brown-skinned, brown-eyed woman, with small, delicate features entered the bedroom. This was Rhoda's beautiful mother, Michelle Jacquelyn Nelson. Mr. Boatwright said she dyed her reddish brown hair to cover the gray. Scary Mary said Mrs. Nelson had to have had her face lifted because there was not a wrinkle in sight. Scary Mary also said that Mrs. Nelson spent most of her spare time in Miss Rachel's, the most exclusive Black beauty parlor in town, or shopping for clothes she didn't need. Pee Wee said she was probably having affairs behind the undertaker's back. I liked the lady immediately and didn't believe a word of all that gossip. She gave me a big smile.

"You're that sweet little girl from across the street!" the pretty woman squealed. Her Southern accent was more pronounced than Rhoda's. She tickled my chins and put her arm around my shoulder. I was so moved I had to fight to hold back my tears. This was the nicest any grown person, other than my mama, had ever been to me. "Gimme some sugar!" I almost fainted when Rhoda's beautiful mother leaned over and kissed my cheeks with hungry little kisses. Rhoda and her mother had given me the validation I needed to feel whole and important. This validation, this attention and sincerity, as fulfilling as it was in my dreams. *I was somebody.* No matter what happened to me after this day, nobody could take away this feeling of importance I felt since meeting Rhoda.

"Yes, Ma'am. I'm Annette," I said, almost out of breath. You could have knocked me over with a feather.

"Gussie Mae's sweet little girl. My, what a pretty smile you have," Mrs. Nelson told me. The Rapture could not have impressed me more.

"Muh'Dear, guess what," Rhoda said. She ran up to her mother and threw her arms around her waist. "Annette's got a real live, peg-legged man livin' in her house." *Muh'Dear.* Among Black kids, that title was the equivalent of Your Highness.

"Oh, I know that saintly Brother Boatwright. How is Brother Boatwright gettin' along, Annette?" There was a look of genuine concern on Mrs. Nelson's face.

"He's fine," I said stiffly. He even had this smart woman fooled! If only she knew all the mean and nasty things he had said about her.

"I must get to the kitchen to supervise supper. Mr. Nelson is preparing a leg of lamb." Mrs. Nelson sighed. A blanket of sadness seemed to cover me. Mr. Boatwright was cooking up another coon for our dinner. "You must join us for a meal sometime, Annette."

"Yes, Ma'am," I managed. I was so stunned and impressed I couldn't think straight. Mrs. Nelson seemed to float out of the room, leaving the scent of her expensive perfume behind.

"How come she's got on a housecoat this time of the day?" I whispered, my eyes still on the door.

"Oh she's got a bad heart and has to rest a lot. She can't drink alcohol or dance or anything like that. It could kill her."

"Who takes care of the house?"

"We do. Me and Jock and my daddy. Uncle Johnny helps out when he's not in jail. And whenever Aunt Lola comes to visit, she takes over." Rhoda was talking as she moved across the floor and flipped on a radio on her dresser. Soft classical music filled the room.

"How come you all don't get a maid? Your daddy is rich."

"A maid? No way. No stranger is goin' to come into this house and start bossin' us around. You lucked out gettin' somebody like that one-legged man to take care of your house. What's his name again?"

"His name is Mr. Boatwright," I mumbled, my eyes on the floor.

"He was supposed to come live with us, but Daddy had to turn Reverend Snipes down because my uncle Johnny decided to move in with us around the same time and needed the room," Rhoda revealed. I tried to imagine what would have happened if Mr. Boatwright had moved in with the Nelsons and did to Rhoda what he was doing to me.

"I never knew about that," I gasped.

"Too bad we couldn't take him in, huh?"

"Yeah. Too bad," I mouthed.

CHAPTER 15

I was so excited when I got home from the Nelsons' house, I didn't care what Mr. Boatwright did to me. He did attempt to have sex with me but was unable. Something about his back going out. Of course he blamed that on me, saying I was getting too fat for him to try and turn over in the bed. He dismissed me with a wave of his hand and a threatening look. He headed for the kitchen, and I went to bathe.

After I ate dinner I put on my robe and waited in the living room for Mama to come home. I didn't know what part of the house Mr. Boatwright was in, and I didn't care. I was still on cloud nine from my visit to the Nelsons.

I met Mama at the door with a hug.

"What's wrong with you, girl?" she wanted to know. She had never seen me like this before, and it startled her. She held me back and gave me a long hard look. "Did you get in trouble at school today? You pregnant?"

"Oh no, Mama. Guess what? I went to Rhoda Nelson's house this evening after school. It looks like a palace over there. And it smells like one. I met her mother and saw her mink coat and baby grand piano and everything. Mr. Nelson's friend, that Italian man—the one who owns Antonosanti's restaurant—was there and I met him. I even met Uncle Johnny. They were all real nice and proper. I met her big brother Jock. He . . . uh . . . now he was *kind of* mean, but Rhoda told me he's really kind of nice when he's not mad about something. Oh,

Mama. I'm so glad we moved on this street. The Nelsons are too good to be true." I was almost out of breath by the time I shut up. Mama was looking at me with her mouth hanging open. She didn't seem the least bit impressed, just suspicious.

"Listen." She sighed tiredly. She gently removed my arms from around her waist and pushed me away. This annoyed me. I wanted her to be more like Rhoda's mother. "Anytime somethin' seems too good to be true, it usually is. Ain't you done heard all the talk about that family?"

"Yeah, but I don't believe any of it. People are just jealous of them—"

"I ain't jealous of nobody."

"Then what do you mean?"

"Them Nelsons ain't normal like us. Scary Mary done told me all about 'em. Caleb say he think Brother Nelson is involved in all kinds of illegal scams."

"Unspeakable! Them Nelsons think they white," Mr. Boatwright croaked. He had slipped into the living room so quietly I hadn't heard him. "And the way they strut around, you would think that house of theirs was Graceland complete with Elvis." He paused long enough to sit down on the couch and drink from a bottle of beer and let out a belch. "Why they ain't even clean," he said, wiping his mouth with the sleeve of his shirt. "One day I was over yonder and I seen a roach big as me crawlin' up the lamp shade. They too good to ride the bus like the rest of us. They got to ride around in a Cadillac? Nelson's supposed to be helpin' the poor."

"Would it help the poor if Mr. Nelson got out of his Cadillac and got on a bicycle?" I asked. Mr. Boatwright and Mama just glared at me. Mama gasped, and for a minute I thought she was going to slap me, but she didn't. She just sat down on the couch next to Mr. Boatwright, looking at him in awe as he continued.

"I tell you, Sister Goode, them Nelsons ain't like us," he barked.

"They sure are not like you!" I screamed. "They are the nicest people I've met since we moved to Ohio. They are not uppity or gangsters or crooks and all those mean things you and Caleb and Scary Mary say—" I shouted. I knew I was probably going to get a whupping for my outburst, but I didn't care this time.

"That boy Jock's bound to ruin you first chance he get," Mr. Boatwright predicted, nodding in my direction.

I glared at Mr. Boatwright and felt like I was on fire. "Jock and no other boy in this town never looked at me! The only one ever did any-thing was—"

"Say what?" Mama gasped. Mr. Boatwright gasped, too, and almost fell off the couch. He took another long drink from his beer bottle. His stiff gray hair seemed like it suddenly stood up on his head.

"Nothing," I mumbled, bowing my head.

"The only one what, girl?" Mama mouthed, giving me an incredu-lous look. She sat with her mouth open so wide I could see the back of her tongue. "What boy been tryin' to take advantage of you? You tell me the scoundrel's name, and we'll pay his mama a visit tonight. Won't we, Brother Boatwright?" She snapped her head around fast to look at him, but not fast enough to see the threatening look he gave me.

"Uh-huh," he said meekly. "I don't know what the world comin' to."

"You ought to be up in your room praisin' God you so blessed. Now git!" Mama advised. She dismissed me with a wave of her hand.

CHAPTER 16

Iwas surprised that I didn't get a whupping for sassing Mr. Boatwright with my outburst earlier that evening, though I did have to read the Bible for twenty minutes and mop the bathroom. I ate dinner in silence, but as soon as I felt things had settled enough, I started chirping about my visit to the Nelson house again.

"Like I said, the Nelsons and everything about them seem too good to be true," I announced. I was in the living room sitting on a footstool by the front window, and Mama and Mr. Boatwright were on our lumpy old couch watching television and drinking beer. They looked toward me at the same time.

I heard Mr. Boatwright let out this long deep groan. The kind that told me he was disgusted.

"Ain't I done told you, girl, anytime somethin' seems too good to be true, it usually is." Mama sighed, fanning her face with the *TV Guide.*

"Amen," Mr. Boatwright added, with his paws up in the air and his head shaking from side to side.

"I don't care. I still like the Nelsons," I stated.

"I heard Jock got a girl pregnant," Mr. Boatwright snapped, waving his beer bottle like a weapon.

"So?" I shot back. I folded my arms and crossed my legs and looked Mr. Boatwright straight in the eyes.

"Brother Boatwright here is just concerned about you, Annette. Me and him both advise you to watch your step when you over there and that boy Jock is in the mix. He might drug you with one of that Johnny's margaritas and take advantage of you," Mama said seriously. "Now go in that kitchen and wash them dishes."

Two-faced, mean-ass Mr. Boatwright drank, raped, gambled, and considered himself a holy man! I let out such a deep sigh, my chest felt like it wanted to explode. Instead, I stood up. "Um . . . they asked me to eat Thanksgiving dinner with them, Mama. Can I?" I stood in front of her and Mr. Boatwright with a pleading look on my face. That sorry old bastard rolled his eyes at me and shook his finger in my face.

"Didn't your poor mama here tell you she got to work on Thanksgivin' Day, girl? Who gwine to be here to hope me get dinner cooked?" he whined.

"You cook all the time when I'm not here—"

"Annette, you on thin ice, girl. Don't you know your family come first?" Mama muttered. I knew that she was tired after working so many hours, and I did feel bad about that.

"Well . . ." I mumbled with resignation. They had won this round. There would be other holidays I could spend at the Nelson house, I told myself.

"It ain't easy for me to hop around that hot kitchen for hours on end, day after day. What if I was here alone and stumbled and dropped a skillet of grease or somethin' on my toe? What if I slip and fall and bust up my hip?" Mr. Boatwright knew exactly how to get his way. He reminded me of a cunning child. "What if I was to—"

"OK. I'll stay home and help with the dinner." Once again, I was defeated.

"You can chop the onions, brown the gizzards." Mr. Boatwright paused long enough to give me one of his knowing looks. When he saw that Mama was not looking at him, he winked at me. Then he said, "I'll find plenty for you to do." Mama patted his shoulder and nodded.

I was ready to leave the room for sure then. But there was one more thing I had to say to Mama.

"Why you lookin' at me so strange, girl?" Mama smoothed the lap of her housecoat and stood up in front of me. She slapped her hands on her hips and leaned over so that our eyes were just inches apart.

"From now on, I'm going to call you Muh'Dear," I told her.

"I been blessed." Mama smiled proudly. One hand went up to her forehead. Her other hand patted my back. "Blessed."

Not to be outdone, Mr. Boatwright grunted, and told me, "You bet-

ter get them dishes done so you can get to bed. You know you got to
go to that schoolhouse in the mornin'."

I slept like a baby that night. The next morning I got up on my own
and was in the kitchen making breakfast by the time Mr. Boatwright
approached me. Mama had already left for work.

"You don't watch your step you gwine to suffer, girl," he warned.

"What do you mean?" I asked, too exasperated to really care.
Hardly anything this man ever said made much sense. I spent a great
deal of my time trying to interpret his ramblings. I stood in front of
the stove and just stared at him. I gave him the meanest look I could
come up with. And it must have been pretty effective because he had
to look away. I was amazed at the way I now sassed grown folks.

"You and Jock," he mumbled, nodding.

Next to Mr. Boatwright, Jock Nelson was the last male on earth I
would involve myself with willingly. "After what you've done to me, do
you think I'd go out looking for some other funky, *nasty* old man or
boy to do even more? I hate all men and boys. I wish every last one of
your motherfuckers' dicks would rot and drop off in your funky drawers. I wish there was nothing but females on this planet. We don't
need men. At least *I* don't. You old goat. How long do you think
you're going to get away with what you do to me?"

You would have thought that Satan had appeared in person right
in front of him the way he whimpered and fell into a chair at the
kitchen table, shaking his head. Then his whole wretched body
started shaking, and for a moment I thought, and hoped, he was having a heart attack or something equally devastating. He babbled inco-
herently at first. Then he stuttered, "Blood of Jesus...I...I...
thought...I thought..." He stopped, closed his eyes, and started
shaking his head slowly from side to side.

"You thought what? That I liked it? You must be crazy. You nasty
thing you!"

After he opened his eyes and stopped shaking, he wiped sweat
from his face with the back of his hand and continued in a normal
voice. "I guess Scary Mary was right when she told me about you," he
said casually. He sucked in his breath and gave me a peculiar look.
"Caleb told me the same thing," he teased.

"What did Scary Mary and Caleb tell you about me?" I had a big
spoon in my hand that I didn't even realize I was waving at him like I
was going to hit him until he told me.

"Stop wavin' that long-handled spoon at me, like you goin' to bop me. I ought to call the juvenile authorities. They got a place for big old strappin' teenage girls that attack disabled elderlies. Special homes." He lowered his head and started looking at me with his eyes narrowed and his lips pursed.

"What did they say about me?" I dropped the spoon back into the big pan of grits I had cooked.

After he swallowed a few Anacins he croaked, "It don't matter. I bet it's true."

"Forget Caleb and Scary Mary. All they do is gossip and tell lies about people. What do they know about me?" I attempted to leave the kitchen, but he grabbed my arm.

"You ain't goin' no place 'til I'm through with you." He paused, narrowed his eyes, and whispered, "You . . . you unnatural they say. You and that Pee Wee."

"Funny? Scary Mary and Caleb think I'm funny?" I said in a low voice. According to everybody I knew, homosexuality was way up there on the list of sins. It was rarely discussed out in the open, and even then in whispers. Suspected of being homosexual was the reason Pee Wee had no friends. I didn't mind having unnatural thoughts about Rhoda as long as nobody else knew. Especially Mr. Boatwright. The thought of somebody like him having that kind of information about me made my flesh crawl. Did I look funny? Did I act funny? It had to be the comments I'd made to Mr. Boatwright about hating males and the gossip he said he'd heard. "Well, you and Scary Mary and everybody else that says that is wrong." I couldn't and wouldn't say any more on the subject. Whether I was funny or not, it wasn't something I was ready to share with the world yet. News like that would destroy Muh'Dear. I left the kitchen and ran to my room to finish getting ready for school. I didn't even shut my bedroom door because I knew that he would join me.

"How could you even think about a female with *a man like me* in this house, girl?" he rasped with a smug look on his face as he entered my room. His sweaty age-spotted hands were already tugging at my clothes.

I was tired, so very, very tired. This was one time I didn't feel it was worth it to fight with him. I eased myself down on my bed. Before he got inside me, I told him, "I'm not funny, Mr. Boatwright."

After he was done with me, he escorted me to the front door as I was about to leave for school like nothing had happened. He patted my shoulder and hugged me, then opened the front door and walked me out to the porch.

"Feel like we might get our first snow today, huh?" he observed, looking around, scratching the back of his neck.

"Uh-huh," I mumbled.

He gasped and patted my shoulder again. "Don't you move, I'm gwine to get your snow boots—"

"Oh no, that's OK. It won't snow that much if it does snow. I don't know where my left boot is anyway," I told him, grabbing his arm.

"Well, you come straight home after school this evenin' and we'll hunt that left boot." Right after he finished his sentence, the Nelsons' front door opened and Mrs. Nelson came out onto the porch, followed by Mr. Antonosanti. They waved as they walked toward Mr. Antonosanti's car, a big shiny gray Buick.

"Queen of Sheba and Al Capone," Mr. Boatwright clucked, rolling his eyes.

"Who?" I asked.

"Yonder there across the street. You ain't blind. Brother Nelson better keep his eyes on that sneaky Jezebel he married to." Then he yelled, "How y'all doin' over yonder?"

"Mr. Boatwright, you're so mean," I said boldly. I knew that I could sass him and get away with it at this point. I was on my way to school, and he would not have time to whup me.

His eyes drifted then focused on me. "Mean? I ain't mean. Who said I was mean?" he whined.

"Yeah you are. Those people haven't done anything to you to make you talk about them so bad."

For once he was speechless. He just stood there with his hands on his hips, glaring at me, trying to come up with an appropriate response. I knew that whatever it was, it would be something mean.

"By the way," he began slowly, his head bobbing, "pretty girls like Rhoda across the street yonder, they just hang around with mud puppies like you to make them look better. They don't like no competition. Everybody in town talkin' about y'all. Callin' you and her Beauty and the Beast. Have a nice day." I didn't even respond to his comments about Rhoda, but I was hurt and concerned. Concerned because I wasn't sure if what he said was true. Most of the pretty girls in my school *did* have plain best friends.

I saw Mr. Boatwright peeping out of the window after I left the house to go across the street to pick up Rhoda. I rang her doorbell just once before Jock snatched open the door and greeted me with, "What's wrong with you, girl? Makin' all this goddamn noise! You wake up my granny, and I'm goin' to kick your butt halfway across town!" He was a good-looking boy, but his hostility was overwhelming.

"I'm here to pick up Rhoda," I said firmly. If I could stand up to Mr. Boatwright, I could stand up to Jock. I told myself that if Jock got too mean, I'd run.

"Oh," he said. I couldn't believe how fast he softened. His scowl disappeared as he opened the door wide enough for me to enter. "She'll be down in a minute. You know how she is with all that makeup and shit. You want some hot cocoa?" Mr. Boatwright would have died if he had heard that. Almost every morning he served me this deadly concoction called pot liquor, which was the juice from turnip, collard, or mustard greens with hog fat and chunks of some kind of meat stirred in. Each time, he groaned about not being able to afford cocoa but once a month.

"Cocoa?" I mouthed.

"Yeah. We drink it every mornin'," Jock informed me.

"Uh . . . no thanks." I was startled by his sudden gentleness. He excused himself, very politely, and left the room. Moments later, Rhoda joined me in the living room.

"Greetings!" she said to me, displaying her award-winning smile.

"Do you want me to be your friend because I'm ugly and it would make you seem even prettier?" I blurted.

"What?" Rhoda gasped. She even stumbled back a few steps. She picked up her book bag from the coffee table, not taking her eyes off me. "What in the world are you talkin' about, Annette?"

"Well, somebody told me pretty girls don't like competition."

She stared at me with a look of confusion on her face. "Listen here, I don't know who you've been talkin' to, but I want you as my friend because I like you. And who said you were ugly?" She motioned for me to follow her to the door.

"Oh some old busybodies. They call me and you Beauty and the Beast."

Once we got outside, we stopped on the porch for a moment. Mr. Boatwright was still peeping out our window. He was so tacky, he didn't even try to hide it. Not only were the curtains moving, his whole face was in full view.

"Horsefeathers." Rhoda laughed, dismissing the thought with a wave of her hand. She tried to hide it, but there was a look of concern on her face. "Fuck whoever told you that shit. Why should we care what they say or think? You're my friend because I want you to be.

And as far as you bein' ugly, well my brother Jock said you were cute."
She smiled at me.

Either I had lost my mind and slipped into a fantasy world and this
relationship was all part of my imagination, or God had finally taken
pity on me and made Rhoda part of my life. Either way, I now had the
best friend in the whole wide world, and I would do anything to keep
her. I wanted to grab her and kiss her hand and then hug her and kiss
her on the jaw. But I didn't want to overdo it. Instead I just smiled
back at her.

"Jock-the-Ripper? Your nasty, mean big brother? He said that about
me?" I was concerned and flattered at the same time. Not only was
Rhoda telling me I wasn't ugly, but a handsome, popular boy like Jock
said I was cute. Boy or not, compliments like that from him went a
long way with me. I couldn't wait to rub this information in Mr.
Boatwright's face.

"Uh-huh. Jock-the-Ripper said that about you, girl," Rhoda told
me.

"Oh. Well, I heard something else about you, Rhoda. From that
same person that said you like me around because I'm ugly."

Rhoda gave me a thoughtful look, then she bit her bottom lip before speaking. "I don't want to hear any more of this mess," she said,
shaking her head with disgust. "I don't give a shit what that person
thinks. Let's haul ass, girl." We started walking. I turned around to see
Mr. Boatwright standing on our front porch with one hand on his hip.

The schoolday started out typical enough. That morning Lena
Cundiff caught up with me, and said, "This is for that toilet thing
Rhoda done to me, bitch." Then she tripped me, and I fell down a
flight of stairs and busted my lip.

During lunch I ate most of Rhoda's food. She kept looking at my
bruised lip, but not once did she ask me about it. I had to volunteer
the information. I lied and told her I'd tripped over my own two feet.
She wiped dried blood from my lip and told me to be more careful.
She just about scared me to death when she called me Sugar.

CHAPTER 17

During the study period after lunch, Pee Wee, who worked in the principal's office, came rushing into the room and whispered something in Mr. Brown's ear. Mr. Brown was one of the whitest people I had ever seen in my life. When he turned red, he literally turned red. That lasted for a few moments then he turned blue in the face. He snatched a handkerchief from his pocket and wiped his face. His eyes seemed to sink into his face right before us. Then Pee Wee fainted. Several girls ran to him and started fanning his face as he lay stretched out on his back in the middle of the floor.

"Class, President Kennedy has been shot," Mr. Brown informed us. Girls gasped, boys cussed. I grabbed my books and ran out of the room. I found Rhoda in a near-catatonic state squatting on the floor outside of her music class.

"He's goin' to die," she moaned. "I just know President Kennedy is goin' to die." All the Black people I knew loved Kennedy because he was helping us get equal rights. I embraced Rhoda. Before I could speak, Mr. Rhodes, our principal, came on the loudspeaker. He was all choked up, and it took him what seemed like a real long time to tell us all to go home right away and take Monday off, too.

We didn't discuss it, but I followed Rhoda to her house. Her pretty mother was watching TV in the living room and crying when we arrived. She had on a pretty pink dress and black high heels. She was wiping her tears with a white-silk handkerchief.

Rhoda hugged her mother and greeted her with a kiss on the

hand. "Who did it? Who shot President Kennedy, Muh'Dear?" Rhoda asked quietly, her voice choking.

"They don't know yet. I just hope it wasn't one of *us*," Mrs. Nelson sobbed. She blew her nose and took a long deep breath. Even with her eyes red, she was pretty. Her voice was soft and gentle. "If a colored man is responsible, we'll be set back fifty years."

"I bet it was the Russians," Rhoda said angrily. She motioned for me to follow her to her room, where she turned on her portable TV. Every station was covering the Kennedy shooting. "Do you want a snack or somethin'?"

I shook my head. "I don't feel like eating," I replied sadly, my eyes on the TV.

"I guess I don't either." She waved me to her bed, where I made myself comfortable, and she curled up next to me. We didn't talk for several minutes but twice out of the corner of my eye, I saw her wiping away tears. I wanted to cry, but I was too embarrassed to do it in front of her.

"I can't believe somebody actually shot the president and in the head," I said, clearing my throat. I had to do that several times to keep from crying.

"Just like my brother David," she said sadly, not looking at me.

"I hate guns," I said seriously. I talked out of the side of my mouth, not taking my eyes off the TV screen.

"Me too, and I hate people who hurt other people," she admitted.

"What did your brother do?"

"Somethin' about a pregnant girl."

"He got somebody pregnant?"

"No. He couldn't have." Rhoda shrugged.

I sighed and looked away. "Pee Wee warned me not to bring it up. You don't have to talk about it."

"This policeman's daughter got pregnant and blamed my brother." Rhoda acted like she had not heard me. "The bitch wanted to get married, but he didn't. He had a fight with her daddy. One thing led to another. One night the police kicked in our front door and came lookin' for David. He fit the description of a robbery suspect, they said. He was in the bed. I used to sneak in his room to steal candy, so I was there the night it happened." Rhoda paused. Walter Cronkite, with tears streaming down the sides of his face, informed us that President Kennedy had died. We both gasped and kind of stared off into space. A sudden lump formed in my throat, and it hurt for me to swallow. I returned my attention to Rhoda. Her eyes were back on the television screen. She was blinking real hard and breathing through her mouth.

"My mama didn't vote for Kennedy," I said hoarsely, my eyes on the TV screen. "She said a 'teenager' like him didn't know enough to run the most powerful country in the world," I added with a dry chuckle.

"My folks voted for Nixon. It wasn't long before they were sayin' they wished that they had voted for Kennedy."

"'I hope they catch the man who shot the president,'" I muttered.

We waited for more news, but the announcers kept repeating the same things over and over again.

Not only was Rhoda's house frighteningly quiet, I couldn't hear a thing outside. No cars, no kids, no dogs barking. It seemed like the world had come to a standstill because of the assassination. I had written an essay on Abraham Lincoln and his assassin's background and motive a week earlier. Mrs. Windland, my English teacher, cried when I read it out loud in front of the class. She told the whole class that none of us would probably experience the pain of a presidential assassination in our lifetime. Even though I was holding back my tears, a sad smile appeared on my face. I turned away so Rhoda wouldn't see it. I was glad when she started talking again.

"Anyway, about my brother, the police came in his bedroom with guns. I was six and real little, so I could hide easy. Nobody knew I was even there 'cause I was all the way up under the covers bunched up with the pillows. Even if they had, I wouldn't have been scared for myself. I am not afraid of anythin'." Rhoda paused, and I looked her over with great admiration. She swallowed hard as she continued talking. "Do you think I'm normal?"

"What?"

"Me not bein' scared of anythin'?"

"Well, no. I wish I could be more like you," I said firmly. "I never knew another girl like you. Not even in any of my books. And I read a lot of fairy tales and science fiction."

"OK." Rhoda smiled dryly. "Anyway, there I was, hidin' under my brother's blankets. It happened so fast. It was late, but I was still awake. He was, too. They kicked open the door and started hollerin' at David. He never said a word. The next thing I knew, the one policeman started shootin'. I threw back the covers and jumped down on the floor with my brother. There were five cops in the room. Just one was black. He was the one who had done the shootin'." Rhoda stumbled over her words, but she continued, with her eyes staring straight ahead.

"You remember all that?"

She nodded. "As long as I live I'll never forget that night and that man and what he did to my family," she said through clenched teeth. "Anyway, my brother's blood splashed all over that room. He was still alive when I grabbed him and hugged him. Strangest thing is, he smiled at me for about a second. Then . . . he died."

"I feel sorry for your family," I muttered. I attempted to put my arm around Rhoda, but she held up her hand and shook her head.

"My whole family had nightmares for years. Uncle Johnny had just accepted his Black relatives, and David was his favorite." Rhoda paused and wiped tears from her face with the tail of her dress. We still had our jackets on. "My granny was so afraid that Uncle Johnny was goin' to go kill that po'liceman 'cause he kept sayin' he was as soon as he saw him on the street. He was carryin' a gun around and everythin'. Uncle Johnny has not run into that bastard yet after all these years. What's so messed up is, I see that motherfucker all the time—at the carwash, the shoppin' center, in restaurants. The funny things is, it's never any of the times I'm with Uncle Johnny." Rhoda let out her breath and shook her head sadly.

"I'm really sorry about your brother," I moaned. I didn't know what else to say. I just listened as she continued.

"My mama was so overcome, we had to put her in the hospital for a few days. Aunt Lola scrubbed and scrubbed the carpet tryin' to wash away David's blood, but those stains wouldn't go away. She pulled up the carpet and blood had seeped through to the wood floor. She scrubbed the wood floor and even painted it."

"What does the floor look like now?" I asked.

"Not only can you still see David's blood, you can smell it. At least I can."

"You can still smell it after all this time?"

Rhoda nodded. "When it started smellin', Daddy said leave it be. Somethin' about that must be some kind of sign from David. Like he's tellin' us he'll always be here." She wiped her nose with the sleeve of her blue-leather jacket, and I pretended not to notice that she was upset. Her hands were trembling.

Hearing about what happened to Rhoda's brother was depressing me more, and I was already depressed beyond belief over the president. I didn't want to hear all the details surrounding her brother's

death, but I let her keep talking about it. It took my mind off the assassination somewhat. "What happened to that policeman?"

She looked at me and narrowed her eyes to where they looked like
slits.

"He got off," she replied. "That Black bastard got away with murder! He claimed he *thought* my brother was reachin' for a weapon.
The closest thin' to a weapon in the room that night was a empty pop
bottle on the nightstand. They did this half-ass investigation and decided that the shootin' was justifiable. The other cops backed that
motherfucker, and nobody wanted to hear anythin' I had to say. Some
old social worker had the nerve to come to our house to tell Daddy to
get me some counselin'! Daddy took David's death real, real hard.
One night I heard him talkin' to Uncle Carmine about how he
wanted to take care of the po'liceman and my uncle said somethin'
about 'his people' would have it taken care of if Daddy wanted him to.
I figured between Uncle Johnny and Uncle Carmine, there'd be
some justice."

"What did they do?"

"NOTHIN'! The fucker is still walkin' around alive. He did move a
few blocks away though. His wife died, and that lyin' whore daughter
of his ran off with some woman's husband. The rest of his folks live in
Detroit, and he doesn't have any friends. He had the nerve to come
to our church the first few months after it happened, tryin' to get
saved. Most of the congregation was so cold to him, he stopped
comin'. He retired, and now all he does is get drunk and go fishin'."
Rhoda tossed her jacket on a chair by the TV and stretched out on
her bed and propped herself up with her elbow.

"So, do you think your daddy's friend would have really killed that
policeman?" I wanted to know. I sat down with such a thud the bed
squeaked and shook so hard, Rhoda lost her balance.

She swung her legs around and sat up on the side of the bed next
to me. "Yeah. But Daddy must have told him to let it go because he's
still alive after all these years." Rhoda wiped tears from her eyes. "That
motherfucker shot my brother and got away with it. I hate guns and
anybody that fools around with them."

"I know somebody like that," I told her in a quiet controlled voice.
At first, she said nothing. She just seemed deep in thought. Then I repeated myself.

"You know somebody like what?" she asked.

"Somebody who messes with a gun."

Rhoda shrugged. "I'd stay out of his way if I were you," she warned. We watched the TV for another five minutes before I continued.

"Remember that time I told you about this girl and rape and stuff by some grown person?"

"Yeah. And I asked if it was you. You finally goin' to tell me?"

"Well, there is this real old man and . . ."

"And what?"

"He um . . . makes me do things with him." I couldn't face her. I couldn't believe I was finally telling somebody about what Mr. Boatwright was doing to me. For a split second I thought I would go no further. But Rhoda looked at me in such a way I knew I had to tell the whole story.

"What things?"

"You know . . ." I could not look in her face. I knew that she was angry from the tone of her voice.

"You mean like sex?" Her lips snapped brutally over each word.

"Uh-huh," I muttered. I looked at her for a moment and saw that same look I saw on her face the day she attacked Lena in the locker room. The devil.

"For real? Who?"

"Mr. Boatwright rapes me." I was amazed at how easy the words seemed to slide out of my mouth.

"Mr. Boatwright? That one-legged old man who always sits in the back of the church and falls asleep? A man like that can't—"

"He can and he did. He's been doing it to me since I was seven," I said flatly.

Rhoda gave me an incredulous look, then her eyes shifted from side to side for a few seconds. She shook her head. "That nice old man?"

"He's not a nice old man, he's a dirty old man," I insisted.

"The man's got a peg leg. And—I don't believe you!" Rhoda stood up and stood over me with her arms folded.

"Why not?" I wailed. "Why would I lie about something like this?" I stood up and got so close up in her face I could smell her hot breath. Our eyes locked. She was the first to look away.

"Why—he must be a hundred and three years old!" Rhoda managed, returning to the bed.

Sitting back down next to her, I said, "Old men can still do *it*."

Rhoda let out a long sigh and looked toward the wall in stunned disbelief, then she looked at me.

"I know I'm ugly and boys don't fight over me, but girls like me still get raped, if that's what you're thinking," I said firmly.

"I wasn't thinkin' anything like that. I know anybody can get raped, even guys. It's just that . . . well, I can't believe a man like Mr. Boatwright is the type." Though we all went to the same church, Rhoda had never met Mr. Boatwright because she always slipped out of church early if she came at all or he was tied up talking to the preacher or somebody else. "Why do you let him do it?"

"He . . . he makes me." I shrugged.

Rhoda blinked hard, then narrowed her eyes to look at me better. The disbelief in her eyes had intensified. "And you don't tell on him?"

"He's got a gun. He puts it up against my head and tells me how he is going to shoot my brains out and stuff like that."

"What about his peg leg? Doesn't it get in the way?"

"Sometimes we take it off, sometimes it falls off."

Again, Rhoda stared at me incredulously with her eyebrows raised. "Do you think he would really do somethin' crazy? Do you really think he would shoot you?"

"I don't want to find out," I replied.

Rhoda let out her breath and touched my hand. "Well, he can't keep doin' what he's doin' to you!" I opened my mouth to speak, but she stopped me before I could get a word out. "I know what we can do." She held up her hand and gave me a critical look. "We can tell a teacher. Miss Tripp, the music teacher. Last year a white girl told Miss Tripp about her daddy molestin' her, and Miss Tripp called the po'lice." Rhoda was excited, almost hysterical. All on my account.

"What happened to the white girl?"

"Miss Tripp adopted her. The girl's whole family was a wreck. White trash to the bone. They didn't even care about what the daddy was doin'. Come to find out, one of the girl's brothers was doin' it to her, too! My God," Rhoda hollered. "It was even in the newspaper. That nasty daddy of hers went to jail, where he belonged."

"I can't get my name in the paper. A scandal like that would kill my mama. Anyway, so many people like Mr. Boatwright somebody would bail him out and he'd come after me before they could really punish him. I don't even know if they would. I can't prove a thing. It would be my word against his." I shook my head so hard it hurt. "No. I sure can't tell anybody but you. He said he would kill me. Knowing him, I bet he would make it look like an accident." We remained silent for about two minutes. I could hear both our hearts pounding. "If . . . if an accident happens to me, have the police investigate," I choked out. "Tell them everything I told you about Mr. Boatwright. Hear?"

"That motherfucker!" Rhoda brought her dainty fist down so hard on her nightstand it almost fell over.

"And if I do die, tell my mama I didn't tempt him like he said I did. He peeped through the keyhole in my bedroom door and tempted himself."

"Damn." Rhoda sighed heavily and turned off the TV. "What are we goin' to do about him?"

We? I trembled. I smiled. "I don't know."

"I guess I could get Jock to beat him up." Rhoda sighed. "Or Uncle Johnny. I just couldn't tell them why. Hmmmm."

"If you told them why, and they told Mr. Boatwright why they were beating him, he would only take it out on me. He already thinks Jock's messing around with me. He might even shoot Jock, and I would have to live with that."

"How long are you goin' to keep lettin' him mess with you?"

"He is old. Maybe he'll die soon."

"Not soon enough." Rhoda gave me a curious look. It was a look I would never forget for the rest of my life. It was like she was looking through me instead of at me. It scared me and made me feel safe at the same time. "Let's go to your house," she told me.

"What for?"

"Because I want to see this hound from hell up close, and I want him to see me."

CHAPTER 18

"Mr. Boatwright! I'm home," I hollered. I walked through the hallway toward the living room of my house with Rhoda so close behind she was stepping on my heels. "He must be asleep," I explained. "He sleeps like a dead man."

We found him stretched out on his back on the sofa in the living room sound asleep, snoring like a buzz saw. There were five empty beer bottles and three of his pill bottles on the coffee table next to his dog-eared Bible. It was fairly cold in the house, but there were beads of perspiration all over his batty face.

"Chick-en skin," Rhoda whispered with her eyes bugged out.

"The only things missing are a horn and a tail," I said seriously.

"I've never seen him up this close before. I never would have guessed that he was this spooky. You . . . *fuck* him?" Rhoda exclaimed.

I nodded.

"Yech!"

"And I have to kiss him, too," I moaned. "Sometime I have to kiss him before I leave for school."

"*Your kids are gonna be born with hooves!*" Rhoda replied. "Eiyeeee! His hands look like bear claws," Rhoda growled, and looked at me. Then she reached over like she was going to pinch his gnarled hands.

"Don't do that!" I slapped her hand.

"Wake him up," she ordered.

"NO!"

"I just want to see his eyes. I want to know how in the world can you not tell your mama?"

"I told you. He said he would shoot me dead."

"She-yit!"

We looked at Mr. Boatwright's chest rise and fall with each breath. Rhoda stabbed his chest with her finger as if to make sure he was real.

"Maybe somethin' bad'll happen to him," she whispered.

Mr. Boatwright groaned and turned over like he was about to wake up. We jumped back a few steps and waited. He kept snoring. Now he was clicking his teeth.

We moved quietly to the kitchen and sat down at the table. I was feeling too bad about Kennedy and my own predicament to be embarrassed about Rhoda seeing our cheap, tacky furniture. She didn't seem to notice the dog-eared, paper place mats on our kitchen table.

"I know one thing that might take care of him. Prayer. Uncle Johnny says prayer can move mountains. It got him out of prison. We can pray for somethin' to happen to nasty old Mr. Boatwright," Rhoda whispered.

"We can't ask God to make something bad happen to somebody," I insisted, shaking my head.

"We'll pray for somethin' like a stroke or a heart attack or paralysis or somethin', not somebody shootin' him or poisonin' him . . ." Rhoda's voice trailed off. I thought her plan sounded pretty stupid and far-fetched.

"We can't ask God for things like that. Maybe something a little more subtle. Like impotence." I was glad nobody was listening to our rambling conversation.

"Well . . . yeah," Rhoda shrugged. "OK. Heart attacks and strokes are pretty extreme. There must be somethin' else God can do to him that'll make him let you alone. Ooh! I know." Rhoda jumped up, waving her arms, looking like she was about to fly. "My dead brother couldn't have gotten that po'liceman's daughter pregnant. Her or any other girl."

"Why not?" I narrowed my eyes to see Rhoda's face better.

"He had one of those dick problems men get and had some kind of surgery."

"Did they cut his dick off?"

"No, but he couldn't get a hard-on. He couldn't do anythin'. Cut Buttwright's dick off—now that's what I would like to do. Cut off this old man's dick with a dull knife. Then that dickless motherfucker would be tame as a duck, huh?" As dainty and petite as Rhoda was, it was hard to believe that she could turn into such a pit bull so easily.

"Exactly what kind of surgery did your brother have? What all was wrong for him to have to go through that?"

"I never could figure it out. Nobody would tell me. But I used to hear the doctors talkin' to Daddy and Muh'Dear. They told them he would be lucky to pee with his thin' let alone do you-know-what."

"Fuck?"

"Fuck." Rhoda nodded, making a face like it was the most disgusting thing in the world. As far as I was concerned, it was. "We could pray for that same affliction to happen to this old man here," Rhoda said excitedly. "Whatever it was. That or somethin' worse."

"What's worse to a man than him not being able to fuck?"

"Don't worry. *I'll* think of somethin'," Rhoda promised.

CHAPTER 19

Every year on New Year's Eve Reverend Snipes gave a late-evening service called Watchtower, open to anybody who wanted to attend. During this service people were asked to stand up and tell everybody what a good or bad year they had had and what they wanted God to do for them in the New Year. On New Year's Day everybody who wanted to increase their chances of having a good New Year ate black-eyed peas. Mr. Boatwright attended this service every year, and every New Year's Day he cooked a huge pot of black-eyed peas that usually took us three or four days to finish.

No matter who Muh'Dear happened to be working for, every New Year's Eve, she had to work. This year it was the judge. He was combining a poker party with a New Year's Eve party.

Mr. Boatwright was planning to attend Reverend Snipes's Watchtower until Uncle Johnny came to the house around 10 P.M. that December 31, 1963. He almost knocked me down trying to get in our front door so fast. Mr. Boatwright was on our living-room couch waiting for a cab. He was wearing the one suit he owned that I hated the most, that white fleecy thing he had on the first time I met him, and he had on that same black fedora. He always wore this suit to funerals, weddings, and the special church events.

"Oh, the judge is entertainin' in style this evenin', Boatwright! The stakes'll be high, the drinks'll be plentiful, and all you eat!" Uncle Johnny hollered, strutting into our living room wearing a seersucker suit and already smelling like a distillery. I followed him into the living room. He stopped in the middle of the floor in front of Mr. Boatwright, trying to talk him into accompanying him to the judge's house.

I planned to go to bed as soon as Mr. Boatwright left. The only reason I was still up was I didn't want to give him any excuse to come to my room, not that he needed one. He didn't have to come to my room to get what he wanted from me. He often tackled me in the living room and wrestled me to the floor or the couch and did whaever he wanted. It made me sick when I thought of Muh'Dear sitting on the same couch where I got violated on a regular basis.

As much as Mr. Boatwright trashed Uncle Johnny behind his back, oddly they had become running buddies. Their main connection was Judge Lawson's poker parties. Uncle Johnny didn't have a car of his own or even a license. He had to rely on public transportation or wait for somebody with the time and patience to drive him wherever he wanted to go.

Mr. Nelson had purchased a blue '61 Ford for Jock a few weeks earlier. According to Rhoda the agreement was, Jock was to let Uncle Johnny drive the car, too, when and if he got his license back, other relatives when they visited, and once Rhoda turned sixteen and learned to drive she could use the car. On several occasions Uncle Johnny had Mr. Boatwright drive him around. Mr. Boatwright was only too glad to do it. He and Johnny were usually headed in the same direction anyway, the bars and Judge Lawson's poker parties, so the arrangement worked out well for both of them. If Uncle Johnny wanted to go to the New Year's Eve poker party, he had to find somebody to do the driving. Once, out of desperation because Mr. Boatwright was in bed with the flu, Uncle Johnny asked Scary Mary to drive him to Judge Lawson's house. First she got mad, and then she laughed. "Do I look like a damn chauffeur?" she hollered.

"Oh, I don't think I can make it tonight, Johnny," Mr. Boatwright told him, holding up both hands. I went into the kitchen, but I could still hear Uncle Johnny trying to talk Mr. Boatwright into going to the party. Ten minutes into his visit I heard Uncle Johnny say something about some cabaret dancers the judge had invited to entertain his guests. The next thing I knew Mr. Boatwright was running out of the door ahead of Uncle Johnny. I watched out the window and waited until I saw them speed off, then I went to bed.

Rhoda always spent her New Year's Eves enjoying a quiet evening with her family. I had been invited, but family gatherings like that depressed me. As far as I was concerned, my family tree had only two branches left on it, my mama and me. I really envied the kids who not only had parents living with them but grandparents, numerous siblings, and an assortment of miscellanous relatives like cousins and aunts and uncles in their lives. Pee Wee had attended his family reunion in Erie, Pennsylvania, the summer before, and he had returned with pictures of a family that had over two hundred members! He and Caleb were from Erie and talked about it from time to time. "If I ever leave Richland, it'd be to go back to Erie," Pee Wee told me. Not only did I not have a family to visit, I didn't even have a hometown I could go back to anymore. My Aunt Berneice had recently left Florida and moved to New Jersey, and I still didn't know of any other relatives.

I was actually glad when the holiday ended and we returned to school. By the end of January everything was back to normal, and people had stopped talking about Kennedy, Oswald, Jack Ruby.

For the next few months all we talked about was a new band from England called the Beatles. Rhoda was one of the few Black girls with Beatle albums. Pee Wee was the only Black boy we knew that had enough nerve to admit he liked the Beatles. He was even brave enough to wear a Beatle wig. But the wig was not attractive on him at all. It was too big, so it sat on his head at a lopsided angle with the bangs more on the side than in the front. It looked as bad as, if not worse, than the wig Scary Mary wore. He looked pretty gross, but Rhoda and I didn't have the heart to tell him. He was happy. He wore the wig to school a few times but stopped when he got tired of kids snatching it off. Now, he just wore it on weekends and after school.

I spent as much time at Rhoda's house as I could even though Mr. Boatwright tried to sabotage that.

"Brother Boatwright feels that you spendin' too much time at that Rhoda's house. Wearin' all that makeup, she just beggin' to get herself raped," Muh'Dear told me in the kitchen one Sunday night after church.

Scary Mary was sitting at the kitchen table with us decked out in a pair of gold-nylon stretch pants with stirrups and a black turtleneck sweater with the sleeves rolled up to her elbows. She had put on about fifty pounds over the years and had no business squeezing into a pair of stretch pants. She was kicked-back, with a can of beer in her hand and her bare feet on the table. She winked at me and surprised me when she came to my defense.

She made a sweeping gesture with her hand in Muh'Dear's direction. "Oh, Gussie Mae, lighten up. Rhoda's a little angel. When one of my girls up and got herself killed walkin' out in front of that bus, Rhoda helped her daddy dress the body. As dainty as that pretty little girl is, she stood there and manicured Sandra's nails and gave her a egg facial. Now, who would have thought to give a dead woman one more facial?" Scary Mary said firmly. She put her feet on the floor, finished her beer, and let out a great sigh. "I wouldn't have."

"That was nice of Rhoda," Muh'Dear admitted. She was darning a pair of Mr. Boatwright's socks. Her can of beer sat in front of her next to her sewing-paraphernalia basket.

"Me, I wish I was as lucky with my girl as you is with yours. Your girl, she is near perfect. No matter how old Mott get, she goin' to have a baby's brain just like her daddy, my seventh husband. She'll have to be looked after like a baby 'til the day she die. I got a itchin' to take in a foster daughter, and I want her to be just like Annette."

"You're adopting a daughter?" I gasped. I had removed the long drab black shift I had worn to church and had slid into the bright yellow housecoat Judge Lawson had given to me.

"Not adopt, foster. Sometime in the distant future after I get off probation. The girl can keep a eye on Mott and keep my house clean," Scary Mary announced with a quick nod. She paused long enough to finish her beer. "I ain't got time to do that kind of stuff. I'm a busy woman."

"What about all those nasty men?" I asked with my eyes stretched as wide as I could stretch them. With her background and her record I could not imagine anybody giving Scary Mary a foster child.

"What nasty men?"

"Uh . . . the ones that come to your house all the time." I glanced at Muh'Dear, and she was giving me a mean look. "Um . . . never mind."

"Like I said, I want my foster daughter to be just like Annette," Scary Mary insisted. She snatched another beer out of a bag on the table in front of her.

I smiled broadly. Despite what Mr. Boatwright told me Scary Mary had said about me being funny, she was OK in my book.

"Muh'Dear said I could be like you one day," I replied. I smiled and tried to look composed, but my whole body was nervous with energy.

Scary Mary held up her hand, and a sad look appeared on her face.

"When they give me my foster girl I'm goin' to raise her up to be better than the mess I turned myself into," she said, her voice crack-ing.

I just smiled at her again, grateful that she thought I was important enough to speak up for.

"Rhoda's a nice girl, too," I added. I had not brought Rhoda to meet my mother and Mr. Boatwright yet because I was too embar-rassed. Compared to our house, hers was Camelot. I was also ashamed of Mr. Boatwright. Since Muh'Dear's work schedule kept her so busy, she was never available to attend any of my school events, like PTA meetings and Parent/Teacher meetings. Once when I asked if she could take a day off and come meet some of my teachers, she sent Mr. Boatwright in her place and the kids talked and laughed about him for days. I never mentioned any school functions again.

Muh'Dear, Scary Mary, and I moved from the kitchen to the living room to watch *The Lawrence Welk Show,* one of their favorites. It baffled me the way almost every Black person I knew worshiped certain TV shows. Their allegiance to *Lawrence Welk* was probably the most baf-fling. *Perry Mason,* the comedies, and *Ed Sullivan* I enjoyed. I only sat through *Lawrence Welk* because I had no choice if I wanted to watch anything on TV.

When we gathered in the living room to watch TV we only talked when a commercial came on or if there was an emergency. "I wish we had another TV set so I could watch wrestling," I complained. "Like Rhoda," I added.

"Speakin' of Rhoda, she such a good friend of yours, how come she ain't got time to come over here and introduce herself?" Muh'Dear asked, adding with an amused look, "Tell her we ain't gwine to bite her."

I frowned; Scary Mary cackled.

"The girl must have somethin' to hide," Mr. Boatwright said. It was amazing how he often appeared out of nowhere. "Good evenin'." Entering from the kitchen, he nodded to Scary Mary, who was sitting next to Muh'Dear on the couch with her feet on the coffee table. I was glad the commercial was short.

When *Lawrence Welk* went off, I left them in the living room dis-cussing Scary Mary's plan to take in a foster daughter. I could hear them from the kitchen. Scary Mary was going on and on about how angry she was about the fact that there were so many Black kids in need of new homes. She had lived in several foster homes when she was a child she claimed. "As a Christian, I feel duty-bound when it comes to our young'ns. Black folks got a obligation to he'p less fortu-nate Black folks. Sister Goode, you takin' in Brother Boatwright is a good example. Just think how Annette might have turned out if he hadn't been around to keep his eyes on her all these years," Scary Mary said firmly.

They jumped from discussing Scary Mary's future foster daughter to Caleb and how he overcharged his customers. Caleb arrived right after Scary Mary left. As soon as he got comfortable, they started gos-siping about her missing so much church.

Mr. Boatwright said she just wanted a foster daughter so she could collect money from the state, and he would pray for the white folks to give her an ugly one so she'd be less trouble. Pretty girls got men in trouble, he said. After Caleb left, Muh'Dear and Mr. Boatwright de-cided that Caleb probably didn't have a bullet lodged in his head. It was most likely water on the brain. He just said that it was a bullet be-cause a bullet commanded more sympathy and attention than water.

Later, Scary Mary returned with more beer. By then, Pee Wee had joined in, and the subject was white folks. Judge Lawson arrived a half hour later. "Good evening, everybody!" he yelled, rushing in after I opened the door. "Hey there, judgie wudgie. How about a little drink?" Caleb slurred. "How about a big drink!" the judge howled. The next subject they discussed was the mysterious undertaker across the street and his family. I couldn't stand to listen to them trash my best friend and her family.

I called Rhoda on the kitchen phone and told her about Scary Mary planning to take in a foster daughter when she got off proba-tion.

"That'll be good for Mott. But knowin' Scary Mary, she'll have the girl cleanin' that whorehouse and baby-sittin' all the time." Rhoda chuckled.

"Yeah. But with Scary Mary being a madam having a police record, do you really think they'll let her have a foster child?" I whispered, glancing every few seconds toward the kitchen door.

"Miss Pimp always gets what she wants. Anyway, the white folks would give Black kids to Godzilla just to get them off their hands," Rhoda snarled.

I gave this information some serious consideration. "You're proba-bly right. But with all those nasty men in and out, it'd be a miracle if the girl doesn't get raped, huh?"

"If the girl is smart, she won't let that happen," Rhoda said angrily.

"Like I should have been." I sighed. "Mr. Boatwright said Scary Mary just wants a foster child so she can collect money from the state," I added.

Rhoda sighed with disgust. "Does that mean old goat trash everybody?"

"Yep," I said quickly. Then I told Rhoda some of what Mr. Boatwright had said about her and her family. She insisted on coming to meet him and Muh'Dear that next day.

An hour before Rhoda arrived, I sprayed our downstairs with Glade air freshener. Glade was no match for the potent, lingering smell of cabbage greens.

I cleaned all the floors downstairs, but there was nothing I could do about our cheap furniture.

After I had worked on the house, I went to my room and stood in my front window watching Rhoda's house, waiting for her to walk out her front door. I waited for more than an hour. Uncle Johnny and Mr. Antonosanti climbed into Mr. Antonosanti's car, a shiny blue Buick, and sped off. Mrs. Nelson came out to sprinkle water on her rosebushes. I got misty-eyed when Mr. Nelson came out and kissed Mrs. Nelson before roaring off in his car. Finally, Rhoda appeared. She kissed her mother, then skipped across the street. I ran downstairs to make sure I got to her before Mr. Boatwright and Muh'Dear did. *Ed Sullivan* had them mesmerized. They didn't even look up when I ran across the living-room floor to open the door for Rhoda.

"Sorry I'm late. My facial took longer than I expected," she apologized, looking around the room, wiggling her nose. Muh'Dear and Mr. Boatwright turned at the same time to stare at Rhoda.

"Y'all shet that door before them mosquitoes come in here and eat us alive!" Mr. Boatwright ordered, stomping his foot.

Muh'Dear's eyes rested on Rhoda's expensive black-leather boots. Mr. Boatwright leaped up and put his hands on his hips. "Is that your real hair, girl?" he asked suspiciously.

"Yes it is." Rhoda smiled, shaking that gorgeous mane of hers.

"It look like a wig hat," he added, turning to Muh'Dear. "Don't it, Sister Goode?"

Muh'Dear rose and stumbled over to Rhoda and tugged on her hair. "It's real all right. I bet Miss Rachel charge you double to straighten this horse's tail," Muh'Dear mouthed. I was glad she had on a nice dress, a green shirtwaist she often wore to church.

Rhoda turned to me with her mouth hanging open. I cleared my throat and introduced her. Mr. Boatwright took a few steps back, fanning his face with his hand like he had just had a hot flash.

"Um . . . Annette tells me how she helps you with your peg leg. I help my daddy prep the dead folks," Rhoda said casually. She walked over and shook Mr. Boatwright's hand. He looked at her like he didn't know what he was looking at and shook his head.

"Girl, young as you is, ain't you scared to be 'round all that . . . death?" he asked, screwing up his tortured face like somebody was pinching him. "Oooooh!"

Rhoda shook her head, and said seriously, "Dead people don't faze me." The room got uncomfortably quiet. Mr. Boatwright and Muh' Dear were staring at Rhoda like she was a circus freak. I could see that this was making Rhoda nervous. I was trying to think of what to say next to get the conversation going again, but Rhoda beat me to it. "Mr. Boatwright, you look a little wobbly standin' there. Here, let me help you to a seat." He seemed surprised that she was so gracious.

Muh'Dear gasped and smiled.

I stood back and watched as Rhoda helped Mr. Boatwright back to the couch, holding on to him by his arm. Part of the reason he was wobbly was because he had been drinking.

"Is this real leather?" Muh'Dear asked when Rhoda handed her her jacket to hang up. "Yes it is," Rhoda said proudly.

"Did you buy it new?" Mr. Boatwright wanted to know. Like me and Muh'Dear, most of the things he wore came from secondhand stores.

"Yes sir." Rhoda nodded, giving him an incredulous look.

"How much you pay for a *new* leather jacket like this?" Rhoda didn't answer him right away. She sighed, pressed her lips together, and scratched her head. Mr. Boatwright looked around, impatiently waiting for her to answer.

"I wouldn't know. My mama picked it up for me when my daddy took her to New York to shop last month."

"They went all the way to New York just to go shoppin'?" Muh'Dear wailed, then covered her mouth and shook her head in disbelief.

"Yes. We do it all the time." Rhoda was not revealing this information to be bragging. This was the life her family lived.

She stayed for dinner and even helped us prepare it. She made Mr. Boatwright nervous. He kept rolling his eyes at her and dropping things. Rhoda was such a distraction he removed the skillet with the corn bread out of the oven without using a potholder and burned his hand. He squealed like a stuck pig and started hopping like he had to pee. Rhoda applied butter to his burn.

During the conversation at the dinner table, Muh'Dear and Mr. Boatwright asked Rhoda a lot of nosy questions. All of them about her family, like how much money her daddy was worth, her family's relationship with the Antonosanti family, and how much her daddy spent on his white relatives. Rhoda answered every question, giving answers so vague she confused Muh'Dear and Mr. Boatwright so much I think they got mad. *"Lassie* fixin' to come on," Mr. Boatwright said, looking from our wall clock to Muh'Dear. They both sighed, with relief I assumed, when I told them Rhoda and I would stay behind to do the dishes.

She didn't stay long after helping me clean up the kitchen, and, under the circumstances, she had stayed longer than I expected her to. She excused herself just as *Bonanza* was coming on. Muh'Dear smelled Rhoda's leather jacket before handing it to her. "It even smell new," she commented, inspecting it like she was searching for a flaw.

"This evenin' was . . . um . . . interestin'," Rhoda whispered when I walked her out to the porch.

"I'm sorry. I didn't know they were going to jump all over you like that. They had no business asking some of the questions they asked you," I told Rhoda. She made a dismissal gesture with her hand, chuckled, then trotted off our porch. I waited until she went inside her house.

"She sure is grown for fourteen," Muh'Dear remarked, after I closed the door and sat down in the living room across from her and Mr. Boatwright. "You need to be more like her, Annette. I bet she don't squall like a panda about housecleanin'. And she eat like a bird. Why she barely touched all that good food Brother Boatwright put on her plate."

"I wonder why," I mumbled under my breath low enough so they couldn't hear me. I couldn't imagine a girl as pampered and sophisticated as Rhoda gnawing and smacking on neckbones like we had. I was surprised that she had eaten the corn bread and turnip greens.

"I heard she threatened to cut a white teacher's throat last year," Mr. Boatwright said quickly, nodding and fanning his face with a newspaper. "She'll wind up in either a room in the state penitentiary or a room at Scary Mary's place one of these days and start takin' advantage of men. No wonder Scary Mary like her so much. You seen the way that little hussy was swingin' them little narrow hips of hers, Sister Goode?"

"Just beggin' to get herself raped." Muh'Dear sighed and shook her head.

"What were you doing looking at her hips, Mr. Boatwright?" I asked under my breath.

"What you say?" he grunted, then belched.

"Nothing," I whimpered. I couldn't get to my room fast enough.

CHAPTER 20

About two weeks after Rhoda's first visit to my house I accompanied her to her house, where we had planned to study.

She left me in the living room going through her records while she went to the kitchen to get me some of the peanut candy she had made the night before.

"You heard the new Beatles song?" It was Jock talking. I whirled around to see him walking into the room smiling. Fresh scabs ran the length of his face on both sides. There was a Band-Aid on his chin. I knew he got into a lot of fights so the scabs and the Band-Aid did not surprise me.

I looked at him, stabbing myself in the chest with my finger. "Are you talking to me?"

"Yeah," he said, nodding, his smile gone. "Rhoda told me you're a big Beatles fan, too."

"I am. Do you like them?"

"They're all right." He let out a short chuckle and waved his hand. "I think they're more for girls though. And white kids. I'm into Motown." He turned on the stereo and put on an album. "Where's Rhoda?" he asked, looking around the room, snapping his fingers to Marvin Gaye's latest.

"She went to get some of that candy she made," I told him. I was nervous. I kept looking toward the door, praying that Rhoda would return before I started sweating through my cheap blouse.

Just then an elderly, heavyset white woman in a plaid nightgown entered the room, walking with a cane.

"Jock, did you—" She stopped and looked at me leaning over the stereo with an album in my hand. *"Whose little nigger is this?"*

I could hear Jock snicker. I gasped and dropped the record. Lucky for me, Rhoda returned a few seconds later.

"Granny, now you know you ain't supposed to get out that bed. You could fall down the steps and break your hip again," Jock said, shaking his head, facing the old woman with his arms folded.

"Granny Goose, this is my friend Annette from across the street," Rhoda told the old woman, then turned to me. "This is our grandmother. The doctor told us to make her stay in bed as much as we can, but as you can see, she sneaks out." Rhoda laughed nervously.

The woman looked me up and down, frowning. Her hair was as white as snow, and her pale face was heavily lined and dotted with moles and age spots. It was hard to tell if she had ever been attractive. Her nose seemed too big for her face, and her green eyes were too far apart. She had almost no lips. "You leave them albums and that stereo just like you found 'em," she barked at me, waving her cane threateningly. For a brief moment I had a flashback. She looked like mean old Mrs. Jacobs, the woman who had whacked Muh'Dear with her cane. I had to close my eyes and count numbers in my head to keep from losing my cookies.

"Sit down, Granny Goose." Jock attempted to lead the old woman to the couch, but she raised her cane and swung at him, missing only because he ducked. Rhoda tried not to, but she laughed.

"Get your black hands off me!" the woman cried.

Uncle Johnny came running into the room. "Mother, don't get excited. Come on with me now so you can take a pill and get some rest. You ain't got no business gettin' out of bed after what Dr. Thompson told you. You ain't well, sugar." He had on a pair of plain black pants and a leather apron with a bib over a white shirt. I had a feeling he had been in the room helping Rhoda's daddy prepare some deceased person for burial. He smiled and nodded at me. "How you doin', Annette?" Before I could answer he turned to Jock, "Boy, get back yonder where your daddy's waitin' on you!" The old woman ranted and raved and swung her cane as Uncle Johnny steered her out of the room. Over his shoulder he yelled, "Jock, get a move on!" I looked at Jock, hoping he would leave the room immediately so that my heart could stop jumping around in my chest. The boy just stood there like he had not even heard a word his uncle said. Then he picked up another stack of records and sat down on the floor.

"That's daddy's and Uncle Johnny's mama," Rhoda explained.

"I thought so." I nodded. I eased down on the floor and crossed my legs at the ankles.

"None of her other kids will have much to do with her," Jock added, looking at me. "Just Daddy, the only Black one and the only one she rejected."

"Didn't she raise him?" I asked. Like Mr. Boatwright there was a lot about Rhoda's family I didn't know.

"His daddy's mama raised him. Once Daddy got back from the army and the Antonosanti family put up the money for his trainin' and to get him started, his white relatives had a sudden change of heart." Jock shrugged. "None of them had a pot to piss in and didn't know where the next meal was comin' from. Right away Daddy started helpin' out his poor white relatives. To make a long story short, Granny Goose got to be too much of a problem for the rest of her kids. They wanted to put her in the state old folks' home. We were all up here by then. About eight years ago Daddy left the house one mornin' while we were all still asleep and when he came back two days later Granny Goose and Uncle Johnny were with him. She's been here ever since, and so has Uncle Johnny off and on."

"What does Uncle Johnny do for a living?" I asked. I had heard a lot about Rhoda's favorite uncle, but nobody had ever mentioned his line of work.

"That's a good question," Rhoda said seriously. "He works as a dishwasher at Antonosanti's, off and on, and of course he helps Daddy out, off and on." Rhoda nodded. "He's been tryin' to preach the gospel for years, but he keeps backslidin'."

"I'm glad he's here. With Muh'Dear bein' so sickly, Uncle Johnny takes a big load off her helpin' with Granny Goose." Jock shrugged. I looked toward the door, praying he would leave.

"Nobody else in her family would take her in," Rhoda said. "Uncle Johnny wanted to, but he was always in jail or somethin'."

"Granny Goose left her husband for Daddy's father," Jock revealed. "She said that's why her family is so mean to her now."

"Where is he now? Your father's father?" I asked. Rhoda motioned for me to join her on the black-leather couch.

She and Jock looked at one another, giving each other pained looks. Then, suddenly, Rhoda looked down at the floor. Jock took a deep breath and tilted his head.

"When we were still little, he disappeared one evenin' on his way home from the sawmill where he worked," Jock told me in a voice so low I could barely hear him.

"They don't know what happened to him?" I gasped.

"Nope," Jock said with his jaw twitching.

"The Klan had been sendin' threats, then they stopped. I guess they did that so Grandpa would let his guard down. Even though it was years after the threats when he disappeared, we all knew that the Klan had done somethin' to him. We just didn't know what, and we couldn't prove anythin'," Rhoda told me, her words cracking.

"The sheriff, that pot-bellied, rednecked motherfucker had the nerve to say Grandpa probably got sick of the way thin's were and went off to another city or state to start a new life like some people do. Bullshit!" Jock shouted, his hands balled into trembling fists.

I nodded sadly. "The Klan used to come after my daddy so much in Florida, we had to move every few weeks," I told them.

"Well . . . we got somethin' in common after all." Jock winked on his way out the door.

CHAPTER 21

"What's it like?" Rhoda asked me.

"What?"

"Doin' it."

"Doing what?"

"Um . . . sex. I think I should learn all I can now."

"Sex?"

Rhoda nodded and looked me over thoughtfully. "Sex," she replied.

"I don't know." I shrugged. "All I know is sex is the biggest joke God ever came up with. It's the nastiest, most ridiculous-looking . . ." My voice trailed off. The sex act was so unbelievable I couldn't come up with a good enough description.

"But you do it with *Butt*wright."

"He has sex. I just lie there making faces."

"Oh. Well can't you at least tell me what it feels like?"

It was the middle of May. It had taken me all these months to talk Muh'Dear into letting me spend the night at the Nelsons' house. I was convinced she had said yes only because Jock was spending the night in Cleveland with Uncle Johnny visiting one of Uncle Johnny's friends. Mr. Boatwright had her believing that Jock was waiting to pounce on me.

"Like a tampon that moves." I shrugged. That was the best description I could come up with. "The first few times you feel crampy and sore. You bleed—just that first time though. And to be honest with you, it looks right ridiculous while you're doing it. I don't know what God was thinking when he came up with sex! He should have stopped with hugging and kissing."

Rhoda frowned. "If it's that bad, I'm goin' to ration it to my husband. What about you?"

We were lying across her bed in our nightgowns. She had on something pink and frilly that tied with a sash around her waist. I had on a baggy, blue-flannel thing with a collar up to my chins and sleeves with buttons. I looked at the floor. "I'm never getting married," I said levelly.

"Why?" Rhoda gasped. "My God, girl. Don't you want to have kids?" Rhoda asked, a surprised look on her face.

"Yeah. It's just . . . I don't like boys. I've told you that already." I don't remember, but somewhere along the way, the last few months, my crush on Rhoda had disappeared. I still adored her, but in a different way, a way I couldn't explain, but a way that I guessed people considered normal. Now I was really confused as to whether or not I was funny. Even though I was not head-over-heels in love with Rhoda anymore, I still didn't like boys in a romantic way. Now they just scared me. After Mr. Boatwright, I would have to be paid to get involved with another male.

"What about Pee Wee?"

"What about him?"

"He's a boy. At least by nature. You like him."

I let out a deep breath. "He's safe. He can't hurt me."

Rhoda touched my shoulder. "All males are not like Buttwright. Look at my daddy. Look at my uncle Carmine. They are not out to hurt women."

"Look at your uncle Johnny. Look at your mean brother Jock," I said, hand on my hip, head tilted.

Rhoda laughed. "Well, yeah, but you don't have to get involved with men like them."

I removed my hand from my hip and went to the window and looked across the street at my house. Our living-room curtains were open, and I could see Mr. Boatwright stretched out on the couch like he didn't have a care in the world. In a lot of ways I guess he didn't. He had a fairly nice place to live, all he could eat and drink, friends, an open invitation to Judge Lawson's poker parties, and free pussy. I felt such a sharp pain in my side I returned to the bed and sat down so hard, Rhoda almost rolled off. "Mr. Boatwright said if I ever look at another man besides him, he'd kill me. Pee Wee is the only boy I'm allowed to socialize with."

We didn't talk for a moment. I could hear Rhoda breathing through her mouth as we lay sprawled across her bed with leftover snacks, including a large pepperoni pizza and half a dozen teen magazines. The TV was on, but neither of us was paying any attention to *The Donna Reed Show.*

Then she started talking. "I knew this girl down South. She belonged to our church. She was real cute, had a real big butt. One day she went to this house down the road, and one of the sons just home from the military raped her. His name was Ernest. A woman came to our house, and said, 'Y'all, Louise done *finally* got herself raped!' "

"Did they catch him? Did he go to jail?" I asked, reaching for the last piece of pizza. Out of ten slices, Rhoda had eaten only two—I'd eaten the rest.

"The girl got a whuppin' from her daddy for goin' around the boy."

"What about the boy? Didn't he get punished?" I sat up fast.

"As far as everybody was concerned, he hadn't done anythin' wrong. I kept hearin' people say, 'boys will be boys.' Everybody was goin' around makin' excuses for him. Me, I wanted to castrate the son of a bitch." Rhoda stopped and shook her head with disgust.

It really bothered me when Rhoda talked about doing violent things. I think one reason is the fact that I knew she was not just talking. I'd seen the devil on her face more than once, and somehow I knew I would see it again.

"Go on about that girl down South," I told her.

"They kept sayin' the girl was askin' for trouble. Just because she was pretty and had such a big butt. That's what puzzled the hell out of me. They say she was askin' for it 'cause she looked so nice. But what about ugly girls that nasty men and boys rape?"

"Like me?"

Rhoda either didn't hear my comment or didn't know how to respond.

"People started rollin' their eyes at her when she came around. Grown women threatened to beat her up if she tempted their husbands," she continued.

"What do we have to do to keep from being raped? We can't be pretty. We can't wear short dresses and low-cut blouses. What are we supposed to do with ourselves in this world?" I asked. Rhoda still liked to watch me eat. Her eyes were on the lower part of my face as I chewed.

"I don't know, girl." She shook her head and sighed. "I remember overhearin' some of the ladies down the road from where we lived talkin' about havin' Louise arrested for prostitution! I got so mad! Guess what I did?"

I looked in Rhoda's eyes. There was a sparkle of mischief there. "What?"

"I set Ernest's house on fire with him in it! I lit a rag and threw it in a basket of clothes in their kitchen. He was the only one home." My mouth fell open as I stared at her. "Oh, don't worry. He didn't die. He was able to put the fire out. But his hands got burned real bad."

"Rhoda, you could have killed that boy," I said nervously.

"I know I could have. And I would have if I had wanted to." I looked away from her as she continued talking. "That girl down South, the only thing she had done wrong was be born a girl."

"None of it makes any sense."

"Now, back home when a white girl got raped, everybody and his brother started runnin' around lookin' for a rope to lynch somebody with. If they couldn't find the guilty one, they got the first man that looked like he had lust on his mind. Anybody, as long as he was Black."

"You mean to tell me they would hang the wrong man and know it?"

"Oh, girl. Where have you been? A Black boy was lynched for just *whistlin'* at a white woman a few years ago. It was all over the news."

"I remember that. I read about it in *Jet* magazine," I told her, swallowing the last of the pizza.

"Finish telling me about that girl." I sighed. The story was making me sick, but I wanted to know it all.

"Well, as soon as the motherfucker's hands healed, *he raped her again.* Him and two of his friends. Her daddy beat the livin' daylights out of her again right in front of a bunch of us kids. My mama called the sheriff. He came to our house and cussed her out when he found out what she had called him for. He was truly mad that he had left a baseball game on the TV for some 'raped colored gal.' Oh God, I was so confused. Just three days earlier a white prostitute had cried rape. The sheriff, his deputies, everybody but the FBI, they searched the woods with hounds and everythin' lookin' for a man that had escaped from the chain gang and alleged rapist. I was playin' with these kids whose daddy was a bootlegger. The white woman was in his house talkin' about the rape. She admitted she hadn't been raped. I heard her say so. The escaped convict had just gotten him a little bit and refused to pay her. They never found him, but two other Black men were found hangin' from trees that same week. Back to the girl from our church. After the boys finished with her, she was all bloody and her clothes were all torn up and everythin'. Again, she was the only one that got a whuppin.' "

"What happened to the girl after that?"

"She walked into Mobile Bay."

"And?"

"She never came out. She left a suicide note sayin' that she didn't want to live in a world that treated its Black women the way she had been treated."

"Every now and then I feel the same way, suicidal," I said sadly. "But I don't have the kind of nerve that must take," I admitted. "And I don't think I could do that to my mama."

Rhoda gave me a hard look, as if she was trying to imagine my pain. "Is gettin' raped really that bad?" Rhoda gasped.

"It is to me. I used to trust people. I used to like everybody. I don't anymore. One time this boy, a boy three grades behind me and half my size, felt on my butt when the cafeteria was crowded. I peed on myself when I should have kicked his ass," I growled. Rhoda was stunned. She had never seen me this angry before.

"A boy did that to me one day at the movies," Rhoda told me, with an evil look on her face I'd seen before.

"What did you do?"

"Jock was with me. I didn't have to do anything. It took four people to get Jock off that boy. That was two years ago, and he's still walkin' with a limp."

"Mr. Boatwright is real old, and he can't have that many years left. All those pills can't keep him going forever. He could die tomorrow," I said seriously.

Rhoda nodded, and told me in a strange and hollow voice, "He sure could . . ."

CHAPTER 22

It was our first day as sophomores at Richland High, the town's only high school, when we saw Otis O'Toole for the first time. Pee Wee, Rhoda, and I were sitting on the big gray school's front lawn comparing our schedules when this tall dark boy wearing white pants and a black shirt strutted by. "Haylo!" He had the cutest accent and was attractive, with a headful of the blackest, curliest hair I'd ever seen on a Black person. He was about the same shade of dark brown as Rhoda and me, and he was muscle-bound like Jock. He had a narrow face and slanted, jet-black eyes, almost like an Oriental.

"Did y'all see that?" Rhoda gasped. She stood up and shaded her eyes to see him better. The boy glanced over his shoulder at Rhoda and smiled, but he kept strutting and bobbing his head. When he nodded at me, still smiling, I gave him a blank stare and was tempted to give him the finger.

"What? That old boy with that long mule face?" I said nastily. I hated for Rhoda to pay attention to boys. Unless it was some boy on television or in one of our movie magazines. Her words hurt me like a knife. I actually felt a sharp pain in the middle of my chest. I couldn't wait to get home to my bedroom, where I could have myself a good cry.

"That was not just a boy! That's a walkin' dream! He ought to be served on a platter!" Rhoda exclaimed.

She belonged to me. I had never seen her behave this way over a boy before, and I sure as hell didn't like it. My heart started beating real fast. The last thing I wanted to share her with was some funky-tail boy. Where would that leave me? I was horrified when she threw the strange boy a kiss. The only reason I didn't say what was on my mind was because Pee Wee was with us. It hurt, but I had to keep my feelings and thoughts to myself.

"Isn't he cute?" Rhoda squealed, looking at me and grinning like a fool.

"Uh . . . I guess," I managed, looking around the schoolyard admiring the nice new outfits some of the other girls had on. I had on a gray-flannel jumper with a black sweater underneath. Rhoda had on a blue-silk dress, and Miss Rachel had permed her hair the Saturday before. As painful as it was to think about, I knew that someday she would go her way, and I would go mine. She wanted to get married and have a family. I wasn't sure what I wanted to do with my life after Mr. Boatwright. When people asked me about my plans for the future I told them I planned to go to Hollywood and become an entertainer. I got a lot of surprised looks and looks of disbelief, but people stopped asking me after a while so I didn't care.

"That new boy lives in that green house on the corner of Fourth Street across from Antonosanti's," Pee Wee informed us. Fourth Street was just a few blocks from our street. The boy's family had to be well-off to be able to afford that neighborhood. "He just moved here from Florida. His folks come from one of them islands. Like we need more Black folks in America to be gettin' fucked over. His mama wears tight clothes. I seen his daddy sneakin' into Scary Mary's whorehouse already—just last night, and they just been here a week!"

"He's skinny," I said harshly. "Like somebody with a disease."

"I bet it's syphylis," Pee Wee said eagerly.

"Or cancer," I suggested. Rhoda ignored our comments. I was concerned that I was beginning to behave like some of the other gossipmongers we knew.

"Well, I'm goin' to marry him and have his babies," she announced. I almost lost the double helping of grits I'd eaten for breakfast.

The *very next day* while on the bus sitting next to Mr. Boatwright on our way home from the slaughterhouse, I saw Rhoda walking down Young Street with that beast, and I had to admit to myself, they looked like they were made for one another. They made such a striking couple people turned to stare at them. A few days later I was in a stall in the girls' room and I overheard some jealous girls, ugly ones at that, grumbling about Rhoda and how she had pussy-whipped Otis before any of them had a chance to. I met him the following day. He was also a sophomore so he ate lunch when we did. When I walked into the cafeteria and saw him sitting next to Rhoda, grinning like he'd won a blue ribbon, I wanted to cut his tongue out. As soon as I sat down across from them, I started rolling my eyes at Otis and belching on purpose. I had to admit, he was polite and very friendly, and he was liked by everybody but me.

"What's he really like?" I asked on the way to school one day, hoping she would tell me Otis was not her type after all. Rhoda had been dating the Jamaican for two weeks. One Saturday I called her house four times and was told that she was out. I found out later that she had spent the entire day with Otis. They had gone swimming at Sun Tan Acres, the Mt. Pilot to see the latest beach party movie, eaten dinner at Antonosanti's, and, according to Pee Wee, they spent three hours in the Princeton Motel, one block from the church we all attended, doing the unspeakable! Pee Wee told me Caleb told him. A woman Caleb kept company with worked as a maid at the motel, and she had told Caleb. "They got a lot of nerve *fuckin'* that close to the church!" Pee Wee said right after he had told me.

"He's got a few rough edges, but I can smooth them out by the time we're old enough to get married," Rhoda said thoughtfully. "And guess what, he's been to Paris and the Bahamas, too."

"Who cares!" I snapped.

"You don't like him, do you?" She sounded sad and serious.

"NO!"

"Why not?"

"Because he's a boy, and he's going to ruin everything for me—just like Mr. Boatwright!"

Rhoda sighed and touched my shoulder and shook her head. "No he's not. I . . . listen, this thing with Buttwright is destroyin' you, girl. If you won't expose him, maybe we should find you a good therapist to see you through it."

I bristled. "A therapist? Me? I'm not the one that's crazy. Mr. Boatwright's the one that needs mental help. I—let's change the subject. Um . . . that Jamaican, you're serious about marrying him?"

Rhoda took her hand off my shoulder and gave me a look of pity. I was spoiled and selfish where she was concerned, but it was her fault. She had me believing I was finally somebody important. The thought of the one thing I feared the most, a male, taking her from me made me crazy. I didn't want to know what she was really thinking about me now. I couldn't risk making her mad enough to sever our relationship.

"Well who wouldn't be? He's cute, he's smart, and his folks are well-off. They run an orange grove in Florida. That's what he's goin' to do after graduation. Go back to Florida and run the family farm with his grandfather. He really likes you. He asks about you all the time. He thought maybe we could all go out together sometime."

"Why?" I gasped, my heart fluttering. I refused to let her see my face. I couldn't hide my disgust. I looked toward the street and started counting cars.

"You're my best friend, and I've told him all about you—"

I looked at her fast and hard. "I hope you didn't tell him about me and Mr. Boatwright."

"Heck no. I promised I would never tell anybody about that, and I won't."

"I don't think I want to go out with him. What kind of fun do you expect to have with him breathing down our necks?" I said, shaking my head and giving Rhoda the most serious look I could.

"Oh come on. He wants us to go to the drive-in movies. Him and me and . . . you and Jock."

Horrified, I stopped in my tracks. "Jock? What's wrong with you, girl?" I roared. I had never raised my voice to Rhoda until then. "You must be out of your mind! Next to Mr. Boatwright, Jock is the meanest, nastiest male alive! I wouldn't be caught dead in a car at a drive-in movie at night with Jock!" I noticed people in passing cars looking at me. I lowered my voice and wiped sweat from my face. Rhoda's face was a mask of incredulity.

"Buttwright wouldn't have to know. I won't tell anybody," she said tiredly with great sadness in her voice.

"It's not just Mr. Boatwright. You of all people know I hate boys— especially Jock. Him with his tattoos and nasty ways and beer and gang friends. He sasses grown people, he passes gas in church just to be funny, he cusses—"

"I cuss. Pee Wee cusses. I've even heard you cuss."

"You and me cussing is different. We only do it when we get provoked. Pee Wee, well he's not a real boy anyway, so he doesn't count. Let's change the subject."

"What do you want to talk about?"

"Anything. Anything but boys . . ." I replied.

CHAPTER 23

The first time I went to the movies with Rhoda and Otis I felt uncomfortable, but not as uncomfortable as they looked. Otis kept clearing his throat, and Rhoda kept shifting her body in her seat. We occupied a back row at the Mt. Pilot Theater watching a Hells Angels movie. I hated biker movies so much I didn't even know the name of the one we were watching. I was with Otis and Rhoda because I believed that my presence was important to maintain the relationship I had with her. It was not long before they stopped inviting me to go out with them, but that didn't matter—I just invited myself.

Otis was nice to me at all times, no matter how much my presence annoyed him. When he didn't think I was looking, out of the corner of my eye I saw looks of exasperation on his face. His parents gave him plenty of spending money and he spent as much of it on me as he spent on Rhoda.

It was then 1967 and Vietnam was a household word. Jock was threatening to join the army. The Nelsons, especially Rhoda and Mrs. Nelson, were horrified. Three boys from Richland had already died in that war. Uncle Johnny was the only one who supported Jock's plan. "The military makes men outta boys," Jock announced with an exaggerated salute one evening in the Nelsons' kitchen in front of Rhoda, me, and Uncle Johnny. "Yeah. Look at me," Uncle Johnny hollered, raising his fist. Rhoda had told me that Uncle Johnny had been dishonorably discharged from the army for sexually harassing

WACs on several occasions, then punching an officer in the nose when he confronted him.

For the past few weeks, Jock had been trying to teach Rhoda how to drive. She was having a hard time learning, and it drove him crazy. She told me, "Oh I can get the hang of it if I wanted to. I'm just fuckin' up so that Jock will be around longer. At least until that damn war is over. It would kill Muh'Dear if he did end up in Vietnam and somethin' happened to him." Each time after Jock and Rhoda returned from the Pine Street cemetery where he took her to practice, she called me up. "I almost hit a tree, I almost knocked over a headstone, and I backed into a truck on the way home," she complained to me one Saturday evening. Otis and Uncle Johnny, who had his license, didn't want to be bothered trying to teach Rhoda how to drive. She had a learner's permit and could drive as long as there was a licensed driver in the car, which was usually Uncle Johnny or Pee Wee. One Saturday a few days before Labor Day, she invited me to join her for lunch. I got in the front seat of the Ford with her and Uncle Johnny got in the back.

"Where are we going," I asked. Rhoda was treating me, and I was hoping she would say we were going to Antonosanti's or one of the other nice restaurants. It was warm and I had on a sleeveless blouse and jeans. For some reason my weight had remained the same for more than a year now, 254, even though I ate as much as I normally did. Muh'Dear said it was because my hormones were changing. Rhoda said it was the stress I brought on myself over her and Otis. I didn't know and I didn't care what it was that was keeping my weight at bay.

"I feel like some soul food today," Uncle Johnny yelled, his arms on the back of the front seat, his hot foul breath on the back of my neck.

"Sounds good to me," Rhoda chirped, wrestling with the steering wheel. It seemed like the car was all over the road. She stopped so abruptly to avoid hitting a man riding a bike on the sidewalk, my head barely missed the windshield. Uncle Johnny's head hit the back of my seat.

"Girl, pay more attention to what you're doin'! I ain't ready to die yet," Uncle Johnny yelled at Rhoda, rubbing his forehead.

She pulled into the parking lot of the Buttercup restaurant located in the same run-down neighborhood I had moved from in 1963. There were several Black-owned soul food restaurants in Richland, but everybody said that the Buttercup was the best one. Some Black people insisted that it was just as nice as Antonosanti's, even though they had never been inside Antonosanti's. I didn't know what to expect. The owner, a man named Robert King, had relocated the restaurant from Cleveland years before Muh'Dear and I moved to Ohio. Unlike some of the soul food restaurants I'd seen, with paint falling off the building and boarded-up windows, the outside of this restaurant was impressive. It was a small well-cared-for gray building with large clean windows and a big black sign out front printed in fancy script, **THE BUTTERCUP**. Once inside, I realized that the Buttercup was nothing more than a glorified rib joint and could never compete with Antonosanti's. The brown tables and chairs were cheap and plain, the maroon carpet was so old it had rips and holes and the smell of assorted barbecue sauces was overwhelming. On the wall facing the door were autographed pictures of obscure Black entertainers who had eaten at the Buttercup while passing through Cleveland. It was a clean and organized place with friendly waiters, and I knew that the food was good because on several occasions Mr. Boatwright and Judge Lawson had brought take-out platters to the house.

Uncle Johnny and I ordered combination plates that included pork ribs, pork links, beef, chicken. The only meat Rhoda could order was chicken or beef. She steadfastly refused to eat pork no matter how much Pee Wee, Otis, and I tempted her.

"Annette, you the closest to the cigarette machine. Go yonder and get me a package of Camels," Uncle Johnny told me, dropping a pile of coins into my hand. I had never bought cigarettes before and wasn't sure how to operate the machine a few feet from our table. Almost all of the dozen or more tables were occupied. Surprisingly, most of the other patrons were white. Even in a Black establishment, white people and a few Blacks turned and stared at me and Rhoda accompanying Uncle Johnny just like they did when Muh'Dear, Mr. Boatwright, and I went to Antonosanti's with Judge Lawson. While I was standing in front of the machine, feeling stupid and confused, my stomach growling, a tall Black man in his fifties wearing a pair of bibbed overalls and a blue-flannel shirt walked up and stood next to me.

"You havin' a problem?" he asked. He had a receding hairline and more than enough wrinkles, but I could tell that he had once been a handsome man.

"I don't know how this works," I told him, assuming he was Mr. King, the Buttercup's owner.

"What do you want?" the man asked, taking some of the coins out of my hand.

"A package of Camels," I replied. I watched him simply insert enough money and push a button under a picture of the Camel cigarette package in the display. The cigarettes popped out right away. "Thank you, sir." I smiled, backing away. He nodded and proceeded to select his choice. When I got back to the table, Rhoda and Uncle Johnny were staring at the man with cold, hard, trancelike looks on their faces. They didn't even notice when I placed the Camels in front of Uncle Johnny on the table. They were looking at the man at the cigarette machine. "Y'all know him?" I asked, dying to get my hands on my four-way combination plate. When neither of them spoke, I waved my hand in front of Rhoda's face. "Wake up." Their eyes followed the man out the door. "Who is that?" I wanted to know. Just then, the waiter rolled a tray over to our table that contained our orders.

"Let's get the hell outta here," Uncle Johnny said, rising.

"Why? We haven't eaten," I cried, talking to Rhoda's uncle, my eyes on the food the waiter had just set in front of me.

"That son of a bitch!" Rhoda seethed. The startled waiter almost dropped her plate.

Uncle Johnny whipped out a fistful of dollars and dropped more than enough to cover our lunch on the table. "Let's get the hell out of here, I said!" he roared.

"What in the world is going on?" I had to run to keep up with him and Rhoda. We had not touched the food, and Uncle Johnny had left the cigarettes behind. Outside on the sidewalk, Rhoda started crying, and Uncle Johnny put his arms around her. "Will somebody tell me what is going on?" I asked, now angry, my hands on my hips. The same man they had been glaring at, who never even acknowledged Rhoda and Uncle Johnny, climbed into a white van at a parking meter a few meters ahead of the Ford. There were some fishing poles sticking out of his back window.

"That's . . . the man who killed my brother," Rhoda sobbed, wiping her face with a handkerchief Uncle Johnny had handed to her.

"Oh," I mumbled. All of a sudden I wasn't hungry anymore, and all I wanted to do was go home and roll this information around in my head.

"Let's get the hell out of here before I kill somebody," Uncle Johnny said angrily.

On the way home, Rhoda sideswiped a fire hydrant. The Ford had to go to a body shop to have the dent in the fender removed, which was the first of several dents Rhoda would be responsible for. Her daddy wouldn't let her drive his Cadillac, and her mother was reluctant to let Rhoda use her car. One day Otis let Rhoda use his car, a shiny red Chevy Impala that he worshiped, to take me to the slaughterhouse, where she scraped the side of a parked bus. From that day on, he refused to let her borrow his car, but he was usually available to take us wherever we wanted to go.

"There is nutting I like better than seeing a girl enjoy herself," Otis informed me. I shared the front seat of his Chevy at the drive-in movies with him and Rhoda one Saturday night, a week after the incident at the Buttercup. Rhoda's seeing the man responsible for her brother's death had upset her greatly. She was depressed for the next couple of weeks. Part of the excuse I used to continue going on dates with her and Otis was so I could be there to soothe her in a way only another female could. I could not help the fact that I was jealous of Rhoda's relationship with Otis, and I did feel bad about it, but I still followed them around every chance I got. It had taken me years to find Rhoda and I was not about to let a boy take her away from me without a fight. I even encouraged Pee Wee to dig up gossip on Otis so we could tell her. He didn't know that he was part of my plan to hijack Rhoda.

"He must be livin' a clean life, goddammit! I can't find out nothin' juicy on that goddamn boy for us to talk about!" Pee Wee reported angrily after trying for weeks.

"Damn!" was all I could say. I followed Otis and Rhoda to the movies another Saturday afternoon. Because Otis's car was being repainted after Rhoda's accident with the bus, they had taken the bus. I'd taken a cab with money I'd earned from going to the Food Bucket for Scary Mary and arrived at the Mt. Pilot Theater ten minutes ahead of them.

A week after that I was in the kitchen peeling potatoes to make French fries. I'd only been home from school for about ten minutes. Right in the middle of peeling the potatoes, I remembered that Muh'Dear had left money for me to pick up some stew meat from the Food Bucket. "Shit!" Before I could make up my mind what to do about the forgotten stew meat, somebody knocked on the kitchen door. It was Jock, grinning like he'd just won the lottery.

"What do you want?" I was surprised, nervous, frightened, and suspicious. He had never come to our house before.

"Can I come in?" he asked.

I looked over my shoulder. Mr. Boatwright was taking a nap on the living-room couch, Muh'Dear was still at work.

I let Jock in, and he followed me to the counter. I didn't take my eyes off of him. "What is it?" I snapped, trying to appear more annoyed than I really was.

"I could see you from outside through the window—"

"Peeping in our window? That's just like a man! You nasty buzzard." I was annoyed, but not as angry with him as I wanted him to believe I was.

He threw up his hands. He had on a black-leather jacket, and I could smell beer on his breath. Just being alone with him made me feel faint. "I wasn't peepin'. Your curtain is wide-open. That's what I really came here for. To tell you that. One of them sex maniacs comin' out of Scary Mary's could peep in, see you, and bust down the door."

I closed the curtain and turned to face Jock with my arms folded. I had on a thin green-cotton nightgown I had picked up at a yard sale. Because it was so old and I had washed it one time too many in water that was too hot, it had shrunk a lot and was now too tight and too short. I didn't like the way he was looking me up and down at all.

"OK," I said with a strong, impatient voice. "The curtain is closed."

"One other thing," he continued, his finger poised in the air. "You like Marlon Brando?"

"Why?"

He shrugged and scratched the back of his neck. "Um . . . I heard how much you like movies. I was wonderin' if you would like to go with me to see Brando's new—"

Before I knew it, I held the butcher knife in front of his face.

"Ai-yee!" he yelled. His hands went up in the air again, and he started to back away.

"What's wrong with you, boy?"

"What the—?" Jock's mouth dropped open, and his eyes got so wide I thought they would roll out of his head. I never expected somebody as tough as Jock to look as scared as he did at this moment. Especially with me.

He gasped and turned around so fast he fell. He left the house running at an incredible speed. My heart was beating and sweat appeared on my face within seconds. I started to cry. The thought of going out with a regular boy made me sick.

"That was real nice." Mr. Boatwright entered the kitchen clapping his hands, his housecoat dragging the floor.

"I—I thought you were asleep." I dropped the knife and folded my arms, then wiped my eyes and nose with the sleeve of my gown and took a deep breath. It had been over a month since my last sexual encounter with him. He had come to my room while I was still asleep that morning and was on top of me before I could wake up good enough to put up a fight.

"You thought wrong." He walked over to me and ran his hand along the side of my face, then he kissed me on the lips.

CHAPTER 24

It had been an hour since I pulled a knife on Jock in the kitchen. I was still in a foul mood when Scary Mary barged in without knocking. With her was a tall, reddish brown-skinned girl with curly brown, shoulder-length hair, a crooked smile, and the strangest-looking eyes I'd ever seen. Her clothes were stylish and cute, but cheap. Scary Mary's seventeen-year-old foster daughter couldn't have arrived at a worse time.

"Y'all, this here is Florence Belle. My gal," Scary Mary said proudly, brushing the girl's hair off her face. "Florence, this here is Annette and Brother Boatwright. Now you better mind Brother Boatwright just like you would me. Don't sass him, and do everythin' he tell you to do. Do you hear me?"

"Yes, Ma'am," the girl said in a low voice. I could tell from the look on her face, she didn't like hearing that.

"Johnny just left my place. I told this girl here to call him *Uncle* Johnny like all the rest of the young'ns around here do," Scary Mary said, looking at me. "It makes him feel good."

Mr. Boatwright was on one end of the couch with a can of Strohs beer in his hand and a scowl on his face that had increasingly become the demeanor he presented. I was on the other end wringing my sweaty hands because I had just argued with him long and hard enough for him to lose interest in fucking me a second time that night.

"Hi," I managed, barely opening my mouth. I was too flustered to offer the girl a smile. I noticed Scary Mary's eyebrow rise, and she gave me an exasperated look.

"God sure is good," Mr. Boatwright stated, bobbing his head, jumping up from the couch. He strolled over to the girl and hugged her so hard she frowned. I just sat there glaring at him. "You 'bout our gal's age, ain't you?"

"I'll be eighteen in November." Florence smiled shyly. Then she looked at me just sitting there like I was paralyzed. "I hope we can be friends."

"Me too," I muttered, still unable to smile. My peculiar behavior puzzled Scary Mary.

"Annette, you all right? You constipated?" she asked with concern. She was looking at me so hard I could feel it.

"I'm gwine to spoon her a dose of castor oil before she go to bed," Mr. Boatwright croaked. "I bet it's all them crunch bars she gobble up that that busy Rhoda be cookin' up all the time."

"I am not constipated," I insisted, rising. "I'm just a little tired."

"If she spent less time runnin' amok, she wouldn't be so tired—"

"I don't run amok, and you know it, Mr. Boatwright!" I snapped. I had never behaved so badly in front of a stranger before, and I was ashamed of myself. I gave Florence a pleading look, and she nodded knowingly.

"Now that's the very thing I done just warned you about," Scary Mary told Florence, shaking her finger in Florence's face. "Don't you never sass Brother Boatwright like this girl just done. Annette, shame on you for showin' out in front of my gal here first time you meet her! I feel like a fraud after all the brags I done on you to Florence!"

"I'm sorry." I finally smiled. I looked at Florence again. For a brief moment our eyes locked. A sad look appeared on her face. "Where are you from, Florence?"

"She from Cleveland, but she been shuffled all over the state, one home after another. Lord, when I think about all the abuse this girl done endured with them foster daddies, I go crazy. One thing about it—ain't no man goin' to molest this girl long as she livin' in my house!" Scary Mary exclaimed, raising her fist over her head and shaking it. "I'll put somethin' on him a doctor can't take off."

I looked at Florence again. There was a faint smile on her face, but her eyes were staring at the floor.

"Oh, we one big family 'round here. I'm gwine to do all I can to make Florence feel right at home." Mr. Boatwright grinned, bobbing that head again.

"Excuse me," I mumbled. "Um . . . Florence, it was nice meeting you." I rushed to my room before any of them could say anything else. As soon as I got there, I regretted being back in it so soon. My bed was still messed up from my latest romp with Mr. Boatwright. The sheet was damp, and grease from his hair was all over my pillow.

I changed the bedding, then crawled into bed, canceling my plan to eat dinner with Judge Lawson and Muh'Dear at the kitchen table like I'd planned to do. Oddly, I dreamed about Florence and what Scary Mary had said about her foster daddies abusing her. I felt bad about the way I had acted toward her. I made a promise to myself that I would get to know her as soon as I could. The more I thought about it, the more I decided it was important for me to hear about her abuse and how she had handled it.

Scary Mary was surprised to see me at her front door early the next morning. "What the hell you doin' bangin' on my door this time of mornin', girl?" she hollered, then yawned in my face. She was in her housecoat, a yellow-silk one like one I'd seen Rhoda's mother wear. "I don't allow nobody but our tricks to be comin' here this early."

"Well . . . I just came by to see if Florence wanted to walk to school with me and Rhoda," I babbled. Out of the corner of my eye I spotted a white man in a gray business suit walking fast toward Scary Mary's house.

"My gal done already got her diploma. She smart," Scary Mary announced proudly.

"Oh? She's graduated already?"

"If you had kept your tail downstairs last night, you'd know that."

I moved so the man could get in the door. Scary Mary smiled at him, slapped him on the back, and motioned him down a hallway. Over her shoulder I noticed a half-naked woman grab the man as soon as he got close enough. Then Florence appeared. She was fully dressed but also had on an apron. She had that same strange look in her eyes that I had noticed the night before. She stumbled a few times walking toward the door.

"Hi, Florence." I smiled broadly. "I was going to invite you to walk to school with me and my best friend Rhoda, but Scary Mary just told me you've already graduated."

"Yes. I studied at home," Florence told me gently. I was impressed because she spoke so properly. She was not ugly or fat, but she wasn't really pretty either. I guess she was about as average as a girl could be. She just seemed unusually reserved for a girl of seventeen. She looked young, but she seemed a lot older.

"Oh. Well . . . uh . . . maybe you can go to the movies with me and Rhoda sometime," I told her.

"This girl don't go to no movies," Scary Mary snapped.

"I'd like to, but I'm legally blind. I wouldn't enjoy a movie much," Florence said softly.

"Blind? Oh." I felt so awkward. "I never would have guessed it." That explained the strange look in her eyes. "Well, I better be going so I won't be late." I started backing off the porch. I bumped into another man, this one a Black man in a black suit, rushing toward Scary Mary's house with a grin on his face.

"Maybe you can come over and listen to records some time," Florence hollered.

"OK," I replied. I let out a groan and trotted across the yard that led to the back of our house. Mr. Boatwright was peeping out our kitchen window, so I didn't go back in. Instead, I went to pick up Rhoda.

"You're late," Rhoda complained. She was already on her front porch fussing with the ribbons in her hair.

"Scary Mary's foster daughter arrived last night. I went to Scary Mary's house to see if the girl wanted to walk to school with us this morning."

"Oh forget it." Rhoda laughed as we headed down the street. "Scary Mary brought her to our house last night, too."

I glanced over my shoulder toward my house. Just as I suspected, Mr. Boatwright was peeping out the front window now.

"Well, did you like her? She seems nice. I was in a lousy mood when I met her because Mr. Boatwright had just jumped me again. I was rude to the girl when I met her. That's why I went to Scary Mary's this morning."

"Yeah, she seems OK, but not the kind of girl I want hangin' around me."

"Why not?" I gasped, looking at Rhoda with wide eyes. "What's wrong with her?"

"The girl's half-blind. I don't have time to be draggin' around with a handicapped girl. I don't have that kind of patience. I'd go crazy."

I was surprised at Rhoda. In some ways I felt handicapped, but she had patience with me.

"She'll just slow us down," Rhoda added. "Let Scary Mary dump her on Pee Wee. Then maybe he won't crowd us so much anymore."

"OK," I mumbled. I didn't want to jeopardize my relationship with Rhoda. I couldn't afford to lose her. Especially for an abused, orphaned, legally blind girl.

CHAPTER 25

Even though I had told Florence I'd spend some time with her, it seemed like every time she called on me, I had something to do. Housework, homework, or I just wanted to be in my room by myself reading. I had just finished *Love Story* and was anxious to start *Valley of the Dolls*.

No matter how many times I was not available, she didn't stop asking me to come over.

One day, a Sunday after church, I wanted to talk to Rhoda. I had not seen or heard from her in four days. I was surprised when she didn't come to church with her parents. Like with me and most of the other Black kids I knew, we attended church whether we wanted to or not. Since Mr. Boatwright only sang a solo on holidays now, church was not as much fun. I was home alone; Muh'Dear and Mr. Boatwright were visiting the family of a recently deceased church member. I dialed Rhoda's number.

"Hello?" Granny Goose answered in a voice that was more like a croak.

"May I speak to Rhoda, please?" I didn't know if the old woman was hard of hearing or not, but I spoke in a real loud voice anyway.

"Hello!" she shouted again.

"MAY I SPEAK TO RHODA, PLEASE?" I yelled louder. She slammed the phone down so hard in my ear I heard ringing for the next five minutes.

I called Pee Wee's house next, and Caleb told me he was at the shopping center. Out of sheer boredom I invited Florence over.

"You get around real good for a blind girl," I told her. She had pushed my hand away when I attempted to lead her to my room. Once we got there we sat on the bed.

"Oh I'm not completely blind. I just have cataracts on both eyes. But as I get older, my vision gets worse. I'm sure I'll be completely blind by the time I'm thirty," Florence said seriously. "When a person loses one of their senses, another one gets stronger. I can't see as well as you, but I can hear better than most people."

"Uh-huh," I replied.

"Like one night when I was in your living room and you and Rhoda were in the kitchen, I heard her tell you I was no fun." Florence laughed.

"Oh you did. Well I didn't say anything bad about you—"

"I know you didn't. I heard you defend me." She laughed.

We got silent for a moment. I could hear Mr. Boatwright roaming around outside in the hallway. I thought I would die when I spotted his eyeball peeping through my keyhole! I was glad Florence couldn't see that or the burning shame on my face. I waited until I saw him leave. I moved closer to Florence and started talking again, in a lower voice. Even though Mr. Boatwright's eye was gone from the keyhole, I knew he was probably still outside my room with his ear against the door.

"So . . . uh . . . you were abused, too?" I was whispering, but Florence had no trouble hearing me.

"Too?"

"I mean . . . somebody . . . molested you."

"Oh yeah. But it was a long time ago, and I'm completely over it." Florence waved her hand and shrugged.

"Who?" I asked gently, anxious to hear the details.

"I was twelve the first time and had just started losing my vision. As if that wasn't enough of a burden to me then, my stepfather held me down on my bed and raped me. That's why they took me away from my mama."

"You told on him?" I gasped.

"Of course I did. Who wouldn't? The same day, right after he did it, I told Mama. When she didn't do anything about it, I went to the police."

"Weren't you scared he'd do something to you? I know he must have threatened you? They usually do—I mean, I bet they do."

"Oh he threatened me all right. He said if I told on him he would kill me. Ha! As soon as I got my panties back on I went to my mama's work and told her. She said we couldn't afford to lose 'a good man like Harry.' We needed his paycheck, and she needed his attention. She just told me to make out like it never happened. He cried like a baby when she casually mentioned it to him. That son of a bitch stood there in front of me and claimed because he'd been drunk, he didn't remember doing it and asked me to prove it was him that took my cherry and not some boy I was probably sneaking around with. At that time, I had about as much interest in a boy as I had in a goat."

"Damn," I muttered.

"Mama told me if I brought it up again, I'd get a whupping. That same night is when I went to the police. A doctor examined me, a shrink talked to me, and the next thing I knew I was on my way to my first foster home."

"And what was that like?"

Florence let out a great sigh before responding.

"Like jumping from a frying pan into a fire," she groaned. "A month after I got to that first foster home, my foster father raped me. There were three other girls in the house that he had already raped. None of them had told at that point, but I sure did. They took all of us girls out of that home and that son of a bitch went to jail. My next foster father was all over me a week after I moved in with him and his wife. I was all right for the next few years. My last foster father was an honorable, decent man. Then he and his wife died in a car crash. Now I'm with Scary Mary." Florence let out her breath so hard I saw her chest rise higher than it should have.

"Do you . . . hate men now?"

"No. Why should I? I can't give up on the rest of the male population because of something three of them did to me. I loved my last foster father, and I'll never forget him."

"But aren't you mad like I . . . um . . . raped girls must be?"

Florence shook her head and smiled. "Life is too short. I don't want to waste any more energy thinking about what happened to me. It's a done deal. I've moved on with my life, and I want to enjoy what's left of it. I'm looking forward to attending trade school this fall."

"Trade school? For what? I mean, being legally blind and all—what can you study?"

"Anything you or Rhoda can study," she told me, leaning back, an amused look on her face. "The only difference is, I'll have to work harder and I will have to learn by using alternative methods, like braille."

I was disappointed when Florence excused herself. Scary Mary called to remind her she had to give Mott a bath.

After she left, Mr. Boatwright knocked on my door so hard it shook. It was locked, and I didn't let him in. When Muh'Dear got home, I went back to the living room. Rhoda and Pee Wee had just arrived. Rhoda was scowling and already sprawled across the couch next to Muh'Dear. Mr. Boatwright was on the love seat, also scowling and fanning his face with the *TV Guide*. Pee Wee was sitting on the arm of the couch next to Rhoda.

"Where've you been?" Rhoda pouted. "I thought you were comin' to my house to help me give Granny Goose a bath."

"Oh, she been upstairs shot up in her room borin' that poor little old blind gal to death." Mr. Boatwright laughed. "That blind gal left here runnin' like somebody ablaze." Mr. Boatwright hadn't said it, but I knew he didn't like Florence. He rolled his eyes at her when she came to the house, and he trashed her just as often as he did everybody else.

"I've told you that blind girl is too much trouble to be gettin' too friendly with," Rhoda reminded me, waving her finger in my face.

"Oh you just jealous, Rhoda," Pee Wee teased. "Sister Goode, can I have a bottle of pop?"

Muh'Dear waved Pee Wee to the kitchen with a tired hand. I never would have thought Rhoda was jealous of my relationship with Florence if he hadn't brought it up. But it made sense. Even though she had Otis, I realized now that Rhoda needed me but probably not as much as I needed her. Other than her boyfriend and Pee Wee, the other kids still didn't want to be her friend, which is the way it still was in my case. In almost every class I watched invitations to all the junior parties get passed around, and there was never one with my name on it. I often wondered what I would have done if I had not met Rhoda. I didn't waste too much time thinking about that because I would never know.

I wanted to remind Rhoda that she was with her boyfriend all evening when I tried to reach her, but I didn't. I didn't want to make her any angrier with me than she already was. I liked Florence but not enough to risk losing Rhoda. I decided then not to encourage Florence to incorporate herself into my life any more than she already was.

"Do you still want me to come over and help you give Granny Goose a bath, Rhoda?" I asked, looking at Muh'Dear for approval.

"Uncle Johnny's already done it, but you can come help me do it tomorrow," she answered, rising. I walked Rhoda to the porch.

She looked over my shoulder back into the house first to make sure nobody could hear us talking. "Now don't you let that blind girl ruin everythin' between us. Do you hear me?" Rhoda shook her finger in my face. She was grinning, but I knew she was serious. This was the first time since we had begun our friendship that another girl had entered our lives the way Florence had.

"Nobody can come between us, Rhoda. Not Florence or anybody else," I mumbled with my head bowed submissively.

"You see that she doesn't. I'd hate to think that I've wasted all these years developing our friendship for nothin'," Rhoda told me. I was confused, wondering what she considered Otis O'Toole's position in our lives.

CHAPTER 26

I avoided Florence the next few days. But a week later, I got desperate for company after Rhoda stood me up to go to a drive-in movie with her boyfriend. I let Florence come over mainly because I didn't feel like being alone in the house with Mr. Boatwright. We sat next to one another on the couch. Mr. Boatwright sat across from us on the love seat rolling his eyes and tapping his foot impatiently. He often used a rolled newspaper to swat flies. There were no flies in the room, but he had a newspaper in his hand that he kept hitting at the air with anyway.

"I love Liz's old movies," Florence said thoughtfully, looking alongside the wall.

"How did you know it was an Elizabeth Taylor movie? Can you see enough to tell?"

"I can barely see the screen, but I know Liz's voice. I know most of my favorite actors' voices," Florence said proudly, her chest stuck out.

"I like her movies too. She's so beautiful," I said longingly. "No wonder so many men fall in love with her."

"That hot-box, Jezebel movie star goin' to get her comeuppance sooner or later. She ain't got no shame atall the way she be runnin' amok all over Hollywood with other women's husbands. It's a wonder Debbie Reynolds didn't whup the shit out of her for stealin' Eddie Fisher," Mr. Boatwright said seriously. Nobody escaped his wrath, not even Liz Taylor

I ignored his comments.

"I can think of a lot of people who are going to get their comeuppance," Florence said seriously. "The men who raped me are going to burn in hell."

Mr. Boatwright gasped, and his eyes got big as he looked over at Florence. He opened his mouth, but nothing came out. Then he shook his head and started fanning his newspaper furiously.

"I hope they burn in hell, too," I mumbled. I cleared my throat and glanced at Mr. Boatwright. He was still staring at Florence. Suddenly he stopped fanning and snapped his head around to glare at me.

"Annette, can you go upstairs and roll my bed kivvers down," he bleated, rubbing his fake leg.

"Now?" I asked.

"Now," he wheezed, rising.

After I helped Mr. Boatwright to bed and returned to the living room, Florence told me, "There's something about that old man I don't like . . . something I can sense."

"What do you mean?" I asked nervously. I moved a few inches away from her on the couch.

"I don't trust him," was all she said.

I let it go at that. If I had been smarter, I would have confided in her then about me and Mr. Boatwright, but I didn't. I was just that afraid. I still couldn't believe that I had told Rhoda.

"He is ugly and mean," I muttered, looking from the newspaper he had left on the floor to the steps leading upstairs.

"Oh, I can't see him well enough to say if he is ugly or not. But he feels ugly."

"What about me?" I asked.

"What about you?"

Most of the time when Florence looked at me, her head was turned to the side so that I'd be staring at her ear.

"Can you see me well enough to know whether or not I'm ugly?"

"Oh yes. You're a beautiful person, Annette. I can see it, and I can feel it."

As soon as Florence stopped talking I heard a car outside. I ran to the window just in time to see Rhoda kissing her boyfriend good night.

"Um . . . you should go now. I have to tell Rhoda something real important," I blurted. I felt bad about giving Florence the brush-off again. Especially after what she had just said about me.

"OK," Florence said, rising. She felt around the couch for her scarf.

It had fallen to the floor, so I ran to get it for her. "Tell Rhoda I said 'hi,' " Florence said on her way out. After she was gone, I immediately called up Rhoda.

"Mr. Boatwright's condom broke this evening," I blurted as soon as she answered the phone. "All he said was 'Oops.' "

"Don't worry. Otis breaks condoms all the time." Rhoda sighed. "Tonight he broke two!"

My mouth dropped open.

"You really have done *it?*"

"Well, yes. Actually, Otis does most of the work. I just lie there and holler," Rhoda confided. The conversation was making me sick.

"What if you get pregnant?" I growled, clenching my fist.

"I don't care if I get pregnant by the man I'm goin' to marry," Rhoda replied casually.

"Well . . . it's late," I mumbled, thoroughly disappointed with Rhoda. I never thought I'd live to see the day she would let sex come between us. "I guess I'll go on to bed."

"Me too. I still have to give myself a facial and wash Granny Goose's hair. Oh! Sorry I canceled goin' to the bookstore with you. I didn't know my man was comin' over tonight."

"Oh that's all right. Florence came over." There was an awkward moment of silence.

"Florence? Florence who?"

"Scary Mary's foster daughter, Rhoda," I said in a harsh tone that I wanted her to know about.

"That blind girl? Are you still draggin' around with her? Didn't I tell you not to get too involved with a handicapped person? She's goin' to drag you down to her level of depression, talkin' about her blindness and all."

"Rhoda, Florence is not depressed. She's the most upbeat person I ever met. She only talks about her blindness when I bring it up. It doesn't even bother her."

"She's the reason I had to wrestle Granny Goose into the bathtub by myself the other night. Because you were with her you forgot to come to my house in time." Rhoda let out a deep breath. Uncle Johnny, Rhoda, and her daddy took turns giving Granny Goose baths. Like a fool I had volunteered to help Rhoda when it was her turn, and now she depended on me. It was a chore I regretted volunteering for immediately. The first time I'd helped her bathe Granny Goose, the old woman bit my hand. "What do you have in common with her?"

"Rhoda, you stood me up tonight to be with Otis. The night I was supposed to help you bathe your grandmother, you took off with him, too."

"I asked what you had in common with that blind girl?" she snarled.

"That blind girl, she's . . . she's been molested, too, by three different men."

Rhoda's silence made me nervous.

"Rhoda, you still there?"

"Yeah." Her voice suddenly seemed weak and small. "I'm sorry to hear that." She sighed deeply. "That's all the more reason why you should avoid her. Don't tell me she won't depress you when you guys start comparin' rape stories."

Rhoda was right. When Florence told me her abuse history, it depressed me.

"Did you tell her about Buttwright?" she asked in a whisper.

"Not yet." I sighed, rubbing the side of my thigh.

"I don't think you should, Annette."

Three weeks later I left home with my coat on over my pajamas. I had been waiting for Rhoda to return from a date with that Otis boy.

"You look like you seen de devil," Otis told me as I rushed into the Nelsons' living room, where he was all hugged up with Rhoda.

"I feel like it, too," I mumbled, pulling Rhoda into the kitchen where Mr. Nelson was fixing tea for Mrs. Nelson, who was in bed with God knows what.

"Girls, would you like some tea?" he asked.

I shook my head. As Rhoda grabbed a cup, I stood back and looked her over. She was flushed, her eyes were dilated, and her makeup was smudged. Her hair was matted, and there were still leaves in the back of her head, telling me that she and Otis had been rolling around on the ground.

"I gotta talk to you," I whispered across the table. Mr. Nelson was standing over the stove with his back to us.

"Annette, how is your mama and Brother Boatwright?" Mr. Nelson asked. He sat down at the table and looked me up and down and frowned when he saw the bottom of my pajamas hanging below my coat.

"Um . . . they both are OK," I said impatiently. "Excuse me, Mr. Nelson, but I need to talk to Rhoda in private—"

He shrugged and started to rise.

"Oh no, don't leave." I held up my hand and smiled. "We can go to Rhoda's room. Rhoda looked over my shoulder at Otis and Jock entering the kitchen. Jock avoided me whenever I visited the Nelsons' house since the night I had pulled a knife on him in our kitchen. When he did look at me, it was just to roll his eyes.

"Got anyting strong to drink?" Otis asked. He didn't see Mr. Nelson right away. Rhoda tried to warn Otis by clearing her throat. Jock covered his mouth to keep from laughing.

"There's plenty of strong cider in the refrigerator," Mr. Nelson said. "Jock"—he turned to Jock and waved his hand—"pour this boy some cider."

Rhoda pulled me out into the hallway leading upstairs. "What's up?"

"I'll tell you in your room." I started to cry before we even got to the top of the stairs. Rhoda gasped, grabbed my arm, and pulled me to her room, where she quickly slammed the door shut. Before we could sit down on the bed someone came banging on the door, then snatched it open before Rhoda could answer. It was the grandmother. She had wandered from her room next door, naked.

"Oh God!" Rhoda grabbed the old woman's wrist and pulled her into the room. She led the woman to her bed, where she snatched off her white chenille spread and wrapped it around Granny Goose.

"I can't find my clothes, Rhoda," the old woman whined. She ignored me completely. "I think the dawgs got 'em."

Rhoda gave me an apologetic look and took her grandmother back to her room. I could hear the old woman fussing and cussing. Rhoda was yelling back at her. After about five minutes, I could hear the whole family in Granny Goose's room trying to subdue her. Rhoda was gone for ten minutes.

"Bitch!" Rhoda spat when she returned and joined me on the bed, rubbing her hand. "She bit me."

"Poor old Granny Goose," I mumbled, shaking my head. Right after I said that I heard Jock cry out in pain and cuss at the old woman.

Rhoda started to laugh at Jock's outburst but stopped after a few seconds. She turned to me. "Why were you cryin' a while ago?" She put her arm around me and smiled.

"I'm going to have a baby . . . by . . . by Mr. Boatwright," I wailed.

CHAPTER 27

The day after I revealed my pregnancy to Rhoda, I hid in the Nelsons' kitchen closet and cracked the door open just enough to peep out while Rhoda talked to Jock.

"Say there, Jock-o. Um . . . what if somebody was to get pregnant and didn't want to have the baby. You must know um . . . certain types of individuals that could do somethin' about it. For a generous fee, of course. There must be some greedy doctor or nurse around town that could use a few extra dollars on the side," Rhoda began.

"That foreigner get you pregnant?" Jock roared. "I'll kill him! I warned that motherfucker!" Jock slammed his fist against the wall so hard utensils crashed to the floor.

"Shhhhh! Shush up." Rhoda grabbed his arm and pulled him closer to the closet. I closed the door about an inch and tried not to breathe so loud. "It's not me. It's this girl from school."

"Oh." Jock seemed relieved. He snatched open the refrigerator and started pulling out things to make a sandwich. "What girl?"

"Some new girl from Cincinnati. A white girl." Rhoda followed him to the counter and was all but standing on his foot.

"Tell her to drink some vinegar down straight. Like she would a shot of gin."

"Vinegar? How much vinegar?"

"A big glassful." Jock slapped some meat on a piece of bread and started to eat. I could see that he was anxious to get away from Rhoda, but she blocked his way.

"Is that all it takes? A big glass of plain vinegar?"

"Yep."

"How do you know it'll work?"

"Um . . . I know this girl at school that tried it when she got herself pregnant. Some dizzy white girl. She said one of my boys did it." Jock paused and took a big bite from his sandwich.

"Uh-huh. But what if that doesn't work? Don't you know some shady doctor or somethin'? You've been hangin' out at that pool room since you were a kid. Or, what about this coat-hanger trick I heard about?"

"Uh . . . that coat-hanger thing is dangerous. Uh . . . this white girl I told you about, I um heard that she tried that first and got real infected. Now there is this other girl . . . I um heard about down at the pool room. She drunk a whole bottle of hundred-proof whiskey while she was settin' in a bathtub full of hot water."

"And that worked?"

"Yep. That's what I heard," Jock said quickly. "She was white, too."

"Can I talk to this white girl? I won't tell her you told me."

"What's wrong with you, girl?" Jock dismissed Rhoda with a wave of his hand. Rhoda was determined. She refused to let him out of the kitchen. She grabbed the tail of his shirt to stop him. "This girl, she's real shy and maybe even a little retarded or somethin' like that," he said. "Tell your friend to try that whiskey in the bathtub trick. It's quick, and she won't get no infections or nothin'."

"So that's what the white girl did, huh?"

"You deaf? What did I just tell you, girl? My man that got her pregnant, he seen her do it. Now get out my way." Jock pushed Rhoda to one side and strutted out of the kitchen chomping on his sandwich. As soon as I heard him stomping his way upstairs, I flew out of the closet.

"Get ready for one hell of a hangover, girl," Rhoda told me.

The next day was Sunday. I was already awake when Muh'Dear eased open my door and walked softly over to my bed and sat down at the foot. I lifted myself up on my elbow. "What time is it?" I asked, yawning.

"We got a little problem with Brother Boatwright, and we need your help," Muh'Dear told me.

I pressed my lips together and looked in her face. Mr. Boatwright was the last person on earth I wanted to help resolve a problem.

"What is it?" I asked, my heart racing. With him it could have been just about anything.

"As you know, he attended Judge Lawson's poker party last night. Well, you know how he is. He won a little money and got mighty reckless with his drinkin'. Somewhere along the line he misplaced his . . . dentures."

I sat up straight, my eyes still on Muh'Dear's face. "He lost his teeth?"

"Uh-huh. Now I know they somewhere in the judge's house. I'm gwine to wake up the judge, have him come pick us up, and we'll go hunt 'em," Muh'Dear said.

"Why can't Mr. Boatwright go? They're his teeth," I wailed.

"Well, he's too embarrassed to go out the house without his . . . dentures. He don't want to miss church service today on account of this little problem here."

"I don't believe that man!" I said through clenched teeth. If Mr. Boatwright wasn't screwing me one way, he was screwing me another.

"Now you know Brother Boatwright would do it for you. He'd do anythin' you or me asked him to do, and you know he would. If you'd rather, you can get Rhoda to drive you to the judge's house and she can he'p you hunt them dentures. You got to hurry so you can get back in time to eat and get ready for church."

Just then the phone rang. I left Muh'Dear sitting on my bed while I ran to the hallway to answer it. It was Rhoda. "It's not time yet," I whispered. "They haven't left for church yet." We had planned to perform my "abortion" as soon as Muh'Dear and Mr. Boatwright left for church.

"I know. I know our plan, but that's not what I'm callin' about." Rhoda was serious.

"What is it?"

"Buttwright and Uncle Johnny used the Ford to go to the judge's poker party last night. Daddy said nobody who has been drinkin' can drive the car. Uncle Johnny and Buttwright got too drunk to drive, so Uncle Johnny called me at 3 A.M. this mornin' and told me to put Jock in a cab so he could drive them home. Well, Jock all but bit my head off when I woke him up. I called a cab and went myself. This mornin' when I went to move the car out of the driveway, these nasty false teeth rolled off the backseat!"

"Mr. Boatwright's teeth," I breathed.

"I figured that. They're not mine, and Uncle Johnny's are real."

"Muh'Dear thought he had lost them at the judge's house. She was just telling me I had to go look for them."

"I'll bring them with me when I come over to do . . . you know," Rhoda whispered.

"No! You have to bring them now. He can't go to church without them," I told her. I got off the phone and went back to my bed, where Muh'Dear was still sitting, looking toward the door with an anxious look.

"Who was that on the phone?"

"Rhoda. Mr. Boatwright left his dentures in their car last night. She's bringing them right over."

Rhoda delivered Mr. Boatwright's false teeth in a plastic sandwich bag. As soon as she dropped them off, she left. "Tell Rhoda I owe her a quarter next time I see her. She left here so fast I ain't had time to pay her," Mr. Boatwright said. He was in the kitchen rinsing his dentures in the sink, his body wrapped up in so many bedclothes he looked like he was in a cocoon.

Muh'Dear had started preparing breakfast. "Thank God we didn't have to wake up the judge." She sighed, dropping a huge chunk of margarine into the simmering pan of grits. "Annette, you got plenty of time, but you should start figurin' out what you gwine to wear to church." Muh'Dear sat down at the table with a groan.

"Um . . . I'm not going to church today," I said, backing out of the door. Muh'Dear and Mr. Boatwright gasped and looked at me at the same time.

"You gwine to miss Brother Boatwright's solo? Reverend Upshaw consented to let him do one on this Sabbath on account of one of the Hawkins boys gettin' baptized today," Muh'Dear told me.

"Um . . . I got the cramps," I lied, placing both hands on my stomach. I stopped in the doorway, looking from him to her.

"Cramps is the Lord's way of chastisin' you for somethin' you shouldn't have done . . ." Muh'Dear accused, popping a piece of crispy bacon into her mouth and looking at me out of the corner of her eye.

"You ain't never had no cramps before in your life," Mr. Boatwright said in a loud voice, clamping his teeth together to secure them in place. His dreaded fleecy white suit looked stiff enough to stand up by itself. He had on a black tie that looked more like a baby's bib.

"Well, I got them now," I yelled back.

"Girl, don't you raise your voice to a grown man again on the

Sabbath as long as you live on this planet," Muh'Dear warned. She looked good in the blue-silk dress Judge Lawson had given to her for Mother's Day. "Brother Boatwright the only daddy you'll ever know. Ain't that right, Brother Boatwright?"

"That's right," he said, grabbing a piece of bacon with one hand, hitching up his pants with the other. His suit coat was open revealing a pair of plaid suspenders from Judge Lawson for Father's Day.

"I'm going back to bed," I said impatiently.

"And you better still be in that bed when we get back from church services," Muh'Dear warned. Mr. Boatwright didn't add anything, but he gave me a threatening look. Right after they left, the phone rang.

"Hello, Annette. It's Florence. I was wondering if—"

"I'm busy, Florence!" I snapped. Just looking at the bacon left on the platter made me nauseous.

"I just heard from your mama that you not feeling well. Is there anything I can do? Is there anything I can bring you?" she asked. I had expected Rhoda on the other end of the line.

"No! Uh . . . I'm fine," I answered impatiently.

"I've got plenty of Midol and ginger tea. That always helps me when I have cramps," Florence said sweetly. It amazed me how my rudeness never seemed to bother her.

"No, that's all right. Rhoda's bringing me some," I told her firmly.

"I see. Well, when you see Rhoda tell her I said 'hi.' " Even though Florence knew Rhoda didn't like her that much, she always told me to tell her hi. I hung up abruptly, sorry that I was being unnecessarily rude to Florence.

Rhoda was hiding between some boxes on our back porch waiting for Muh'Dear and Mr. Boatwright to leave. As soon as I let her in the kitchen she ran to the refrigerator without a word. She had to open one of Mr. Boatwright's root beer pops and take a long swallow first.

"What took you so long to answer the door?" she barked, shaking the pop bottle at me threateningly.

"I was on the phone with Florence—"

"Again?"

"Well yes—"

"I squatted down on your dusty, musty back porch on my knees in a pair of twelve-dollar tights waitin' for you and you were on the phone talkin' gibberish with that Florence?"

"Stop it, Rhoda! She hasn't done a thing wrong for you and Mr. Boatwright to talk about her so bad every time I mention her name.

You're beginning to sound just like him! She's always telling me to say 'hi' to you."

"I'm sorry," Rhoda said contritely, bowing her head. "I truly am sorry. I don't mean to trash the girl. She is a sweet person. I don't even know her that well." Rhoda blinked hard and took another swallow. "God knows I don't want to sound like Buttwright."

"Florence can't help being blind. No more than I can help . . . being the way I am," I mumbled.

"When you see Florence . . . tell her I said 'hi.' " Rhoda smiled. She put her arm around my shoulder, and we walked upstairs to the bathroom next door to Mr. Boatwright's room.

"How long will it take?" I asked between gulps of whiskey as I sat naked in a bathtub full of hot water. Rhoda had brought over a whole bottle of her daddy's best whiskey. As expensive as it was, it tasted awful. It took me the longest time to get it all down without throwing up, and I got drunk as hell. I could not imagine what the cheap whiskey tasted like.

"I don't know," she answered. She was standing over the bathtub, shifting her weight from one foot to the other. She didn't even remove her coat. I figured she wanted to be prepared to run if something real bad happened.

I don't remember much. All I remember is Rhoda helping me from the bathtub and into my gown and saying, "Gee, I hope you don't get alcohol poisonin'."

I woke up in the city hospital two days later. Muh'Dear, looking like she had not slept in a week, and a blank-faced Mr. Boatwright were standing over me.

"Who done it?" Muh'Dear whispered, glancing over her shoulder toward the door and wringing her hands.

I closed my eyes and groaned. Now was as good a time as any to pretend I was too sick to speak.

Muh'Dear asked me over and over, "Who done it? Who done it?"

Mr. Boatwright was frighteningly silent. He looked away every time I looked in his direction. He looked at the floor most of the time, twitching and shifting his weight from one foot to the other. He cleared his throat and in a low, meek voice, told me, "Annette, I'm prayin' for you. With God's help, we gwine to pull through this mess unscathed."

I was not in that much pain but I was weak and disoriented. All I could do was remain still and listen. Finally, I spoke, "I don't know who got me pregnant," I said. What else could I say?

Muh'Dear gasped and threw up her arms. She fell back against Mr. Boatwright, almost knocking him down. "Lord, it's worse than we thought, Brother Boatwright. The girl done fooled around with so many, she don't know which one got her in this mess." Muh'Dear had to fan her face and catch her breath before continuing. Her face had become a mask of rage. "Bride of Satan!" she shrieked.

"Sister Goode, we just gwine to keep a tighter hold on the girl, that's all. She runnin' with the wrong kind of kids," Mr. Boatwright added, humbly.

I saw red. I pulled myself up and glared at him. There was a burning sensation in my nostrils, and my flesh crawled. "I don't care what you do to me, I am not going to stop being friends with Rhoda," I said evenly. Muh'Dear was stunned. She threw her arms around Mr. Boatwright.

"The girl ain't responsible. It's all that medication," he mouthed, fumbling with his shirt pocket, reaching for his handkerchief so he could fan his sweaty face.

"Rhoda is my best friend. The only friend I've got." I started to cry. The hospital room was cold and impersonal, but I was glad I was in it and not in my room, where I'd probably conceived Mr. Boatwright's baby.

Muh'Dear let out a weak sigh and looked at her watch. "I got to get my tail to work. Judge Lawson will think I skipped out on him." She paused and looked at me, shaking her head so hard her scarf came untied. "Where did I go wrong? I'll tend to you when you come home," she said, as they prepared to leave.

I was propped up in bed watching TV when Rhoda arrived and handed me a get well card later that day.

"Thanks," I mumbled.

"It's from Florence."

"Oh." I set the card on the nightstand without reading it. I wanted to read it, but not in front of Rhoda.

"She gave it to Pee Wee to give to me," she informed me. "Are you OK?" She smiled.

"I guess so." I nodded. "That baby is gone. I'm sorry I had to do that to a poor little innocent baby." I truly was sorry. Even though Mr. Boatwright was the father, I was still the child's mother.

"Girl, it wasn't a real baby. We're talkin' about a *Rosemary's Baby.* How could you love a child like that?" Rhoda said, waving her arms.

"You're probably right," I said thoughtfully, nodding. "I probably would have ended up mistreating it or deserting it or something."

"Well, it's over with now." Rhoda moved closer to the bed. She leaned over and felt my forehead. It was colder in the room than it was before, but I felt hot. There was even sweat on my face. "How'd your mama take it?"

I just frowned and shrugged. "Well, you know my mama. She's just a country woman. She's not sophisticated like your mama. There's no telling how she's going to behave toward me after I get home. They'll probably make me memorize the whole Bible."

"I bet they do," Rhoda agreed.

"And you should have heard that son of a bitch Mr. Boatwright."

Rhoda started talking with her eyes looking at the floor. "We have got to do somethin' about him. Real soon."

CHAPTER 28

"Everybody thinks you have the flu," Rhoda informed me the next evening. I was home alone, so I could talk freely on the kitchen wall phone. I had been released from the hospital just two hours earlier. "Even Florence."

"You've been talking to her," I asked, unable to hide the fact that I was surprised.

"Well no, not really. She's been talkin' to Pee Wee. He's been talkin' to me."

"What about that loudmouth Pee Wee? You don't think he'll go around and blab, do you?"

"He doesn't know anythin' about you bein' pregnant. Not unless he's pyschic. I sure as hell didn't tell him," Rhoda answered. My fear was that Mr. Boatwright would get drunk and start running his big mouth at Scary Mary's one day or while he was with Uncle Johnny, and of course Uncle Johnny would blab. Rhoda and I were quiet for a moment. "What are you thinkin'?" she finally asked.

"Rhoda, I've made up my mind. I'm going to leave home as soon as we graduate. Erie, Pennsylvania, sounds like a nice place to start a new life. I am not going to wait around like I figured I would."

"That's not such a bad idea. What about your mama? She won't like that at all."

"She can't stop me."

"Well what about lover-boy? Do you honestly think Buttwright's goin' to just sit back and let you walk out of his life? Especially to

move to Pennsylvania, a state so close to—as Buttwright would probably call it—a Babylon like New York."

"Well, once I turn eighteen, nobody will be able to tell me what to
do. Not Muh'Dear. Not Mr. Boatwright. I think I've suffered enough.
I don't see things changing if I stay here. The only thing I can change
is myself, and I can't do that here as long as that motherfucker is
alive." I paused, expecting Rhoda to agree with my last comment. She
remained quiet too long for me. "Hello."

"I'm still here." She sighed. "I tell you what. As soon as you feel well
enough to talk to that old asshole, casually mention to him about
movin' to Pennsylvania right after we finish school and tell me how he
reacts."

"Well, he knows I want to get a real good office job. He must know
that office jobs don't pay much here in Richland, Ohio. All his talk
about doing something to make me sorry if I leave home I think is
just a bluff. I am just going to have to call him on it."

"Yeah. He probably is just bluffin'. As stupid as he is, even he must
be smart enough to know he couldn't get away with doin' somethin'
crazy like shootin' you or your mama. Unless . . ."

"Unless he does something and makes it look like an accident?
What if he tells people he was cleaning his gun and it went off? They
would all probably believe anything he'd tell them," I wailed. "And I
bet Judge Lawson would make sure he didn't go to jail."

"All I can say is, if we don't do somethin' drastic and soon, you'll
end up in that nuthouse where Scary Mary sent Mott that time."

"You said we. Are you really going to help me come up with a plan
to get Mr. Boatwright off my back?" I couldn't imagine what we could
do to scare him enough so that he would let me alone.

"Yeah."

"You sounded so funny just now, Rhoda. Is there something in your
throat?"

"No. I'm just cookin' up a plan."

"OK. Well let me know what it is real soon. I'll mention to him tomorrow right after Muh'Dear leaves for work about me moving to
Erie, and I'll make it clear he can't stop me. OK?"

"OK."

"I'll let him know that I am leaving after graduation, and only
death is going to stop me. Hear?"

"Yeah."

The next morning, I was all set to tell Mr. Boatwright about my vague plans. Muh'Dear had just left for work. Before I could even get dressed and out of my room, that son of a bitch yelled from across the hall for me to join him in his room. Before I reached his room, all ready to cuss him out and fight him if I had to, the phone rang. I ignored the one in the hallway upstairs and ran to the kitchen. I heard Mr. Boatwright laugh then cuss all the way from his room upstairs when he heard me run to answer the phone before coming to his room.

"Why are you crying, Rhoda?" I asked.

"My . . . my grandma died last night," she sobbed with a trembling voice.

"Oh I'm so sorry to hear that. Did she die in her sleep?"

"Um . . . no." Rhoda paused and cleared her throat.

"Did she fall and hit her head on something?" I asked.

"Um . . . yeah. Uncle Johnny forgot to lock her bedroom door, and she got up durin' the middle of the night, wandered out to the hallway, stumbled and fell down the stairs and . . . broke her neck," Rhoda choked.

"Oh no," I breathed. I wasn't too crazy about the mean old white woman, but I was sorry to hear about her accident. "Do you want me to come over?" I moved to the refrigerator and removed a carton of buttermilk and filled a large glass. Then I snatched a piece of toast from a plate Mr. Boatwright had set on top of the stove.

"Uh-huh. Our white folks from Alabama are on their way up here. They are all in an uproar. They'll be in an even bigger one when they find out Granny Goose left all her insurance money to Daddy."

"I bet they will," I said boldly. "Well, like I said, I can help get the house ready. It's already spic-and-span, and I know there is not much to be done, but whatever you need me to do, I'll be there, Rhoda."

"Um . . . I think we're goin' away for a couple of weeks right after the funeral."

"Who? You and Otis?"

"Oh no, he's not goin'. Just me and my family. As soon as we get Granny Goose laid to rest and everythin' settled, we're goin' to the Bahamas. We've been plannin' to do this for a long time. But . . . Granny Goose was such a burden, we couldn't take her with us and we couldn't leave her here by herself or with a nurse. None of her white family wanted to be bothered with her, not even for two weeks."

"Well, she was kind of mean, but you can't blame her. Old age does strange things to people's minds," I said, trying to imagine Mr. Boatwright twenty years down the road.

"I know," Rhoda admitted.

"I'll call my mama at her work and tell her what happened, and I'll let her know I'm going to be at your house." I hung up. I turned around and there was Mr. Boatwright standing in the doorway with his hands on his hips, his housecoat open so I could see his naked body.

"You ain't gwine no place, least of all to that cesspool across the street," he informed me.

"But Granny Goose died—"

"Goosey Loosey! Your mama told me not to let you out my sight 'til you heal. Here you is volunteerin' to go over there and clean somebody else's house and your own house lookin' like a crime scene. Wash them dishes, mop this kitchen floor, and save me some of that buttermilk yonder. When you done, meet me in my room."

"Rhoda's grandmother just died," I gasped, talking, drinking my buttermilk, and chewing the bacon at the same time. "How in the world can you be thinking about sex at a time like this? I just had a miscarriage, too! I'm going to Rhoda's house."

"You ain't gwine over there right after gettin' over that baby mess with that boy Jock settin' around waitin' on you like a spider—"

"Jock already left for the army, and what's he got to do with me getting pregnant? You're the only one who has ever done anything to me!"

"In a pig's eye! What little bit of sap I got left wouldn't get a flea pregnant, let alone a big old strappin' ox like you. I know how Jock is, and I know how weak you is!"

I was horrified by his comments.

"I've never looked at a boy that way. I've never been with a boy in my life, and you know it," I snapped. I couldn't believe that he believed I would let some boy do to me what he did. Before I knew it, Mr. Boatwright hobbled up to me and slapped me so hard across the face, I almost dropped my glass of buttermilk. I set the glass on the counter and we wrestled for a few moments. I kicked his peg leg, and he lost his balance. He had me by my arm, so when he fell, I fell to the floor with him. Somehow, I got up and left him lying on his back, wheezing and shaking like he was having a spasm. I leaned over and helped him up and led him to a chair at the kitchen table. He was sweating so profusely my clothes got wet.

"You all right, Mr. Boatwright?" I asked, genuinely concerned. I'd have a lot of explaining to do if he'd been hurt enough to require medical attention. "Can I get you something?"

"Get a switch!" he rasped, fanning his face, blinking fast and hard.

I said as calmly as I could, "I am not getting any switch for you to whup me with. Not this time or any other time ever again." As common as whuppings were among Black kids, they usually ceased around eleven or twelve years of age. At my age, I felt it was time for Muh'Dear and Mr. Boatwright to stop sending me to a tree to get a switch. I sucked in my breath and continued, still using as calm a voice as I could. "Mr. Boatwright, this thing we do, it's got to end right here and now. I am not a scared little girl anymore. I'm almost a grown woman. How long do you think I am going to let you continue abusing me?" I was standing over him with my arms folded.

"I ain't never abused nobody before in my life!" he mumbled. He attempted to stand but was so shaky he had to sit back down.

"You're taking advantage of me—"

"I ain't never took advantage of nobody! What you think you got I want to be takin' advantage of?" he managed, fanning his face with a wet dishrag he had grabbed from the table.

"Raping me. Or whatever you want to call it!"

"It ain't rape what we do!" He was so mad, spit was flying out of his mouth, but I stood my ground.

"Then what is it?"

"It's . . . it's just, you know . . . one of them things." He stumbled over his words.

I stared at him in stunned disbelief. "Is that what you think you're doing to me? I'm just 'one of them things'? Why me, when you can do it to any of the women at Scary Mary's house! *One of them things* is what they do for a living!" I said, stabbing him in his chest with my angry finger.

"Cause I really do like you, girl," Mr. Boatwright whimpered, not looking at me. He sounded almost like a little boy with his hand caught in a cookie jar.

"You can like me all you want, but you can't touch me again," I said firmly.

"You picked a fine time to start actin' crazy," he gasped. "I shoulda never took up with you in the first place," he told me, shaking his head sadly.

"Look, let's forget everything you've done to me. I won't tell anybody anything. After I move to Pennsylvania—" I stopped when he interrupted me with a loud cackling laugh.

"You ain't gwine noplace," he assured me. "Pennsylvania'll be your final restin' place . . ." He paused and pointed his finger at me, and said, "BANG BANG!"

CHAPTER 29

Iwas lying across my bed on my back counting the cracks in the ceiling with my door locked when Muh'Dear got in from work around 8 P.M. The depression caused just by being in my bedroom, the room Mr. Boatwright had tainted with his presence and actions, gripped me like a vise. There were times I fantasized about blowing up the house just to destroy my bedroom, the room that had become a Chamber of Horrors for me.

"Why you all locked up in here, girl?" she wanted to know. "Brother Boatwright say he real worried about you. He say you been delirious."

"I didn't want to be disturbed," I replied, letting her into my room. She had pounded on the door so hard the room shook.

"By who? What if you had fainted and hit your head on the end of the chifforobe or somethin'? How would Brother Boatwright have got to you in time to prevent brain damage with the door locked up?"

"It won't happen again." I sat up in my squeaky bed with Muh'Dear, still wearing her coat, standing over me waving both arms.

"It sure enough won't. First thing in the mornin' I'm goin to have Brother Boatwright remove the lock from your door completely."

"Yes, Ma'am."

"Now. How you feelin'?" She placed her hand on my forehead and frowned.

"I'm fine," I told her.

"I need to know who done it so I can talk to his mama." She removed her coat and draped it over her arm.

"I told you I didn't know."

"How many was there?" she asked impatiently.

"I don't remember," I said mechanically, refusing to let her see my eyes.

"Do you mean to tell me you done fornicated so much you done lost count?"

"No. I think there were three. Or five." I sounded like I was reading cue cards.

"Next thing you'll be tellin' me is you was drunk or on dope."

"I was drunk." My face was on fire. I had let my own mother down in the worst way. I could easily clear myself, but telling her the truth was unthinkable.

"Uh-huh. Brother Boatwright told me he smelled alcohol all over you when he found you all passed out. I got a call in to the Reverend Upshaw and Reverend Snipes." Muh'Dear sighed. She sounded so tired and looked worse than she sounded. She had become an old woman right before my eyes.

"For what?"

"For you, girl. If I don't get you some spiritual counselin' now, you liable to wind up pregnant again . . . or on that slab in Brother Nelson's house." She sighed and turned to leave.

"I guess you heard about Granny Goose dying last night?" I asked. She stopped in her tracks and whirled back around to face me, walking fast back toward my bed.

"Granny Goose died? Last night? Well how is Rhoda and her family holdin' up?" Muh'Dear wanted to know.

I shrugged. "I didn't go to the house yet."

"What? How long have you knowed?"

"Rhoda called me right after you left for work this mornin'."

"Well if you was well enough to make that big mess in the kitchen I seen, you was well enough to go pay your respects."

"She too busy layin' in there gobblin' up chicken wings and readin' pornographic books," Mr. Boatwright yelled from the hallway. I'd been reading *Peyton Place* for most of the day. Within seconds he was in my room. His housecoat belt was tied securely and he was buttoned all the way up to his neck.

"Shame on you, Annette. I thought Rhoda was your best friend," Muh'Dear gasped, waving a finger in my face. "I bet she right frantic. I can't believe you ain't over there to hug her."

"Can I go over there now?" I asked, looking at Mr. Boatwright from the corner of my eye. He glared at me.

"I guess so. I'll be over there as soon as I bake 'em a cake," Muh'Dear said.

"There's a whole chicken in the freezer we can donate, too," Mr. Boatwright offered. "My bum leg wasn't in such misery, I'd go with y'all. I leave the house bad as I'm feelin' now, I might be the next one to wind up on that slab in the undertaker's house."

CHAPTER 30

The Nelsons' flag had been lowered to half-mast, and there were several unfamiliar cars parked up and down the street. Mr. Boatwright ended up going with us, walking with me holding him by one arm and Muh'Dear holding him by the other. I don't think he was as helpless as he claimed to be, he just liked being in control when he was upset. I was convinced that he had changed his mind about going to the Nelsons' house with us was because Muh'Dear kept going on and on about how handsome Jock must look in his army uniform.

"What took you so long?" Rhoda asked, looking directly at me when she opened the door.

"I was resting," I said.

"From that flu bug that put her in the hospital," Muh'Dear said quickly.

As soon as we got inside, Mr. Boatwright started jerking his head from left to right, looking all over the place with an expression on his face that reminded me of a deer caught in the headlights of a speeding car. I heard him mumble to Muh'Dear, "Is that rum I smell?"

The mob in the living room was mostly people from various churches and the neighborhood. Florence greeted me but kept her distance because she knew Rhoda didn't like seeing her with me. Three white boys under ten were running throughout the house punching one another.

Rhoda introduced us to her white relatives from Alabama, then led me to a corner, where she whispered something about each one.

I squinted to look across the room resting my eyes on Uncle Johnny standing in the middle of the floor with a drink in his hand and swaying like he was about to fall. "Uncle Johnny's drunk. Your daddy's not afraid he'll get loose in here?" I asked.

"Oh, Uncle Johnny can handle his liquor," Rhoda said seriously. Out of the corner of my eye I saw Mr. Boatwright hugging Rhoda's mother and crying like a baby about how Granny Goose was going to be missed. Every time the door opened his head snapped around toward it. I knew he was looking for Jock to appear.

Rhoda's mother, wearing a long black hostess gown, left and came back into the room a few minutes later carrying a tray of mixed drinks. "Brother Boatwright, would you care to have a drink?" she asked. He was on the couch with Muh'Dear and a woman I didn't know.

"Don't mind if I do," he said quickly, reaching for the tallest glass.

"Don't worry, this batch is nonalcoholic," Mrs. Nelson assured him. As usual, her hair and makeup were flawless.

"Oh," he grunted, looking at the glass like he wanted to shatter it. As soon as Mrs. Nelson walked away, he walked over to Uncle Johnny and they left the room. Minutes later they returned and Mr. Boatwright had a different drink in his hand that I was sure was alcoholic.

"See that thin, blond-haired woman standin' there talkin' to Scary Mary? That's my aunt Lola," Rhoda said. I looked at the woman, who appeared to be in her fifties. She was pale and tired-looking, but she had nice features. Her face was small and oval-shaped like Rhoda's. She had big pretty green eyes that had more than enough eye shadow and mascara on them.

Rhoda sniffed. "She might move in with us after she sells her house down South. Lookit the lipstick on her teeth. She used to be a whore in a house in Montgomery. I bet Scary Mary is tryin' to recruit her old as she is. These wild kids runnin' all over the place are her grandkids. Their mother, my cousin Donna, she ran off with some woman's husband. Aunt Lola got out of the whorin' business and settled down."

To be in mourning, Rhoda was talking a lot. Talking was one thing most of the grieving people I'd been around didn't want to do.

"Did she get religion like Uncle Johnny did a long time ago, too?" I asked.

"No. She robbed one of her tricks and he stuck a pair of red-hot marcel curlers up her coochie. She never sits down for too long. She can't! She sleeps on her stomach like a seal. Scary Mary wouldn't get much mileage out of her."

"Ouch!" I felt a tingling in my crotch.

"Ouch is right." Rhoda shuddered.

Like a lot of the people in the house, including me, Rhoda kept a plate of rich food in her hand and was eating like this was the Last Supper. This was out of character for her. In all the years we'd been friends, Rhoda had always been weight-conscious. I was convinced that Rhoda was behaving the way she was to avoid an issue deeper than her grandmother's death, but I couldn't imagine what. She was so frisky and animated I was convinced that she had been secretly sipping one of those mixed drinks. She was acting like it, and smelling like it.

I got up to go to the kitchen where all the food had been laid out to refill my plate and had to pass the parlor to get there. Mr. Nelson, Mr. Antonosanti, and Judge Lawson, each of them dressed in a dark suit and tie, were in the parlor, with Mr. Boatwright standing among them. He looked so out of place in his dingy dungarees, plaid suspenders, and house shoes with the backs removed. I stopped outside the door, curious to hear what an oaf like Mr. Boatwright would have to say to men like these particular three. They were discussing women and minorities in politics.

"I envision a woman in the White House before a Black man or an Oriental," Mr. Antonosanti said.

"Oh I hope not!" Mr. Boatwright laughed. "A woman president would mean the end of the world, sure enough. She'll get in one of them PMS moods and every month she'll push a button and nuke a foreign country."

I gasped and shook my head. I leaned over just enough to see the expressions on the men's faces over Mr. Boatwright's stupid ramblings. They looked at him like he was less than nothing. I truly felt sorry for him. He wanted to so badly, but he could never fit in with men like Rhoda's daddy, Judge Lawson, and Mr. Antonosanti.

I got more food and returned to the living room, to discover more people had arrived. I was kind of glad when Mr. Boatwright, still babbling nonsense, returned to the living room a few moments later, tagging behind Mr. Antonosanti.

Rhoda's father's older sister Moline was a washed-out, sixtysomething white woman with blond hair and the same green eyes as

Rhoda. She looked a lot like Lola but was heavier by at least fifty pounds.

Moline cornered me and started talking in a low nasal voice. The alcohol on her breath was so strong, I had to cough. "I'm just so impressed with the way my little colored brother turned out. This fine home, this fine family, all these fine friends and neighbors, the world sure enough has changed. Laurette wouldn't come. She's my oldest girl. My old shoe wouldn't come neither. I been tryin' to divorce him for twenty-five years, but he keeps hidin' the divorce papers. Him and Laurette ain't as modern as the rest of us. You'll never catch them two in no Black household. They're superstitious. They look down on y'all, Jews, Spanish-speakin' peoples, Asians, and," she paused, then whispered, "fags and bull dykes." She paused again to suck in her breath, then she looked me up and down and shook her head. "Johnny tells me you and Rhoda is best friends. Is that a fact?"

"Yes, Ma'am."

"Rhoda's such a smart girl, she could do anything she want. Thing is, she ain't interested in college or climbin' no corporate ladder. She just wants to be a happy married woman, like me. What about you?"

"I'd like to have a secretarial career," I said proudly, but in a low voice. I noticed Mr. Boatwright tilt his head in my direction.

"Secretaries make good money, especially in the bigger cities," Moline commented.

"I know," I agreed.

"See Lola there—she used to be in the sportin' business. She was a damn good whore. Ain't nothin' wrong with a good pesterin', especially when you gettin' paid for it. I know this old gal from Mississippi that done it 'til she was sixty-four. *Sixty-four*, girl. Lola could have done it longer than that. However, a freak accident forced her into early retirement. She works in the gum factory now."

Rhoda finally rescued me and pulled me to the other side of the room. She introduced me to her seventeen-year-old twin cousins Alice Mae and Mae Alice. They were blond, blue-eyed versions of Rhoda.

"Rhoda tells us you plannin' to jump on a corporate ladder," Mae Alice said.

"As soon as I get out of school," I replied. Rhoda kicked my foot. Mr. Boatwright was just a few feet away.

"Where do you plan to work, Annette?" Rhoda said real loud. "Cleveland? Uh . . . Cincinnati?"

"Nowhere in Ohio. I've been thinking about Pennsylvania," I said in a low, shaky voice.

Right after I said that, Jock strode in flanked by two of his former gang brothers. He slapped five with Uncle Johnny and embraced the Moline woman and the twins. Lola threw her arms around him and pulled him down next to her on the couch. I guess he was still mad because he rolled his eyes at me.

"Honey chile, you look better than a government check! Don't he, Annette?" Lola squealed, kissing Jock all over his face.

"Yes, Ma'am," I managed. I looked at Mr. Boatwright, and, just as I thought, he was staring at me with a cold, angry look on his face.

In less than a minute, Muh'Dear was in front of me whispering. "We better leave. Brother Boatwright's bum leg is givin' him trouble, and that use-to-be-whore Lola keeps flirtin' with him, makin' him nervous. He want us to he'p him home," Muh'Dear informed me.

"Can I stay a little longer?" I begged. "Can Pee Wee or Uncle Johnny help you get him home?" Everybody had surrounded Jock as he started talking about signing up to go to Vietnam to "kick butt" legally.

"Now you know thin as Pee Wee is, he ain't able to hold up Brother Boatwright as good as a big old strong thing like you. And Johnny way too drunk to do hisself any good, let alone a stout man in Brother Boatwright's condition," Muh'Dear said firmly.

"Please let me stay," I begged.

"You ain't well yourself," Muh'Dear told me, still whispering. "Besides, you don't want these nosy folks to start askin' you questions. You might let somethin' slip about gettin' yourself in that mess, and I wouldn't be able to show my face in church or on the street. Let's go. You look like you need a dose of castor oil anyway."

I moved as slow as I could across the room to where Mr. Boatwright was sitting in a La-Z-Boy and helped Muh'Dear pull him up. Lola attempted to help, but Mr. Boatwright pushed her away. The way he was struggling, his leg couldn't have been bothering him that much.

"Brother Boatwright's feisty. Just like my third husband was," Scary Mary slurred from a stool at the bar in the living room. She had not stopped drinking since she walked in the door.

As soon as we got off the Nelsons' front porch, Mr. Boatwright started saying mean things.

"They sho nuff was stingy with them drinks!" he roared. "I been waitin' all my life for a margarita, and when I finally get me a few, they give me ones so weak you could wean a baby on 'em. How they expect a grievin' man to relax at a time like this with a sip that won't fill a thimble? Y'all seen how Lola kept flirtin' with me." He said it like he was bragging, grinning and sticking his chest out. "I bet—Ouch! Don't pinch my shoulder, Annette," he yelled. Just as we made it across the street, Rhoda, Pee Wee, and the twins came running after us.

"Annette, you left your scarf," Rhoda informed me. I met her in the middle of the street, and she whispered, "Come back if you can tonight."

CHAPTER 31

Muh'Dear was the type to fall asleep as soon as her head hit a pillow, so I didn't have to worry about her. But I had to wait a half hour for Mr. Boatwright to start snoring.

By the time I returned to the Nelsons' house, most of the visitors were gone. I was glad Florence was one of them. I did want to talk to her, but not in front of Rhoda. The only people left were family members. The kids were still chasing one another around the house knocking over plants and chairs, and nobody was saying a word. But the look on Rhoda's mom's face told me she was not too happy.

"The young'ns are all in Rhoda's dollhouse in the backyard," Mr. Nelson told me as soon as I got inside.

"I'll get 'em," Uncle Johnny said, jumping up from his chair.

He was gone for ten minutes before anybody said anything.

"I hope Johnny didn't go out that back door and fall and break his neck like Mother did," Moline whined. "Gal—go see," she ordered me.

I was glad to leave. But as soon as I stood, Lola did, too.

"I want to see this dollhouse everybody done run off to," she said, stretching her arms. "I done heard so much about it."

We heard the giggling before we even got to the dollhouse. Lola and I peered in the window and witnessed all the teenagers, except Rhoda, passing marijuana cigarettes around. Uncle Johnny snatched one from Pee Wee and stuck it in his mouth. That's when Lola pushed the door open with her foot.

"Johnny Goose! Gimme that thang here!" She rushed up to him and grabbed the cigarette and put it in her mouth and started puffing furiously. I liked Lola. She was friendly and fun to be around, just like Uncle Johnny.

After we all got back to the Nelsons' living room, Lola wanted me and Rhoda to accompany her to the shopping center, where she and Rhoda could pick up some feminine products to accommodate all the extra females staying at their house. We left in Mr. Nelson's big fancy Cadillac, a white one he had just purchased a month earlier. Rhoda had not had an accident in weeks with the Ford, but Lola's driving scared me even more. She was driving through town like a bat out of hell, speeding, weaving in and out of traffic and running red lights.

"Aunt Lola, pull over and let me drive," Rhoda begged, a desperate look on her face.

"Uh-uh. We're almost there. I got to go drive lickety-split, so we'll get there before the drugstore closes," Lola told her, humped over the steering wheel. It was a miracle we didn't have a serious accident.

After we left Hardy's Drugstore loaded down with tampons, Kotex, butt spray, and douche powder, Lola ducked into a nearby bar to have another drink. Rhoda and I went back to the drugstore, where she looked for new makeup and I leafed through movie magazines. The car was parked outside in front of the bar. Rhoda did not purchase any new makeup but she bought me a bag of candy. By the time we left the drugstore again, headed for the car, Lola was good and drunk. She was staggering toward us wearing one shoe, carrying the other in her hand, and with her eyes rolled back in her head.

"Look at Miss Lola!" I hollered. At first, I thought somebody had beaten her. There was blood on her lip and the front of her blouse. We ran to her just in time to keep her from falling to the ground.

"I'm . . . DRUNK!" Lola slurred. "Rhoda, girl, you got to drive the car. Your daddy'll bust my brains out all over the place if I was to wreck that big old mobile of his'n."

"What? My daddy won't let me drive it. He thinks I'll ram into another light pole or a tree," Rhoda wailed, struggling with her aunt to keep her from falling to the ground. "Annette, you have to do it."

"You know I don't know how to drive, girl." I laughed, looking at her incredulously. The thought of driving that big, intimidating car was beyond my imagination.

"But you got to drive. I'll tell you everythin' you need to do," Rhoda insisted.

We managed to slide Lola into the car on the front seat. Rhoda got in on the passenger's side and I got in under the wheel so nervous I started sweating immediately.

I followed Rhoda's instructions and the car took off like a bullet, jerking and weaving. Before I knew what was happening, a police car came roaring out of nowhere with the siren blaring. Lola had passed out, and the whole bottom part of her face was covered in blood. The police car blocked the Cadillac, then the cop jumped out and ran up to the driver's window with his hand on his gun.

"WHERE Y'ALL GOIN' WITH THAT WHITE WOMAN?" he hollered, jerking his head side to side, looking in the car. "Oh it's you?" he sighed, wiping his forehead with the back of his hand. Suddenly, he smiled at Rhoda.

"Hello, Officer Proctor," Rhoda said calmly, smiling. The girl never ceased to amaze me. This man no doubt thought we were trying to kidnap a white woman, and here she was all but kissing him. "As you can see, my aunt Lola here had a little too much to drink and we were just tryin' to get her home safe and sound." Rhoda was not even nervous. The policeman leaned back and inspected her face, running his tongue across his bottom lip and squinting. All during this time, Rhoda was smiling like she had a secret. The policeman returned his weapon to its place, then wiped sweat from his big red face again this time with the sleeve of his shirt.

"Uh-huh. Well, y'all get her on home before she get herself ruined. The streets are full of rapists these days." The policeman moved back from the car, tipped his hat, and told Rhoda, "Tell your daddy I said 'hi,' you hear?"

I was stunned.

"You're so lucky, Rhoda," I said, starting the car again.

"Why? Because of who my daddy is?"

"Uh-uh," I said, shaking my head. "Because you're so pretty. Pretty girls can do just about anything they want in this world and get away with it. I bet if you killed somebody, you would get away with it, huh?"

"Well," Rhoda began slowly, "I might, and I might not."

CHAPTER 32

Muh'Dear was not able to get off work to attend Granny Goose's funeral on Saturday, but she did send three sweet potato pies and some poke salad. Mr. Boatwright, who had developed a severe cold, went with me.

After the burial, most of the mourners returned to the Nelsons' house. Jock took all his young white relatives to meet some of his friends, and Rhoda and I hid ourselves in her room. Mr. Boatwright was busy going on and on to anybody who would listen about how much he was going to miss Granny Goose to pay much attention to me.

"I'll be glad when they all leave," Rhoda said as soon as she shut her bedroom door.

"I know exactly what you mean." I sat on the bed and watched Rhoda stand in front of her door mirror and fuss with her hair and smooth the sides of her black jumper.

"Now we can take our trip to the Bahamas for Christmas." She yawned.

"Do you have to go with them?" I groaned. I wet the tip of my finger with spit and tried to remove a grease stain from the navy blue woolen suit I'd worn to Granny Goose's funeral.

"What's wrong with you, girl? The trip was my idea! Mine and Aunt Lola's. Of course I have to go with them. I'm the one who has been on Daddy about it so much. Why?" she said, still standing in front of her mirror.

"The next few weeks are really going to be rough for me," I moaned.

Rhoda sat next to me with a concerned look on her face.

"We did get rid of that baby you were carryin'."

"I know, and I'm glad. But Muh'Dear is really going to be on my case now until I can get out of that house. Mr. Boatwright's been staring at me a lot more than usual."

"Has he . . ." She nodded, and her eyes became slits.

I shook my head. "Not yet. He hasn't done *it* to me again, yet."

"You want to come to the Bahamas with us? I'll pay your way out of my savin's. It'll be my Christmas present to you this year."

"Don't make me laugh. I'm not even allowed to go to the movies anymore for a while; do you think I'd be allowed to go on a trip halfway around the world."

"I can call you every day from down there," Rhoda offered with a sigh of defeat.

"That's not the same as you being here. For two weeks we'll be on Christmas break. For me that means two weeks alone in the house with Mr. Boatwright."

Rhoda gave me a thoughtful look. "You know how much I care about what you've been goin' through, Annette. But I can only do so much. You can't tell on him because he has a gun and said he'd kill you. What else is there to do?"

I shrugged, then stood up. "Nothing I guess."

"Did you tell him you're movin' to Erie after graduation?"

I nodded. "He's not going to let me go. I'll have to wait a while. I'll let him and my mama think I've changed my mind, then I'll sneak away."

I returned to school the Monday after the funeral. I didn't even have to make up any lies to tell the kids as to where I'd been; nobody asked.

Rhoda and Otis cut classes right after lunch and sneaked off to a motel, so I had to suffer through the afternoon without seeing her between classes. I was thoroughly disappointed that sex had become such an important thing with her.

When I arrived home Mr. Boatwright was not in. I didn't know how much time I had to myself, but I planned to enjoy it. Before I could decide what to do, the phone rang.

"When you get out the hospital?" Pee Wee asked.

"Four days ago."

"If I had known that I could have been over there sittin' with you, updatin' you," he whined.

"Don't worry about it."

"Let me put my clothes on. I'm comin' over there right now. I ain't got nothin' else to do tonight. I been spendin' all my spare time with Florence, and she ain't no fun at all. Walkin' into walls and shit."

"Pee Wee, you don't have to come over—"

"OK. Well, I guess I'll sit here and eat this *large* pizza all by myself or share it with Florence after all . . ."

I sighed, and told him, "I'll turn the porch light on."

Pee Wee was only with me for ten minutes before Caleb called and made him come home to sweep hair off the barbershop floor. I went to my room, read a few chapters of *In Cold Blood,* then dozed off.

I heard muffled voices downstairs and got up to put my ear to the heat register on my bedroom floor. My room was directly over the living room so it was easy to hear people talking downstairs. Rhoda was in the house. Muh'Dear was going on and on about it being too late for her to be out visiting. She gave in when Rhoda promised to come back the next day to deliver some of the food left over from Granny Goose's funeral.

"Some of that cracklin' bread, if you don't mind," Mama purred.

"Oh yes, Ma'am. I'll bring you a whole pan of it," Rhoda said in a sweet, humble voice she used only with grown folks. Her voice was getting louder as she got closer to my room. "Matter of fact, I'll bring two pans." I pictured her walking backwards, all the while grinning and nodding for my mother's benefit.

"Don't you stay up there too long, Rhoda. Annette's got to get up early for school tomorrow, and I know you do, too," Muh'Dear yelled.

Rhoda rushed in and sat down next to me on my lumpy bed and crossed her legs. I frowned when I noticed a gold chain from Otis wrapped around her ankle.

"My God, girl. You look like hell," she told me, shaking her head.

"Thanks, Rhoda. I needed that."

"You're welcome." She yawned and stretched her arms high above her head, shaking her hands. Then she started blowing on her nails.

We stared long and hard at one another.

"Well," I said, shrugging. Her unexpected but welcome visit was a surprise.

"Well, is he pesterin' you again yet?" Rhoda whispered, motioning with her head toward Mr. Boatwright's room.

I sighed heavily and looked at the floor. "No. Not yet. But I know he will. I saw his eyeball peeping through my keyhole last night," I mumbled.

Rhoda gave me an incredulous look and gasped. In a hard, controlled, throaty voice she said, *"That-piece-of-shit."* She made a fist and brought her hand down so hard on my precarious nightstand, my goosenecked lamp fell off.

I called Rhoda's house the following Saturday morning around ten, and her mother told me she was at Miss Rachel's beauty parlor at the shopping center. I was alone in the house with Mr. Boatwright. Right after I hung up the phone, he joined me in the kitchen.

"You want some more breakfast, possum?" he asked, gently placing his hand on my shoulder. Even though he abused me, I appreciated the pleasant times we shared.

"Yeah," I replied, looking up from my seat at the kitchen table.

"I'll call you when it's ready," he said. He smiled at me, and, to my own amazement, I smiled back.

"I'll make us some popcorn, and I'll have 'em deliver us a pizza," he said. The pleading look on his face and the promise of popcorn and pizza weakened me.

"OK," I muttered. My addiction to food was probably my biggest downfall. Later, I sat on the living-room couch next to Mr. Boatwright watching *American Bandstand.*

"Watchin' white folks dance is as much fun as watchin' wrestlin'. Just look at 'em! Hoppin' around like they tryin' to stomp out a fire, ain't they?" He chuckled, his mouth full of pizza.

"Uh-huh." I laughed, nodding. The coffee table in front of us was covered with snacks. The whole time, he had one arm around my shoulder like any other lover. A few times he leaned over and kissed me on my cheek. Surprisingly, he didn't want sex that night.

I didn't see or talk to Rhoda for two days. She didn't call me or come to my house and was "out" each time I attempted to reach her.

"I needed some time alone," she explained a day later at school. She approached me in the hallway right after fourth period class, and we walked to the cafeteria together for lunch. "I really want to help you out of this mess with Buttwright. I've just been tryin' to come up with a plan."

"It better be soon." I sniffed. "Can you come over this evening?

He's got that look in his eyes . . . like he wants to do something," I added. I was afraid to tell her how nice he had been acting the last few days. I thought that if I did, she would back out of helping me. I knew Mr. Boatwright well enough to know that his niceness was temporary.

"I can come and stop him tonight. But I can't come every night," Rhoda replied.

"Well, anytime you can stop him would make it a little easier on me. I can't . . . I'm *not* going to let him touch me again," I said. My words surprised Rhoda more than they surprised me.

"How are you goin' to stop him?" she asked.

"He won't bother me as long as somebody else is in the house. You can come over when Muh'Dear's not home, and I can get Pee Wee or Florence to come when you can't come."

"OK." Rhoda sighed tiredly. I sensed that she was finally getting impatient and maybe even frustrated with my situation. Something had to happen soon.

My scheme only lasted six days. Two days in a row, Rhoda stayed with me from the time school was out until Muh'Dear came home. Pee Wee and Florence came over the next four days. Mr. Boatwright must have figured out what I was up to because he went to Muh'Dear with his complaints.

"Them kids been spendin' more time over here than they should. All that activity is makin' Brother Boatwright nervous," Muh'Dear told me.

"They come over to keep me company," I defended.

"You tell 'em the longest they can stay durin' a school night is one hour," Muh'Dear said firmly, shaking her finger in my face. "Now go to bed."

I didn't sleep much that night. I couldn't wait for morning so I could talk to Rhoda.

"I knew that son of a bitch would sabotage everything first chance he got!" Rhoda seethed when I reported Mr. Boatwright's tattling the next morning on the way to school.

"We'll come up with another plan," I said quickly. I had to run to keep up with Rhoda she was stomping down Reed Street so hard and fast.

"You're damn right we will!" she assured me through clenched teeth. "Because I'm beginnin' to take this shit personal!"

CHAPTER 33

Two days after Rhoda and her family left for the Bahamas, I got lonely enough to visit Florence around seven that evening. I was horrified when Scary Mary told me Florence was out on a date.

"A *date?*" I shrieked. "With who?" I was on Scary Mary's back porch. She was in the doorway removing rollers from her new wig, the reddest one yet.

"She at the church Christmas dance with her boyfriend, girl!" Scary Mary shouted, stomping her foot. She placed her hand on her hip and gave me an exasperated look.

"I . . . I didn't know Florence had a boyfriend," I pouted. "When did this happen?" It was cold, and there was at least a foot of snow on the ground. But I'd left my house in such a hurry I had not bothered to put on my coat or boots.

"Oh, she been keepin' company with one of them Hawkins boys a couple of weeks now."

"Oh. Well, tell her I came by." I rushed home to my room and threw myself across the bed and howled. I figured I'd have a good cry, then invite Pee Wee over.

"Florence's got a boyfriend," I told him as soon as he arrived.

"I know; Jimmy Hawkins. The one with the harelip," Pee Wee announced, falling down sideways onto our living-room couch.

I was amazed. Florence had never given me the impression she cared about boys enough to date one.

"But she's blind!" I wailed.

"So?" Pee Wee said with a smirk. "Blind girls need love, too. So do harelipped boys." He gave me a thoughtful look and continued. "Wonder how they kiss? She almost ain't got no sight, how she goin' to find the lips he almost ain't got?"

Pee Wee babbled on for a while, but I wasn't really listening. I just felt so lonely with Rhoda gone and now . . . Florence.

When Rhoda returned from the Bahamas, everything returned to normal for the next few months.

On a rainy Saturday morning I called her up and asked if she could give me a ride to the slaughterhouse. Fooling around waiting for buses in the rain was something I avoided every chance I got.

"Sure. Meet me in front of my house in ten," she said cheerfully. I was surprised when she led me to her mother's car in the driveway.

"Where's the Ford?" I asked, climbing into the passenger side. Rhoda didn't like her mother's two-month-old Volkswagen because of the way it looked. I didn't like it because it wasn't designed to accommodate obese people comfortably. But I didn't complain. It was still better than the bus, and it was free.

"Um . . . it's in the body shop *again*. I ran into a mailbox to avoid a cat the other night," she explained, not looking at me. She adjusted her seat, then checked her makeup in the rearview mirror. "Damn pimple. My period must be comin' early again." Finally, she turned on the ignition. The radio came on, and she started humming along with Diana Ross as we pulled off.

"You're in a real good mood," I commented. I waved to Mr. Nelson, who had come out on the front porch.

"Why shouldn't I be? Hey—how is the beast?"

"Mr. Boatwright's about the same." I sighed. "I bit his hand the other day when he tried to . . . you know."

"That miserable old fucker. I'm goin' to go home with you when we leave the slaughterhouse. My presence pisses the hell out of him." Rhoda started laughing so hard she almost drove up on the sidewalk. "Oops!"

Even though she now had a boyfriend, too, Florence still called me up and came over on a regular basis. I saw her when I felt like it, but Rhoda still came first in my life. A few times I even stood Florence up to be with Rhoda, but every time I did, I felt bad about it later. What puzzled me was, as inconsiderate as I was with her, Florence was always nice to me. I knew the Hawkins boy from church, but I never followed him and Florence on their dates the way I did Rhoda and Otis.

On April Fool's Day, a week after my last trip to the slaughterhouse with Rhoda, Pee Wee snatched open our front door without knocking and ran into the kitchen where Mr. Boatwright and I were eating collard greens, pig ears, and corn bread, and announced, "The radio news just said that po'lice that killed Rhoda's brother is dead."

Just fifteen minutes earlier, Mr. Boatwright had wrestled me all over the living-room couch, laughing and cussing at the same time because even with what he described as a "hat-rack hard-on," he couldn't perform. The bottle of Thunderbird I had encouraged him to drink had slowed him down.

"What happened to him, Pee Wee?" I was no longer hungry. Just thinking about how Rhoda and Uncle Johnny had reacted that day in the Buttercup restaurant when they saw this same man made me lose my appetite. I stopped eating, but Mr. Boatwright kept gnawing on pig tails like a hound.

"They found him layin' along the side of the road off the Sampson River Bridge in the bushes. He been layin' there a few days, and they say it look like a hit-and-run. I bet he was drunk and staggered out in front of a Mack truck. Them greens and them hush puppies sure lookin' good, y'all." Pee Wee grabbed an empty plate off the counter and snatched the lid off the pot containing the greens. "Brother Nelson already got the body," he added, almost out of breath. Instead of sitting at the table, he chose to stand in front of the stove and eat with his fingers.

Mr. Boatwright grunted and nodded. "That's what he get for shootin' Brother Nelson's boy like he done." Mr. Boatwright paused long enough to grab a bottle of beer on the table next to his plate and take a long swallow. When he set the bottle back on the table and let out a great belch, I frowned. "I knowed sooner or later it was gwine to catch up with him. Everybody oughta know by now God don't like ugly, and you gwine to reap what you sow," he announced, his head tilted to one side.

Pee Wee confirmed this information with a nod.

"So true," I said levelly, looking Mr. Boatwright straight in the eye.

He turned away immediately. "Pee Wee, go turn on the TV. The wrestlin' matches is about to come on," Mr. Boatwright said.

I was curious as to how Rhoda had reacted to the policeman's death. I didn't even finish dinner. As soon as Mr. Boatwright and Pee

Wee left the kitchen, I jumped up from the table and ran to the phone on the wall and dialed her number.

"Uh . . . Hi, Uncle Johnny. Um . . . Pee Wee just told us about that policeman that killed your nephew getting himself killed," I said.

"And may he burn in hell!" Uncle Johnny roared.

"Can I speak to Rhoda?" Rhoda must have been sitting on Uncle Johnny's lap because she got on the phone seconds later. "I just heard about that policeman that killed your brother getting killed," I told her.

"Uh . . . huh." She sounded disembodied. I could still hear her uncle in the background cussing the dead policeman's soul.

"Are you OK? You don't sound like yourself," I said. Even though I was using the phone in the kitchen, I had to talk loud. Pee Wee and Mr. Boatwright were in the living room in front of the TV yelling at the screen.

"I'm fine. I'm just havin' a hard time absorbin' this news," Rhoda admitted.

"I bet." I let out a long, deep breath. "I'm surprised your daddy is handling the body. The man did kill his firstborn son."

"My folks forgave him. They're even goin' to attend his funeral." Rhoda sighed with disgust. "But Muh'Dear's all depressed about it anyway. She's been in the bed on the verge of a nervous breakdown ever since we heard the news. I'm goin' to help Daddy prepare the body because Uncle Johnny won't help. He's still mad about what happened to David."

"Rhoda, have you forgiven that man for killing your brother?" I asked.

"I'll *never* forgive him," Rhoda hissed. I heard some muffled sounds on her end, and then she excused herself.

Martin Luther King was assassinated the same day as the policeman's funeral. I was glad they closed the schools for two days to honor Dr. King because his death hit me hard, and I got so depressed I couldn't eat. I removed a picture of him from my bedroom wall because I cried every time I looked at it. I had no way of knowing, but I was sure that wherever my daddy was, he was crushed. Long before I'd heard of Dr. King, I'd heard Daddy make public speeches similar to the ones Dr. King had made.

"Nobody is going to fight as hard for civil rights as Dr. King did," I said to Mr. Boatwright on the couch, watching the TV's coverage of the shooting.

"As if colored folks ain't got enough of a cross to bear," Mr. Boatwright commented. He sat next to me fanning his face with a rolled-up copy of *Ebony* magazine. He had actually shed a few tears. "We fightin' in them wars white folks started and still can't eat and live where we want to. It wasn't enough devilment for them white devils to blow up that church in Birmin'ham and kill them four little colored gals and lynchin', beatin', shootin' at, and turnin' dogs loose on them civil rights workers down South every time I look up. If killin' Dr. King don't satisfy 'em, nothin' will." He wiped tears from his face with his sleeve.

His words moved me. He was showing a side I'd never seen before.

"You want me to get you a beer?" I asked, patting his shoulder.

He shook his head and rose. I watched until he disappeared up the stairs.

A minor riot broke out in Richland. By the end of the third day after the assassination, two local Blacks had been killed and several people had been arrested for looting.

Muh'Dear still had to work, but because of the racial uproar we were experiencing, the cabs stopped running at 6 P.M., and the bus she normally took stopped running for a few days. When Judge Lawson was unable to provide transportation, she had to walk to work, leaving the house two hours earlier to get across town and getting home two hours later.

It was a few minutes before 10 P.M. four days after the assassination, when Mr. Boatwright hopped into my room and jumped into my bed and started kissing up and down my neck. I had been in bed since 7 P.M., but I was still wide-awake. I was still mildly depressed. In addition to the assassination, there was so much on my mind: the policeman's mysterious death, the riot, my uncertain future, and my relationship with Mr. Boatwright. "How could you be thinking about sex at a time like this?" I asked. I sat up and pushed him away as hard as I could. When I was younger, smaller, and weaker he used to get real mad and threaten to whup me when I resisted him. Now when I did it, he still got mad, but his age and failing health had slowed him down tremendously. I was as strong as he was now, maybe even stronger. I had pushed him so hard he almost rolled off the bed.

"You tryin' to kill me or what?" he asked, more startled than angry. He sighed with exasperation and slid off the bed, struggling with the bedpost to balance himself.

"Get the hell out of here!" I ordered. "Martin Luther King might not have meant much to you, but I cared about him." I stood up next to my bed and put my hand on my hip, facing him angrily.

There was a look of absolute astonishment on his face. "Don't flatter yourself. Who said I came in here to pester *you*? I'm upset over Dr. King, too. The whole mess got me feelin' real befuddled. Just like that Kennedy thing. All I wanted was a hug from somebody," he whined.

I looked at his pleading eyes for a long time. In my confusion, I leaned over, wrapped my arm around his shoulder, and patted him. Then, surprisingly, he let out a long sigh and left my room without another word. I don't know how much time passed, but I had dozed off when he returned to my room later and shook me awake. "Slide over," he ordered. "I done run out of condoms," he complained, crawling back into my bed.

"I . . . can't wait until I get out of school so I can leave this town and get away from you," I said tiredly, trying to push him away with no success.

He didn't say anything else until after he had entered me. "You ain't . . . gwine no place," he muttered between thrusts. "You do, you . . . you might . . . not never see your mama alive again . . ."

I was wide-awake by the time he had satisfied himself. He left the room without a word. I put on my housecoat and went downstairs to the kitchen and dialed Rhoda's number. Uncle Johnny answered and yelled at me for calling so late, but he called Rhoda to the phone.

"He did it to me without a condom," I blurted. "I hope I don't get pregnant again." I stared at the phone for a moment, waiting for Rhoda to respond. "Did you hear me, Rhoda?"

"I heard you." She sounded as detached as she did when I talked to her about the policeman's death.

"He didn't say it, but I think he was tellin' me he would do somethin' to my mama if I leave home. Besides, after we do graduate, I'd still have to get a job and save enough money to leave home with. That could take another year." I moaned. "I can't go through this for another year. I've had it, Rhoda. I was still a little depressed, and he knew it but still did me," I wailed.

Rhoda cussed under her breath, and I could hear her shifting around in her seat

"Where is he now?" she asked.

"He went to bed. Can you come over? I wouldn't be surprised if he came at me again before Muh'Dear comes home. I can't ever let him touch me again."

"He won't," Rhoda said calmly.

I heard her let out a long sigh first. Then she told me, "As soon as I finish helpin' my daddy and Uncle Johnny clean up the mortuary, I'll come over. But first I have to help Aunt Lola unpack. She got back up here a little while ago. She's here to stay."

"For good?"

"Uh-huh. In David's room. She's much happier here, and Uncle Carmine said he'll give her a job waitressing at Antonosanti's." Rhoda paused and sucked in her breath. "I'll be over as soon as I can."

She arrived ten minutes after we got off the phone. "Buttwright still got that gun?" she asked, before I even closed the door behind her.

"As far as I know," I told her. "Why?"

"Nothin'," she replied, making herself comfortable on the living-room couch. She placed her coat on the back of the couch. I sat down next to her, and we didn't talk for five minutes. Instead, we watched more TV news reports about Martin Luther King's assassination.

"So you think he's still got that gun, huh?" She spoke without taking her eyes off the screen.

"Yeah. But he hasn't had to show it to me in a long time."

I could feel Rhoda staring at the side of my face. "I see," she said hoarsely.

We didn't talk for another five minutes, and I'm glad we didn't. A portion of Dr. King's "I Have a Dream" speech was being broadcast. I didn't have to look, but I knew she was crying just like I was. Out of the corner of my eye, I saw her wipe away her tears.

"Muh'Dear loves to hear that speech," I managed, blinking hard.

"I think everybody does," she said stiffly.

We got quiet for another few minutes. Suddenly, Rhoda tapped my shoulder, and I turned to face her. "Y'all got any herbal tea?" she asked.

"Yeah," I told her. I stood up and started backing out of the room.

"I'll get it. You want a cup?" she said, rising. She grabbed my arm and pulled me back to the couch and pushed me down.

"Yeah," I muttered, puzzled. Rhoda liked to be waited on when she visited. It was not like her to volunteer to do anything when there were no grown folks around for her to impress. I didn't question her. I was still overwhelmed by what we had just seen and heard on TV. Besides, I was tired and didn't want to be running back and forth to get refreshments anyway. I was glad she offered to do it.

She was gone for at least twenty minutes. The kitchen was less than a minute away, and the tea was the instant kind. All she had to do was heat some water. Just as I was about to go look for her, she returned, holding a tray with two cups of steaming tea.

"What took you so long? I was getting scared," I told her, as she handed me my cup.

Instead of answering, she just shrugged and set the tray on the coffee table, then started drinking her tea. We sat in silence for another two minutes watching TV.

"He's dead. He is actually and truly dead," Rhoda whispered. I assumed she was talking about Martin Luther King. I patted her knee and watched as she stared at her cup. *Dead, dead, dead,* she chanted.

"I was planning to do my next book report on him," I said in a hollow voice.

"I meant Buttwright," she informed me. "He's gone."

"What did you say?" I turned my head so fast and hard my neck cracked, and I spilled tea on my lap. I had never seen such coldness in Rhoda's eyes before, not even the day she saw the former policeman in the restaurant. I got a chill, and a sharp pain shot through my chest like a blazing sword. "What do you mean by that? Mr. Boatwright's gone where?"

Rhoda nodded slowly. With a strange look on her face, she told me, "He's . . . he's finally gone to hell."

I set my cup on the coffee table, wiped my lips with the back of my hand, and stood up. "What are you talking about?" I hollered. I could still hear the television, but I couldn't understand anything being said. It was like my mind had drifted into another dimension. "Mr. Boatwright's dead?"

Rhoda stood up too and looked me straight in the eyes, and told me, "Yep. I-just-killed-Buttwright." I couldn't believe my ears. We just stood there staring in one another's eyes. Neither one of us even blinked.

Suddenly, I ran from the living room toward the stairs, with her close behind still holding her cup of tea. Mr. Boatwright's door was closed. I knocked so hard my knuckles hurt.

"Oh, he won't answer," Rhoda told me casually. She gently pushed me aside and opened the door and we went in. "See there. I told you so." She motioned with her head toward Mr. Boatwright on his bed.

He lay on his back with the bedcovers pulled up to his neck. He appeared to be asleep, but he was not snoring like he always did. Nor did I see any movement. Suddenly his eyes opened.

"See—he's alive! He opened his eyes! Mr. Boatwright, get up!" I hollered with relief, and shook him so hard he almost rolled to the floor.

"That's just a reflex," Rhoda informed me, waving her hand like she was dismissing the whole situation. "One time a dead man sat up on the slab even after he had been dead for two days. I saw it with my own eyes," she added.

I looked from Mr. Boatwright to her, then back to him.

"How do you know he's really dead?" I mouthed, trembling. I shook Mr. Boatwright again. He still did not move.

"My daddy's the undertaker, girl. Remember? I know a dead person when I see one," she said evenly.

I shook Mr. Boatwright until my arms got tired. There was no doubt about it. The man was dead.

I stood up straight and sucked in my breath, turned to Rhoda, and said, "Girl, *what have you gotten yourself into?*"

CHAPTER 34

"Rhoda, Mr. Boatwright *is* dead!" I hollered. Not only was the room ominously quiet, there was nothing going on outside on the street like it usually was particularly at this hour. No loud cars, no voices, no barking dogs, nothing. It was like Rhoda and I were the only things making a sound in the night.

"See. I told you," Rhoda mouthed.

"And *you* killed him?"

"Uh-huh." She nodded slowly, closing her eyes for a moment.

"How?"

"I put that pillow there over his face and held it down," she confessed.

My ears were ringing. The fact that Rhoda was so casual was making me sick. I could feel the bile rising in my throat. I moved a few feet away from her, but she moved so close to me I could feel her breath on my face.

"Why, Rhoda? Why did you kill Mr. Boatwright?" I gasped.

"Why? What do you mean why? Because of what he was doin' to you, that's why," she exclaimed.

"But did you have to *kill* him?" I waved my arms to keep from grabbing her and shaking her.

"What else could I do?" she asked with an incredulous look.

"Oh God! What are we going to do? Oh God . . . oh God!" I shifted my weight from one foot to the other and looked around the room. "We better call the police. We'll tell them it was self-defense, but you're going to go to jail for a little while no matter what—"

"For what?" Rhoda gasped. She leaned back and looked at me with her eyes stretched open.

"For what? What—girl—*you just killed a man!* You killed Mr. Boatwright."

"Did you see me kill him?" Rhoda drank more of her tea.

"You told me—"

"He was probably drunk. You can still smell that cheap wine on him. Maybe he got tangled up in his blankets and smothered accidentally. I heard about a drunk man that died 'cause he choked on his own tongue. Freak accidents happen all the time. I just happened to come say good night to the man and found him . . . like this." Rhoda made a sweeping gesture with her hand. We looked at one another for a brief moment.

"Is that what happened? Please tell me that's what really happened," I pleaded.

"It could have," she shrugged. "I could say that's the way it happened."

"But it's not the way it happened, is it, Rhoda? You did kill Mr. Boatwright, didn't you?"

She didn't hesitate, she just shrugged and nodded. I was surprised when a sad look suddenly appeared on her face.

"Oh no . . . no," I moaned. I covered my face with my hand because I didn't want to look at her at that moment. I was startled when she pulled my hand away from my face.

"You can't tell anybody what happened, Annette."

"Well . . . what do we do now?" I asked feebly, wringing my sweaty hands.

"Nothin'."

"Nothing?" I wailed. I couldn't even feel my feet or my legs. But I was sweating from head to toe.

Rhoda looked around the cluttered bedroom and shook her head, then went back downstairs. I looked at Mr. Boatwright again. I shook him one last time and got no response. Finally, I closed his eyes with my fingers.

I went to his bedroom window and looked up at the sky. My head was throbbing so hard I could hear bells ringing that were not there. "God, you listen here . . . You *know* what happened here tonight . . .

So You know . . . I didn't have anything to do with it," I whispered. "Don't chastise me for something I didn't do," I prayed.

I returned to the living room and sat next to Rhoda on the couch. For five minutes we did not talk; we just stared at the TV screen. Every time I heard a car I ran to the window and snatched the curtains back. Each time, I reluctantly returned to sit next to Rhoda, making sure not to touch her. I didn't know what to do, but I knew that I didn't want to touch a person who had just committed murder.

"Stop shakin' so hard. People get murdered all the time, girl," Rhoda said firmly, rubbing the side of my arm.

"Yeah, but not in my own house."

We watched TV in silence for another ten minutes.

I could not focus on anything but Mr. Boatwright. "Rhoda, I don't know if I can go through with this . . . not tell anybody what you did." I heard a car door slam, and I jumped off the couch and stood in front of her.

Rhoda stood up with her face close to mine. I moved away so we wouldn't have to touch.

"But you can't tell anybody, now can you? He was old. Real old. He was goin' to die soon anyway, I bet." The way Rhoda stumbled over her words, I think she was trying to convince herself more than she was trying to convince me.

"Well what do we do now? We have to call somebody." I could not stop shaking no matter how hard I tried.

"We aren't goin' to do anythin'. Your mama's goin' to come home and see us sittin' here cryin' like babies over Martin Luther King, then she'll go hunt up Buttwright and find him dead in bed."

"She'll ask us what happened. The police will come. They'll do an autopsy—"

"Let them do all the autopsies they want. Just like I told you, he just stopped breathin'. That's what they'll say."

Muh'Dear was surprised to come home and find Rhoda still at our house close to midnight sitting stock-still on our living room couch with a blank expression on her face.

"Rhoda, you all right, child?" Muh'Dear asked tiredly as she unbuttoned her coat. She was so used to seeing a dramatic and animated Rhoda. "Your mama and daddy know where you at?" A flat ponytail was matted to the side of Muh'Dear's face.

"Oh yes, Ma'am. My mama told me I could stay here 'til you got home so Annette wouldn't be by herself."

Muh'Dear looked around the room and asked, "Where is Brother Boatwright? At Scary Mary's, with Johnny, or is he at that special church service for Dr. King singin' one of his hymns?"

"No Ma'am. He's in the bed," I said quickly. "He wasn't feeling too good."

"He wasn't lookin' too good either," Rhoda commented.

"Let him rest. I have some rhubarb I was goin' to let him sample tonight." Muh'Dear sighed. "If y'all don't mind, I'm goin' to turn in." Muh'Dear's voice trailed off. We sat still until we heard her bedroom door slam.

"Oh God. She won't find him until tomorrow," Rhoda said, rising. "I guess I better get on home now," she added, sounding nervous for the first time since Mr. Boatwright's murder.

I stood up, too. "I'll call you as soon as she finds him," I managed. "OK?"

"OK. If you cry—" She paused and stabbed my chest with her finger for more emphasis. "Cry when she tells you. Don't faint or anythin' drastic like that. He wasn't a blood relative, so everybody is goin' to expect your grief to be limited. Do you hear me?"

"Uh-huh," I mumbled, nodding my aching head. "I'll try."

"What do you mean, you'll try?"

"It'll be hard," I told her, rubbing the spot on my chest where she'd jabbed me.

"You make it sound like a game. A man is dead because you killed him."

"Well, you're finally free, Annette. Isn't that what you wanted more than anythin' in the world?"

"That's what *you* wanted. I just wanted him to stop molesting me."

Rhoda let out a long sigh of disgust and glared at me.

"You drag me into your mess and beg me to help you and I did. Oh it took me a while, but I did. Would it make you happy to see me in jail? And what about your mama? If I go to jail, I will have to tell the whole world *why* I killed Buttwright. You know what a scandal that would cause? Whose goin' to want your mama workin' for them when they find out she moved a rapist into her house?"

"Muh'Dear didn't know what he really was," I reminded, my hand in the air.

"It won't matter that she didn't know. She'll still be part of this mess."

"I hadn't thought about all that." I sobbed. I took a deep breath and looked in Rhoda's hard, angry face.

Suddenly, she seemed to soften right before my eyes. "Just remember, now you can live a normal life like me." She smiled, caressing my face. Her touch felt as cold as ice.

I nodded so hard my neck hurt. "I'm just so scared, Rhoda," I choked out.

"This'll be our secret 'til the day we die. Nobody but me and you will ever have to know," Rhoda said, talking in a slow, controlled manner.

"God'll know," I whispered. A pensive look appeared on Rhoda's face. She blinked hard, but tears still formed in her eyes. "Rhoda?"

"What?"

"Did you hear what I just said?"

"Yeah . . ." she mumbled, lowering her head.

"God knows what you did to Mr. Boatwright," I said firmly.

"I know He does." She tried to sound casual about it, but I knew she was worried about what kind of payback we would have to deal with down the road. I know I was.

CHAPTER 35

I didn't sleep at all the night Mr. Boatwright died. Instead, I moved back and forth from my bed to my bedroom window. On the bed I just sat with my hands on my lap with Rhoda's confession repeatedly going through my head. My fear of getting caught was so intense I had to run to the bathroom three different times to throw up. Each time I forced myself to go to Mr. Boatwright's room to check on him. Now his body was cold, and he was starting to turn gray. The light was still on, and I left it that way. When I got tired and numb from sitting on the bed in the same position so long, I stood in front of my window looking up toward the sky trying to picture God and figure out what He planned to do to me for my part in Mr. Boatwright's murder.

"I noticed Brother Boatwright's light still on around 2 A.M. when I went to the toilet. It's still on," Muh'Dear commented as we ate break-fast the next morning. I had gotten up and prepared grits and coffee.

"Uh . . . he's left his light on all night before," I said quickly. "The assassination really upset him."

Muh'Dear nodded and sipped her coffee. "Oh, it's got everybody upset. Even Judge Lawson can barely get out the bed. Oh well, since Brother Boatwright the one that pay the light bill, he can keep his bedroom light on much as he wants to." She finished her coffee and rose. "I got to walk to work again, so I best start steppin'." She left the kitchen and returned a few minutes later clutching her purse and buttoning her coat. I was still sitting at the kitchen table with half the food left on my plate untouched. "What's the matter with you, girl?"

Muh'Dear asked. She stopped buttoning her coat and walked over to me and looked in my face.

"Ma'am?" Since I had not gone to bed the night before, I still had on the same clothes from the day before and hadn't taken a bath or even washed my face.

"You just sittin' there daydreamin', ignorin' all that good food. What's on your mind?" She moved back a step and placed a hand on her hip. "If it's boys, get 'em off right now," she warned.

"It's nothing, Muh'Dear."

"Well whatever it is, you better watch your step." Muh'Dear moved closer to me and leaned over and kissed my forehead, then smiled. "When Brother Boatwright wake up tell him I'm sorry I ain't been around to say nothin' to him in the mornin' lately. I'll be walkin' to and from work 'til this riot mess is over with and the buses get back on route."

"Can I go to Rhoda's house later on, Muh'Dear?" I begged.

She started shaking her head right away. "I don't think that's a good idea. Them Nelsons got enough on they hands with that Johnny and Lola livin' there now." Muh'Dear started to leave but turned around fumbling with her purse. She opened it and removed two five-dollar bills and dropped them on the table next to my plate. "Go over to the Food Bucket today and pick up some poke salad greens, neckbones, and whatever else Brother Boatwright wants to cook for supper."

I slid the money into my blouse pocket. "I'll stay in Rhoda's room watching her TV. Maybe I can get her to drive me to the market, too," I said, blinking hard at Muh'Dear as she gave me an exasperated look.

"I don't want you to leave Brother Boatwright alone today at a time like this. Rhoda's mama and daddy there to keep one another company. Plus Lola and that stooge Johnny. You tell Rhoda to come over here. That way you and her both can keep Brother Boatwright company."

As soon as Muh'Dear left, I called Rhoda. "She didn't find him yet! I can't come to your house today, but she said you can come over here."

"OK. Let me finish my perm." Rhoda agreed tiredly.

She arrived a half hour later with a pan of freshly made candy for me. Before she sat down, she ran up to Mr. Boatwright's room and felt his forehead. I was right behind her.

She looked around the room, then ran to his dresser and snatched open the top drawer. "Where is that gun he used to pull on you?"

"I don't know. I haven't seen it in a long time."

Rhoda searched until she located the gun in the drawer of his nightstand. She sucked in her breath and looked at it for several minutes. Then she glanced at me and nodded, "It's a fake! All this time he was threatenin' you with a fake gun!"

I moved over to her and looked at the gun as she held it up in front of my face. "How do you know it's not real?" I asked in a scratchy voice, unable to take my eyes off the gun.

"Because I know guns like I know the back of my hand. Uncle Johnny's got a gun. My daddy's got three. Uncle Carmine's got a roomful. If anybody knows a real gun when they see one, it's me."

I touched the gun. Without another word Rhoda placed it in my trembling hand, and I inspected it thoroughly. "It is fake," I mumbled, looking in Rhoda's eyes.

We left Mr. Boatwright's room and went downstairs, where we sat on the living-room couch most of the day going over the situation and staring at the TV between pauses in our conversation. "I can't believe he's dead," I kept saying. "Well he is, and there is nothin' we can do to change things," Rhoda repeatedly told me. Around 2 P.M. we moved to the kitchen and finished what was left of the tea.

"What do we do now? There's nothin' but news programs on TV, and I'm gettin' real bored," Rhoda said, stretching and looking around the kitchen.

"I almost forgot. Can you drive me to the Food Bucket to pick up a few things for Mr. Boatwright to . . ."

"Sure," Rhoda said, rising. She touched my shoulder, and said firmly, "He's dead, and he won't be cookin' or doin' anythin' else anymore." Rhoda brushed off her silk blouse and let out a low whistle. "That Food Bucket is such a dump."

"I don't have enough money to go to Kroger's or the A&P," I wailed, rising.

"I'll pay for it," Rhoda indicated.

She drove me to the A&P, and we were back in my kitchen within an hour staring at a pizza we had picked up but now couldn't eat.

"We're goin' to have to act normal. We're actin' like zombies," Rhoda told me.

"I'm not hungry," I mumbled. The food I'd picked up from the market was still in the bag on the counter. Around four, Rhoda's mother called.

"I have to go home to help Aunt Lola do the laundry," Rhoda

breathed. She placed the phone back into its cradle and just stood in front of me staring at the pizza container. "I shouldn't have told you, huh?" she said softly, her voice cracking.

"Shouldn't have told me what?" I asked, not looking at her.

"What I did to Buttwright. You would never have known, and you wouldn't be feelin' the way you are now."

"But you're feeling sick, too. You didn't even touch that pizza," I told her, searching her eyes.

I think Rhoda was feeling the way she was because of how I was feeling more than she was about killing Mr. Boatwright.

"I can't stay in this house by myself with a dead man," I wailed. Rising, I grabbed her wrists. "Call your mama back and ask if you can do the laundry later," I begged.

Rhoda shook her head. "We have to act normal so nobody will get suspicious and start askin' questions. Don't be afraid to be in the house alone with him." She smiled and shook her head slowly. "He can't hurt you now."

"But he's dead! I'm scared of dead people."

"Girl, I'm always in my house alone with dead people. Sometimes two and three at a time."

"But I'm scared—"

"Then come to my house. You can help do the laundry, then we can watch TV in my room. Buttwright's not around to tell your mama, so she won't know you came over. Besides, I got some new paperbacks I'm ready to pass on to you," Rhoda said impatiently.

"I can't. Muh'Dear might call or come home early. She told me to stay in the house."

"All right. I'll bring some more tea when I come back," she promised. She called an hour later.

"When are you coming back?" I asked, sobbing. My hand was shaking so hard I could hardly hold the telephone. The longer Mr. Boatwright remained undiscovered, the more nervous I became. Every little noise made me almost jump out of my skin. There was a knot in my stomach and a lump in my throat.

"I have to help Aunt Lola finish the laundry, then go to this political gatherin' with my folks that I just found out about. I can't see you again until tomorrow."

"Oh no," I mumbled. A long silence followed.

"Did you hear what I said? I gotta go somewhere with my folks."

"Yeah, I heard you. What time will you be home, Rhoda?"

"I don't know. If it's not too late, I'll call you."

Three hours later, Muh'Dear wandered in, dropping her coat on the kitchen floor. Before saying a word, she lifted the lid off the pot I'd cooked the greens and neckbones in, grabbed a fork off the counter, and started fishing greens out.

"Brother Boatwright in the bed already?" she asked with her mouth full. It was odd for him to be in bed two nights in a row when she got home. "He sick?" She talked with her back to me.

"Um . . . he didn't get out the bed at all today," I told Muh'Dear. She whirled around and looked at me for what felt like an eternity, still chewing. "He is an old man, now, Muh'Dear. He needs all the rest he can get . . ."

I can't say how I really felt about what had happened to Mr. Boatwright at that moment. My feelings changed from one minute to the next. I was relieved that my abuse had ended, but I was afraid that sooner or later somebody would find out Rhoda had killed old Mr. Boatwright and that I knew about it all along. As strange as it may sound, I missed that old goat. He had become a part of my life, and in many ways he had replaced the father who had abandoned me. For those reasons, I felt like hell. One fear I had was, what if another man entered my life and took up where Mr. Boatwright left off? Would Rhoda kill him, too?

"I guess you right. Let him rest, bless his heart." Muh'Dear swallowed, yawned, stretched her arms, then leaned down and picked her coat up from the floor. "I'll check to see if he need anythin' in the mornin' before I leave."

I spent another night just sitting up. This time in front of the TV in the living room instead of my room looking out the window at the sky trying to bargain with God. The television didn't hold my attention, but I kept it on anyway. Every time I heard a car outside, I ran to the window to see if it was Rhoda.

I was desperate for something to happen, and it had to happen soon. I did manage to doze off for a brief moment around eleven but woke up as soon as I started having a dark dream about Mr. Boatwright chasing me with his fake leg.

Another hour went by before I heard another car. Rhoda and her folks had finally returned. I watched them get out and as soon as I saw Rhoda go in the house I called. "Muh'Dear didn't find Mr. Boatwright yet," I told her. Even though there was nobody in the room to hear my end of the conversation, I was holding the telephone receiver close to my face, and I was whispering.

"Hmmm . . . Uh . . . I can't talk about that right now." Rhoda lowered her voice and continued, "We'll figure out somethin' in the mornin'."

"It can't wait until morning. I'm about to have a complete nervous breakdown, girl," I hissed, looking over my shoulder. My head was pounding, my ears were ringing, and my stomach was in knots. This mess was making me sick. I held the phone away from my face and just looked at it. "Rhoda, I've got to do something soon, or I'll go crazy." A frightening silence followed.

"What are you goin' to do?" Rhoda asked.

"I'm goin' to go tell my mama that Mr. Boatwright died."

"And?"

"And what?" I asked.

"And that he died in his sleep?" Rhoda wailed.

"O . . . K," I managed.

"That is what happened, isn't it?"

"Yes, Rhoda. That is what happened," I agreed.

CHAPTER 36

I was already in the kitchen making breakfast when Muh'Dear walked in the next morning. She was dressed for work and seemed in a hurry. She had her coat on and it was already buttoned. "I swear to God, Brother Boatwright sleepin' so hard he wouldn't know if the house was on fire," she muttered, a pensive look on her face. "Between you and me, Brother Boatwright's room smell like a out-house! I cracked open a window to let in some fresh air. I ain't never smelled nothin that loud..." A puzzled look appeared on Muh'Dear's face.

I dropped my plate to the floor.

"You went in his room?" My lips snapped brutally over each word.

Muh'Dear looked from the floor to me, shaking her head. "You clean them grits up off that floor and rewax it just like it was."

"Yes, Ma'am." I grabbed a towel off the counter and dropped to the floor so hard I skinned my knees.

"I left him a note and told him to call me at Judge Lawson's house if he want me to brin' him somethin' home. Hmmmm. I don't rightly know what ails him, though. Do you?"

"No, Ma'am."

"He ain't told you nothin'?"

"No, Ma'am."

"He ain't got no color to him, and he so cold." Muh'Dear poured herself a cup of coffee and shrugged. "Bless his soul." She finished her coffee and left.

I called Rhoda immediately. She was at the door within minutes.

"OK. She's got to find him tonight. He's goin' to smell before long. Then he'll start to rot. Lord, what a mess that would be." Rhoda moaned.

Somehow I made it through the schoolday. Rhoda was waiting for me in front of the school after my last class.

Looking around first, she moved close to me, and said, "I'm goin' home with you. I'm goin' to be there when your mama comes home. We've got to figure out a way to get her to realize that man is dead, and we've got to do it tonight," she informed me stiffly.

Rhoda and I were sharing the couch when Muh'Dear got home around 9 P.M. She was so tired, I had to help her remove her coat.

"Did Brother Boatwright cook them oxtails I left on the counter this mornin'?" she asked.

"No, Ma'am. I cooked them when I got home from school," I said.

"I guess I'll eat me some oxtails, then crawl in the bed myself. Brother Boatwright doin' any better?" Muh'Dear wanted to know. "It's strange I ain't talked to him in days or seen him."

"He must really be sick," Rhoda said quickly. "Maybe he needs a doctor . . ."

"Except for his foot doctor, he don't believe in doctors," Muh'Dear replied, walking out of the room headed for the kitchen.

"Maybe he *can't* get out the bed. My uncle Henry in Alabama had a stroke one time and couldn't budge. He laid in his bed for three days before somebody went to his house to check on him." Rhoda looked at me. "You remember me tellin' you about that, don't you, Annette?"

"Uh-huh," I agreed. I had no idea what Rhoda was talking about.

"I'm so tired. Annette, you and Rhoda go take a look-see at Brother Boatwright," Muh'Dear suggested. "And listen here, don't y'all leave his room 'til you get a reaction out of him. Hear?"

"Maybe he's playin' possum," Rhoda said.

"For three days?" I shouted. Muh'Dear laughed and dismissed us with a wave of her hand and disappeared into the kitchen.

Rhoda and I rushed to Mr. Boatwright's bedroom.

"I can smell him now," I gasped, standing in the middle of the floor. The foul odor of his body wastes and death overwhelmed. The insides of my nostrils felt like they were on fire. I almost vomited.

"I can smell him, too." Rhoda coughed. Holding her nose, she moved closer to the bed. "My daddy gonna have a mess on his hands with this toad. I hope it's a closed-casket funeral . . ."

We stayed in the room for just a minute before we went running back to Muh'Dear in the kitchen.

"Sister Goode—he's not movin'!" Rhoda shouted.

Muh'Dear didn't say a word. She whirled around, dropping the lid to the pot containing the oxtails and ran upstairs with a plate in her hand and us behind her. As soon as we reached Mr. Boatwright's room, she handed me the plate and leaned over and shook him.

"Brother Boatwright! Say somethin' . . . anythin', Brother Boatwright!" She stopped after a minute, then stood up straight with her hand covering her mouth.

"What's wrong, Muh'Dear?" I shouted. I grabbed her arm and shook it. "Is he all right?"

"The man's dead," she whispered.

"The poor thing died in his sleep." I heard Muh'Dear telling somebody on the kitchen telephone the next morning. "Brother Nelson from 'cross the street got the body, and the funeral is pendin'."

Mr. Boatwright had no family that we knew of. Even Reverend Snipes didn't know of any, and none of us knew exactly where he came from or why he'd come to Richland. According to Reverend Snipes, Mr. Boatwright just showed up at one of his tent revivals one night babbling about how lost he was since he had strayed from his church. The preacher took Mr. Boatwright to the seedy Richland Rescue Mission behind the police department downtown, where he stayed for about six months. With his fake leg and other ailments, taking care of him got to be too big a chore for the people at the mission. That's why we'd ended up with him.

A day after Mr. Nelson and Uncle Johnny had carried Mr. Boatwright from our house to the mortuary, around 5 P.M. I entered our living room from upstairs just as Mr. Nelson, Lola, and Rhoda walked up on our front porch. People had come and gone all day to drop off food. Our kitchen table and counter were covered. We expected a huge crowd later that night.

Judge Lawson had given Muh'Dear a week off with pay. He decided to eat his breakfast and lunch at Antonosanti's and dinner at our house until she returned to work. Lola had agreed to clean the judge's house for that week.

"Hi," I said, opening the door. Mr. Nelson smiled and tipped his hat. Lola touched my shoulder. Rhoda refused to look at me. Mr. Nelson, his arm around her shoulder, led Rhoda to the living room, where Muh'Dear was on the couch dabbing her swollen red eyes with a handkerchief. Lola walked alongside me, sobbing softly.

"Have you decided what he should wear?" Mr. Nelson asked Muh'Dear.

Her eyes got wide as if she had forgotten we had to provide a burial outfit for Mr. Boatwright. "Uh . . . I hadn't decided," she trembled, looking at me.

"Well, did he have a favorite suit?" Lola asked, moving to the couch. She sat down and placed her hand on Muh'Dear's shoulder.

"That white fleecy one," Rhoda offered, glancing at me. Out of the corner of my eye I saw Mr. Nelson and Lola look at one another and frown at the same time. "He told me that was his favorite suit," Rhoda said.

"Well"—Muh'Dear began looking from face to face—"he did just have it dry cleaned a few days before he . . . passed." She sniffed, wiped her nose, and turned to me. "Annette, go to his room and get his white suit."

Without a word I went upstairs and removed the suit I hated so much from a coat hanger in his closet. They hadn't asked, but I assumed he would need shoes and undergarments. It took me five minutes to gather everything and slide them into a shopping bag sitting on the floor by the door. The living room was deathly quiet when I returned. I immediately handed the bag to Lola.

"I'll be goin', Sister Goode. I can see you're tired and need to be left alone. Mrs. Nelson and I, and the rest of the family, will see you and Annette later tonight." Mr. Nelson paused and lifted the shopping bag and gently shook it. "We can work out the rest of the details tomorrow." He gave Muh'Dear a big smile, then squeezed her shoulder. "Lola and Rhoda are going to stay here to help you and Annette handle your guests."

Rhoda looked at me with a blank expression on her face, then she watched her daddy until he was out the door.

It was an uncomfortable evening. With the exception of the Nelsons' white relatives from Alabama, the same people came who had attended the gathering for Granny Goose, but I guess they didn't stay as long because we didn't have any alcohol. Rhoda, offering me weak smiles, stayed close to her mother most of the evening. Even though there was a mountain of food in the kitchen, I never saw Rhoda with a plate.

Several people stood around in the living room making glowing remarks about Mr. Boatwright like they did for everybody, even deceased pimps and dope dealers.

"I'll never forget the times me and him shared a cab or he drove me to Judge Lawson's poker parties," Uncle Johnny managed. This was one of the few times I'd seen him sober.

"I used to like to go to church just to hear him sing," Pee Wee muttered, smiling sadly, toying with a chicken wing on his plate.

"I'm sure enough goin' to miss settin' with him on the front porch shootin' the breeze," Caleb wailed, rubbing the bullet spot on his head.

"We done lost us a good man," Scary Mary whined plaintively. She had had a few drinks before coming over, accompanied by several of her current and former whores. The women with Scary Mary were all dressed like they were going to a nightclub. I had never seen so many tight, short dresses and spiked high heels in my life.

"I was supposed to cut and shape his hair yestiddy," Caleb said. "What little bit he had left."

"I never understood Mr. Boatwright. He was a complicated man," Florence said thoughtfully.

"The next poker party will be in his honor," Judge Lawson announced, forcing himself to laugh. "He would have wanted it that way." Almost everybody in the room agreed with him.

"Rhoda's goin' to help Annette pack up Brother Boatwright's stuff for Johnny to take to the Salvation Army." Rhoda's mother coughed. Rhoda glanced at me, and our eyes locked. People kept saying good things about Mr. Boatwright, but Rhoda kept her eyes on me. After a few moments more, I went to the kitchen. I wasn't there a minute before Lola entered.

"Imagine Scary Mary lettin' all them strumpets come over here advertisin' at a time like this," Lola complained, sitting down hard at the table. I was in front of the kitchen window with my back to her. I turned just enough to see her with a huge plate in front of her on the table. "When I was in the business I didn't even dress that slutty when I was workin'." Lola sucked on a piece of meat, her eyes on me.

I just smiled and shrugged.

"When I was a workin' girl, things were different. Of course bein' down South, things were different anyway." Lola gave me a thoughtful look. "Look at me now," she said sadly.

"You look fine, Miss Lola. I heard you got a job working at Antonosanti's." I sniffed. I was glad it was she who had come into the kitchen and not Uncle Johnny or Pee Wee.

"I'd rather still be in the sportin' business," Lola admitted with a wink. It had been a while since I'd seen somebody eat as fast as she was. She was getting as much food on her as in her.

"Ma'am? You mean you'd rather be a prostitute instead of a waitress?" I asked.

"Annette, I'm a lot older than you, so I know a lot more. Take it from me, when it comes to us women, pussy is the best card we got left to play. Ask any successful woman." Lola let out a short chuckle and got up to leave with her plate in her hand. As soon as she was out of the kitchen I turned back around and started staring out the window again. I remained in that position for ten more minutes. When I finally turned around, Rhoda was standing in the doorway with a look on her face I will never forget. Her eyes were fixed on me, and her lips were quivering like she was in a trance.

"How long have you been standing there?" I gasped. I was so startled I stumbled and fell against the wall.

"Since Aunt Lola left," she said evenly.

"Do you want to go upstairs so we can talk or something? I don't think I could stand that crowd anymore," I said, still standing in my spot.

"I really came to say good night," Rhoda told me.

"Good night, Rhoda," I responded. Then she left.

Mr. Boatwright had left his life insurance policy made out to Muh'Dear. She never told me how much it was for, but she used some of it to cover his funeral expenses.

I didn't go to the calling hours the next day. After the gathering at our house, I didn't think I could stand a wake and a funeral for Mr. Boatwright, too. "It won't look right if you ain't there. Everybody thought of him as part of our family," Muh'Dear said when I told her I wasn't going. "I know, but these cramps are killing me," I lied, feigning a moan.

That Saturday there was a brief funeral service in Reverend Snipes's church with the same grief-stricken crowd.

It was hard to look at Mr. Boatwright lying in that coffin with his paws resting on his chest, looking like somebody's harmless old grandfather. It was hard to believe that this was the same man who had abused me for so many years.

The night before the funeral I had dreamed that Mr. Boatwright had come into my room, stood over my bed, and told me, "I'm sorry, possum." For reasons I didn't understand, I forgave him in the dream.

Now I was scared to death that somebody would find out that Rhoda had smothered Mr. Boatwright with one of his own pillows and that I knew all about it. Both of us could go to jail.

I didn't know how, but I had to keep this mess a secret until I died. My conscience was what I was worried about. How long would it be before I broke down and spilled everything? How long would I be able to continue attending church and facing our preacher and Muh'Dear knowing what I knew? What if Rhoda snapped one day and thought that I'd tell. Would she kill me, too?

CHAPTER 37

Rhoda wasn't available to help me pack up Mr. Boatwright's stuff until three days after the funeral. She finally called and came over around six that evening.

"Let's get this stuff boxed up as fast as we can," she suggested with a deep sigh. We were drinking tea in the kitchen while Muh'Dear was visiting Scary Mary.

I didn't like Rhoda's tone of voice or the fact that she had taken three days to come over again. "You know you really don't have to help me if you don't want to," I whined even though I was terrified of being in Mr. Boatwright's room alone with his things still there. "Florence said she would help me. And I bet Pee Wee would, too, if I asked him."

"I never go back on my promise, and I did promise your mama and my folks I would help you." She smiled, but I questioned her sincerity.

"You should be the main person who would really want to get this thing over and done with," I said angrily, giving her a hard look.

"What's that supposed to mean?" she gasped. Her mouth remained opened after she had finished talking.

"You're the reason he's dead!" I snapped, shaking my cup in her face.

"No, honey! You are the reason he's dead." Her voice was hard and even. She spoke while stabbing me in the chest with her finger and shaking her head so hard her curls fell from the side of her face to the front, almost covering her mean eyes.

"What?"

"You should have told somebody on him."

"Is that what you would have done?"

"Hell yes! The first time he put his hands on me I'd have gone straight to my mama."

A great sadness came over me, and suddenly it was hard for me to speak but I did. "I was scared of what he would do to me," I rasped, staring at my empty teacup.

"Well, he can't do anythin' to you now. How come you won't tell your mama now? She's got a right to know. Maybe if she did, she and everybody else would stop goin' around talkin' about him like he was some saint. The man was a rapist, and he didn't deserve havin' all these people around here feelin' the way they did about him," Rhoda snarled.

"I can't hurt my mama by telling her what I went through. What good would it do now? She would die of guilt for putting me in that position in the first place. She would never get over it. I want her to be happy. And you know how people treat rape victims. What about that girl you told me about down South that ended up killing herself because people blamed her for getting raped? Who would believe some man would rape somebody that looks like me?"

"Rape is not about the way you look, Annette. You know that."

"Well, I am not going to have people whispering behind my back blaming me for it. Mr. Boatwright said I brought it all on myself. If he believed that, Lord knows what everybody else will think. Let's get this stuff packed up, girl."

We picked up large boxes Muh'Dear had left in the upstairs hallway and went to the bedroom Mr. Boatwright had occupied, leaving the door open after we got inside. The room smelled worse than it smelled when he was in it alive.

Rhoda stood behind me as I pulled back the bedcovers. I almost fainted from the stench.

"Shit!" I growled. He had soiled the bed.

"I forgot to tell you, that's one of the first things a dead person does when they die. They shit," Rhoda informed me. "All their butt muscles relax."

"Muh'Dear said we can throw his bed things in the trash," I said, frowning as I looked over the bedding. "Burn them."

"If you ask me, I say burn everythin' in here," Rhoda said angrily, kicking the side of the bed.

"We're giving the good stuff to the Salvation Army."

"What *good* stuff?" Rhoda gasped, giving me an incredulous look.

"Well, the stuff somebody might be able to use, I guess." I shrugged.

"And who would want any of this shit?" Rhoda snarled. She held up one of Mr. Boatwright's shirts. There were pins up and down the sleeves and buttons missing.

I shrugged again.

"What if they decide to dig him up later and do an autopsy?" I asked, hugging myself. I was shivering hard, even though the room was not cold. "These Ohio detectives get awful suspicious."

"My God, girl. Since when do these detectives care about old Black men enough to dig one up just to see if they can find some foul play?" Rhoda marched over to me and stood with her hands on her hips. "What reason would anybody want to kill Buttwright? He didn't have any money to speak of. No enemies. No nothin'. Why would a detective busy with real criminals start investigatin' Buttwright's death?"

"They might think Muh'Dear did it for his insurance money, like the women who kill their husbands in those old murder movies, Rhoda."

"Those women usually have handsome young lovers lined up to help 'em spend the insurance money. Your mama used Buttwright's insurance money to bury his black ass. Besides, your mama got old Judge Lawson's nose open so wide, she could get every dime he got. Why would she need to kill anybody to collect a few insurance dollars? And another thing. I bet Judge Lawson loses more money playin' poker in one night than Buttwright's whole insurance policy must be worth."

"I guess you're right." I sighed with resignation. The smell in the room was getting worse by the minute to me. The insides of my nostrils felt like they were on fire.

"Now like I said, let's get this shit boxed up," Rhoda ordered.

We started grabbing clothes from the floor and out of the drawers that we hurriedly stuffed into the boxes. Every time I looked toward the bed I tried to imagine Rhoda holding the pillow over Mr. Boatwright's face.

"Don't you feel something for him?" I asked her.

"I don't know . . . do you?" Her mouth remained open.

"I don't know. I don't think I really hated him. I hated what he was doing to me."

Rhoda sighed. "Well, I did feel kind of bad right after I did it, but now that he's in the ground, I don't know. I would have rather talked to him and made him stop by threatenin' to tell the po'lice, but he threatened to kill you. At least that's what you told me."

"Yeah. He did."

"Did you mean what you just said about not hatin' him?"

I nodded. "I only hated what he was doing to me."

A sad look appeared on Rhoda's face. "I see," she mumbled.

"Mr. Boatwright was real good to my mama at all times," I admitted.

"Uh-huh. But he treated you like hell."

"Not all the time."

"What do you mean?"

"When he first moved in he was a good man to have around. One time I was sick in bed with the flu, he came to my room and I pretended to be asleep. He patted my forehead and pulled the covers up around my neck."

"Was he drunk?"

"I don't think so. Another time he came all the way to the school to bring my snow shoes. His leg bothered him so much from that long walk in the snow he had to stay in the bed for a week."

"Well, he was goin' to die soon anyway. Just like Granny Goose. The doctor said she could go any day. Fallin' down the steps just took her out of her misery that much sooner," Rhoda insisted. I think she was trying to convince herself more than she was me.

"I won't ever tell what really happened, Rhoda. But you'll know what you did."

"I know," she responded dryly. Rhoda got real quiet, then gave me this funny look. "I want to say somethin' . . ."

"What?"

"Annette, I never saw Buttwright molest you. I never heard him threaten you. All I heard was your side of the story. *How do I know you didn't make all this up to get attention?*"

"You don't," I told her.

"Then it is all true?"

I gave her an incredulous look and gasped, "Well, it's a little late for you to be asking questions now, don't you think. You already killed the man. Everything I ever told you about Mr. Boatwright and me is the absolute truth. Who would want attention this bad?"

Rhoda sighed and nodded. "Oh well." She shrugged. "The thing is, nobody knows I killed Mr. Buttwright but you and me." She looked in my eyes for a long time.

"And God," I reminded her in a whisper.

CHAPTER 38

It was Rhoda's idea for me to go make some tea. I left her in Mr. Boatwright's room alone. There was some already made so all I had to do was reheat it. I guess I finished faster than she expected. When I returned to the bedroom I saw her on her knees with her head bowed, her hands cupped. She was praying! Nothing Rhoda did surprised me anymore. She had crossed a line, and I had crossed it with her. We could never turn back now. I admitted that I was feeling guilty about Mr. Boatwright's murder, even though I had not actually done it myself or even been present when she did it. I was scared to death that we would either get caught or that Mr. Boatwright's ghost would come back and haunt me. I had been sleeping with my lights on and my Bible under my pillow since his funeral.

I gasped and moved back to the steps and returned to the kitchen. I waited a few minutes, then went stomping back up the stairs making as much noise as I could. Rhoda was snatching stuff from the closet when I returned to the room.

We drank the tea in silence. All I could hear were our spoons clicking against our cups.

"You can go when you finish your tea," I told her.

"I'll stay until we finish," she replied. "I have something to show you." She removed a box from the closet with a brown folder. I opened it and saw a stack of newspaper clippings that were so old they had turned brown. "I've only read two of them. They are from some unheard-of Mississippi publication," Rhoda told me. "I thought you should be here to read the others with me." Just then the door slammed shut. We both whirled around at the same time. "What was that?" Rhoda asked.

"The wind?" I said, shaking.

"There was no wind," Rhoda insisted.

I got up to open the door and looked out in the hallway. "See. Nobody's out here. It *had* to be just the wind."

"Yeah. It was the wind," Rhoda agreed weakly.

I returned to the bed. I couldn't tell which of us was shaking the hardest.

"Our minds are playing tricks on us, but we can't freak out now," I told her. "We're in this thing too deep."

"Yeah. Let's read," Rhoda said in a hollow voice. Her mood had softened considerably.

We put the clippings in chronological order, then we sat on the bed and began to read them one by one. After the first few sentences I forgot about the mysterious way the door slammed shut.

BATTERED COLORED CHILD FOUND

An unidentified colored male, approximately three years old, was found unconscious by a state trooper in an abandoned shack on Dabney Road last night.

The boy had been sexually assaulted and savagely beaten. A white mule doctor, who asked that his name not be revealed, amputated the boy's left leg this morning.

The boy was unable to identify his assailant or the weapon used to damage his leg beyond repair.

The boy is currently in the care of the Reverend Buck Poole, also colored. Police are investigating the matter.

On the back of the first item was a girdle ad that took up more space. We read on.

CRAZED COLORED WOMAN SLAIN BY POLICE

A wild-eyed colored woman, wielding a butcher knife, entered the home of the Reverend Buck Poole last night through a window and forcibly removed a child she claimed was hers. The boy was also colored.

This boy, possibly retarded, was found abandoned, abused and unconscious last week.

Four hours after the boy was taken by the woman, police scanned the immediate area. The woman was tracked to Howard's sawmill by the police hounds. The boy had been slashed over ten times about his tail and stomach area.

Officer Jackson Cramer, white, was forced to shoot the woman five times after she jumped from a tree, made threats against his life, sassed him using foul language, then went after him with the bloody knife.

ABANDONED COLORED BOY ABANDONED AGAIN

A routine patrol possibly saved the life of a six-year-old colored boy. The boy, who gave his name as Doolittle Boatwright, has known nothing but a life of despair since the day he was born.

The boy first made the news about three years ago when patrolers found him naked and near death.

In this incident, the elderly colored preacher who had taken the boy in dropped dead after being kicked in the head area by a frisky rogue mule.

The boy is currently being held in the town jailhouse while police investigate rumors of an illegal still on the property of the only colored orphanage in the county.

Police encourage members from any colored church to offer their services regarding this boy.

We skipped over a few of the clippings that seemed to be repeating some of the incidents.

"Let's read this one. This is many years later," Rhoda said. Her voice cracked, but I pretended not to notice.

COLORED SPORTING HOUSE RAIDED

Local police raided a house on Jersey Street being used for fornication by a woman who is well-known by the law. A Miss Lucille Boggs, an ex-convict, refused to give her age, and had several young colored girls in her company as well as ten colored prostitutes between the ages of eighteen and fifty.

A colored boy, Doolittle Boatwright, age fifteen, tipped off the police after the Boggs woman evicted him from a room he had been living in since age eight. One-legged, the boy has never attended school, and learned to read on his own and is unusually smart for a colored boy.

The boy retaliated after the Boggs woman beat him in front of her guests and turned her dogs loose on him.

According to eyewitnesses, all colored, Boggs removed the boy's makeshift peg leg and struck him with it about his head area.

Everybody involved in this mayhem was colored. Except the police.

If the articles weren't depressing enough, the unsophisticated journalism made them seem worse. "Those old time Southern redneck reporters sure have a shabby way with words," I told Rhoda.

"Damn crackers. Probably some of my Caucasian relatives," she spat.

"I can't read any more," I mumbled. I felt so bad for the way life had started out treating Mr. Boatwright. No matter what he had done to me, he was still a human being, and that made him one of God's children. Just like me and Rhoda.

She skipped ahead anyway.

"Let's read this last one. This one is dated only about twenty years ago from today."

"OK, but after this one let's burn them. We have enough to worry about," I said, trying to sound firm.

"Yeah. Let's put all this behind us," Rhoda said seriously. "All this mess . . ."

We sighed and unfolded the last one we were going to read.

ONE-LEGGED COLORED MAN ATTEMPTS SUICIDE FOR THE THIRD TIME

Bad luck and misfortune continue in the life of Doolittle Boatwright, age unknown.

The one-legged man is well-known in the area by the police. He has been convicted for robbery, vagrancy, disturbing the peace, battery, attempted rape, vandalism, and breaking and entering.

After being evicted from a colored mission house for disorderly conduct, Boatwright jumped off the Lexington Bridge, where he hit a rock and landed on the riverbank.

Two weeks earlier, Boatwright jumped in front of a truck that ran out of gas before it reached him.

Police subdued Boatwright with a hose and the dogs. Boatwright was later escorted to the county mental facility in a straitjacket. Authorities summoned a specialist from the county seat to examine the man. It was determined that he suffers from a variety of mental disorders. The man was released into the custody of Ike Townes, a colored man known for taking in hopeless cases. Ike Townes, twenty years on the chain gang and a respectable fortune-teller, has had some luck with redeeming hopeless Negroes. Townes predicted that Boatwright would one day find a woman and live a normal life.

"I would say that the woman the fortune-teller predicted was your mama." Rhoda put the last clipping we read back into the folder and slapped it shut.

"What a bum deal," I sobbed, wiping my eyes and nose with the back of my hand.

"Too late to be cryin' for him now, Annette." Rhoda stood up and looked away, but not before I saw tears in her eyes. "I'll get the rest of the stuff from the closet." She went to the closet and pulled out the fake brown leg and burst into tears.

CHAPTER 39

Three days went by and I didn't hear from Rhoda and I didn't call her. I had almost stopped calling up Florence. She was out with her boyfriend most of the time when I did.

"Things just ain't the same since Brother Boatwright left us," Muh'Dear said at breakfast one morning. He had been dead two weeks. Ironically, now that he was gone, she had cut her hours, and I saw more of her than I had in over ten years even though it meant she brought home less money. But there was still some of the insurance money from Mr. Boatwright's policy that helped us a lot (as did Judge Lawson's mysterious generosity). "We done lost us a good man."

"I miss his cooking," I said. I couldn't think of anything else good to say about Mr. Boatwright. He was a good cook, and once upon a time he was a good man. "Muh'Dear, how much did you know about him?"

Muh'Dear gave me a sad, thoughtful look, then she smiled. "I knew he was the kind of man I wish I had met when I was a young girl. Except for that missin' leg, the man was flawless, irreplaceable."

"I mean about where he came from. Do you know anything about his background?" I held my breath and blinked hard, trying to figure out why Muh'Dear kept looking away.

"His mama died when he was a baby, and he never knew his daddy. His granny raised him. Then she died. He joined the army, where he got his leg blowed off. Then he traveled the world on a merchant ship for many years before he found Jesus, then us."

"And you believed everything he told you?" I asked, pushing a piece of sausage around on my plate with my fork.

"Why wouldn't I? Brother Boatwright was a righteous man that didn't believe in lyin'. That man read the Bible every night before he went to bed."

"He never married?"

"He was engaged when he went in the army. When he lost his leg, he lost the girl. He was too shy from then on to approach a woman." Muh'Dear paused and laughed, then she cried. She stopped after a minute. "I had to approach him."

"What do you mean?" My body tensed as I waited for her response. So far I didn't like much of what I was hearing.

"I asked him to marry me after you finished school."

"What did you say?" I almost choked on a piece of sausage. Muh'Dear reached over and patted me hard on the back.

"He was goin' to marry me. Well, you old enough to know now. We was like man and wife anyway. That devil." She cackled and shook her head. "He used to hop into my room just about every night after he thought you was asleep."

"You mean . . . for sex? With you?"

Muh'Dear nodded. "He was so hurt when you got yourself in that mess with that boy."

"I bet he was." My body was on fire after hearing Muh'Dear's confession, and I didn't want to face her. I was not hungry anymore, and I wanted to leave the room, but my legs felt too heavy for me to move from the table.

"I wanted to send you to Florida to live with your Aunt Berneice I was so upset over you gettin' yourself pregnant. The shame was so overwhelmin'. I'd die if the congregation found out. He talked me out of sendin' you down South. He said wild as you was, you'd be pregnant again within a week down there."

"I don't think so. I was stupid for letting something like that happen to me. I knew better," I muttered.

"The way you lit into old lady Jacobs when you was a little girl that time for hittin' me with her cane, I never woulda thought you'd be the type of girl to let anybody take advantage of you," Muh'Dear said with her eyes sparkling.

"I didn't either." I shrugged, looking toward the wall.

CHAPTER 40

It was not easy, but I put Mr. Boatwright and what had happened to him out of my mind as much as I could. Graduation was a few weeks away, and we all had a lot of studying to do. One thing that was occupying most of the minds of the class of '68 was the senior prom. Going to the prom was something girls in my position didn't dare think about. So that's why when I got asked to go, I almost swallowed the piece of chicken I was eating.

"What did you just ask me, Pee Wee?" I gasped into the phone. Muh'Dear was at work, of course, and Rhoda was shopping with her mother and Lola.

"I asked if I could escort you to the senior prom. This is a once-in-a-lifetime thing, you know," Pee Wee said.

"Can I call you back?" I asked, barely able to breathe.

Pee Wee was silent for a moment.

"You gotta think about it, or somebody else asked you to go?" he asked.

"Um . . . no. I have to make sure it's OK with my mama."

"OK. Well let me know as soon as you can."

It took me five minutes to compose myself after I got off the phone. Then I called Judge Lawson's house to ask Muh'Dear if I could go to the prom.

"Judge Lawson's residence," she announced, answering on the second ring.

"Muh'Dear, it's me," I said with a shaky voice.

"What's wrong?" she asked. I heard Judge Lawson in the background ask who was on the phone. "It's Annette," she told him. This was the first time I'd ever called her at Judge Lawson's house since she'd started working for him.

"Can I go to the senior prom?" I said quickly, then held my breath.

"Can you what?" she choked out.

"I got asked to the prom. I'll be out real late, and I'll need a new dress. I just wanted to make sure it was OK with you before I accepted the invitation." I couldn't believe those words were coming out of my mouth.

"My girl got asked to the prom," Muh'Dear said, talking to the judge. I heard him clap his hands and whistle. "Of course you can go, baby," she said excitedly. There was some muffled sounds on her end for about a minute. "We'll talk about it when I get home tonight," she told me.

I had to compose myself again. I waited another five minutes before I called Pee Wee back. "Yes," I told him, glad he couldn't see my face and feel my excitement. I never thought I'd see the day I'd get excited over being asked out by Pee Wee.

"Cool. I'll be over later tonight, or I will talk to you in study hall tomorrow," Pee Wee said eagerly.

I couldn't wait to tell Rhoda. I didn't want to tell her over the phone, so I went to her house with my coat on over my housecoat. Uncle Johnny sent me upstairs to Rhoda's room, where she was stretched out on her bed.

"Rhoda, guess what?" I closed the door with my foot and rushed over to her bed. "What's the matter? You don't look too good." I sat down on the side of her bed.

"I'll be OK . . . in about seven months," she whispered, looking at her stomach.

My heart sank. She didn't have to tell me, but I knew she was pregnant. I'd been expecting that to happen. Surprisingly, I was not as disgusted as I thought I would be. "Do you want me to come back later?" I asked.

"No, stay. What's up?" she asked, struggling to sit up.

"You're going to have a baby aren't you?" I asked, saddened. Things were happening too fast for my weary brain. Mr. Boatwright was dead, I was about to graduate, Rhoda and Otis were getting married right after graduation, and now here she was pregnant. Not only would I have to share her with Otis, I'd have to share her with a baby. "Are you and Otis still going to the prom?"

"Of course!" She sat up straight and smiled broadly. "This'll be my one and only time to go to one. I wish you were goin' to be there," she told me, patting my shoulder.

"That's what I came to tell you. Pee Wee asked me to go with him." I was in a fever. A grin I could not hold back took over my face.

Rhoda gasped, then let out a short laugh. "You're kiddin' me!"

"No, I'm not. He just called a little while ago. Muh'Dear said I could go, and I'm going to get a new dress." I couldn't stop grinning. Just then Mrs. Nelson entered the room with a cup of tea for Rhoda.

"Muh'Dear, Annette's goin' to the prom, too," Rhoda told her mother, reaching for her cup.

Mrs. Nelson stood back and folded her arms. "Well isn't that nice! I hope you both have as much fun at your prom as I had at mine." Rhoda perked up immediately and decided that Pee Wee and I would ride with her and Otis. I thought I would faint when Mrs. Nelson told me she was sending me to Miss Rachel's to get my hair done. This was another night I didn't sleep at all.

The next few days were the most hectic of my life. Judge Lawson let Muh'Dear take another day off with pay so she could take me shopping for my prom dress. I wanted to buy the first one I saw at one of the cheap downtown dress stores, but Muh'Dear didn't like it. It was blue chiffon with lace across the top. "We could find somethin' much nicer at the shoppin' center where Rhoda got her dress," Muh'Dear insisted. "We can't afford those stores," I reminded her. "Um . . . this is a special occasion. We'll figure out a way to afford one," Muh'Dear assured me.

I didn't ask Muh'Dear where the money came from for the expensive blue chiffon I picked out at Stacy's, the same shop where Rhoda got her pale pink chiffon.

I had been doing my own hair since the age of thirteen. Cheap perm kits, straightening combs that were too hot, and not enough general care had damaged my hair badly. The prim and impeccably groomed Miss Rachel had a time bringing it back to life. "You've got nice thick hair. You should take better care of it," she told me. I felt like a princess sitting in the most exclusive Black beauty parlor in town right along with some of the other Black girls preparing for the prom. I knew that things were going too smoothly. So when Lena Cundiff, the bully Rhoda had pushed into a toilet in the eighth grade, entered Miss Rachel's salon to get her hair done I wasn't surprised. "What the hell are *you* doin' in here, Bertha Butt?" she barked at me.

Two of her equally loathsome girlfriends were with her, and they all snickered. Over the years, I had had several more minor run-ins with Lena since the toilet incident. I knew her schedule, so I was usually able to avoid her a lot the last couple months of school. "I came to get my hair done for the prom," I announced proudly, walking away before she could hurl another insult my way.

Judge Lawson brought Muh'Dear home early the evening of the prom so she could help me get ready. My understanding was, Pee Wee and I would ride with Rhoda and Otis in his car. I was shocked when an hour before we were to leave from my house, a black stretch limousine, compliments of Judge Lawson, stopped in front of our house. We took a dozen pictures at Rhoda's house and then a dozen at mine. I had never seen Muh'Dear look so happy when she hugged me, and said, "See, I told you if you was good to God, God'd be good to you." She stood on the porch with Judge Lawson and Caleb waving until the limo turned the corner.

The auditorium looked spectacular. Shiny silver stars of various sizes hung by pastel-colored crepe ribbons from the ceiling. The tables had silver tablecloths with a large dark blue star in the center of each one. A band that played both soul music and soft rock entertained. One of my favorite soft rock tunes was playing, "I Want to Make It with You" by Bread. As soon as we sat down at our table near the bandstand, I spotted Lena standing nearby with a few of her vicious girlfriends. As lovely as they all looked in their beautiful dresses and nicely done hairdos, there was an ugliness about them. Their stares were so cold I wish I had worn the shawl Lola had offered me.

Muh'Dear had warned me and Rhoda not to drink any alcohol, but Otis and Pee Wee started drinking from flasks they had smuggled in right away.

I had never attended a dance before and didn't know if I had any rhythm or not. But I surprised myself when I got on the floor with Pee Wee to jump around like everybody else to the Motown tune "Do You Love Me?" The first hour went fine. I got up and mingled. Kids who had never acknowledged me before smiled, hugged me, and wished me well. A few asked what my plans were. "I'm thinking about leaving Ohio," I told Charlotte Harper, a girl who used to sit behind me in junior math class. Before she could respond, Lena Cundiff bumped into me from behind with so much force I fell against Charlotte, almost knocking her down. "That's what happens when they allow cows in here," Lena said in a loud, drunken voice. Everybody around us heard the snickering coming from her and her friends. Rhoda witnessed the incident and came to stand next to me.

"You want me to take care of that?" she asked.

"No, I'm OK." I wanted to say more, but I didn't know what. The eighth grade locker room was a long way from the senior prom scene. "In a couple of weeks I'll never have to deal with Lena Cundiff again," I told Rhoda, letting out a sigh of relief.

"Unfortunately, there are a lot of Lenas out in the real world," Rhoda observed. I returned to our table with her for a few minutes before we went around the room hugging our favorite teachers.

As much fun as I was having, I was glad when it was getting close to time to leave. Right in the middle of the four of us at our table making a toast, I was bumped into from behind again. Lena glared at me and deliberately spilled her punch over the top and lap of my dress. "You bitch!" Rhoda hissed, starting to rise; Otis grabbed her by the arm and forced her back into her seat.

"Lena, why don't you get a life," Pee Wee yelled.

"Why don't you get a real woman and not a bull," Lena taunted, cackling. Two girls near me handed me napkins to sponge punch off my dress. I was glad none of the teachers witnessed the incident. The last thing I wanted to risk was a confrontation this close to graduation.

"Let's get out of here," Rhoda said, rising. Otis held on to her arm as he led her toward the exit. Pee Wee, more than a little drunk, walked along next to me, cussing under his breath over what Lena had done to me.

The night air was cool. With that huge wet stain on the front of my dress, I was feeling pretty chilly and started to shiver. Pee Wee took off his tuxedo jacket and was about to drape it around my shoulders when I held up my hand. "Just a minute," I told him.

"Where are you goin'?" Rhoda asked. We were several yards away from our limo. In the opposite direction near the side of the school building stood Lena with several of her male and female friends. Rhoda, Otis, and Pee Wee followed as I took my time walking up to Lena.

"Lena, this is for *everything*," I said calmly. Nobody said a word. I closed my eyes for a second and pretended that Lena was Mrs. Jacobs, the mean woman in Florida who had beaten Muh'Dear with her cane. My fist connected with her mouth with so much force she stumbled backward past two other limos before falling to the ground out cold, leaving several of her teeth on the ground next to my feet. I turned to my friends. Pee Wee and Otis were grinning. Rhoda's mouth was hanging open, and she was clutching her chest. "Let's get out of here," I said evenly, forcing myself not to smile.

Rhoda hugged me as soon as we got into the limo, "Attagirl!" she yelled. Our dates slapped five with me until my palms hurt. All the way home, the conversation revolved around my well-aimed fist. "I'll talk to you in the mornin'," Rhoda told me. Otis went in with Rhoda, I thanked Pee Wee, and he went into his house next door, then I went in. Muh'Dear was on the couch waiting for me.

The only light on in the house was a small lamp on an end table in the living room. That and the fact that Muh'Dear was so groggy prevented her from seeing the ugly stain on my dress as I stood over her and told her what a great time we had had.

My last two weeks of high school were the most pleasant days out of the whole thirteen years I'd been going to school. All because I'd finally stood up for myself. Kids who had never said "hi" to me before smiled and spoke to me. In the last three of our gym classes, the ball team leaders all but fought to choose me to play on their sides. I was not impressed when a good-looking boy who had stared at me at the prom asked in the cafeteria a few days later if I had a boyfriend. To avoid complications, I told him yes. Lena didn't return to school after the prom, and, according to the grapevine, it was because of her four missing front teeth. I thought about her receiving her diploma through the mail when I marched across the stage in my cap and gown to receive mine.

"If only Brother Boatwright had lived to see this day," Muh'Dear sobbed afterward on the way home from the graduation ceremonies in Judge Lawson's car.

The night I graduated was another sleepless night for me. I sat up wondering what I was going to do with myself from that point on.

Rhoda and Otis were married in her parents' living room three weeks after our graduation.

Moline, Lola's grandkids, and the twins came from Alabama again, in addition to some relatives on Rhoda's mother's side from New Orleans as well as the usual neighborhood crowd.

Jock came home for Rhoda's wedding but was scheduled to go to Vietnam in a few days, so Mrs. Nelson paid him more attention than she did Rhoda.

"Don't you worry none, Annette. Somewhere in this universe there's a man that's goin' to marry you," Caleb told me during the reception, patting my arm.

I smiled sadly and thanked him.

It was getting late, and people had started to leave. I had not had a chance to talk to Rhoda privately.

I finally got to do so when she summoned me to her dollhouse.

"I don't know when I'll see you again. We're leavin' tomorrow night, and we'll be real busy 'til then," Rhoda told me. Her daddy was sending her and Otis to Jamaica for two weeks, where they would combine their honeymoon with a visit to some of his relatives. From there they would move to their own house near Miami.

"I am going to miss you so much." I cried and smiled at the same time.

"I'll only be a phone call away," she said, looking at me, then squeezing me real tight. Then her body suddenly tensed, and I heard her suck in her breath. "Um . . . you won't forget to keep our secret will you?"

"What secret?" I mouthed.

"You know . . . Buttwright?"

I looked away and spoke like I was talking to myself. "Poor Mr. Boatwright . . . died in his sleep."

CHAPTER 41

I spent the next week mildly depressed. Not counting her trip to the Bahamas with her family, this was the first time Rhoda and I had been separated since we had become friends. Even though I was feeling strangely independent, I had no idea that I was going to miss her as much as I did. Then she called me from Florida. As soon as I heard her voice, I broke down and cried like a baby.

"Why can't you live up here?" I sobbed.

"I have to go where my husband goes, girl. I love him. And besides, we can't grow oranges in Ohio." She laughed.

We talked for twenty minutes, but I was still a little depressed after we got off the phone. We had not discussed anything profound. She told me all about her new location and what it was like being a married woman. I was happy for her on one hand but jealous and bitter on the other. It didn't seem fair that a girl like Rhoda, who had everything going for her, always got what she wanted, whether she deserved it or not.

I missed going to her house. I missed sitting on that lush couch in her living room watching her sophisticated parents parade in and out with their equally sophisticated friends. I was sorry that school was out. I had no job and very little to do with myself. As much as I enjoyed reading, watching movies, and eating, there was a limit. There was more to life, but whatever it was, it wasn't going to come to me; I had to go out and find it. I had the whole house all to myself when Muh'Dear was at work, but I still spent a great deal of time in my bedroom trying to put Mr. Boatwright and the horrible way he died out of my mind. I tried to imagine what it must have been like for him to have that pillow pressed down on his face cutting off his air until he died. Nobody deserved to die the way he did. On more than one occasion I had been tempted to ask Rhoda if he had suffered, but I'd stopped myself.

To make matters even worse, Pee Wee joined the army the first week in July. Before he left he told me it was to prove that he was a real man. The rumors about him liking boys had reached him years earlier. Though he laughed it off, it clearly hurt him. I missed him immediately. Then Florence moved to Toledo to go to a school for the handicapped, then on to teach blind kids. I felt truly abandoned. Rhoda, Pee Wee, and Florence were the only close friends my age I had ever had in my whole life, and now they were all gone. I knew that if and when we all got back together to sit around and gossip and hang out, things would never be the same.

I hid my depression from Muh'Dear. As a matter of fact, I don't think she ever knew I was ever depressed in my life. I pitied my mama, but in some ways I envied her ignorance.

A few days after my conversation with Rhoda I started my first real job as a telephone operator. I was still depressed but I pretended to be excited about it. Even though I was going to dress up and take the bus and or a cab to one of the nicest areas in town to get to the phone company five days a week, my life seemed like it was going nowhere without Rhoda around to share it.

I hated the job at the phone company immediately. It was boring, and the pay was low. I couldn't save much money because I spent most of my paycheck on a new wardrobe, transportation expenses, and expensive lunches. I was the only Black operator, and though there were a few other big-boned women, I was the only one that weighed 244 pounds. I was too self-conscious to try and make friends with any of my coworkers. None of the other operators invited me to lunch or talked to me during our breaks, unless it was work-related. I blamed that on the way I looked. Muh'Dear didn't agree with my theory when I told her what I thought. "Annette, one thing I know is, you can't blame everythin' on them two factors, being fat and Black. In some cases yeah, but not in all cases. With God you can override the devil. With Him all you need is the right attitude. That's the key to success, not what you look like. Change your attitude, go after what you want, and if you don't get it, make a detour and go after somethin' else you want. With the right attitude, you'll eventually get all the rest of it anyway. Look at me. Me and you done been through so much since your daddy run off. And buhlieve me, God ain't through with us yet!"

Sometimes some of the things Muh'Dear said made a lot of sense. Even before she told me, I knew that I would have to make an attitude adjustment before I could find happiness. I was smart, and I knew it. But there's a certain level of stupidity in everybody. So that's why to this day, I believe it was pure stupidity that made me go to Scary Mary thinking she was my only hope.

CHAPTER 42

The bottom had dropped out of my precarious world, and I was hanging on by the skin of my teeth. As much as I hated men, or as much as I *thought* I hated them, I was willing to sleep with them for money.

A few weeks earlier I would never have considered prostitution. Lord knows I was too timid, and my self-esteem was too low for me to approach men on most levels. But Mr. Boatwright's murder had elevated my desperation level to an all-time high. I needed money, and I was ready to do whatever I had to do to get it.

With Rhoda gone, I was on my own. The first step was to move away from the environment that had robbed me of my innocence in the first place. Turning tricks seemed to be the quickest and easiest way for me to put my clumsy plan in motion.

It took me an hour of practicing what I was going to say before I went to Scary Mary's house. I was nervous and unsure of myself. I had no other options to consider. If she rejected me, I would be right back where I started. From there I didn't know which direction I'd go.

"Look, Scary Mary, I need some serious money, and I need it fast, like by the end of next week. I need at least a thousand dollars to move out on my own with," I told the madam.

"What's that got to do with me?" Scary Mary was wearing a red-silk housecoat and already drinking whiskey from a coffee cup at 8 A.M. on a Saturday morning.

"I want to work for you," I explained. I was standing in her kitchen doorway. She and her daughter Mott were sitting at the table. Mott was wrestling with a big plate of assorted breakfast items. She threw her spoon at me. Scary Mary never tried to discipline her retarded daughter. She didn't even react to Mott throwing the spoon and getting grits all over my clean dress. I picked up the spoon and gave it back to Mott.

"WAH!" Mott yelled at me.

I moved farther away from the table and returned my attention to the madam. I just looked at her real hard through narrowed eyes with my heart racing a mile a minute, waiting for her to respond to my proposal.

"You want to work for me? Doin' what? Dustin', moppin', sweepin', and or cookin'?" Scary Mary laughed, cackling like a hen. "You want to leave the phone company to do all that?"

"No, Ma'am," I said, shaking my head.

She raised both eyebrows and whispered, "What then?"

"Turning tricks," I announced boldly. "I know enough about the business, and I'm old enough now," I said, unable to conceal my impatience.

Scary Mary looked me up and down, in a mean, critical way that made me feel like less than nothing. I certainly felt like nothing the way her eyes were blinking and her head bobbing up and down. I got a lump in my throat just recalling that day when Mr. Boatwright was on top of me, and I told myself that if I reached adulthood I would share my life only with women and cats. Well, my life had taken an odd turn. I never truly developed my lesbian tendencies, and Muh'Dear had never let me own a cat.

Scary Mary laughed like a hyena for two minutes. "I don't know who you been talkin' to, girl. What makes you think *you* can make a thousand dollars in a week turnin' tricks? Even *I* couldn't make that kind of money turnin' tricks in no one week. And what do you know about . . . um . . . the um . . . *my* business?"

"Well I . . . might be a lot of things, but I am not stupid and I am not blind, Scary Mary. Muh'Dear and I used to live with you. Remember?"

The old crow gave me a long, hard look. "All that don't mean nothin'. What I meant was, what you know about pleasin' a man?"

I looked at her just as long and just as hard as she looked at me. "I've had a lot of experience. I know what men like," I said seriously. Our eyes locked, and her bottom lip trembled.

Scary Mary drank from her cup before responding. Then she laughed again. "In the first place, you ain't no Liz Taylor," she informed me, shaking her head.

"I know that. Like I said, I am not blind," I mumbled. I had never tried to fool myself. I knew that I was not beautiful. But fucking was not about beauty. Besides, I had seen Scary Mary's girls over the years. She had never had any you could call beautiful. When I was around eight she even had one who was almost as retarded as Mott, but who knew how to get what she wanted from men. And then there was the one with polio. The one I liked most was Lula, the crazy one. Lula had worked for Scary Mary for just a few weeks, like most of her girls, when I was eleven. Lula looked and even acted normal most of the time. But when she didn't take her medication, she ran out of the house naked. Two or three times a week Lula would run out of the house naked, pluck a switch from one of Scary Mary's trees, and run until she found a school playground, where she'd beat and chase the kids. Scary Mary and some of her other girls would have to chase her and throw a sheet over her. Scary Mary currently had five women working for her. Two were over forty, one weighed fifty pounds more than I did, and the other two were just average.

No matter how I begged and pleaded, Scary Mary would not let me work for her as a prostitute. She said I could look after Mott, run errands, and do a little cleaning around the house. I agreed to do all that; I just didn't tell anybody.

I quit the telephone operator job and started working for Scary Mary the next day without telling Muh'Dear.

A week after I started working for her, Scary Mary moved five blocks away to an even larger and grander house. Her new place, a five-bedroom, red-shingled building, had a birdbath and a flower bed in the front yard. It was right around the corner from Antonosanti's, where most of her prosperous customers dined. "Now the menfolk can get here even quicker," she said to me and Muh'Dear the day after she moved.

I cleaned that big house, emptied funky trash cans filled with used condoms and whiskey bottles, washed and pressed the prostitutes' work clothes, and performed other duties, like running to the store and going to pay bills. I also baby-sat Mott.

One day it rained hard and one of the men, a former Black preacher I had run to the store for a few times, offered to give me a ride home. Five minutes after I'd gotten into his car, he propositioned me, and I accepted without hesitation. He paid me fifteen dollars just to masturbate him.

"You be a good little girl and make 'Daddy' feel nice . . . hear?" he slobbered in my ear. He was no worse than Mr. Boatwright. In fact, he was better-looking, and he certainly smelled better. Even though my skin was crawling, I forced myself to smile and promised him I would and I did. He was so hot he couldn't even make it to a motel just five more minutes away. I did it in his car in an alley behind the city library. It took two minutes.

When I got home I plunged the hand I had jacked the ex-preacher off with into the hottest bowl of Clorox bleach and water I could stand. That night I was in such a state of disbelief over what I had done, I had to sleep with the lights on.

I felt nothing for men so far, so it didn't faze me one way or the other if I made them pay for me to make them feel good. I justified my actions by telling myself, if I've got to do it anyway sooner or later with a husband, if I ever got crazy enough to get married, why not do it now and get paid for it. The money would make up for the times I'd have to do it with a husband for free.

This ex-preacher and several others became my regulars. Before long, I didn't even need the other odd jobs, the things Scary Mary had me doing. I quit, but I didn't tell her why.

With Mama still working so much, I was alone most of the time. My tricks just called me up at home and told me what they wanted and where to meet them. Motels, hotels, their cars, alleys; I didn't care. More and more each day I despised what I had become. I was selling the very thing that had made most of my life so miserable, sex. Like Rhoda's aunt Lola had told me, it was the best card a woman had to play.

I had always believed that Mr. Boatwright was probably the biggest, weakest motherfucker in the world when it came to sex. Well when I saw the way some of my tricks carried on over a three-minute blow job, I began to see men in an even more disgusting light. Most of them were mature, married, and successful in whatever their business was. But they were subhuman. They had to be! They were risking losing their lives, their families, and their children over an orgasm that lasted only a few moments.

It took me two months of prostituting myself to save enough money to leave home. I went through it all in a mild daze. I didn't feel a thing and didn't give it much thought when I was doing it. During that dark period of my life I thought of it as just a job.

Because of a minor stroke, Judge Lawson was now almost exclusively confined to his bed and a wheelchair. He still had his poker parties, but he couldn't drive anymore, and when he left the house it was in a specially made van driven by a chauffeur. He needed round-the-clock care. Another woman and a driver had been brought in to help Muh'Dear. In a way I was glad. Not glad about the judge's failing health, but glad because Muh'Dear didn't have to spend so much time at his house. In addition to all that, Muh'Dear got involved in two things. One, the most important of the two in my opinion, night school! "You the first and only one in my family to graduate from high school. I want to be the second one," she told me shyly one evening. I had encouraged her and even helped her select the appropriate courses and school.

"I'm so glad you got that telephone-operator job. I can finally cut back on my hours even more," Muh'Dear told me.

Since the judge was not in the picture as much as he had been, the other thing Muh'Dear involved herself with was another man. I think of my mother as some kind of a magnet. Like Mr. Boatwright, he just showed up at our house one day out of nowhere. I had never seen him around town before even though Muh'Dear told me he had lived in Ohio longer than anybody else she knew.

The whole business just about scared me to death, but I didn't tell her how I felt. All I wanted was for her to be happy.

"This here is Mr. King," Muh'Dear introduced him that Sunday night. "He *owns* the Buttercup restaurant."

I was amazed at how much emphasis she put on the word *own*. Her face lit up like a lamp as she talked. I had just returned from performing three tricks in an alley across town, with almost two hundred dollars inside my bra.

I recalled the day I came home from school when I was six and found out that Muh'Dear had moved Mr. Boatwright in with us. At first, I figured that this Mr. King was going to move in with us, too, and it pissed me off. If that was the case, I'd have to work overtime so I could move out even quicker. There was no way I was going to risk going through another episode like the one with Mr. Boatwright with another man Muh'Dear had moved in with us to help out.

"Where you been all day, girl?" Muh'Dear asked me.

"I was visiting some friends from work," I lied. I had not bathed yet and could still feel the men's sweat on my body. I hated it, but my need for money kept me from stopping. I had two more men lined up for the next day. "Is he moving in with us?" I said quickly.

The man gasped.

Mama rolled her eyes at me.

"Naw, he ain't movin' in with us. Mr. King got him a big old house all to hisself right next door to his restaurant."

"Oh, that's nice," I mumbled uneasily.

"My girl here is a phone operator," Muh'Dear told the man. "I'm so glad she such a good girl. Oh now she's strayed off the track a mite. When she was a young'n, got herself in the family way by mistake. The Lord saw fit to make her miscarry and, praise Him, she been on the straight and narrow ever since."

"Give thanks," the man nodded. "My girl got herself in the same fix when she was fourteen. Now she twenty-five, married to a serviceman, and I got me two grandbabies runnin' around somewhere out there on that island of Hawaii." The man and Muh'Dear groaned at the same time. He was her age, tall and tan and rather handsome. He still had most of his hair and a nice set of pearly white teeth. His thick black mustache was streaked with gray.

"I ate at your restaurant one time, Mr. King," I said shyly.

"Well I do hope you enjoyed the food and the service!" he told me with great excitement, standing to shake my hand. My hand felt too dirty for anybody to be shaking it. My whole body felt dirty. No matter how many baths I took, I could never wash away the nastiness that went along with being a prostitute.

Muh'Dear's new friend started babbling on about something, but I wasn't listening. My mind was on too many other things. Like the men I had spent the last few hours with. I could hardly look in Muh'Dear's face without wanting to throw up. But every time I felt that way, I justified what I had resorted to by telling myself that after all the times Mr. Boatwright had used me and paid me only a nickel I deserved as much as I could get from other weak men.

I sat with them in the living room and listened to Muh'Dear talk about her schoolwork.

"As soon as I finish school, get my GED, I'm goin' to start lookin' for a night college!" she hollered. "I ain't goin' to be no simple simon the rest of my life."

"College?" I mouthed. College was something I had never even considered for myself.

"I want to study business administration. I'd like to have some business know-how, so I will be ready to run my own business." Muh'Dear paused and looked directly at Mr. King, sitting next to her on the couch. "My girl is goin' to get her a fancy office job and make lots of money. She goin' to finance me a restaurant when she make her first million." She paused again and this time, she turned to face me. "Ain't you?"

"Uh-huh. A restaurant and that long-overdue trip to the Bahamas," I added.

CHAPTER 43

What made my life even more miserable was the fact that *another* man had somehow come between Muh'Dear and me, and I didn't want to have to live around that again. I wanted my mother to be happy, and if she could find happiness with some man, I would force myself to accept it.

"Me and Mr. King thinkin' about takin' a little trip ourselves one day soon," Muh'Dear told me. She had only known him a few weeks!

I was shocked and horrified when Muh'Dear took a day off from her work and went to an amusement park with Mr. King. I was at "work" when they left, so I didn't see what she had on until she got home. A pair of shorts!

I called Rhoda as soon as Muh'Dear and Mr. King left to go out to dinner. "My mama's been drinking like a fish!" I yelled into the phone. "Not just beer, but whiskey and brandy."

"What's wrong with that? I wish my mama was well enough to get out and enjoy herself." Rhoda was so calm she made me angrier.

"She's never done that kind of stuff before that hard and heavy!"

I heard Rhoda let out a loud sigh.

"You better hurry and get yourself to Erie, Pennsylvania. You're goin' nowhere fast. Pee Wee is gone, I'm gone. Even Florence is gone. Why are you still hangin' around Richland?"

"I'm saving money for my ticket."

"You've been workin' long enough to have saved your fare. Look, you sit down and decide what day you're leavin'. I'm not goin' to talk to you again until you call me from Erie." Rhoda hung up on me. I felt bad because I had not even asked her about her pregnancy, and since she hung up on me, I was too afraid to call her right back to ask.

I cried for a while, then I sat down and figured out how much money I had saved up. Fifteen hundred dollars. The next evening when Muh'Dear got in from the movies and came to my room to tell me what a good time she had had with Mr. King, I told her. I told her, "I'm moving to Erie soon. I don't know exactly when yet, but it'll be before Thanksgiving, so I can avoid the holiday crowds." A sad look appeared on her face. She let out a deep sigh, and then she sat down on the side of my bed. I had already turned in for the night.

She just looked at me for a moment, like she was studying every inch of my face.

"You really leavin' me?" she rasped. Tears had already formed in her eyes. "You don't have to go nowhere if you don't want to. You can live with me the rest of your life if you want to."

I shook my head. "I can't, Muh'Dear. It's time for me to get out in the world and see if I can make it on my own," I said with a forced smile.

"You just got out of school. Lots of kids don't leave home 'til they get in their twenties," she informed me.

"I'm ready now, Muh'Dear. I've been ready for a long time."

Muh'Dear sighed and looked around the room. "This room sure could stand a new paint job. Uh . . . I'll get you some new suitcases in the mornin'." She returned her attention to me and gave me a big smile, though there were still tears in her eyes.

"OK, Muh'Dear." I smiled and gave her a bear hug.

I packed everything I wanted to take the Sunday night before my departure date, almost four months after my eighteenth birthday. I didn't really have a plan as far as my future was concerned. I figured a few months or maybe a year or two in a place where I didn't know anybody would give me the time I needed to get a grip. Besides, turning tricks, even for the short time I had, had worn me out. I felt dirty and cheap. Even though it was all behind me, I still took two baths a day, gargled frequently, and douched before going to bed every night.

Muh'Dear arrived home unexpectedly in a cab from Judge Lawson's house around 5 P.M. "Why are you home so early? I haven't even put dinner on yet," I said.

For once she didn't look tired after working most of the day. She gave me one of her biggest smiles and gripped my shoulders. " 'Cause

I want to send you off with a bang. Get your coat. The cab's waitin'. We got a reservation at Antonosanti's."

Muh'Dear and I didn't talk much during the cab ride. In fact, I sat up front with the driver on purpose, hoping I could carry on a conversation with him instead. Muh'Dear asked me over and over if I had packed my Bible, my good dress, toothbrush, things like that. In addition to those items, I had also packed things that I would never use again, particularly clothes I'd outgrown, but that reminded me of special events I'd shared with Rhoda. Things Rhoda had given to me, like some stiletto heels her Aunt Lola had given to her that she didn't want. I had worn the shoes only once, to the prom. I had also packed my prom dress, which I had not had cleaned on purpose. I would never wear it again, so the stain made by Lena Cundiff's punch didn't matter. I left it stained because I never wanted to forget what she did to me and what I did to her.

After we entered the restaurant, Mr. Nelson was the first person I spotted, sitting at the bar. He had an unlit cigar in one hand and a shot glass full of whatever he was drinking in the other. Sitting next to him was Mr. Antonosanti. He was smoking his cigar, and there was a full shot glass in his hand, too. I would have gone over to speak to them if Uncle Johnny had not appeared, staggering from a side entrance near the men's room. Antonosanti's was the nicest restaurant in Richland, but it was too expensive for average people. It was a large, dimly lit place with live plants leaping out from big vases on the floor. On the walls were paintings of Roman soldiers in uniforms hugging thick-bodied women. Music, women wailing in Italian, filled the main dining area.

The place was crowded with well-dressed white patrons stretching their necks and shading their eyes with their hands to look at me and Muh'Dear as we strutted proudly across the floor. I was glad Muh'Dear requested a booth near the back for privacy. "Let us try to stroll into a place like this in Florida. Them white folks would set the dogs on us so fast," Muh'Dear said under her breath.

The only thing I felt a little uneasy about was the fact that we were so casually dressed. Under my trench coat I had on blue jeans and a gray smock. Muh'Dear had on her black-and-white maid's uniform. We didn't check our coats at the front. We didn't remove them and place them on the other side of the booth until we had ordered. "Add a bottle of your best champagne," Muh'Dear told the waiter. The friendly young man hesitated, then looked at me with his eyebrows raised. "Don't worry, she's twenty-one. You can ask your boss, Mr. Antonosanti . . . good friend of my boss, Judge Lawson," Muh'Dear told him, speaking out of the side of her mouth. The waiter nodded and winked before he left. "They better not give me no stuff in here. I'll sic Judge Lawson on 'em and make 'em lose their liquor license. Straighten your collar, girl."

I straightened my collar and brushed off my dingy smock. "I guess we could have dressed up a little," I said with a sigh.

"We didn't have time. I wasn't sure I could get away from the judge, so that's why I didn't call you at the house earlier to tell you we was goin' out." Muh'Dear smiled as our waiter returned pushing a cart with a bucket on top of it. I didn't know one bottle of champagne from another. But since Muh'Dear had requested the best, I was sure this would be something good.

"Compliments of Mr. Nelson," the waiter told us.

I gasped and turned to look toward the bar. Mr. Nelson had left, but Mr. Antonosanti and Uncle Johnny were still nursing their drinks.

After the waiter popped open the champagne, poured it into our glasses and left, Muh'Dear took a long swallow and let out a great belch. "It's too late for me, but I hope you marry a man like Brother Nelson someday."

I took a long swallow before I answered, frowning at the way the liquid burned my throat "I hope I do, too," I replied, covering my mouth with my hand to silence a burp I felt coming on.

Muh'Dear refilled our glasses. "We forgot to toast." She laughed excitedly, waving the bottle in the air. After we toasted to "nothin' but good times in our future," Muh'Dear set her glass on the table and fished a handkerchief out of her purse, blew her nose, and dabbed both eyes. "I guess now is the time for me to let you know just how good a man Brother Boatwright was."

"What?" I had to finish my drink to handle whatever was coming. Muh'Dear put her handkerchief back in her purse, then pulled out a long white envelope.

She cleared her throat and blinked real hard a few times first. "This is for you from Brother Boatwright." She opened the envelope and pulled out what I thought was a money order and slid it across the table to me.

I didn't say anything right away because I didn't know what to say. It was a ten-thousand-dollar cashier's check made out to me.

"He had told me, bless his heart, if he died before me, I was to use his life insurance money to pay for his funeral and split the change fifty-fifty with you. But he told me not to give yours to you until I felt it was the time you needed it the most."

"I . . . I don't . . . know . . . know what to say," I stuttered. I didn't know what to say. If Muh'Dear could have read my mind, she probably would have fainted. I was thinking about all the whoring I'd done to scrape up the money I needed to finance my relocation. My hand started shaking so hard Muh'Dear got a worried look on her face and filled our glasses again.

"As soon as you get to that Erie, put it in a bank. And whatever you do, don't go around blabbin' to *nobody* about it. Folks get crazy when they know you settin' on a gold mine. It would be just like some smooth-talkin' con man like that Johnny yonder there at the bar to try to take it from you to drink and gamble away and spend on some other woman. Some men is like that. I know 'cause I seen 'em do it. Don't slouch in your seat, girl. You'll get a humpback."

I was glad the waiter arrived with our steak and spaghetti dinners. The distraction allowed me enough time to catch my breath. I looked at the check for a full minute to make sure I was seeing right. "Ten thousand dollars?" I mouthed. "This is for ten thousand dollars!"

"I know how much it's for. I'm the one that went to the bank to get it. Don't buck your eyes out like that with all these white folks lookin' at us, girl."

"Oh what am I going to do with all this money?" I asked, waving the check in the air.

"You're goin' to carry it with you and save it for when you really need it. Now put it in your pocketbook before somebody come snatch it."

Mr. King drove Muh'Dear and me to the bus station the next morning. "I'll wait in the car," he told us, after giving me a big hug. Muh'Dear insisted on waiting inside with me until I got checked in. He started to leave, then turned back with a silly grin on his face. "Go with God, Annette." I just smiled and waved to him.

"I have a feelin' I won't see you again for a long, long time," Muh'Dear said. She looked so tired and old, even with the makeup. Working for so many years and such long hours had taken its toll. It was only at this moment that I was truly glad she had Mr. King. "At least, not the little gal that's gettin' on that bus today. You ain't goin' to never be the same."

"You're right, Muh'Dear. I'll never be the same again," I said sadly. I promised myself that the old Annette Goode was dead. My rebirth had been a long time coming. I was leaving behind all the ugliness I had known for eighteen years.

We stood in line behind seven other travelers, and the line was moving so slow Muh'Dear and I got a chance to talk a lot.

"I knowed it. You ain't never goin' to be the same no more after you leave here today."

"How did you know?"

"Oh, just a feelin'. You'll get a fancy job workin' for the mayor or a politician and eventually forget all about us little people. It happens all the time. Your Aunt Berneice's latest old man called me the other day from New Jersey, where him and Berneice moved to work for the Piaz family and told me you'll be home in a month beggin' for a piece of toast, standin' in the welfare line, or holdin' a tin cup. Like he would know. He ain't never even met you. What he don't know is Berneice is on the verge of gettin' a divorce from his sorry ass. I know you was too young then to remember, but the Piaz family the ones what had the old granny you used to set with on the porch."

"I remember that old lady," I said, smiling sadly. I recalled the many times the old woman and I sat on the porch throwing rocks at cars and chasing kids with switches.

"You remember old lady Piaz? You wasn't but three," Muh'Dear said, a surprised, amused look on her face. "You can't remember back that far."

"I remember a lot that happened when I was three and four years old. All that walking to get to your work, my squirrel with the white paw, that old woman that hit you with her cane, that tornado, and most of all those dreadful clodhoppers we found in a trash can that you made me wear."

Muh'Dear gave me a strange look, and said, "You don't remember your daddy, do you?"

"Oh yes I do. He left the morning after that tornado with a white woman in a green car. You told me a long time ago he moved to Texas and that we would never see him again," I said, my eyes staring off to the side.

"And we won't, I hope!" Muh'Dear snarled. "Anyway, I know you'll do good in that Erie, Pennsylvania. Me and you, we natural-born survivors. Brother Boatwright comin' into our lives was just the beginnin'. God ain't through with us yet. Look what He done for us—He got

Brother Boatwright still lookin' out for us from beyond the grave . . . leavin' us all that insurance money."

"I know. I know," I said with great sadness and my head lowered. "And I'll show Aunt Berneice and her old man, whoever he is. Them and everybody else," I said firmly. And I would. I just didn't know what I was going to show people.

"You ain't got to show me nothin'. I'm your mama. I don't care if you make a fool out of yourself or what. I just want you to be happy. I'll tell you one thin'. Mr. Parker at the hardware store, you remember I cleaned for his mama before Judge Lawson hired me. He told me to tell you if things don't work out for you in that new city, he'll give you a job behind the counter at his hardware store."

"Tell him thanks." We both had tears in our eyes, but somehow we both managed a smile.

" 'Course you could always go back to the phone company if you have to move back to Richland. Everybody always tellin' me what a nice proper voice you got. Like the girls on TV." Muh'Dear grinned proudly.

The line moved forward a little. I pushed my luggage along with my foot.

"I wish Brother Boatwright was alive. Things would be so different."

I stiffened. "They sure would be," I snapped. Muh'Dear gave me a surprised look, then she straightened the collar on my tweed coat and brushed the sleeves. Even though he was dead, I didn't have the nerve to tell Muh'Dear about Mr. Boatwright abusing me. I didn't know if she would believe me. And if she did, would she blame me? I knew that if I ever did tell her, our relationship would never be the same again, and I liked it the way it was.

"Brother Boatwright was right proud of you. Everythin' he advised me on was for your benefit. His real concern was keepin' you in line 'til we got you a husband. So many girls in Richland had to give up their dreams to raise babies alone. Brother Boatwright's the one that persuaded me—"

"Let's not talk about him anymore."

"It's too painful, ain't it?" Muh'Dear sighed.

"Uh-huh," I agreed, looking around.

"What I wouldn't do to be young again so I can do better with my life," Muh'Dear commented, giving me a thoughtful look.

"What would you do differently?" I asked, looking in her sad face.

"There's somethin' I'd *never* do if I had it to do over again. I had men usin' me like they had paid for me by the pound. Don't never let no man use you . . . for money. It ain't worth it. There's always a better way. I am so proud you ain't the type to end up doin' . . . what I done, what the girls in Scary Mary's house do . . ." Muh'Dear shook her head as hard as she could. "It's the worst thing a woman can do to her body."

"I know it is, and I'll never do it," I said, nodding and deliberately looking away so she couldn't see my lying eyes.

We didn't talk for a few moments.

"Did I tell you Judge Lawson's havin' a little birthday celebration for me next Friday before his poker party?"

"No, Ma'am. You didn't tell me."

"Well he just told me day 'fore yestiddy." Muh'Dear paused and chuckled softly. "Poor thin'. Dyin' right before my eyes, but he still havin' his parties and guzzlin' his highballs. See how good God'll be to you when you do right by God? That's the one thin' I hope you never forget."

I nodded. "I'll call you for sure to wish you happy birthday."

"Fifty-two." Muh'Dear sighed. "Sometime it feel like a hundred and fifty-two."

"Fifty-three," I corrected with a chuckle.

Muh'Dear shrugged and shook her head. "Fifty-somethin' years old and the white folks *still* call me *girl*." Muh'Dear paused and looked me up and down. "Don't you forget that." Her eyes watered.

"What?"

"To the white folks you'll always be a girl. You can't never sass none of 'em don't care what they do to you. I'll never get over the way we used to have to hide from the Klan 'cause your daddy was the outspoken kind always sassin' white folks back in Florida. Lord, the way he took off with that white woman that mornin' was suicide. I bet they didn't make it two miles. I bet his carcass layin' rotten in the Everglades with a rope 'round his neck right as we speak." Muh'Dear sobbed, then fished her handkerchief from her bosom and wiped away a tear and blew her nose.

I don't know why I said what I said next. "Muh'Dear, the way things were for you, did you ever wish you'd never been born? Or that you were dead?"

"Never in my life." She closed her eyes for just a moment, and her lips curled up at the corners. "I'm glad I was born. And I sure ain't

ready to lay down and die. At least not until I get to see the Bahamas,"
she said longingly.

"And get that restaurant," I added.

"And get that restaurant." She smiled, and with a mischievous glint
in her eye, added, "Just like Mr. King's."

CHAPTER 44

I arrived in Erie on a gloomy morning just before noon. The trip had taken a little more than two and a half hours, with several stops along the way.

I stumbled off the bus, retrieved my luggage, and crawled into the backseat of the first available yellow cab.

"Is there a cheap but nice motel close to the downtown area you can take me to?" I asked the middle-aged East Indian driver.

"There is many cheap motel, hotel."

"Well can you take me to one. As long as it is near the downtown area. The nearest Travelodge will do," I instructed.

Erie looked a lot like Richland. The bus station was located in a fairly nice-looking area, but once we drove across some train tracks the houses and everything else started looking pretty shabby. One street we drove down reminded me of the street in Richland we had lived on before moving to the nice house on Reed Street. Boisterous, disheveled people looking bitter and tortured were standing on street corners drinking alcohol straight out of the bottle. "Did you have to go *this* way to get to a downtown Travelodge?" I asked.

"I take best route!" the man snapped, waving his hand impatiently.

I had taken a lot of cabs to get from one place to another in Richland. I knew how some greedy cab drivers purposely drove people out of the way so the meter would go higher.

"Well I've only got ten dollars," I lied. The meter was already up to eight dollars and sixty cents. The driver didn't say anything. He just let out a long sigh.

We passed some of the same factories and the same grocery stores a second time. Then, miraculously, two blocks over was the Travelodge. The meter was up to nine dollars and eighty cents. I grabbed my two suitcases and got out as fast as I could. The driver made no attempt to get out to help me. I handed him a ten, and said, "Keep the change." He looked at the crumpled bill, rolled his eyes at me, then sped off.

I had never stayed in a motel or hotel before in my life. This one reminded me of most of the shacks we had lived in in Florida. The room was small and dark, but it was clean. I had a decent bathroom with plenty of fluffy white towels, a mini refrigerator, and a color TV. Before I even took off my coat, I called Muh'Dear and was glad she didn't answer. I needed time to gather my thoughts and continue to try and come up with a plan. Caleb had offered to give me some phone numbers of some of his relatives, but I didn't take them. After some of the things I'd heard about his relatives from Pee Wee, they didn't sound like the type of people I wanted as new friends. Some had prison records, and some were violent and couldn't be trusted he had told me.

Walking two blocks I discovered a decent-looking restaurant near the motel. I ate a roast beef dinner and picked up a newspaper on my way back to my room. I was not impressed with the *Erie Review* want ads. Most of the office jobs required some college and experience, and the restaurants wanted waitresses with experience. I couldn't drive that well, so the ad for cab drivers was useless. There were two types of positions listed that I was qualified for: housekeeper and factory worker. Well, I was not wild about becoming a housekeeper. I had come too far for that. Even though I knew that Muh'Dear loved cooking and cleaning and raising other folks' kids, I didn't. I circled an ad for the Erie Manufacturing Company, where they assembled garage-door openers, and a place called Bolton's, where they assembled airplane-engine parts.

I waited another hour before I called Muh'Dear again. This time Mr. King answered the phone. "It's me. I just wanted to let Muh'Dear . . . and you know I made it all right. Is my mama there?"

"She in the shower," Mr. King told me. "But I'll sure and tell her you called." I chatted with him for a few minutes, then hung up.

I guess I was more tired than I realized. I fell into a deep sleep and didn't wake up until noon the next day. I could survive without work-

ing for a few months if I lived cheaply with the money I had. I picked
up the newspaper again and turned to the section advertising places
for rent. Even though Erie didn't look too much better than
Richland, the rents were surprisingly high. I didn't see a single ad for
a studio for less than a hundred dollars. In Richland you could rent a
fully furnished studio in a fairly nice neighborhood for fifty dollars or
less, and that would include utilities! My Travelodge room was fifteen
dollars a day, and I had no cooking facilities. After looking through
the want ads, I wasn't sure I would find an affordable place and a job
in one week. I pulled out the yellow pages and called a dozen more
downtown motels looking for cheaper ones, or at least one with a
kitchenette. Seven of the dozen charged ten dollars a day but none of
them had cooking facilities. Five told me I'd be allowed to use a hot
plate and I could store perishable items in the office refrigerator.
They were all located on the same downtown area street. I was told
that all I had to do was come with enough money and sign in.

I called a cab and had him drop me off at one of the seven motels I
had called. Since they were all offering pretty much the same things,
I figured I'd just check into the first one on the list.

The cab left me in front of the Prince Street Motel, next to a large
sign advertising vacancies. I took my time looking around the immediate area. It was a tree-lined, clean, and busy street. From where I
stood I could see the few office buildings that made up downtown
Erie. There were bus stops on both sides of Prince Street, but downtown was within walking distance. It was a bright dog day but chilly
like Richland the day I left which was why I put on my fall coat instead
of packing it. It was my favorite time of the year. During this time of
the year the leaves on the trees in states like Ohio and Pennsylvania
turn all different shades of brown, gold, and yellow and fall to the
ground, covering it like snow. When I was very young, before Rhoda
entered my life, Mr. Boatwright used to rake up the leaves from the
trees in our yard. He would shape them into mounds or sometimes
pyramids as tall as I was and I would play in them for hours.

My plan was to check into the new motel and stay there until I
found an apartment. In the meantime, I planned to apply for every
job I was qualified for.

Not counting our run-ins with the Klan in Florida, my experience
with motels in Erie, Pennsylvania, was my first real dose of blatant
racism. It was the in-your-face kind that would make anybody want to
get violent.

As soon as I entered the Prince Street Motel office the clerk, a teenage white boy with red freckles all over his face, neck and arms, ran. He disappeared into a back room and was gone for five minutes before he returned with a tall, ponytailed man who looked enough like him to be his father. "Yes—what can I do for you?" the man asked. His deep voice was gruff and impatient. His eyes were so cold I felt a chill. He shifted his weight to one side and folded his arms.

"I called this morning about renting a room," I said, offering my biggest, fakest smile.

"We don't have any vacancies," the man mouthed, his eyes shifted briefly from one side to the other.

"I called this morning and left my name. Your sign even says—"

"We don't have any vacancies," the man repeated. "The sign's out of order."

"I see," I mumbled. The scene was repeated in all the rest of the motels I had called the same morning. There were other motels along the way that I had called, but they were more expensive. I didn't even bother to check with them. My head was reeling, and I was so overwhelmed I couldn't think clearly. I just kept walking down Prince Street toward town. After ten minutes an empty cab stopped at the light I was waiting for. The young white driver smiled and yelled, "Do you need a cab, Miss?" I was just a few more blocks from the Travelodge, but I think the real reason I got into the cab was because the driver seemed so nice. And after what I had just experienced with white folks, his friendliness went a long way with me. "Where to?" he asked. He started whistling along with a tune coming from a small transistor radio on the dashboard.

"The Travelodge on Noble Street next to the Shell station," I told him. The cab shot off like a bullet.

"Think we're gonna have another one of those killer winters like we did last year?" the driver asked. He had his arm hanging out the window and was bobbing his head as he continued whistling.

"I'm from Ohio," I said quietly. "Richland. I just got here yesterday."

"The Buckeye State. Mmmm huh," he nodded. "Well we share the same kind of weather. I lived in Cleveland for a few years when I was around your age. Cleveland's a nice city. But Erie's about as big a city I want to deal with. It's clean, low crime rate, and some pretty nice folks."

"I don't know about all that. Nice folks I mean. I just tried to get a

room in seven different motels on Prince Street, and they all told me
they were full. I had called every single one of them just this morning
and was told that they had vacancies," I said angrily.

I looked up at the rearview mirror. The driver was looking through
it at me with pity in his eyes. "Well, some of us still refuse to accept
certain changes. I know of two Black restaurants on Liberty Street
that suddenly run out of everything I want every time I try to eat
there. Assholes come in all colors." We both laughed. "How long do
you need a room for?"

"I'm not sure. Maybe a week or two. I need a place near public
transportation that's cheaper than the place I'm in now until I find a
job and an apartment." I sighed. Like this stranger cared. I was wrong;
he did care.

"My brother-in-law manages a place downtown right next to the police station. It's cheap, clean, and you'd certainly be safe there."

"Will they let me use a hot plate there? Do they have a refrigerator
in the main office or in any of the rooms?" I asked with renewed ea-
gerness. My hands were gripping the back of the driver's seat as I
leaned forward.

"Well, all the rooms I've been in have little kitchenettes. This is not
a motel but one of those residential hotels run by the state," the driver explained. He seemed as excited as I was.

"Do you know if they have any rooms available? Do you have their
phone number—never mind. I've had enough for one day after that
'no room at the inn' drama I just went through."

"Well if they have a vacancy, and if you've got the money, they will
rent to you. A lot of the residents are Black. Mostly single mothers,
new people in town—like yourself."

"Can you take me there now?" I begged.

The hotel the cab driver took me to was called the Richland Hotel.
The name being the same as the city I had grown up in had to mean
something. Muh'Dear and even Mr. Boatwright would insist, "God
tryin' to tell you somethin'." It was a large, tight, brooding gray building with well-worn gray carpets. The minute I stepped into the lobby I
could hear kids yelling and screaming and radios blaring in the background. But it looked clean, there was a security guard in the lobby,
and I was not turned away. I paid two weeks rent at the Richland and
checked out of the Travelodge all within an hour.

My room at the end of a long dark narrow spooky hallway on the
tenth floor was not impressive. The brown furniture was plain and

musty, and you could see through the plastic curtains. I hung up the few clothes I had brought with me and took a long hot bath in a tub that could barely accommodate my body. The hotel had a restaurant on the second floor, where I ordered a fried chicken dinner. The chicken was greasy, overcooked on the outside and raw on the inside, but I ate the sorry mess, knowing I wouldn't have to eat it again unless I wanted to. I didn't even touch the plastic-looking vegetables that had come with it. I ate the French bread, drank the Coke, then left. "Come again," the waitress yelled after me, smiling at the fifteen percent tip I had left on the table.

There was a convenience store across the street from the hotel. With a kitchenette, I could do my own cooking. I was actually humming when I returned to my room and dialed Rhoda's number. I gave her a brief description of my bus ride and the hotel room. "What's it like down there in . . ."

"Atwater," she answered. "Miami is only a few minutes away by car, the weather's fabulous and—oh I just love it here," she squealed.

"I'm happy for you," I lied, speaking in a weak voice. From the day she met Otis, I'd wanted their relationship to fail so that she would have more time for me like she used to.

"Our nearest neighbors, the Fergusons, are five minutes away," Rhoda continued. "They're white, white trash I might add, and most of the family members are not very friendly." She paused, then added in a whisper, "Klan."

"Oh no," I lamented. Suddenly my sadness turned to concern for her safety.

"Oh don't worry. Uncle Johnny used to be in the Klan before he got religion. That's when he realized how generous his Black half brother was. But even when he was in the Klan Uncle Johnny was pretty harmless he claims. I think this crew is pretty harmless, too," she assured me. "Otis's grandpa just hired one of 'em. Now a Klansman willin' to work for a Black can't be too threatenin'," Rhoda laughed.

"Uncle Johnny's not smart or sober long enough to be threatening. You and I both know how dangerous the Klan can be if you step on their toes. They threw a firebomb in our house one time when I was a little girl."

"Well we're mindin' our own business, so they have no reason to fuck with us. The wife, Betty Lou Ferguson, is real friendly. She's in her mid thirties and already has eight kids. The youngest, the only girl, is this cute little thing named April who follows me around like a shadow. She's more anxious for me to have the baby than I am. Hey! When are you goin' to find a job?"

"Soon. But I've got enough money to last for a while."

"Well, if the goin' gets rough, you need a little money or somethin', just let me know."

"I will." I desperately wanted to tell her about the money I had inherited from Mr. Boatwright but saw no point in doing so. Even though I had eagerly accepted it and planned to spend every penny, I felt somewhat hypocritical. Besides, I couldn't have come up with an acceptable excuse not to accept the money.

"Just put aside enough money for a one-way ticket back to Richland, just in case," she instructed. "I have." She brought me up to date on what was happening with her family, and we had a few laughs over Uncle Johnny and how he was borrowing money like mad from Mr. Antonosanti to play poker at Judge Lawson's house. After we hung up, I sat there looking around the room for about ten minutes before my eyes returned to the phone. I took a deep breath, then I called Muh'Dear.

First, she rambled on about some church activities, how Judge Lawson was dying, and what a good man Mr. King was. "Did you put that money in the bank yet?" she wanted to know.

"No, Ma'am—"

"Well, you better do it soon! The last thing I want is to get a phone call from the po'lice tellin' me to come identify your body 'cause somebody done busted your brains out robbin' you."

"Yes, Ma'am." I laughed, rolling my eyes back in my head.

"And no matter what, if things don't work out, you can always come home. Judge Lawson's done fixed it so we'll always have this house to live in, and Mr. King say you can work in his restaurant if you need a job. You read your Bible today?"

"Not yet," I muttered.

"Well you better. You want God to be good to you, you got to be good to Him. Study His word and live by it . . . best you can. Do you hear me?"

"Yes, Ma'am." After I hung up I pulled out the same newspaper I had previously picked up and stared long and hard at the want ads again. I tore out the section advertising the clerical jobs and placed it on the nightstand next to the phone.

CHAPTER 45

"I'm sorry. We're looking for someone with at least two years experience," the thin young Asian personnel representative at the utility company informed me coldly. I sat across from her wearing a dark blue suit and a white scarf around my neck with my stomach churning.

"What about something that doesn't require two years' experience?" I bleated.

The woman shook her head slowly and sighed again. Before speaking, she rose and extended her hand. "I truly am sorry we can't offer you anything at this time." We shook hands, I mumbled a thank-you, and left.

That was my fifth interview in a week. The phone company had some interest in me, but they had no openings. My application and résumé would remain on file for six months. The others had all told me either they had no openings or that experience was a requirement.

My room at the Richland Hotel was beginning to feel like a cell. I only left it to go out to look for work or to get something to eat. A few of the women in the hotel had attempted to befriend me, but I started to avoid them when they started asking me if I could lend them money or if I could baby-sit.

I had not talked to Muh'Dear or Rhoda in the last week, but both of them had called me several times while I was out and left messages with the front desk. I didn't plan to call them back until I had something positive to report. The last thing I wanted was for them to know what a hard time I was having finding a job.

Two more agonizing weeks crawled by, and I was still going on useless interviews and spending more and more money on the hotel, food, and transportation.

The week of Thanksgiving was one of the darkest weeks of my life. Two more places I applied to couldn't talk to me until after the holiday. The personnel rep at the newspaper office called me up the day before Thanksgiving and invited me to come in to interview for a receptionist position. I couldn't sleep much that night. I got up bright and early, took a long hot bath, and put on the best-looking business outfit I had been able to find. I felt glamorous in my dark red wool suit. I brushed my hair back into a neat bun, put on a little makeup and was on my way, strolling down the hallway on my way to the elevator. I felt that this was the job God had been holding for me. The woman who had called me had even said "no experience necessary." The day before, I had applied at three restaurants and two factories only because I had already applied for all the clerical jobs listed in the want ads and some that were not.

I walked into the newspaper office's front lobby and was directed down a long hallway by a security guard. Across from the personnel office was what appeared to be a typing pool, with about twelve young, attractive women. In just a few seconds I scanned the room. It was a bright, neatly organized place with pictures of young kids and smiling husbands or boyfriends on all the desks I could see. Most of the women were white, but there were two Blacks and one Hispanic woman. Then it hit me. They all looked alike, slim and beautiful. The ad had stated that a "front desk appearance" was one of their requirements. Compared to me, all these women looked like models. A couple of them glanced at me with blank expressions. One of the Black women looked me up and down, then went back to her work without a smile or even an acknowledgment. I took a deep breath and headed for the door marked PERSONNEL and knocked.

The personnel representative was even more beautiful than the women in the secretarial pool. She was a young blonde with hair that reminded me of corn silk and skin that looked like porcelain. Her big blue eyes shifted a lot, which to me usually meant a person's uncomfortable or lying. After a few questions about my expectations, she told me what the job entailed and concluded by saying, "Um . . . do you have at least three references, Miss Goode?"

"Oh, yes, Ma'am." I smiled, my heart beating a mile a minute. I prayed the interview would end before sweat started sliding down my face. I handed her a manila folder with a letter of recommendation and three references from the phone company.

She read my recommendation letter with one eyebrow raised the whole time. "Very nice," she mouthed. "Well," she said, rising. She handed me my folder back, then extended her hand to me. I rose with her, now trembling. "I've got three more interviews today. Thank you for coming down on such short notice." She started walking from around her desk.

"When can I expect to hear from you?" I managed, sweating by now.

"With the holiday and so many people taking time off, I won't be able to make a decision until sometime next week." She patted my shoulder and snatched open the door. I thanked her, gave her another smile, then walked out with my feet feeling so heavy I could barely put one in front of the other.

On the way home I picked up a bottle of vodka and some lemon juice. I didn't really like the taste of alcohol, but it was not the taste I cared about. It was what it would do for me. Back at the hotel I waved to the front-desk clerk and made my way to the elevator.

Holding the door for me was one of the down-and-out men who lived on my floor. "You lookin' mighty nice today," he told me, looking me up and down with wide eyes and a big grin. He was a stocky, dark brown Black man around thirty, with shiny black eyes and a gold tooth in front.

"Thank you," I mumbled, clearing my throat, thinking that if I didn't make too much eye contact he would stop talking.

"You got any plans for Thanksgivin'?" he asked. I was too dazed to realize what he was up to. I just shook my head. "I'm right across the hall from you, and I ain't got no plans neither. All my folks and friends back in Georgia. I just joined this real nice church, reminds me of the one I belonged to back home, that's providin' dinner for the homeless and folks alone like me and you . . . ." His voice trailed off. "They servin' them dinners today instead of tomorrow on account of the church folks with families want to spend the Thanksgivin' Day at home."

I turned and looked him straight in the eye. "What?"

He pressed his lips together and coughed before speaking again. "You welcome to go with me to that church dinner this evenin'. It's the Church of God in Christ over on Patterson Street, six blocks from here. Dinner is at six this evenin'—"

"I can't—I mean I'll let you know," I said. When the elevator stopped I almost knocked him over trying to get out so fast. Normally I would have flat out turned him down. But I had too many other things on my mind. One of the things being the vodka in my purse. I fished it out, opened it, and started drinking straight out of the bottle before I even took my so-called power suit off. The alcohol affected my brain immediately.

By the time I had finished half of the vodka I was not only drunk but depressed as hell. I took off my suit and slid into a pair of blue corduroy pants and a T-shirt. I just knew the lady from the newspaper personnel office had no intentions of hiring a big fat Black oaf like me, and I knew I would not hear from any of the other jobs I had interviewed for. Since the day I was born, this was the first Thanksgiving, or first holiday period, I would spend completely alone. It had started to get dark, and I had not turned on the light in my room yet. But there was enough light shining through my window from a bar and other business neons outside. I sat on the bed and stared at the wall. After a few minutes, I staggered to the window and stared out of it for a while. Both sides of the street had people rushing to and from somewhere. Even though November was a cold month in Erie, I was sweating like a hog. That's why I opened the window, or at least that's what I told myself. With that cold wind slapping against my burning face and hot tears streaming down my cheeks I decided I had had enough. My life had become my worst enemy. Where was God now? The alcohol felt like it had burned a hole in my brain, my stomach, and even my soul, but it made things look so much better. One was the ground below. All I had to do was squeeze through that window and jump. I chuckled, thinking what a mess I'd be for somebody to scrape up off the sidewalk. Seconds later, at the same time, somebody knocked on the door and the phone rang. It took me a few moments to refocus my attention.

"I've left so many messages!" Rhoda began in a piercing loud voice as soon as I grabbed the phone. Whoever was at the door sounded like they were trying to come through it.

"Rhoda, hold on a minute," I told her. I ran to the door and cracked it open. It was the man from across the hall who had talked to me in the elevator. "Yes."

"I just wanted to drop off one of them dinners from the church since you wasn't able to make it. It ain't the best, but it's better than that slop they servin' downstairs at the Richland Hotel Restaurant this evenin'. You have a nice rest of the day, sister, and a happy holiday if I don't see you tomorrow." He handed me a large brown bag that was still warm. Then he nodded and turned to leave.

"What's your name again?" I yelled.

"Levi. Levi Hardy," he replied with a warm smile, letting himself into his room.

"Thank you, Mr. Hardy," I told him, my voice cracking. The food was so potent it immediately filled my entire room with a delicious smell. I set it on the foot of the bed, then sat down and picked up the phone. "Rhoda, I'm sorry. It was this man from across the hall dropping off something," I slurred.

"Well since you take your good old time returnin' calls, I figured I'd keep tryin' until I reached you. I just wanted to wish you a happy holiday."

"Thanks, Rhoda. I 've been meaning to call you back, but I've been so busy looking for a job." My eyes rested on the vodka bottle sitting on the window ledge. "How is your family?"

"Oh everyone is fine. Muh'Dear, Daddy, and Aunt Lola came down. They're goin' to be here until the weekend," Rhoda said cheerfully. "They all said to say 'hi' to you."

"Didn't Uncle Johnny come?"

"Uncle Johnny. He's in jail," Rhoda whispered.

I was blind drunk, and my head was spinning like a top, but I was still able to talk coherently. "My God. What did he do?" It was so good to hear from Rhoda. Already I was feeling better. I shuddered when I looked at the window that was still open. If Rhoda had not called when she did, or if Mr. Hardy had not come by and knocked when he did, I probably would have been on the ground by then. In a whisper to myself I repeated one of Muh'Dear's frequent phrases, "God's trying to tell me something." I had not eaten since before noon. I took the foil-wrapped dinner out of the bag while listening to Rhoda.

"He was drinkin' with Uncle Carmine over at Antonosanti's the other day. Well, Uncle Carmine had to leave, but he told the bartender to keep servin' Uncle Johnny. You know my uncle when it comes to free booze. He got so drunk he fell off the barstool and hit his head. He gets up with this bloody knot on his forehead and has the nerve to ask for another drink. Well, when the bartender turned him down, Uncle Johnny picked up a chair and threw it at him. Uncle Carmine is my daddy's oldest and dearest friend, but I believe Uncle Johnny's goin' to ruin their relationship. Daddy tried to talk Uncle Carmine out of it, but Uncle Carmine had Uncle Johnny arrested."

"Poor Uncle Johnny. That man has such a miserable life." I sighed.

"Yeah. Too bad he's not happy like us."

"Yeah. Too bad," I responded. I started eating the dinner. It was a huge plate with all the trimmings, even corn-bread dressing and cranberry sauce.

"I can't talk long. We're goin' to sit down to eat in a few minutes. We'll talk again next week." After Rhoda hung up I sat looking at the phone and eating. Then I looked at that window again, thinking how close I had just come to jumping out of it. I set my plate down and went to close it.

I called up Muh'Dear and just as I expected, she was out. I finished my dinner and turned on the television. My buzz was still pretty strong, and my head was hurting like somebody had hit me with a brick. It helped when I walked around. But the room was so small, walking around too much meant I had to walk around in circles. To avoid doing that I walked across the hall to Levi Hardy's room. He was glad to see me.

"Come on in, sister, and make yourself at home!" He grinned, opening the door wide. Gospel music was playing softly on a clock radio on his dresser.

Unlike my room, Levi had personalized his. His Bible was on the nightstand, and there were several pictures of various members of his family next to it. His mother looked a lot like him, but the three brothers he pointed to didn't.

"Me and my brothers had different daddies," he confessed, like he had read my mind. He seemed eager to talk, so I let him ramble on for a few minutes without interrupting him. "I'm my mama's outside child by some other woman's husband. Ma's folks didn't accept me. When folks treat you different, you know, not as good as the rest of the family, you grow up with all kind of mixed feelin's. I been on my own since I was sixteen, fifteen years now, and I still don't know what to do with myself. I spent a few years on a merchant." Levi paused long enough to catch his breath. "One of my shipmates talked me into movin' to Erie, where he'd help me get a job in one of the mills. A week after we got here, me expectin' to live with him and his folks 'til I got situated, boom. He had a massive heart attack and was dead at thirty-eight. I had a few dollars on me, so I figured I'd kick around here for a while, rather than go back to a home in Georgia that wasn't a home. I just got hired over at the Davies Body Shop the other day. I swear, sometime it be like God intervene at the right time."

"I know exactly what you mean," I told him. "I only have my mama and an aunt somewhere in New Jersey." I occupied a wobbly chair by his window, and he was on his bed with his short legs crossed with a bottle of beer in his hand. "Thanks again for that nice dinner." I smiled. I could still feel the vodka dancing around with my brain.

"Where your man at?" Levi smiled, scratching his chin and giving me a thoughtful look. He had on a dull brown suit, a dingy white shirt with a stiff tie, and a pair of brown loafers with run-over heels.

"Um . . . in the military," I lied. "We'll probably get married when he gets back from Vietnam," I added.

A sad look replaced Levi's smile. "He a lucky man," he muttered, finishing his beer.

I told him about my futile job interviews. He told me more about places in Erie I'd probably enjoy, like his favorite bar, the nearest movie theaters, the best soul food restaurants, and his church. "I hope I get a chance to take you out before that soldier boy come home." He grinned, raising one brow suggestively.

"Maybe," I mumbled, rising. "Thanks again for the dinner," I continued, moving toward the door.

"You ain't got to run you know. I don't know about you, but this is a lonely night for me, and I am enjoyin' your company," he said, leaping up from the bed with his arms outstretched.

"Well . . ."

"There's a gospel program comin' on Channel Seven in a few minutes." He strode across the floor and turned off the radio, then turned on the small color TV next to it.

I ended up staying another hour, and I am glad I did. He was a nice man. After the program went off I stood up again.

"I really do have to go now. Thanks again for the dinner," I told him one more time, extending my hand.

"Oh, you welcome." He got up to shake my hand and walk me to the door. "Anytime you missin' that soldier boy of yours, my door is always open if you wanna come over and talk. And I wish you'd think about goin' out with me sometime."

I went to bed that night still concerned about my employment situation. But I was in a much better mood. I couldn't believe how close I had come to ending my life. Again, Rhoda had saved me. Rhoda and a strange new man.

CHAPTER 46

I spent most of Thanksgiving Day in bed. The hotel restaurant was open, so I went to pick up one of their dinners. Before they wrapped it I could tell it was a mess. The turkey looked dry, the dressing looked like mud, and the mashed potatoes had lumps big as marbles. "You sure are a brave soul," a petite Black woman with red hair and gray eyes laughingly said as we got into the same elevator. "The last time I ate in that restaurant I spent the next two days in the bathroom, throwin' up from both ends."

"Yeah, I know the food is deadly," I said. "But sometimes anything is better than nothing." The woman I was talking to was one of the ones who had tried to get me to baby-sit. She was just a little older than I, but she had four kids already.

"Ain't you got no family neither?" she asked.

"No not in Erie," I told her.

"Well I'm Jan Kirksey in Room 1142 if you ever feel like talkin' or you just need somebody to lean on." I thanked the woman and got off. Once I got to my room I felt bad about turning down her many requests for me to baby-sit for her. When she knocked on my door later Thanksgiving Day, accompanied by a rough-looking man wearing a do-rag asking again if I would watch her kids while she went to one of the nearby bars, I still said no. As bad as I wanted and needed friends, I promised myself I would avoid anybody I thought was out to take advantage of me. I lied to her about having a date, but as soon as she left, I crawled into bed and ate my dinner with a relish.

I dozed off, but around ten the phone rang. Muh'Dear told me all about the wonderful Thanksgiving dinner she had enjoyed with Mr. King and a holiday service they'd attended at church. Before she asked I told her that I was certain I'd be working any day now. "I've been on several interviews," I revealed. "That's why I was not here all those times you called."

"Well turn it over to God. If you done interviewed all you can interview, it's up to Him now." Muh'Dear babbled on for a few minutes more about Judge Lawson's failing health and what some of the people from the neighborhood were up to. She told me in great detail about Caleb's recent hip surgery, Florence calling to get my address, and Pee Wee's picture in the newspaper because of some medal he had earned. She finally hung up after telling me about how she took flowers over to the cemetery to put on Mr. Boatwright's grave.

I dreamed about Mr. Boatwright that night. He had come into my room wearing a white robe and carrying his Bible. "Don't you be scared of nothin', girl. I'm here to comfort you," he told me. The dream was so real. I woke up around 5 A.M. in a daze the day after Thanksgiving and could not get back to sleep. I was just lying in bed staring at the ceiling when around 9:30 A.M. the phone rang. It was the personnel representative at the Erie Manufacturing Company, one of the two factories where I had applied. They had a job for me.

"When do I start," I yelled. The woman on the other end was silent.

"Are you available to start work a week from Monday?"

"Oh yes. I'm available to start TODAY if you want me to," I said eagerly.

The woman laughed. "That won't be necessary. You'll need to take a physical first, then, of course, there is some paperwork you will need to complete."

After I got off the phone I actually started dancing around the room. I had to share my news with somebody. Rhoda and Muh'Dear were both out. I put on a blouse and skirt and walked across the hall to tell Levi. Before I could knock, his door opened and he walked out with an attractive woman in her mid-twenties. "I'm sorry. Um . . . I just wanted to let you know I got the job I applied for at Erie Manufacturing."

"Praise the Lord!" he yelled. I didn't bat an eye when he hugged me. His lady friend rolled her eyes at me and advised him that they had a cab waiting.

Too excited to sit in my room, I went to the hotel's restaurant and wrestled my way through another one of their fried chicken plates.

CHAPTER 47

I hated my new job at first. Along with seven other women I sat on an assembly line screwing washers, nuts, and bolts onto various parts of garage-door openers. After only a week, it was a chore I could do in my sleep. Because of the oil and dust, we all dressed very casually, so I'd wasted all the money I'd spent on business suits.

The seven dollars an hour and the medical benefits were the incentive I needed to keep me going. Muh'Dear, Rhoda, and everybody else I'd told were happy for me. Florence even sent me a congratulatory card.

"What are your coworkers like?" Rhoda asked. She had just come home from the hospital with a seven-pound baby boy she had named Julian. I could hear him crying in the background.

"Well, I don't know yet. They mind their own business and so do I. I am the youngest one and there are only two other Black women. There is another department in another section where they test and paint the garage-door openers, but I haven't met any of those people."

"You've been sharin' an assembly line for two weeks now with seven women and you don't know what any of them are like yet?"

"Well, the white women hang together and keep to themselves on breaks and lunch. They've all been working together for almost twenty years. The two Black women, well they aren't very friendly. Everybody speaks to me, but none of them have invited me out for break or lunch or anything," I said sadly. It was true none of the women had tried to establish a friendship with me.

"Have *you* tried to develop a friendship with any of them?"

"Well no—"

"Annette, you don't have to wait for them to approach you. Why don't you ask one of them to go to lunch or somethin'? I bet if you made an attempt to get to know them, they'd help you find an apartment," Rhoda told me, sounding almost angry. "You can't spend your life waitin' for things to come to you, Annette. Life's too short."

The next day at work I invited the middle-aged white woman next to me on the line to lunch. "There's a McDonald's down the street I usually go to," I told her. Cynthia Costello, a thin, plain-looking bleached blonde smiled at me and shook her head.

"But I'd love to. With six kids I am on a tight budget. I always bring my lunch unless it's a special occasion." Cynthia had the worst case of acne I'd ever seen on a woman her age, and her teeth didn't look too much better. I ate lunch alone that day but later when it was afternoon breaktime, Cynthia invited me to join her and one of the two Black women. Her name was Viola Jenkins, and she appeared to be in her mid-fifties like Muh'Dear.

"You look a little like my niece in Baton Rouge," Viola informed me. I sat across from her and Cynthia at one of six plastic tables in our lunchroom down the hall from the assembly line. In the lunchroom were several vending machines with chips, sodas, and candy bars. Cynthia opened a thermos filled with coffee that she had brought from home. Viola was even larger than I was. We each had a Diet Pepsi in front of us. She had beautiful bronze skin, small, tired black eyes, and only half of her teeth left. There were at least half a dozen moles on the bottom half of her face, and her salt-and-pepper hair was pulled back into a flat ponytail with a red rubber band holding it together. "I hear you ain't got no family here. What about a church home?" Viola said, giving me an intense look. She had a deep aggressive voice that was almost masculine.

"Well as soon as I get settled into an apartment I'm going to pick a church. A man I met at the Richland Hotel where I rent a room told me about the Church of God in Christ. Have you ever been to it?"

Viola's eyes got big, and a wide grin appeared on her face. "That's the only sanctified church in town, and my stepdaddy is the preacher there," Viola said proudly. "You Pentecostal?"

"Well no. I'm a Baptist, but I've been to Pentecostal churches before," I told her. I felt bad not including Cynthia in the conversation. I turned to her. "Do you go to church, Cynthia?"

She nodded. "I'm Catholic, and you're welcome to attend our services, too." I truly enjoyed talking with these two women. After work, walking to the bus stop a block away together, Viola shared some disturbing information with me about Cynthia. "She's done every drug in the book and drinks like a fish. All on account of that man of hers."

"Does he beat her?" I asked.

"Like he gettin' paid for it, girl," Viola growled, walking with great difficulty. She was breathing hard and lumbering along like a weak turtle, a lot like Mr. Boatwright used to do. "Poor Cynthia. I went to school with her mama."

"What? How old is Cynthia?" I gasped, whirling around to face Viola.

"How old you think she is," Viola muttered, slowing down even more.

"Well . . . with six kids and the way she looks, I'd say she was in her late forties, maybe even early fifties."

Viola laughed and shook her head, fanning her face with a flat straw purse she had in her hand. "The girl ain't but thirty-six." Viola sighed with a groan so long and deep I almost felt it.

Erie Manufacturing was on the opposite side of town from my hotel. There was a bus that stopped a block away that some of the workers who didn't own cars depended on. Viola had a car, but because parking was such a problem she chose to utilize the bus. In fact most of the other employees did also for the same reason. Cynthia's brutal husband brought her to and from work because, according to Viola, he was extremely jealous and didn't trust her in too many public places alone where men were present.

"He beats her, he brings his two kids by his outside woman home for Cynthia to baby-sit while him and the other woman go out and party, and Cynthia can't talk on the phone without his permission. He's even been down here drunk as a skunk tryin' to start some mess. I can't tell you how many times he done almost got poor Cynthia fired."

Viola loved to talk. During the bus ride she told me all about her church, her family, her big house on Noble Street across from her church, and her man. She had four grown children that she had kicked out as soon as they each turned eighteen. She even told me about some new apartments in her neighborhood.

A week after I moved into a furnished one-bedroom apartment on

Maple Ridge, two blocks from Viola's house, I got a call from the personnel rep at the newspaper company. It was a job offer. I thanked her profusely, but I turned the job down. I had gotten used to my assembly-line work and Viola and Cynthia. Two clerical job offers came the following week, but I turned them down, too.

Muh'Dear was ecstatic when I called and told her I had found a church even though it was not of our faith. "God the same no matter which one of His houses you in," she assured me. She didn't seem too pleased that my two new friends were so much older than I. "Can't you find no friends your own age?" she asked, sounding worried. "I will eventually," I said.

I had a life now. I had a job I had grown to like and new friends I adored. The Church of God in Christ was very much like the other Pentecostal churches I'd visited. Most of the frenzied congregation shouted and fell to the floor speaking in tongues every Sunday. I didn't shout or speak in tongues, but I enjoyed the services. It was a small church with not enough benches, so I had to stand for the whole sermon almost every time I went. I often saw Levi and his lady friend at church and each time he was friendly, but the woman, whose name was Nettie, rolled her eyes at me.

Viola's husband, Willie, was a frail brown-skinned man with beady brown eyes and thin lips, whom she controlled completely. Viola did whatever she wanted whenever she wanted, but Willie didn't make a move without her approval. Unlike Cynthia's situation, Viola didn't use violence to control her husband. He seemed to enjoy being told what to do and what not to do. "Vi, do you mind if I go over to the pool room for a while?" he asked one evening when I was visiting Viola at home. "Yeah, you can go," Viola told him with a smile, kissing him passionately before he left.

Even though Viola was old enough to be my mother, and we didn't have much in common, I enjoyed being with her. We spent a lot of time shopping and cruising restaurants. One evening I went to dinner with Viola at Percy's, our favorite soul food restaurant. Her husband, Willie, had come with us to help celebrate Viola and me getting raises at work. On our table were huge servings of black-eyed peas and ox-tails threatening to slide off the plates. Viola paused and wiped her lips and chin with a napkin, and then she shook her head. "I can't believe you ain't got no man," she told me, looking at me across the table. Willie sat quietly next to her, speaking only when spoken to.

"Oh well I have this man in the army," I said. It bothered me when anybody commented on my solo status. Whenever it came up, I consistently told the lie about my bogus military lover to keep them from trying to play matchmaker.

When I wasn't at work, church, or out with Viola, I spent my free time going to movies and bookstores alone. I missed all the people from Richland, but I was glad that the ones I missed the most, Muh'Dear and Rhoda, were just a phone call away. I called them or they called me on a fairly regular basis.

I often ran into Levi at Kroger's, where I bought my groceries. Whenever he was alone he asked me out, and each time I told him I had something to do, which I usually did. He always seemed to invite me to go somewhere on a night I had plans to go out with Viola.

The weeks turned into months, and before I realized it, five years had slipped by and not once had I attempted to visit Richland. I was still working on the same assembly line sitting on the same stool next to Cynthia Costello doing the same job. It was comfortable, I got regular raises, and I enjoyed it. The rest of the women were a lot more friendly toward me now, so I always had somebody to go to lunch with or for drinks after work.

On November 14, 1973, Rhoda gave birth to another little boy. This one she named David after her dead brother and her father. She continually invited me to come for a visit, but each time I made up some wild job-related excuse. I wanted to see her and meet her children but I knew that seeing her in person enjoying life without my presence would depress me severely. She had just as many excuses not to come visit me.

I wrote a few letters to Pee Wee because he sent me so many and, unlike Florence, who didn't complain when I took my time writing back to her, kept telling me I'd *better* write back to him more often or he was going to talk about me like a dog. I did, looking at it as one way to wean myself off Rhoda. Pee Wee was always prompt about responding. In his last letter he told me that he planned to visit some relatives in Erie soon and that if he did, he would visit me as well. So much time went by I forgot about it so I was surprised when he called me on a Saturday morning in the middle of June, seven months after the birth of Rhoda's son.

"Hello, Annette, this is Jerry," an unfamiliar, very masculine and sexy man's voice said.

"Jerry who?"

"Pee Wee from Richland, Ohio."

"How are you, Pee Wee?" I had never called him Jerry and had almost forgotten that was his real name.

"I got your phone number from your mother."

"Where are you?" I asked, so happy to hear his voice.

"Well, I'm in Erie visitin' some of the old neighborhood gang and some kinfolks for a few days. Did you get my last letter? I told you I'd look you up if I made it here."

He sounded so different. I had not heard his voice since the summer after graduation. He finally sounded like a man.

"Yeah, I got your letter. Please do come by!" I didn't have to give him directions. He was as familiar with Erie as he was with Richland.

I didn't know what to expect, but when I opened my front door that Saturday evening around five, I was shocked speechless. Gone was that thin homely boy and standing before me was a tall, well-built man handsome beyond my imagination. His uniform made him even more breathtaking. He was holding his hat in his hand.

"Pee Wee? *Is that you?*" It was hard to believe that a man could change so much in less than six years.

"In the flesh." He grinned. He had even grown a mustache.

I motioned him to a seat on my living-room couch, where he eased down and placed his hand on his knee.

"You've got a nice place," he said, looking around, nodding at my entertainment center, the first thing I had purchased with my first paycheck.

The furniture that came with the apartment was nice. I had a black-leather couch and matching love seat, two large beige lamps on smoked-glass end tables and a glass coffee table in front of the couch. I had purchased the imitation Monet paintings on the beige walls myself.

"Uh . . . you've changed," I muttered and shrugged. "My God— you've *changed.*"

"I sure hope so. The military can make you or break you. In my case, the military *remade* me." He smiled. "And I've been into weight trainin' for about four years now."

He told me about his Vietnam experience and his plans for the future. He was going to finish his commitment, go move back to Richland, go to barber school, and work with his father. "Daddy's plannin' to add two more chairs and will need my help."

I told him about my job and my new friends, but I was reluctant to talk about my future; everything still seemed uncertain at this point.

We drank a few glasses of wine and laughed and talked about some of the people from our old neighborhood. Around eleven, he looked at his watch.

"What time do you have to leave?" I asked.

"Well, the last plane back to the base tonight leaves in a couple of hours. If I miss it, the next one leaves in the mornin' at eight."

"When do you have to be back on the base?"

"Oh I don't have to be back for another two days."

"Why don't you just stay the night then. I would love to have your company," I told him, making a sweeping gesture with my hand.

He stayed and we enjoyed more wine and a late fried chicken dinner I had delivered from Percy's. I made up the couch and around midnight, I went to bed, leaving him up watching TV. I don't know what time it was, but during the night I woke up and found him standing at the foot of my bed. I don't know if it was the wine or if this was something that was bound to happen sooner or later. No words were needed. He smiled. I returned the smile, and then I threw back the covers.

What he did to me and what Mr. Boatwright had done to me for years were two different things. And as far as the men from Scary Mary's were concerned, I couldn't even remember what sex had been like with them. It seemed so unreal when I recalled any of it, which was every day. The shame of prostitution as part of my work experience was overwhelming. He offered to teach me things, telling me, "We got all night." I did everything he told me to do. Afterward, when I shared his joint with him, I couldn't stop grinning. I waited until I was sure he was asleep before I climbed out of bed and ran to the living-room phone to call Rhoda.

"Do you know what time it is?" she barked.

"I know. I just wanted to tell you . . . Pee Wee is here and we . . . you know. I just wanted you to be the first to know we did it!"

"Did what?"

"Pee Wee and I had sex."

"*Our* Pee Wee? You have got to be kiddin'!" Rhoda screamed. She was wide-awake now.

"I am not kidding." I laughed. "And do you know what? I liked it. Now I know why you and Otis were always sneaking off to motels."

"This is too much," Rhoda replied.

"Tell me about it." I laughed again.

We got quiet for a few moments but I wasn't ready to get off the phone. I never got tired of talking to Rhoda.

"Well, what now? Does this mean you and Pee Wee are an item or something?" Rhoda asked.

"He's leaving in the morning to go back to the base. He'll be discharged in a few months, then he returns to Richland to go to barber school so he can work with Caleb." My voice was now low and hollow. My mind was whirling with confusion and a strange sense of joy. My crotch was still tingling. I had finally found out what all the fuss was about.

"I see. So this was just a one-night stand?" Rhoda said accusingly.

"I guess so," I answered, disappointed because I was thinking the same thing.

"I figured that. You know how men are." After Rhoda said that, I felt cheap and used. Now I was ready to get off the phone.

I felt really sad after my conversation with Rhoda. I missed Pee Wee already, and he had not even left. I went back to sleep and when I woke up, planning to fix him breakfast, he was gone. No good-bye, no nothing, just gone! I got depressed all over again. If I could have, I would have kicked my own ass for letting a man make a fool out of me the first time I let my guard down.

Within a week, things were back to normal for me. I put Pee Wee out of my mind and concentrated on my life in Erie.

For the next few weeks I didn't call Rhoda. I felt too ashamed after what Pee Wee had done to me. When Pee Wee returned to Richland he wrote me a brief note and apologized for leaving me the way he did. I wrote him back and told him not to worry, we were still friends. We began to write to one another on an irregular basis.

About three months after I'd slept with Pee Wee, my telephone rang one Sunday night right after I had gone to bed. I figured it was Muh'Dear calling, but it was Rhoda.

"I need you. *I need you here with me real bad!*" she said as soon as I spoke. Something was dreadfully wrong. My first thought was she had confessed to Mr. Boatwright's murder and she was calling to tell me that our gooses were cooked. My heart started beating so hard I was afraid it was going to pop out of my chest.

"Did somebody find out about Mr. Boatwright?" I hollered, out of breath. The long silence that followed scared me even more. "Rhoda, are you there?"

"My son David is dyin'," she rasped. "He has a hole in his heart just like Muh'Dear."

"What did you say?" She repeated herself, and her words were like a sledgehammer slamming against the side of my head. All of a sudden, my problems didn't seem so big anymore. "I'm on my way." I left the apartment with just the clothes on my back and my purse.

The taxi got me to the airport in record time, but the next flight to the Miami area, where Atwater was located, wasn't for another three hours.

I arrived in Miami the next morning at 10 A.M. after a two-hour stopover in Charlotte, North Carolina. A gypsy cab took twenty minutes to get me to Rhoda's country place.

Even though Rhoda had told me all about her house, I didn't know what to really expect. The cab let me out on a dirt road, then I had to walk through some woods for about five minutes to reach a clearing. Surrounded by orange trees was the cutest little white cottage I'd ever seen. A truck and a jeep were in the front yard, along with some hens and a coon dog. A young white girl of about twelve was sitting on the front porch steps crying. Sitting on her lap was a young Black boy, who was a miniature version of Rhoda's husband, sucking his thumb. She had sent me lots of pictures of her older boy, so I knew that this was her son Julian. He whined when I reached out to touch him.

"He's afraid of strange people," the girl informed me.

"Is this where Rhoda and Otis live?" I asked, knowing that it had to be.

The girl gave me a suspicious look, then nodded and stood up. The boy hid behind her.

"Are you April?" I asked.

The girl nodded again and started wiping her nose with the tail of her flowered dress. She was a pretty child, with milky white skin, huge brown eyes, and a single blond braid.

"Where is Rhoda? Where is her husband?"

"Mr. Otis is in Jamaica with his daddy. They're on the way back home now. Miss Rhoda is on the back porch with the baby. She told me to keep this boy here with me so she could tend to the little one."

I snatched open the front screen door. Not being familiar with the house, I didn't know where to run once I got inside. Just as I expected, Rhoda had decorated her home nicely, with wicker furniture, lush green carpets, large white lamps, an elaborate fish tank with an assortment of exotic fish, and a library in the living room that contained hundreds of books.

"I'll show you." April grabbed my hand and led me through the house to the kitchen. Outside on the back porch sat Rhoda in a rocking chair, holding David. Her right nipple was in his mouth, and she was rocking him and humming. Tears came to my eyes when I noticed a squirrel with a white paw like the one I had played with as a child perched in a corner on the porch looking up at Rhoda. I blinked hard to contain myself.

"Rhoda, is he going to be all right?" I asked softly, moving toward her. She looked at me with red swollen eyes. Smiling sadly, she stopped humming and shook her head slowly. Then she looked away and started humming again.

April tugged on my arm. "Lady, he's dead," she whispered. "He died last night."

CHAPTER 48

Since I'd left Erie with nothing but my purse, I took a cab back into Miami the same day I arrived to pick up a few items I'd be needing during my stay at Rhoda's house. The most difficult purchase was a simple black dress to wear to the baby's funeral.

I didn't plan to return to Erie until the weekend. I called Viola from Rhoda's living room phone to tell her where I was and why. "Annette, don't you worry about nothin'. I'll call the shift supervisor right away and tell him where you at and why and that you won't be back to work for a few days," Viola told me.

Right after I finished my conversation with Viola I called up Muh'Dear to tell her about David's death, but she already knew from the Nelsons. "And did Rhoda tell you about that brother of hers? That mannish boy Jock." Muh'Dear whispered.

"What about him?"

"Since he been back from Vietnam, he's been real strange. Shell-shocked, Mr. King called it. Chasin' cars, spittin' on folks. He went up to Scary Mary and slapped her so hard her wig flew off," Muh'Dear told me.

"Rhoda didn't tell me about Jock," I whispered, looking over my shoulder. A doctor had sedated her, but she was up and about anyway.

"Well don't bring it up at a time like this," Muh'Dear pleaded.

"Rhoda'll be fine. I'm going to help her prepare dinner," I said, glad Muh'Dear got off the phone right away.

Rhoda's kitchen was larger than one would expect. So was her living room. The three bedrooms, all neat and brightly furnished, were small, which made them seem congested. "April keeps this place neat as a pin." Rhoda laughed. She was standing over the sink washing collard greens when I joined her after my conversation with Muh'Dear. I was sitting at the table drinking a cup of tea. Before I could speak Otis popped into the kitchen, looking tired and beaten down. While Pee Wee had blossomed so to speak and turned into a real hunk, Otis's good looks had started to fade already. At twenty-five, he looked ten years older.

"Hi, Otis. How are you feeling today?" I said, trying to smile. The funeral had been the day before. His eyes were still red and swollen.

"Oh, I'm getting along as well as can be expected," he mumbled. He went to Rhoda, brushed her lightly across her face, whispered something in her ear, and then excused himself. Rhoda sighed and came to the table with a dishpan containing the greens. Without a word she handed me a knife, and we both started cutting up the greens.

"Men," she huffed. "He'll come back smellin' like a beer garden and finish drivin' me crazy." Rhoda seemed like she was talking more to herself than she was to me.

I cleared my throat. "Um . . . whatever happened to your white cousins Alice Mae and Mae Alice? I was suprised they didn't come down for the funeral," I said.

Rhoda chuckled first. "Oh didn't I tell you? Alice Mae 'married' a woman and is living with her in Detroit." Rhoda bowed her head and looked at me with a strange expression on her face.

"She's a lesbian?" I gasped.

"Always has been. I said I'd never tell you this, but she had the hots for you. The minute she met you when Granny Goose died she told me and her twin. I told her not to waste her time or yours."

I was stunned. So stunned I didn't know how to respond to Rhoda's news. "What about her twin? Where is she?" I was taking my time cutting up the greens. I wanted to savor my moments alone with Rhoda.

"Sellin' pussy all over the state of Alabama like Aunt Lola did for so many years. And the killin' things is, Aunt Lola's the main one tryin' to talk her into quittin'. I don't judge anybody. I say do what you gotta do. All women use their pussy in some kind of way to get what they want. That's how my mama kept my daddy under control. That's what's made Scary Mary so much money."

"Yeah. I got a feeling that's how me and Muh'Dear survived," I mouthed.

"I know for a fact it is," Rhoda said, looking directly into my eyes. "Scary Mary told me your mama used to turn a few tricks on the side when you guys were real down-and-out," Rhoda paused and looked me in the eyes. Neither one of us blinked. "And everybody knows about your mama and Judge Lawson. They've had a thing goin' on for years. Now she's got that Buttercup restaurant man, Mr. King, in her hip pocket." Rhoda's voice got real low, and she looked around before continuing. "And remember those times you'd do it with Buttwright without a fuss just to get money to go to the movies and stuff with?"

I nodded, not looking at her. "Yeah," I muttered, looking at the floor. "But I didn't want to do it."

"Well I am sure no woman in her right mind wants to do it. Like I said, a woman's got to do what she's got to do," Rhoda said firmly. She slammed the kitchen table with her fist for emphasis. "I'd do it if I had to, wouldn't you?"

"I did," I mumbled, then held my breath.

"I know you did. Buttwright—"

"Not just with him." I almost laughed. Rhoda looked in my eyes, and we just stared at one another for so long we both got nervous. "Right after you and Otis left Ohio, I got desperate and I guess a little crazy. I needed money. I needed a lot of money to leave home with," I confessed, trembling so hard I dropped the knife.

"Weren't you workin' for the phone company?" Rhoda asked.

"I quit after just a couple of weeks and . . . and I got involved with some of the men that go to Scary Mary's place."

Rhoda stared at me with an incredulous look on her face, shaking her head. "Girl, you are full of surprises. First, you call me in the middle of the night to tell me you screwed Pee Wee. Now this?"

"Well"—I shrugged—"like you said, a woman's got to do what a woman's got to do. Are you going to judge me?" I asked boldly, cutting up the greens hard and fast.

Rhoda turned away from me, stared at the floor and started talking in a slow controlled manner. "When my baby died my first thought was God's punishin' me for . . . what I did," Rhoda whispered.

I stopped cutting the greens and moved my chair closer to hers. "I thought that same thing. I said to myself, God taking Rhoda's baby was the payback for Mr. Boatwright's murder."

She looked at my face and shook her head. "Not that. I . . . I had an affair." My face felt like it had frozen in time. I couldn't react right away. "Right after I had Julian, me and Otis had some problems in the bedroom. That postpartum shit had me so depressed all I did was eat and walk around in the same musty housecoat all day long. He wouldn't touch me with a stick, and the longer it went on, the more unattractive I felt. That's why I did it."

"Who was this other man? Do you still see him?" I wanted to know. Now I really felt bad thinking about all that time I spent up in Erie wishing Rhoda and Otis would break up. She looked and sounded so sad, I thought she was going to start crying.

She closed her eyes and shook her head. "My husband's best friend," she whispered hoarsely.

"What?"

"He was visitin' from Jamaica for a couple of weeks," she said slowly and so quietly I asked her to repeat it. "We were alone . . . one minute we're drinkin' beer, the next minute we're . . . you know."

"Oh my God!" I shrieked. "Rhoda, how could you? In your own house?"

She nodded. "It gets worse." Rhoda paused and held up her hand. Before finishing her confession, she looked around again to make sure we were still alone. "His name was Bobby. David . . . David was his son."

"Are you sure?" I thought I was going to go into complete shock.

"Oh there's no doubt about it. Otis hadn't touched me in weeks. I was already two months along—the doctor had even confirmed it— when I got Otis drunk and seduced him on the livin'-room couch. I waited just three weeks before I started droppin' hints to him that I might be pregnant again. When David arrived seven months later, right on schedule, Otis and everybody believed me when I told him the baby was premature. Thank God David looked like me."

I put the greens and the knife on the table and stood up to hug Rhoda's shoulder.

"When did the affair end?" I asked.

"When he left. He moved to London and married some English-woman. He never knew about the baby."

"Rhoda, why didn't you tell me before now?" I looked at Rhoda like I was looking at her for the first time. Her lips were trembling, and there were tears in her eyes. In all the years we'd been friends, this was the first time I'd seen her without makeup. She was still beautiful, but in a more natural way.

"Lord knows you and I've got enough dark secrets. I didn't want to burden you with another one," she said. She sucked in her breath and shook her head.

"That's something you really needed to talk to somebody about. You know you can always talk to me about anything."

"I couldn't even tell you before now because I was so ashamed. This makes up for the Buttwright thing, I guess. When my baby died, I knew then I couldn't keep this secret to myself any longer. I had to tell somebody, and that somebody could only be you. I'm just glad you were able to drop everythin' and come down here to be with me."

I hugged Rhoda again. "Our lives are beginning to sound like soap operas," I said. "Any other sordid secrets you want to share with me?" I asked. It did make us both laugh for a brief moment.

"That's it for me right now. What about you?" Rhoda asked.

"Well, nothing. Oh yeah there is. That first Thanksgiving in Erie, I was so lonely and depressed I got blind drunk and was seriously think-ing about jumping out of my hotel window. If you hadn't called me when you did, I would have died that night," I said. Rhoda gave me another incredulous look, then laughed so hard she shook. It took me a moment to realize she thought I was joking, and I left it that way. Right after that, Lola, who was planning to stay another week, re-turned from the graveyard where she'd gone to leave more flowers on David's grave. After a good cry on my shoulder, Lola helped us finish preparing dinner.

After I returned to Erie, the next few weeks seemed to fly by. I did not talk to Rhoda for quite a while. When we did talk, a couple of weeks later, she told me what was happening with her brother. It was a grim situation. Apparently, Jock had become too much for her aging parents to handle. Lola did as much as she could to help out when she wasn't working at Antonosanti's, but that still was not enough. Uncle Johnny was still having his problems with the law and spent more time in jail than out, so he was not much help.

Otis had told Rhoda that Jock could move in with them. By living out in the country like they did, Jock running around outside naked wouldn't be so bad.

"I don't think that's a good idea," I told Pee Wee during a phone conversation.

"Why not? He's gettin' into all kinds of trouble in Ohio. He was in the V.A. hospital in Cleveland and roughed up an intern so bad the man had to be hospitalized. He loves Rhoda and Otis, and they're young and strong enough to handle him better. Besides, what kind of trouble could he get in out in the country? The worst would be to set an orange tree on fire?" He snapped.

I dismissed Pee Wee's comments. I recalled how Jock used to intimidate and beat up Pee Wee when we were kids. It was hard to believe that someone like Jock was now in the same boat with Scary Mary's daughter Mott: mentally handicapped and totally dependent on others.

"I just don't think it's a good idea. Jock was pretty crazy even when he was still sane. Now that he's really crazy, how can they know what to expect? God I wish we were all kids again and back at home gossipin' on the front porch," I whined to Pee Wee, attempting to change the subject.

"Me too. I really miss you and Rhoda. And Lord knows I miss old Mr. Boatwright. What that man could do to a pot of turnip greens! I know you miss all that good home cookin', girl."

"Pee Wee, you don't know the half of it," I told him.

CHAPTER 49

"Who is this?" I muttered into the telephone. It was just a little after 7 A.M. on a Saturday morning.

"April."

"Where is Rhoda?"

"Mr. Otis carried her to the movies, then dinner."

"Tell her Annette called."

"OK. You know Jock lives here now."

"Yeah I know."

I hung up the phone and looked at it. Then I dialed Pee Wee's number. I was horrified when a woman answered. "He's in the shower," the bitch told me. I slammed the phone down, then I got under a blanket on my couch with the *Jet* magazine. Not more than five minutes later the phone rang.

"You called?" Pee Wee asked.

"How did you know it was me?" I said nastily, dropping my magazine to the floor.

"You're the only woman who calls me," he informed me seriously.

"You had company?" I continued.

"Oh yeah. That was Lena."

"Lena who?"

"From school. The one you flattened on prom night," he said, laughing. "She was here to get her hair trimmed, but she showed up early. Daddy let her in, then he left before I could get out of the shower."

I got silent because I didn't know what to say.

"You still there?" Pee Wee asked, clearing his throat.

"Uh-huh. Um . . . I thought that sounded like Lena," I snarled. We only talked for a few minutes more. Things were fairly normal in Richland, and he didn't have a lot to tell me.

I didn't tell Rhoda right away, but I had begun to have more nightmares about Mr. Boatwright, what he had done to me, and what she had done to him.

One night I woke up with my gown soaked with sweat and the insides of my thighs throbbing. Another time I was thinking about him while I was cutting up a chicken and I took the knife and started stabbing the chicken all over. There were times when I showered seven, eight times a day trying to wash away the pain and anger he had caused me. Rhoda was still the only person I could talk to about Mr. Boatwright.

"I'm sorry to be calling you this late," I told her one night after midnight. "I was having another nightmare about Mr. Boatwright and I needed you to get me through the rest of tonight. Please."

"I'm here for you. I'll always be here for you." Rhoda listened to me babble for a whole hour.

"Before I hang up, I just want you to know, I would do anything in this world for you, Rhoda. All you have to do is ask." I meant it. If she had asked me to give up Erie and move to Florida to help them run the farm, I would have. "Do you hear me, girl?"

She mumbled something under her breath.

"Huh?" I said.

"I was talkin' to Jock," she told me. "He is so fucked up in the head sometimes we have to tie him to the bed so we can get some sleep."

"Wouldn't he be better off in one of those army hospitals?" I asked.

"He would. But he is my brother. I promised him I would take care of him until the day I die." I could hear Jock yelling obscenities. "Annette, I caught Jock and April together in the cornfield the other day."

My whole body tensed. Suddenly, my Mr. Boatwright nightmares didn't seem as bad as they seemed before.

"Oh no. She's just a child! A white child in *Klan* country!" I roared.

"She's fifteen goin' on twenty-five and looks it. She wears a 36DD bra and has hips wide enough to balance saucers," Rhoda told me in a low flat voice.

"How could Jock mess with that little girl?" I asked, out of breath.

"Sex is like dope to some men. You were a lot younger than fifteen when Buttwright jumped you. It must be their *fuckin'* nature, pardon the expression," Rhoda said nastily.

"What Jock is doing is slow suicide. You've got to stop him before her family finds out," I wailed.

"I couldn't have said it better," Rhoda said gently.

"What are *we* going to do?" I was ready to do whatever it took to help Rhoda straighten out this mess. "You want me to take Jock off your hands for a while?"

"Oh no, that's out of the question. I wouldn't dump a burden like that on you."

"Well what else can you do?" I hollered.

"Don't worry. I'll fix it," Rhoda assured me.

CHAPTER 50

Seven months after Rhoda's son's funeral I finally agreed to go out with Levi Hardy. He approached me after Easter Sunday church service.

"I seen you at the Blue Note the other night." He grinned, his eyes all over me. He had on a plain gray suit that was too big. The legs of his pants were dragging the ground, and the sleeves on his jacket almost covered his hands. I was feeling good and looking good. I had on a cream-colored two-piece suit that made me look ten pounds lighter, with matching shoes and hat. Being large didn't bother me half as much as it had when I was a schoolgirl and the only girlfriend I had was a size four. Leaving Richland and the limited life I had accepted for so many years was one of the best decisions I ever made. Viola and half of the Black women I came in contact with since moving to Erie were just as big as I, if not bigger. They were popular and happy, and now, so was I. I had tried several diets, including a liquid diet, a rice diet, a grapefruit diet, and a few others, but none had worked. "Girl, God didn't mean for every woman to be a size four. If he did, you wouldn't have so much trouble stickin' to them diets. Pass me the potato salad," Viola told me one day over a barbecued chicken dinner at her house. It wasn't that I couldn't stick to a diet. I did follow them, and still didn't lose weight. Once on a liquid-protein diet, one so extreme I experienced fainting and dizziness, I lost eighteen pounds in three weeks. As soon as I went off the diet and started eating my beloved fried chicken again, I gained the eighteen pounds back plus five more. I told Viola, "You're right. If God meant for me to be a big woman, no diet in the world is going to work for me." I gave up dieting and continued to eat like I always had.

That particular Easter, Viola and most of the congregation were going home to eat ham with all the fixings. She had invited me to her house, but I'd declined. I was still uncomfortable socializing with people and their complete families. Viola's holiday dinners included her four children, her three grandchildren, her parents, and a few other assorted relatives. With each passing year, having only Muh'Dear and Aunt Berneice concerned me tremendously. Knowing that once they passed on I would have absolutely no blood family left saddened me to a point where I fantasized about finding a man and deliberately getting pregnant. I didn't want to grow old alone and end up hopeless, helpless, and dependent on strangers, like Mr. Boatwright. Odd as it seemed, even to me, more than once I regretted aborting Mr. Boatwright's baby. As close as Viola and I had become, I could not tell her about the sexual abuse I had endured. The main reason was whenever rape entered our conversation, unless the victim was a female infant, an invalid, or a nun, she usually said something like, "*She* probably brought it on herself." We had a few things in common, but in many ways Viola and I were as different as night and day. We liked the same movies and TV programs, but the only things she read, other than her Bible and the daily newspaper, were Black publications like *Jet* and *Ebony*. I read everything from the classics to the current best-sellers to the *Enquirer*. Viola, wearing a voluminous, floor-length cotton dress with so many flowers she looked like a parade float, was standing next to me listening and looking at Levi like he was talking to her.

"Viola and I go to the Blue Note all the time," I told him. We were standing outside in front of the church along with about a hundred other members of the congregation all dressed for the occasion. Typically, most of the women had on loud outfits similiar to Viola's and garish hats that included feathers and more flowers. The men were dressed more conservatively in dark, neutral suits.

It was a warm, sunny day, but foul fumes coming from the nearby factories made it hard to breathe. There was a lot of coughing going on, and people were wiping smoke from their eyes. Kids of all ages were running amok. Viola's plump stepfather, Reverend Jackson, was still roaming throughout the crowd shaking hands and hugging babies. Viola had ordered her husband, Willie, to go get the car, which was parked a block away. Viola hated walking more than a few yards at a time and did it only when she had to. When we went shopping, she had to sit down to rest, catch her breath, and fan every few minutes. I thought about Mr. Boatwright almost every day of my life anyway and how some of his habits had annoyed me. Viola's problem with walking was so much like his, I thought about him even more.

"I been meanin' to ask you, you wanna slide through the Blue Note one evenin' for a beer and listen to the band?" Levi continued.

"Well." I bowed my head for a moment and glanced at my feet, frowning at the grass stains and dust on my new beige pumps. Since my passion-filled night with Pee Wee, I had been with several other men I'd met while out with Viola in bars, restaurants, and parties. One Monday morning when I got to work, Viola started teasing me before we'd even had our first cup of coffee. "Willie told me he seen you and that truck driver we met at the Blue Note a couple of weeks ago comin' outta Percy's holdin' hands. I know he the reason I couldn't reach you at home all weekend." I told Viola how I'd spent the weekend in Pittsburgh with Ernest Stamps. I liked Ernest, and we got along real good. Every time he returned from one of his cross-country hauls, I would be waiting for him with a home-cooked meal ready. After a few weeks, the relationship fizzled out, and I moved on to a security guard who worked at Erie High School. None of my relationships ever went too far, and I didn't think one with Levi would either. I had lost everything I had to lose, so there was no reason not to accept his latest invitation. "Uh . . . when did you want to go?" I glanced at Viola; she smiled and nodded.

"What's good for you is good for me. I'm pretty flexible." He laughed, dancing an exaggerated jig. "I'd like to go tonight if you ain't got nothin' to do."

"I don't have any plans for tonight," I lied. I had planned to pick up a dinner-to-go, call Rhoda and talk to her for a while, then watch TV. "We can go tonight if you want to," I told him. We agreed that he would pick me up around seven and we'd go to the Blue Note for a few drinks.

Two years earlier, Levi had moved into a three-bedroom house on Lutz Street, a few blocks from me. He had invited his elderly mother, Clara, to leave the South and move in with him. Before going to the Blue Note, we went to his house to eat the Easter dinner his mother had prepared. Clara was a few years older and heavier than my mother, but she looked a little like her, with the same light brown skin and features. She wore horn-rimmed glasses that she looked over the top of when she talked. Like Muh'Dear she was totally devoted to the Lord.

"I been prayin' for this boy here to slow down and get married so he'll have somebody to take care of him," Clara whined, looking directly at me. I threw up my hand and laughed nervously. Levi cleared his throat to get his mother's attention. She glanced at him briefly, gave him a threatening look, then returned her full attention to me. "How old is you?" she asked me with a gleam in her eyes.

"I'm twenty-four," I told her. Levi's house was too small for all the furniture he had crammed into it. The living-room couch was so close to the love seat facing it you didn't have to lean too far to touch it. None of the furniture matched. The lamps on the black end tables were blue, the couch and love seat were plaid, and there was a what-not stand in a corner filled with tiny plastic animals and clay Oriental people with slits for eyes and exaggerated grins. A big box of a television had a cracked yellow vase full of plastic red roses on top of it. The bottom half of the living-room walls had been painted dark brown, and the top half was pink.

"How come you ain't married yet?" Clara asked seriously. She pressed her legs close together and cupped her hands on her lap. "I heard you had a soldier boy."

"Well that didn't work out," I said, shifting in my seat.

"Oh? What did he do to you?" she asked in a low voice with her eyebrows raised. Then she turned her head and leaned her ear in my direction.

"Oh, he didn't do anything. We just decided to go our separate ways."

"Was he in the church?"

"No, Ma'am."

"Well you didn't need him noway. Levi got reborn when he was a young'n and been sanctified ever since." Clara paused and turned to Levi sitting next to her on the couch. "Ain't you?" She rubbed his arm, then patted it.

"Yes, Ma'am," he said meekly.

Clara sucked in her breath and continued. "Now." She paused and looked from my thick legs slowly up to my face. "I got a feelin' you love to cook."

"I do," I replied with a sigh.

"Well . . . God'll send you a husband long as you believe. Levi, go set the table and let's eat that ham before it 'vaporates," Clara said firmly, fanning her face with a folded newspaper.

Levi and I only stayed at the crowded Blue Note for about an hour. I was impressed when he walked me to my door, shook my hand, and waited until I had gotten inside and turned on the lights in my apartment. I waved to him from my living-room window.

Levi became another bizarre episode in my life. He loved to eat as much as I did and had gained weight since I first met him but I still outweighed him by at least fifty pounds. In the beginning we ate in a lot of restaurants, and some of our most serious conversations revolved around food. "You seen them great big old beef ribs they serve at the Murphy Eat-A-Rama?" he asked one day on our way back to my apartment from a day at a carnival. "Oh yes. The meat's falling off the bone," I said, smacking my lips. He made me laugh without trying, usually at times when he thought he was being serious. Levi didn't read anything at all unless he had to, and he was not the most intelligent man I'd ever dated. One night he called and asked if there was anything I wanted him to bring me. I requested a large pepperoni pizza with mushrooms on one side. He wanted to know "which side." In addition to our visits to restaurants, it wasn't long before I was cooking meals fit for a king two to three times a week. Since I wasn't that crazy about bars, the Blue Note was the only one we ever went to every other week or so.

We attended a lot of movies, church functions, and parties at Viola's house. "That Levi would make you a good husband," she whispered to me at a birthday party for her husband. "He got a good job, he looks clean, he don't cuss, he's good to his mama, and he don't smoke. What more could a woman want?"

"I don't . . . love him," I confessed. Levi was standing in a corner talking to Viola's docile husband Willie, who had a bibbed apron on over his party attire. Most of Viola's guests had left, and the few that remained were on the other side of her living room.

"Love ain't nothin' but a four-letter word, girl. You think I married Willie 'cause I loved him? I married him 'cause he had everything I needed. And in all the years we been married I ain't had to whup him but five times."

"But don't you feel anything for him?" I asked, surprised.

"I guess I do," Viola said, shrugging her huge shoulders. She beckoned Willie, and he darted across the room to where we were on the couch holding our plates and drinks. "Willie, I thought I told you to put more chips in them bowls and more ice in that bucket."

"Oh, I forgot. I'll do it right away!" Willie said quickly, nodding and backing toward the kitchen.

As soon as he was out of hearing distance I whispered to Viola, "What about . . ." I didn't even have to finish my sentence.

"Sex? I let him pester me once a week, and he know better than to complain," she said with a firm nod.

"Is it . . . enjoyable?" I asked shyly. Unless there was money involved, I didn't see any point in having sex if it didn't feel good.

"It is for him. I just lay there thinkin' about what I'm gwine to can next, plums or pears."

Muh'Dear had enrolled in a community college and was studying business administration. Judge Lawson was paying her tuition. I had been dating Levi for two months before I told her about him. "I been tellin' Scary Mary my girl don't get involved with the first man come along. I'm glad you took your time findin' somebody. Now you remember that mess that boy got you into when you was a young'n—make this one use somethin'. Either that or you go get on some pills or somethin'. Do you hear me?"

"Yes, Ma'am," I mumbled.

Levi didn't ask me to have sex with him the first time we did it. He just climbed on top of me on my couch one night after we'd been dating for almost a month. It was quick and pleasant, but I didn't experience the satisfaction I had with Pee Wee. Levi and I never got fully undressed. When he spent the night with me he had on pajamas and I wore a gown and underwear. He just opened his fly and I lifted my gown high enough for us to connect. I never removed my panties. I just slid one leg over to the side. Like Viola's husband he was docile, but without my encouragement. He often insisted on washing my dishes and running errands for me. After a while we developed a routine you could set a clock by. He'd come over without calling every Monday, Wednesday, and Saturday evening to eat one of the lavish dinners I'd prepared. He liked whatever I cooked, but his favorite meal was collard greens, corn bread, fried chicken, and potato salad. That's what I cooked every Saturday. A few times he'd come over just long enough to gobble up a couple of plates of food, then run. "I got to carry my mama somewhere," or "I got a union meetin' to go to," he often told me. Like with Viola, I didn't have too much in common with Levi. We shared our love for good food, movies, and the church. "Girl, it sounds like that man is usin' you," Rhoda teased when I told her about all the dinners and sex I was into with Levi. I didn't want to think that I was being used. Levi's mother lived with him and cooked whatever he wanted her to. He didn't have to depend on me for a decent meal, and I was sure there were other women who would sleep with him, too.

"Oh I don't think so. He brings a lot of food to my place for me to cook that he buys with his money, and he's always offering to do things for me," I told her. He was fun, he never disagreed with me, and, most of all, I was no longer lonely. The closest friend I had in Erie was Viola, but she spent a lot of time with her other friends, family, and her husband, so she didn't have as much time to spend with me as I wanted her to. Levi took up where she left off.

Viola went to visit relatives in Louisiana the week of the Fourth of July. Cynthia Costello showed up at work after the holiday wearing dark glasses to hide a black eye, and there was a Band-Aid on her nose. None of the other women or I said anything to her all morning about her injuries. Two months before she had come to work on crutches because her husband had broken her leg in two places. She had just gotten rid of the crutches. Before that it was a cast on her arm. She chatted along with the rest of us about sales, something that was on TV the night before, and recipes. I felt so sorry for her I wanted to hug her.

"What are you doing for lunch today, Cynthia?" I asked a few minutes before noon.

"I brought my lunch," she mumbled, clearing her throat. It was only when she smiled that I noticed a deep cut on her bottom lip, too. Cynthia brought the same things for lunch every day, either a Spam, liverwurst, or peanut butter with jelly sandwich. I spared no expense when it came to eating out. With my paycheck and five thousand dollars left over from Mr. Boatwright's money, I could afford to. Though Viola and I bought our lunch at McDonald's a lot, we ate like kings at least three times a week at the nice restaurants close to the factory. The nicest most expensive one was Giovanni's, an Italian restaurant that reminded me of Antonosanti's in Richland.

"Would you like to have lunch with me at Giovanni's? The food's great—my treat," I said to Cynthia.

First, she gave me an incredulous look, then a broad smile appeared on her face.

"I haven't eaten in a restaurant in five years," she managed to say.

"You can order anything on the menu," I told her, then I gave her a big hug.

Along with lunch, Cynthia drank five glasses of Chianti. She was a functional alcoholic and nobody could tell when she was drunk unless she told them. I felt good the rest of that day because I'd brought a little joy into somebody else's tortured life. Nobody knew better than I how far a little kindness went.

CHAPTER 51

Three years after I'd started dating Levi he stopped spending the night with me. We talked on the phone a few times a week and he came over without fail every Saturday night to eat and have sex, but he left right afterward. One Friday he called me at work and told me he was not going to be able to come over this particular Saturday. "Somethin' came up," was all he told me.

I cooked the collard greens and fried a chicken anyway when Saturday evening rolled around, then curled up on my couch to watch *The Love Boat* and *Fantasy Island*. During all the time I'd been dating Levi I had only seen his mother Clara five or six times. But I did talk to her on the phone often enough. She called almost every time Levi came over to tell him to pick up this or that from the store on the way home. One reason I avoided going around her too much was I didn't like the way she always brought up the subject of marriage. Levi had never given me any indication that he wanted me to be his wife, and I wasn't sure I wanted to be anyway. However, if he had asked, I probably would have taken him and run. I'd marry him not because I loved him, but because I believed he would probably be my only chance. At twenty-eight, no other man had ever proposed marriage to me, but most of the ones I had dated ended up marrying somebody else.

This particular Saturday, since I was so used to Clara calling the apartment every Saturday, I decided to call her to see how she was doing. A strange woman answered the phone. "She still at the wed-din' reception," the woman told me. I thanked her and hung up.

It was still early, so I called up Rhoda. There was something in her voice that concerned me when she answered. She sounded almost as stiff and detached as she did when she called to tell me her son was dying.

"Are you OK?" I asked. My concern instantly turned to fear. I sat up on my couch, slid what was left of my dinner off to the side of the couch, and leaned my elbow on the arm of the couch.

"I'm fine. How are things with you and Levi?"

"Oh about the same." I laughed. "This is the first Saturday he hasn't come over since we started dating. I need to wash my hair anyway." I yawned, glancing at my recently manicured nails. "How are things workin' out with your brother?" I asked.

Rhoda took her time responding. First she sucked in her breath. "Jock got April pregnant," she told me in a slow and tired voice.

"That young white girl?" I gasped. I jumped up from my seat so fast I knocked the plate to the floor. "Oh no," I moaned, squeezing the phone.

"She's three months along."

For a few seconds I was stunned speechless. Somehow I managed to get out, "What are you going to do now? Her folks will have a fit!"

"She says that if Jock doesn't take her away, Ohio or somewhere, she's goin' to tell her daddy that he raped her."

"Oh no, Rhoda! You can't let her do that! Can't you give her some whiskey and sit her in a bathtub of hot water like you did me or to some doctor and get her an abortion?"

"It's worse than you can imagine. She *wants* this baby, girl. Half of the girl's family belong to the . . . Ku Klux Klan. The child would be my niece or nephew. I'd go crazy worryin' about how that child was bein' treated livin' with all those redneck, peckerwood bastards. That is, if they don't beat it out of her before it's born." Rhoda let out an angry breath. "Lord, what a mess!"

"What are you going to do, Rhoda?" My heart started beating so fast and hard I had to breathe through my mouth.

"Whatever I have to do," she growled.

"Well, is there anything I can do? Do you want me to come down and try and talk some sense into her?"

"If she won't listen to me, she won't listen to you."

"Can you send Jock back to Ohio?"

"She's already said that if he does leave, she'll tell her folks *my hus-band* raped her! She'll blackmail me."

"Just like when I threatened to leave town, Mr. Boatwright said he would kill my mama, huh?"

"Uh-huh. Now I really know how you felt."

"I'm sorry, Rhoda. I just don't know what to tell you to do. It sounds like there's going to be trouble soon no matter what."

"There is. I just don't know what." Rhoda sighed again and cussed under her breath for a full minute.

I waited until she paused before I said anything else. "I'll call you again tomorrow," I told her. I tried to reach Viola so I could talk to her about what Rhoda had just told me, but her line was busy. Since Levi was the next person closest to me, I called his house again. This time his mother answered.

"Naw he ain't here," Clara told me in a gruff voice. She sounded out of breath. "Who is this anyway?"

"It's me, Miss Clara, Annette. Did Levi say when he'd be back?"

There was a long pause. "Girl, Levi just got married this evenin'. Don't you—"

"He what?"

"You deaf? The boy got married. Didn't you know he was gettin' married this evenin'?"

"Well . . . I think he told me he was. I guess I forgot," I managed. I didn't want to hear anything else. I didn't want to say anything else. That's why I hung up right away. I stood in the middle of the floor looking around my living room but seeing nothing but red. Rhoda's chilling news and the news about Levi was more than I could stand. I was glad I didn't have any alcohol in the house. I sat in a dazed state for the next two hours, with Rhoda's words and Clara's words going through my head over and over again.

I didn't go to bed that night. Instead I curled up on my couch and looked at the ceiling until I fell asleep and had one nightmare after another. I was not only being chased by Mr. Boatwright, but by Klansmen as well. Levi's face was in the background laughing at me. It was no wonder I woke up screaming.

It was too early for me to get up and get ready for church, but it was not too early for me to call Rhoda back.

I was going to tell her about Levi, but not until I talked to him and got all the facts. With the mess she had on her hands with Jock I didn't think she was in the mood to hear about my love life at the time anyway. "Have you decided what to do?" I asked as soon as Otis called her to the phone.

"No. Not yet."

"I'll help you in any way I can, Rhoda."

"I know you will . . . I just don't know what to do," Rhoda admitted. "How . . . how is Levi?" she asked. I knew she wasn't really interested in hearing about Levi, but I was glad she was the one to change the subject.

"He got married," I said flatly.

"He did what?" she gasped.

"He got married. That's what his mother told me when I called his house last night."

"Well when did you break up with him?"

"I didn't. He was with me just the other night."

"Do you mean to tell me this happened right up under your nose? Who is this other woman?"

"I don't know. I guess whenever he wasn't with me, he was with her. I won't know anything until I talk to him."

"You know somethin', Annette, I would give anythin' in the world to have the good old days back in Richland. We didn't know how good we had it when we were kids—except that thing you were goin' through with Buttwright."

"Yeah. Except for that, we never had it so good. I'll call you again in a day or so." I hung up and walked around my apartment, trying not to look at the phone, trying not to think about Levi, trying not to think about the mess Jock had gotten himself into. I had planned to go to church, but there was too much going on in my head. I didn't eat anything the entire day or leave the house. I didn't sleep at all that night, and I was glad. I couldn't stand more nightmares.

I went to work the next day with dark circles and bags under my eyes. I got there a little earlier than usual, so by the time Viola arrived I was already in the breakroom with a cup of coffee and my newspaper. She nodded at me, got her coffee, and sat at my table across from me. "I feel the same way you look," she told me.

"I had a rough night. Cramps," I lied.

Viola held her cup up to her lips but didn't drink. She just looked at me and stared. Other coworkers had come into the breakroom and by now the place was crowded but unusually quiet. "I was talkin' about Cynthia Costello."

"What about Cynthia?"

"Girl, you didn't hear?"

"Hear what?" I didn't think I could stand to hear any more bad news. "She got fired didn't she? I saw it comin'. We tried to get her to leave that beast she married. We tried to tell her to get some help." I sighed, feeling a sharp pain in my chest and thinking that there were some people that simply couldn't be helped.

Viola shook her head and let out a long deep breath. "She won't be needin' no help now," she told me.

I froze, staring at Viola with my mouth open and my hand in midair. "He finally killed her didn't he?" I asked softly, tears forming in my eyes.

Viola shook her head again. "She put a pistol in her mouth last night and blew her brains out."

CHAPTER 52

I didn't go to Cynthia's funeral. Not because I didn't care but because I had received too much disturbing news all within a couple of days, and it was too much for me. I was afraid for Rhoda's brother, I was angry with Levi, and I was thoroughly saddened about Cynthia's suicide.

The funeral was the following Wednesday. I still had not heard from Levi, and I was too overwhelmed to call his house again. We had a brief memorial service for Cynthia at work in our breakroom the day after her funeral, and I attended. Viola had taken her friend's death so hard, she had to take off the rest of the week. Just seeing all the grief Cynthia's suicide had caused made me recall the night I almost ended my life. I could not imagine the pain the people who loved her were in. For the first time I tried to imagine the pain my suicide would have caused the people who loved me. I called in sick that Friday. I spent the day going through my apartment gathering up everything Levi had given to me, a cheap clock radio, a few articles of clothing, some Mahalia Jackson albums, a prayer cloth he had ordered from Reverend Ike, and a few other odds and ends. Instead of putting the items in boxes, I stuffed everything into large trash bags. We had taken a picture together at the Blue Note one night. First I tore the portion off with him in it. After thinking about it for a second I tossed the whole thing into the trash, frame and all. Saturday morning I took a cab across town to Seventh Street and left the trash bags at the Salvation Army donation drop-off. After doing that, I rode cabs all over town looking for sales to replace everything that I had just gotten rid of. Before I got into another cab to go home, I went to Kroger's to pick up some greens. I already had a chicken in the freezer. Levi or no Levi, I was still going to enjoy my favorite Saturday night dinner.

Minutes after I had sat down to enjoy my dinner, the doorbell rang. "What the hell are you doing here?" I snapped, my mouth full of food. It was Levi clutching a bottle of wine.

He gasped and gave me an incredulous look before speaking. "What's wrong with you, girl? I come every Saturday," he said seriously, waving the bottle so hard the red ribbon around its neck came undone.

"Except last Saturday when you were off getting married," I seethed, shaking my finger in his face.

He dropped his head and scratched the side of his face. "Oh," he muttered.

"Is that all you have to say?" I swallowed my food and slapped my hands on my hips. "How come you didn't tell *me* you were getting married, Levi? How come you didn't tell me you were seeing another woman?"

He shrugged. "That didn't have nothin' to do with me and you," he said, shaking his head and shifting his deceitful eyes.

Mr. Boatwright was the last person I'd given the cold mean look I gave to Levi. It was a look that was so intense, he flinched and moved back a step.

"I was goin' to invite you to the weddin'," he said contritely. I continued to stare at his face in stunned disbelief.

"How could you do this to me, Levi?"

"Well"—he shrugged casually—"my son needed me."

"Son? What son?"

"I got a boy a year old."

"You mean to tell me *a full year* into our relationship you started up with this other woman and had a baby?" I screamed.

"Somethin' . . . somethin' . . . like . . . like that," he told me.

"You son of a bitch," I said evenly, stumbling against the doorway. I slapped his hand when he reached out to grab my arm. "You better get home to your wife and your son!" I barked, already attempting to close the door.

"I guess that mean we won't be eatin' our Saturday night collard green dinner I can smell all the way outside?" he asked with a surprised look on his face.

"*You* won't! The only way you'll ever get back into this apartment will be if you break in!" I slammed the door and locked it while he was still standing on the steps. I stood with my back against it until I heard his car leave. If there was ever a time I needed to get away it was right then. I called Muh'Dear. "I'm going to go up to New Jersey to visit Aunt Berneice for a week or two," I announced.

I had accrued lots of vacation time. But a week was about all I thought I could stand with my aunt. The day and one-half bus ride was comfortable and it seemed longer, but it gave me time away from everybody to go over things in my head. My job at Erie Manufacturing was comfortable, and I was now making good money, but it was a dead-end situation if ever there was one. The only place left to go at the factory was out the door. Most of my coworkers had made it clear that death or mandatory retirement were the only two things that would make them leave. Once I had asked Viola if she ever considered another job. "It's the same all over," she indicated. Well, I didn't believe that. In my heart I knew it was time for me to leave the new life I had made for myself in Erie.

I had never heard of Englishtown, New Jersey, and I didn't know what to expect. But when my aunt met me at the bus station with a mule-wagon I was horrified. "You live way out in the country?" I asked after she hugged and kissed me for two minutes and told me how wide my hips had gotten since the last time she had seen me.

"Yep. I'm a country girl to the bone. I ain't never lived in no city, and I ain't never goin' to," Aunt Berneice told me. I hadn't seen her since I was a child. Her hair was completely gray, and that pretty lemon-yellow face with its sparkling brown eyes and small, upturned nose I remembered was nothing more than a lot of loose skin and wrinkles. She had on a stiff flowered dress over a pair of jeans. The knee-high, thick-heeled black boots she had on looked several sizes too large. Riding next to her on the mule-wagon reminded me so much of the many times Muh'Dear and Daddy and I had hitched rides in Florida with people driving mule-wagons. "How many kids you got by now?"

"Oh, I'm not married yet," I said, shaking my head. After finding out what Levi had done to me, I felt sorry for the woman who had married him. It could have been me.

"I didn't ask you that. You ain't got to be married to have no kids. If I hadn't fell out a tree and ruined myself when I was a girl, I'd have me at least a dozen by now. Giddy-up, mule!" Aunt Berneice yanked the reins but the mule ignored her and kept lumbering along at the same pace.

It took more than an hour for us to reach my aunt's small, red-shingled house off the side of a dirt road. The inside of her house was better than I had expected. A lot of nice but cheap furniture had been strategically placed throughout the small rooms, and the smell of freshly baked bread filled the air. A thick-bodied man with a bald head and a long sad face was lying on the living-room couch snoring. Aunt Berneice led me past the man into a side room, where I left my suitcase and coat on the small, neatly made bed I was assigned to. "The bathroom is on the other side of the kitchen," she told me, leading me back to the living room. "Get up, Harry James. My niece is here!" Aunt Berneice slapped the man across the top of his head. He let out a sharp, loud yip and sat up real fast.

"Hello," I said.

First he sucked in his breath and swallowed hard. Then he grabbed a Maxwell House coffee can off the floor he was using as a spittoon and coughed spit into it. He leaped up and shook my hand. "How you doin', how you doin'?" He grinned. His thick paw was sweaty and almost covered with hair. "So you the smart young'n I done heard so much about? I hope you stay for a few weeks. We gwine to slaughter two hogs next month." He grinned again, snapping his suspenders. He had on a pair of jeans with patches on both knees and a blue-flannel shirt. There was a pipe sticking out of his shirt pocket.

"I'm sorry. I'm only staying a couple of days," I apologized. I heard my aunt gasp. I turned to her with a weak smile. "I have to get back to my job. We've been real busy lately."

"Maybe you can come back for Christmas," Harry James suggested. "We gwine to put up a live tree and everything. I'm gwine to let you chop one down on Buddy Spool's property."

"When you get tired of that Erie, you oughta move up here so you can keep me and Harry James company since we ain't got no kids," Aunt Berneice mouthed, rubbing her husband's shoulder and drooling at him like he was Mr. Universe.

"I'll think about it," I lied. I was ready to turn around and go back to the bus station on foot. It was time to leave Erie, but I didn't want to move to New Jersey. By leaving Richland I had found what I was looking for in Erie, the real me. I was strong, independent, and no matter what I looked like, I was a beautiful person. The ghost of Mr. Boatwright would follow me no matter where I went even if I moved back to Richland. So that's what I was going to do.

The problems that had sent me running to New Jersey kept me up most of that first night in Aunt Berneice's house. When I got up the next morning Harry James and Aunt Berneice had dressed and eaten breakfast. Harry James was stretched out on the couch. His spit can was on the floor in front of him, and he was already snoring by 9 A.M. Aunt Berneice fixed me a plate of grits and sausages and sat across from me at the table and watched me eat.

"Tell me all about that Erie," she insisted. Between swallows, I gave her a vague picture of my life in Erie. She didn't seem at all impressed with my job and the nice apartment I described, but she smiled when I told her about Levi. I only told her about our dinners, nights out, and how we spent our Sundays in church. "If he was all that, how come you let him go?" Aunt Berneice leaned across the table and shook her finger in my face. "Men like that hard to come by. I never thought I'd find a man like Harry James."

"He . . . he got a job offer in Texas, and I didn't want to go," I lied.

Aunt Berneice shook her head and looked at me with pity. "Texas. That's where your daddy run off to that time."

I lost my appetite. It had been years since Muh'Dear mentioned my daddy, but I thought about him almost every day. I still missed him. I looked off sadly, chewing slowly and blinking my eyes hard so I wouldn't cry. "I hope he's happy in Texas," I muttered. I truly meant it. No matter where my wayward daddy was, I hoped that he was having a good life.

"Oh he ain't in Texas no more," Aunt Berneice informed me. She got up to get a cup of coffee.

"Do you know where he is?" I asked, following her as she moved around the kitchen to get sugar and cream.

"He back in Florida with them half-breed kids that white woman left him with," she said, returning to her seat.

"You've talked to him?"

"I talk to Frank all the time. He called to wish me happy birthday last week."

"Where's the white woman?" I said, clearing my throat and blinking hard. My aunt didn't see the tears in my eyes.

"Only God knows. Her runnin' off desertin' them kids the way she did broke Frank down to a frazzle." Aunt Berneice drank from her cup and shook her head at the same time.

"Now he knows how Muh'Dear and I felt when he left us," I said nastily.

My aunt set her cup down and gave me a look of pity. "I wish you could see him now. He the most repentant man alive. That savage South can be such a jungle for Black folks, especially them that speak they mind like Frank. That woman lured him away with her daddy's money and a promise of a better life. I always said he was gwine to pay in his heart for what he done to y'all. He come draggin' back to Florida lookin' for y'all and started buggin' me day and night tryin' to get me to give him y'all's phone number and address. Your mama told me she'd break my neck if I did. She don't never want to see him again. When he got a job at a sawmill, I kept them young'ns for him for free until he got on his feet and could afford a baby-sitter."

"How many kids?"

"Well there's that Lillimae, the oldest. She twenty-three and got two boys of her own. There's that Sondra." Aunt Berneice paused and scratched her head. "Sondra . . . she around twenty I think. Then there's that boy Amos. He oughta be outta high school by now."

I looked at what was left on my plate. "Do they know about me?" I asked quietly, still looking at my plate, stirring the grits around with my fork.

"Sure they do. I sent 'em pictures. Them girls look just like you." Aunt Berneice laughed. "And is just as fat!"

"Does Muh'Dear know any of this?" I croaked. I was so over-whelmed I experienced a hot flash knowing *I did have a family.*

"Naw." Aunt Berneice shook her head hard and fast. "She don't allow me to mention nothin' about Frank even though I told her God was goin' to chastise Frank for runnin' off and God did by not lettin' him find y'all. How come you stopped eatin'?"

"I'm not as hungry as I thought I was," I mumbled, pushing the plate away.

"I like Frank even after what he done to y'all. Like I said, he repented. When I was between husbands and was tryin' to get well from knee surgery him and them kids saw after me. He such a determined man, always have been." A dreamy-eyed look appeared on my aunt's face. "The way he marched with all them civil rights people back in the sixties was righteous. He even went to Alabama to show support when the Klan bombed that church and killed them little girls." Aunt Berneice wiped a tear from her eye.

"In Birmingham?" I asked.

"Bombin'ham is what we called it then. His only regret was he never got to meet Dr. King or Medgar Evers or none of the rest of the ones doin' all the important protestin'. His brother St. Louis, him and his wife and them six young'ns they got livin' in Florida right outside Miami too, now."

More tears welled up in my eyes. I had a real uncle and real cousins.

"I never met any of Daddy's people. At least I don't remember," I managed.

"Well St. Louis used to come around when you was one, two years old. Then he signed up with the military. Y'all was gone when he got out. It's a shame how families lose touch. Me and your mama, we ain't got nobody left now but a cousin that went to Canada before you was born. Last letter I got from him, he was talkin' about movin' back to Florida when he retire this year."

"I didn't think I had any other family," I said sadly, looking my aunt in her crinkled eyes.

"Well you do. Hmmm. Look like it might rain," Aunt Berneice said, looking out the window at the gray sky. "I better go get them clothes off the line."

"Do you want me to help?" I offered, rising.

"Naw, you finish your breakfast. Men like a little meat on they women." She grinned and winked. I was glad that she had declined my offer to help take the clothes off the line. Being alone for a few moments gave me time to think about what I had just learned.

My daddy was still alive and had been trying to get in touch with me. I had siblings who wanted to meet me. For years I had felt like I had no history and a family tree that was almost naked. My world had started with Muh'Dear and my daddy and ended with me. I didn't think that now.

Behind my aunt's house, separated by a field, were two other shacks occupied by friends of hers. One man was off visiting relatives in Newark. The other one, Clyde Proctor, a stout, slovenly, divorced man in his late thirties, had dinner with us later the day after my arrival. "You ever seen New York City?" Clyde asked with his mouth full of pinto beans and ham hocks.

"No," I said, shaking my head.

"Clyde goes to New York to party all the time," Harry James told me. "He'll carry you over there before you leave."

"She'll love that place in Harlem where they sell them candied ribs," Aunt Berneice insisted, spooning more beans onto my plate. "You gwine to New York this evenin', ain't you, Clyde?"

"Uh-huh," Clyde replied, blinking at me. "I'll pick you up at six o'clock. We'll have to stay over there all night 'cause my truck ain't got but one headlight, and I can't drive it after dark. And dress warm, my truck ain't got no heater neither."

"I can't go. I'm only going to be here another day or so," I said quickly. I really wanted to spend that time with my aunt. I finished dinner as fast as I could, then I ran. I left my aunt, her husband, and Clyde at the kitchen table enjoying peach cobbler, and I went to bed and tried to imagine what my sisters, my brother, and the rest of my relatives were like.

Before she went to bed, Aunt Berneice came into the bedroom, flipped on the light, and sat at the foot of the bed. "You sleep?" She had on a stocking cap that almost covered her face.

"No, Ma'am," I said, sitting up.

"Ain't Clyde somethin'?" She grinned and winked.

"He sure is," I agreed.

"He likes you. He done had a lot of experience with women, so he gwine to make some woman a good husband. He been married four times. You sure you don't want to stay and get to know him? He just itchin' to take you out. You oughta see him in his blue suit."

"I don't think so," I said, shaking my head hard and long.

I had no interest in seeing any more of Englishtown, what little there was. Other than going to a nearby farmers' market with Harry James, I didn't leave my aunt's house during the rest of my short visit. I spent most of that time in the bedroom with bogus cramps to avoid Clyde. He spent more time in Aunt Berneice's house than he spent in his own.

Three days after my arrival, Harry James accompanied Aunt Berneice when she took me back to the bus station on the mule-wagon. Clyde had offered to drive me in his flatbed truck, but luckily the bus was scheduled to leave after dark.

I called Rhoda as soon as I got back to Erie, but she was not in. I thought about calling Muh'Dear, but feeling the way I was about the news Aunt Berneice had passed on to me, I didn't. I knew if I mentioned Daddy, she would say something negative about him, and I didn't want to hear it. I smiled sadly, wondering if he or my siblings would ever take it upon themselves to come to Ohio and try to find me. I wasn't ready to talk to Viola. I had decided I wasn't going to tell her about Levi getting married. I was hoping that by the time she found out, I'd be back in Ohio. I still had the rest of the week and the weekend before returning to work. But once I was certain that I was returning to Richland, I called Erie Manufacturing and resigned over the phone. I spent the next day hauling things from my apartment by cabs and buses to the Salvation Army. I called Muh'Dear that evening and told her I was coming home.

"I been prayin' to hear that," she sobbed. "I ain't seen you in so many years, I honest to God didn't think I'd ever see you again. I can't wait to tell Mr. King and Judge Lawson. Scary Mary told me she had a premonition you was movin' back here, and I called her a liar."

"Well I'm coming home. And I'm coming home to stay," I said eagerly.

Rhoda was home when I called her after my conversation with Muh'Dear. "When are you leavin'," she asked when I told her. She didn't sound the least bit surprised.

"As soon as I can get my stuff packed up."

"Are you serious?"

"I have never been more serious about anything in my life. After I get home, you can come up and we can try and figure out what to do about that pregnant white girl. Or maybe I'll come down to Florida before I get a job. We'll think of something." I tried to sound cheerful, but the seriousness and sadness in Rhoda's voice prevented that. I didn't have a clue as to what I could do to help Rhoda and her brother. Part of the excitement I was feeling was because I was returning to the home where I belonged, but my real excitement was knowing I had a big family after all. I planned to tell Rhoda and Muh'Dear when I felt the time was right. "When things settle, this white-girl mess I mean, maybe you and I can take Julian and go to Disneyworld. We can even bring old Pee Wee along."

"Uh-huh. Let's do that. I got to go now."

Then I called Pee Wee. He was glad to hear that I was returning to Richland to live. "See there. I told everybody The Prodigal Daughter would come back home." Pee Wee laughed. His words made me tingle with more excitement. Richland was no paradise, but I'd come to realize that paradise was just a state of mind.

I had a lease, but my landlord agreed to let me out of it when I told him a fantastic lie about a sick mother. That and the fact that I gave him most of the things I couldn't take with me, like my TV, my clock radio, and especially my entertainment center.

Viola couldn't have been happier for me. "You been like a daughter and I'll miss you, child. But you do what you got to do," she sobbed over the phone. "Me and Willie gwine to take you out to dinner before you leave for one last binge."

After I confirmed my travel arrangements, I called Rhoda. It had been a week since my last conversation with her.

"I'll be home in three days," I said, unable to hide my excitement. I had decided that I would not bring up her brother and the white girl unless she did. "I hope you can come up for a visit soon." We chatted casually for about five minutes. Just as I was about to conclude the conversation, she mumbled something I did not understand. "What did you just say?"

"I said, April's dead," she answered, sounding totally detached.

I had a difficult time forming words and getting them out. First, my mouth opened and closed twice and my throat tightened. "Oh no. What happened?" My heart started pounding so hard, I had to sit on my bed and rub my chest.

"You know how careless kids are. She was takin' a bath with her radio sittin' on the edge of the bathtub. Well, it fell in and . . . she got electrocuted. I saw it happen in a TV movie once."

"Yeah, I saw that Valerie Harper movie on Channel Four, too." There was nothing but silence for the next few moments. I cleared my throat.

"That poor little girl. Her mother must be frantic!"

"She is. I'm prayin' for her left and right."

"I will too," I said. "People rarely die in freak accidents like that. Didn't she know better?"

"I guess not. But . . . um . . . freak accidents happen all the time. My cousin Lester choked to death on a pork chop bone. Did I ever tell you about that?"

"No, you didn't, Rhoda. Well . . . what's going to happen now?" I asked.

"Um . . . the funeral's day after tomorrow."

"What about Jock? What about the baby she was carrying? Did anybody else know about it?"

"Um . . . no . . . uh . . . not that I know of."

Rhoda was stumbling over her words more than she usually did when excited or disturbed. With all her family problems it was no wonder. I pitied the poor thing, but as resilient as Rhoda was, I knew she would bounce back in record time. She always did.

"Oh shit. I'm sorry to hear that the girl got herself killed, but . . . maybe it's for the best. I mean, with her threatening to cause a real big stink about Jock getting her pregnant and all. Maybe this happened for a reason. Can you imagine if she had told her daddy about her and Jock and the baby? I mean so many lives would have been ruined."

"All of us would have been destroyed," Rhoda said in a low voice.

"Muh'Dear tells me all the time God don't like ugly. I guess by God's definition, April crossed that line just by making those ominous threats," I insisted.

"Well . . . that's God for you. Reverend Upshaw kept preachin' about the *mysterious* ways God works in . . ."

"Yeah, he sure did. Every Sunday. Are you going to go to the funeral?"

"Of course! She attended my baby's funeral. Her family wants me there, and they want me to sit with them. When I took a pie over to them, her daddy, Mr. Grand Dragon Klansman himself, even thanked me for all the time I'd let the girl hang around over here. He said I'd kept her from gettin' in trouble like his other kids did. He gave me a bear hug and told me to my face I was a 'do-right' gal, meanin' I was a good nigger."

"Some Klansman," I said thoughtfully. "Hugging a Black woman must have been a first for him."

"Tell me about it. He had the nerve to kiss me on the jaw! Listen— I got to get on over there now and help 'em pick out a dress for her to . . . you know . . . be buried in. Uh, I guess I won't get a chance to talk to you until after you get back to Richland."

"Yeah. Listen, call me as soon as you can at my mama's house. I'm sure we'll all feel a whole lot better by then. You take care of yourself." On one hand I was truly sorry about April's death, but on the other, I felt strangely relieved. "Rhoda, I think everything's going to be all right," I said gently. "For both of us," I added.

"It will be now," she said firmly. For a reason unknown to me, after we hung up I held the phone in my hand and just stared at it for a few moments, going over everything Rhoda had just told me.

CHAPTER 53

After being gone for over ten years, I returned to Richland on Thanksgiving Day, in 1978, with a suitcase in one hand and my purse in the other. In my purse was a cashier's check for almost two thousand dollars, the rest of the money from Mr. Boatwright's insurance. I took a cab from the bus station to the house on Reed Street. The neighborhood had not changed much. A few of the houses had been painted, and different cars sat in some of the driveways, but other than that, things looked pretty much the same.

I found Muh'Dear, Pee Wee, Scary Mary, Caleb, and old Judge Lawson sitting in our living room waiting for me. The judge was in a wheelchair. After the usual hugs and kisses, I fell onto the couch next to Muh'Dear, and she drapped her arm around my shoulder. I was surprised that she had not told me she had bought all new furniture. For the first time, everything in our living room matched, and the house smelled good. Not like mean greens and pork and mold, but like the fresh outdoors. There were even large healthy-looking plants all over the place.

Everybody looked the way I had expected them to—older, heavier, wrinkled, and gray-haired. Judge Lawson looked like he belonged in a mummy's tomb. He was still lucid, but the life was gone from his eyes. He had lost all of his hair, and his whole body shook when he talked. Scary Mary still had on a wild reddish wig and too much makeup, and Caleb was still wearing his plaid shirts and stiff, cheap pants. Pee Wee even had a few strands of gray hair. I did, too, for that matter. There was a time when I didn't think I would live to see the age of thirty. Now I was closer to it than I cared to admit.

In spite of a cold coming on, I felt good. It was good to be home. An old ugly coat rack that used to sit by the front door was gone. I removed my jacket and placed it on the back of the chair Pee Wee was sitting in.

It made me a little uneasy being in the same room with Pee Wee after what we had done when he had visited me in Erie. I would never look at sex the same way again as long as I lived. I didn't know if that was good or bad. I was ashamed to admit to myself that I wouldn't mind doing it with him again. I still couldn't get over how handsome he had turned out. With all the man-eating women in Richland, I was truly surprised that somebody else had not snatched him up.

"Where is Rhoda's white uncle?" I asked. "Is he still in jail?"

"Last we heard he was. What a mess he caused owing Antonosanti money, then refusin' to pay it back. Brother Nelson's relationship with Antonosanti done got real shaky on account of Johnny. Smart as that undertaker is, he shoulda knowed better than to let that Johnny get too close to his best friend. Now he got to mop up Johnny's mess if he want to stay friends with Antonosanti and his bunch. Iffen it was me, I'd beat Johnny like he stole somethin'," Scary Mary offered, waving her beer can in my direction. "It sure enough is good to have you back home. I'm so glad Jesus sent you back here to help me keep my house clean." She looked me over critically, resting her fish eyes on my face.

"I don't think I'll have time to clean your house. I'll probably go back to the phone company," I said quickly. I was through doing a lot of things. One thing I was not going to do much of anymore was hang around Scary Mary's house. And I was certainly not going to clean it for her.

"My girl got good sense," Muh'Dear bragged, screwing her lips up like a coin purse to kiss me on my neck. "She was raised right. Praise God for leadin' Brother Boatwright to me when He did to assist me."

"Uh . . . I think I should go on up to my room and start putting my things away," I said quickly, rising. One thing I wanted behind me in every way was Mr. Boatwright. I didn't want to think about him or hear people talking about him, especially if they were going on and on about what a saint he was.

"I done already made up your bed with fresh sheets, new blankets, a new spread, and some pillows fit for a king," Muh'Dear informed me.

"You want me to help you with your suitcase?" Pee Wee asked, rising from his seat. He had been unusually quiet so far. I had a feeling he was just as uneasy as I was.

"Oh no. It's not heavy. I'm all right." I smiled. For a moment our eyes met, and we held the gaze. Without warning, I experienced a hot flash. I couldn't get upstairs fast enough.

Before I entered my old room, I stopped in front of the room that Mr. Boatwright had lived and died in. A great sadness came over me. I set my suitcase on the floor and gently opened the door.

He had come and gone, and there was nothing in the room to indicate that he had ever existed. Everything that had belonged to him was gone, even his smell, which had lingered for weeks after his murder. Muh'Dear had painted the walls from beige to bright baby blue. One of the windows was opened by a few inches, and a cool breeze made the colorful new drapes flutter. I smiled when I saw a red robin sitting on the windowsill looking at me. It was quite a difference from the owl I'd seen so many years ago on the windowsill in the shack in Florida the day after Daddy left with that woman. I had to blink real hard to keep from crying as I pictured him in that green car. I swallowed and took a few deep breaths before I turned to leave.

Across the hall, I opened the door to my old room. Gone was that haunting bed where I had endured most of Mr. Boatwright's abuse. The old chifforobe, the wobbly nightstand, and the goosenecked lamp were all gone. The walls were still the warm beige I liked, and there was a new four-poster, a dresser with a mirror, and a bookcase containing the hundreds of books that I had left behind in boxes. Not sure what to do first, I sat down cautiously on the bed and just stared at the walls. I was not aware of the time, but I had been sitting for a while when Scary Mary barged in.

"Girl, we thought maybe you had come up here and fainted in the middle of the floor. Why you just settin' here lookin' like you seen a haint? We got us a Thanksgivin' feast spread out on the kitchen table fit for a king, with a turkey with meat so tender it's 'bout to slide off the bone."

"I . . . I was just resting," I explained. "I'm not that hungry now anyway."

"Uh-huh. Well from the looks of you, you don't look like you done missed no meals lately. Heh heh heh."

"Oh, I ate dinner with some friends before I left Erie." In my honor, Viola and Willie had celebrated the holiday a day early. I'd eaten as much as my excited stomach allowed me to.

The old madam strutted arrogantly across the floor and stood in front of me with her arms folded, eyeing me suspiciously. Her cheap stockings had started to roll down her legs, revealing knobby knees covered with hair.

"I couldn't wait to get you by yourself to ask you, you get into any monkey business over there in that Pennsylvania? Bein' that close to New York, I bet the money is real good over there, ain't it?"

"What do you mean?" I asked wearily.

"You know what I mean, girl." Scary Mary cocked her head to one side and glared at me out of the corner of her bloodshot eye.

"I do?"

"Don't play games with me, Annette."

I finally sighed and gave Scary Mary a look that let her know she'd won. "Well . . ." I began, not quite sure what I was going to tell her.

"Speak up, girl." Scary Mary narrowed her eyes and gave me an even harder meaner look. She lowered her voice to a whisper. "Trickin'." I could feel and smell her foul breath on my face.

"Tricking?"

"I heard about what you done with some of my customers before you left town. Every last one of 'em told me. Heh heh heh. Girl, I didn't know you had it in you." Scary Mary started patting her chest, all the while grinning in my face.

I looked at her with my lips pressed close together for a few moments, knowing and liking the fact that my behavior was aggravating her. "You didn't think I could get a bunch of men to pay me to fuck, did you?" I said boldly. I was still pissed off because she had turned me down for a job when I had approached her, and instead made me clean her house and baby-sit her idiot daughter, Mott.

"Oh, child. Looks ain't got nothin' to do with trickin'. Most men would pester a baboon if they could. To them, tail is tail."

"You didn't say that when I tried to work for you," I reminded. "You laughed at me."

"I didn't want you takin' away all my regular girls' business, then runnin' off to God knows where. You bein' all young and all then, my girls would have died. I can't afford no uproars like that in my house. I'm a businesswoman. When I heard you done it anyway, the only thing that pissed me off was you got to keep all the money and cheated me out of a cut. After all, them was *my* men friends." She paused and let out a short sharp chuckle.

I looked toward the door, then back to Scary Mary, who was still standing over me with a scowl on her face. I could hear Muh'Dear and the others talking downstairs.

"Are you still . . . in the same *business?*" I asked.

"Of course I'm still in the same business. What else would I be doin' at my age after all these years, girl?" she gasped. "Business is better than ever. Shit."

"Does my mama know . . . about me and some of your customers?" I asked gently.

"Naw." Scary Mary shrugged. "I ain't got no reason to tell her. What she don't know won't hurt her. Even if she did know, she ain't got no room to talk. Every woman I ever met done turned a trick or two. Your mama wasn't no different. Especially in the old days back in Florida. I ain't gwine to tell her on you. I ain't never told nobody on her yet. One thing about me, I can carry a secret with me to the grave. I ain't goin' to tell nobody what you done."

"You're right. What Muh'Dear doesn't know won't hurt her." I was thinking to myself how my mother would never have to endure the pain and shame of knowing what Mr. Boatwright had done to me. I'd endured enough for us both.

"I'm glad to hear that. Muh'Dear doesn't need to know any of that. Besides, it's all behind me. I want to get on with my life. Rhoda's coming up here so we can make plans to go to Disneyworld before I start looking for a job."

Scary Mary closed her eyes for a moment and shook her head. She sat down on the bed and draped her arm around my shoulder and leaned over so close to my face I got scared.

"Yep. I am so glad the good Lord sent you and Florence on back here so y'all can help me keep my house clean."

"Florence is back in Richland?" I gasped. She had stopped sending me cards and letters three years earlier.

"Oh, she moved back here years ago. She teachin' second grade blind kids," Scary Mary said, beaming. "I'm right proud of my gal."

My heart ached. I felt truly bad because I had never acknowledged any of Florence's letters or cards.

"What about that Hawkins boy she was with?"

"He gave her two little boys, may he rest in peace. Cancer of the brain, God rest his soul."

Florence had married, had children, and lost her husband, and nobody had told me.

"Nobody told me," I wailed.

"Nobody thought you cared," Scary Mary replied, tears in her eyes. "Rhoda was the only friend you ever really cared about. It took Florence a long time to realize that, but she did eventually, bless her heart. I bet that's why she finally stopped wastin' stamps writin' you letters you took your time answerin'."

"I did care about Florence. I just didn't . . . I just—"

"Like I said, Rhoda the only friend you ever cared about."

"I was so confused. Rhoda was jealous of Florence—"

"Florence back livin' with me," Scary Mary told me quickly.

"I'll call her and tell her to come over—"

"Don't bother." Scary Mary held up her hand. "She in Columbus with her fiancé, one of Reverend Snipes's boys, and some of his relations for the holiday. She won't be back 'til next week."

"Tell her I said 'hi' if she calls before she comes home." I smiled. I suddenly felt warm all over.

"And how is that poor little pretty little Rhoda now?" Scary Mary sniffed, blinking her bloodshot eyes rapidly.

"Oh, she's fine. I talked to her just before I left Erie," I smiled.

"The poor little thing. One brother got killed, the other brother crazy as a betsy bug, and now this latest mess, findin' that little white girl the way she did right in her own house."

For a moment I thought that I had just heard bells. I was wrong. It was just Scary Mary's words ringing in my ears.

I jerked my head around so fast to look Scary Mary in the eyes I could hear the bones popping in my neck. I looked at her more seriously than I had in years and mouthed, "In Rhoda's house? April died in Rhoda's house?"

"Yeah. Didn't you know that? Rhoda is the one that found her. She didn't tell you? I hope they don't drink up all that beer before I get back downstairs," Scary Mary said, glancing toward the door.

"No, she didn't tell me that part. I thought April died in her mother's house."

"Naw. She died in Rhoda's house. She had all but moved in with Rhoda and that Jamaican. Every time I seen Rhoda's daddy he was gwine on and on about how every time he called Rhoda's house or went down there, that little white girl was in the mix. She was like one of the family, which is quite a feat considerin' her menfolks is in the Klan. I guess that just goes to show you, ain't nobody all bad. Rhoda even helped piece the funeral together and even had the nerve to get up in church and say a few words in front of all them hateful crackers, her daddy told us." Scary Mary stood up to leave, stretching her flabby arms high above her head. "Come on back downstairs and tell us some more about Erie, girl." I almost fell getting up from the bed. Scary Mary gave me a strange searching look. "What's wrong with you?"

"Nothing. Nothing." What I was thinking was unbelievable. But in my heart I knew it was true. Rhoda had killed April.

CHAPTER 54

I spent another hour with everybody after they had eaten Thanksgiving dinner. I thanked God when they finally started to leave. Pee Wee and Caleb left first to drive Judge Lawson home.

"With so many people not havin' to work day after Thanksgivin' we'll be busy, so we got to get in the bed," Pee Wee explained. "I'll stop by later in the evenin' after work tomorrow, Annette."

"Sister Goode, that sure enough was a world-beatin' meal," Caleb said, grinning and smacking his lips. Muh'Dear walked them to the door and patted both backs as they went out the door, with Pee Wee pushing a snoozing Judge Lawson's wheelchair.

"I guess I better get my old bones on home and rest 'em. Tomorrow is a busy day for me, too." Scary Mary winked at me. I helped her put on her black woolen coat and walked her to the door. There was a cab waiting in front of the house for her.

It was Muh'Dear's idea for me to get to bed. "Suddenly you look like you got the weight of the world on your shoulders. Did Scary Mary say somethin' up there to upset you? Was she braggin' about how Florence doin' so well with a man and kids and you ain't? Did she try to borrow money from you?"

"No, Ma'am. I'm just tired, that's all. 'Night, Muh'Dear."

How I did it I don't know. I climbed into my bed and slept like a baby. I guess I was just that tired. When I woke up the next morning, I tried to make myself believe I had dreamed my conversation with

Scary Mary about Rhoda and the pregnant white girl. I had not dreamed it. I knew that Rhoda had killed again, but I had to hear it from her.

My mind was a ball of confusion, and I stayed in my room for as long as I could. By the time I got downstairs to the living room, around nine, Mr. King had arrived. Like Pee Wee, time had been fairly good to him. He was now more handsome than ever. The deep lines around his sparkling eyes gave him a distinguished look, not a tired, used-up look like Scary Mary's lines or Muh'Dear's. His hair was gray, but thick and healthy-looking.

He gave me a big hug and led me to the couch, where I sat down next to him. "Just look at you. I told your mama, you can work for me anytime you want to. We all one big happy family," he hollered, winking at Muh'Dear. "As attractive and sophisticated as you is, you'll be a good addition to the Buttercup!" Mr. King exclaimed.

Muh'Dear nodded and smiled harder than ever before.

Around ten, Scary Mary returned hugging a bag of beers, straining like the bag weighed more than she did.

The chatter became one long rambling mess. In a way I was glad. They were doing so much talking, I could not have gotten a word in edgewise even if I had wanted to. There was too much on my mind for me to think clearly, let alone speak clearly. I almost jumped out of my skin when Rhoda's name came up.

"Oh she called early this mornin'. She said to tell you she'll be here sometime tomorrow. She can't wait to see you," Muh'Dear told me.

"I hope she bring me somethin' like Pee Wee and Florence done. I treasure my fruit basket from Vietnam and my lamp from Toledo," Scary Mary whined. "Annette, I guess you ain't thought about no souvenirs before you left Erie, huh?"

"I'm sorry. I was in such a hurry to get packed and out of that city, I didn't think about bringing anybody any souvenirs," I explained.

Mr. King had also brought a big bag of beer with him, and everybody was drinking. I managed to eat a light breakfast and watch a little television on a small set Muh'Dear had installed on the kitchen counter, but I could not stop thinking about Rhoda. I didn't know how I was going to approach her about the white girl. But for my own sanity and peace of mind, I had to confront her. If what I believed was true, and if for some strange reason Rhoda got caught, she might break down and confess the Boatwright murder, which would surely include my involvement. I felt sick. I desperately wanted to see her to find out for sure. I prayed that she would tell me and convince me that April had died accidentally.

Scary Mary went with Muh'Dear and Mr. King to his restaurant for dinner. They had all tried to talk me into going with them, but there was way too much on my mind. Once I was totally alone in the house I felt a strange sense of sadness. The last thing I wanted to do was cause a big stink with my best girlfriend. The timing was so wrong. This was supposed to be a time for rejoicing and reunions.

I was thankful to find a few leftover beers in the refrigerator. I drank every one in sight. The mild buzz made it easy for me to go to my room and take a nap. With so much on my mind, it didn't bother me at all being in the very room where I had cried so many tears.

I don't know exactly what time Rhoda blew into town the next day. She came over to our house around 6 P.M. loaded down with gifts. She gave Muh'Dear and Scary Mary handmade earrings she had picked up in Jamaica, and she gave Mr. King and Caleb straw hats. She gave Pee Wee a Bob Marley T-shirt and me a big pan of her homemade candy.

"You look beautiful," she told me. She hugged me so hard, my chest hurt.

"Thanks for the candy," I rasped. I lifted the foil to show it off to everybody, then I set the pan on the coffee table without offering any or even biting a plug off of it myself. Rhoda followed me to the sofa, chattering away about her great life in Florida. She had everybody spellbound. Muh'Dear was especially mesmerized listening to Rhoda go on and on about her frequent trips to the mystical Bahamas. Muh'Dear could have used part of Mr. Boatwright's insurance to enjoy a trip to the Bahamas long before now. But every time I had mentioned her doing just that, she gave me some vague story about how she was waiting on the "right time" to go. While everybody else in the room had aged to some degree, Rhoda had not. She looked the way she had looked at eighteen. In fact, she looked even younger. There was a noticeable glow about her face. It wasn't long before I found out why. She was pregnant again.

"Lord, I hope my girl slow down someday and get her a husband and some kids," Muh'Dear lamented. "Like Rhoda done. And poor, blind Florence 'bout to marry husband number two . . ."

"Uh—Rhoda. Let's go to my room so we can talk." I wasn't ready to confront her. I had planned to drink a few beers first. But I couldn't stand to sit any longer the way the conversation was going.

"Oh let the girl alone. I want to hear more about the Bahamas," Muh'Dear insisted, dismissing me with her hand. I had to endure three more hours of nonstop chatter, mostly praising Rhoda. Just when I thought I was going to scream, everybody but Rhoda decided it was time to go home. It was past midnight.

"Me, I better get my tail on to bed or I won't be good for nothin' in the mornin'," Muh'Dear admitted. She had to work the next day.

Finally, it was just me and Rhoda. I waited until I heard Muh'Dear's bedroom door shut before I looked at Rhoda. She was on the couch with her legs crossed. The rest of her body was sprawled across the arm of the couch. Anybody who didn't know any better would think that Rhoda lived in the house. She just seemed to dominate every place she went. I was standing on weak legs, feeling like shit. I was so uncomfortable and anxious it was hard for me to remain still.

"OK. What's wrong with you?" she started.

"What do you mean?" Now I was folding and unfolding my arms and shifting my weight from one foot to the other.

"I know you better than anybody in the whole wide world. Even your mama don't know you like I know you. You've been actin' funny ever since I walked in that door." She uncrossed her legs and gave me a hard look before continuing. "Did Pee Wee offend you?"

"No," I said quietly. I moved over to the sofa and sat as close to Rhoda as I dared. Her eyes followed every move I made. "Uh . . . why didn't you tell me that April died in your house?"

She gave me a surprised look, then blinked hard a few times before responding. "What difference does it make to you where she died?"

"It makes a big difference to me. Like you just said, you know me better than anybody else in the world; I think I can say the same thing about you. You didn't even mention that part of the story. I had to hear it from Scary Mary."

"I didn't mention it because I didn't think it was important." Rhoda waved her arms dramatically and leaned back as if to see my face better. I refused to take my eyes off her.

"Why was she taking a bath in your house? Did you talk her into drinking a bottle of whiskey like you did me?"

"She wanted the baby, I told you," Rhoda reminded me, blinking hard again. "She took baths at my house all the time."

"Her death was real convenient for you and all that mess going on between the girl and your brother, huh?"

Rhoda sucked in her breath and shrugged. She opened her mouth but didn't speak. Then she just shrugged again and gave me a slow nod.

"I know you did it, so go on and admit it."

The room was deathly silent for a moment. "I had to," she whispered, with a pleading look in her eyes. "What else could I do?"

"I knew it! I knew it!" I hissed, shaking my head, staring at her as hard as she was staring at me.

"Shhhhh! You want your mama to hear?" Rhoda slid over so close to me our knees touched. She seemed surprised and hurt when I moved away from her.

"I don't believe it. I don't believe you did this *again!*"

"Then don't believe it," she snapped. She stood up and stretched long and hard, rolling her eyes making sure I knew that I had annoyed her. "I didn't come here to be accused—"

"Accused? You just admitted it." I jumped up, my face close to hers.

She glanced at her watch, then told me, "It's late and I'm tired. This is not the time to be discussin' . . . this subject. We'll finish this conversation in the mornin' after you've had time to sleep on it."

"No. We are going to finish this conversation right here and now."

"What more is there to say? I did it, I said I did it, you know I did it. Now that's that. Nobody but you and I have to know just like . . . with Buttwright. We've put him behind us, let's do the same with April." She squeezed my shoulder for a moment, then started buttoning her sweater. "After all . . . I was provoked."

"Let's go talk in my room," I said, grabbing her arm. She looked down at my thick hand holding on to her thin arm with an expression on her face that normally would have frightened me. But I was no longer afraid of her. Even though it was fairly late, I could hear people outside on the street laughing and talking and noisy cars whizzing by. My mood was black and anxious. I knew ahead of time that by the end of this conversation, my life would be altered again.

"All right. Let's get this over with so I can go home and get some sleep." Rhoda followed me to my room in silence.

Once we entered my room, she made herself comfortable on my bed. I stood by the front window rehearsing what I wanted to say to her in my mind.

"All right," she announced. "Let's get this over with." She crossed her legs and started moving her foot, making circles in the air.

"Why did you kill that girl, Rhoda?"

"What do you mean? You of all people know why I had to do it."

"Just like Mr. Boatwright, huh?"

"You could say that," she agreed.

"You know if you ever get caught, you'll probably spend the rest of your life in prison. Was it worth all that? I know you're lucky and you're intelligent. But sooner or later your luck and intelligence are not going to be enough, Rhoda."

"I'll worry about that when it happens," she said in a shaky voice. She then uncrossed her legs and started tapping her toe on the floor impatiently.

"You've killed two people, and you're not worried?" I asked incredulously.

"Four," she said quickly, quietly, looking toward the door.

A gasp caught in my throat, and my head dropped forward and low.

"What did you say?" I heard myself ask.

"You heard me. I said 'four.' " Her voice sounded like an echo.

"Who else?" I asked, looking deep into her eyes, searching for something. I just didn't know what.

"Remember the last time my daddy put the Ford in the body shop to have another dent removed?"

"You told me you knocked over a mailbox," I said guardedly. I had to turn away. I could not face her and absorb her confession at the same time. I spoke with my eyes looking at the floor. "Go on."

"Remember that cop that killed my brother?"

"The one they said . . . died in a hit-and-run . . . accident." Now I was looking at the side of her face. Like me, her whole body was shaking. "Who was the other one?" I asked, almost choking on my words.

"Remember when Granny Goose fell down the steps and broke her neck? I . . . I . . ." Rhoda's eyes were on the floor.

"Your own grandmother?" I spoke, looking toward the wall.

"You don't know what a burden she was and how much she was sufferin'. I loved her, but she didn't know me from Moses anymore. I did it for her."

"No!" I whirled around to face her. There was the strangest expression on her face. Her eyes were stretched open wide, and her lips were pressed together in a hard, thin line. Her bright red lipstick gave her a devilish appearance. Her jaw was twitching. "Your own grandmother? I can't believe my ears—"

We stood there for the longest moment just looking in one another's eyes.

"Do you know I still have nightmares and I'm still afraid somebody will find out you smothered Mr. Boatwright and that I knew it. Now all this . . . I . . . I . . . don't . . ." I paused, unable to go on for a moment. I had to fight hard to prevent myself from having a panic attack. "Rhoda," I said firmly. I sucked in my breath and stood up straight. "Rhoda, how can I go on being friends with you now?" My words had a chilling effect on me. These were words I never dreamed I would hear myself saying. But never in my wildest imagination would I have expected to hear what Rhoda had just told me. At first I wanted to call her a liar. I wanted to accuse her of trying to get my goat. But I had known her too long, and I knew her well enough to know that she was not one to make such claims lightly. She stood up, not taking her eyes off me.

"Do you realize what you're sayin', Annette? Is this the way you want to end our relationship after all these years?"

"Do you realize what you've done to me? You've burdened me with information that could destroy me," I said levelly.

"I thought you told me I could tell you anythin'," she snapped.

"Not about one murder after another. What about all that talk about God? What about your children? What about me and this additional pain?"

"Look, you're the one who brought up the subject. I didn't have to tell you about April—"

"But I knew you killed her."

"Well you wanted to hear it and I . . . told you. It's been hard carryin' all this on my shoulders alone. Just like that mess I got myself into by gettin' pregnant by my husband's best friend. It helped ease my mind when I finally told you about him and our affair. I feel better now tellin' you about . . . that cop and Granny Goose."

"Well, I don't feel better knowing all that. If there's anything else, from the past or in the future, keep it to yourself."

"That means I can't talk to you anymore?" Rhoda leaned back and looked me over critically.

"Is that the way you see it?" I asked.

"That's the way it's goin' to be. After tonight, we won't talk or see one another again. Ever," she told me.

"Maybe that's the best thing for us to do now. We've outgrown each other," I asserted, with hot tears streaming down the sides of my face.

"Tell me, Annette. After you've had time to think about this conversation and all we've invested in this friendship and the future we won't have together, will you be sorry then?" she asked. There were tears on her face, too.

I gave Rhoda a quick, halfhearted smile and told her with all the sincerity I could come up with, "I'm sorry now." I was sorry. I never expected or wanted our friendship to end this way.

"I can let myself out." She sighed heavily, dismissing me with a wave of her hand. Without another word, Rhoda left my room for the last time. I waited until I heard her slam the front door downstairs before I allowed more tears to spill out of my burning eyes onto my face. From my front window I watched her strut down our walkway and on across the street to her parents' house. She didn't turn around to look, and I was glad she didn't. I didn't want her to see my face again, and I didn't want to see hers.

It was a few minutes later before I returned to the living room downstairs to turn off the lights and lock up. Before I did, I lifted the pan of candy she had made for me off the coffee table and took it into the kitchen, where I threw it in the trash.

CHAPTER 55

"I just seen Rhoda gettin' in a cab with her suitcase!" Muh'Dear informed me. She had come into my room before leaving for work the next morning. It was so early, it was still dark outside. I had slept well. Not a single dream had interrupted my night. I woke up feeling cleansed and free and strong. The aroma of the grits and bacon Muh'Dear had prepared for breakfast gave me a warm feeling. I couldn't wait to get up and get dressed and eat. Even though I had been baptized more than once, I had never felt what some people described as a rebirth. Until then.

"Uh, yeah. Her husband called up last night and told her to come home. Her little boy is sick," I lied. I sat up in bed. "You look nice, Muh'Dear. Is that uniform new?"

"Well, when is she comin' back? I thought she was goin' to spend some time with you celebratin' your return."

"Uh . . . I'll talk to her and find out when she's coming back. Did you make some coffee?"

"Uh-huh. Oh! Guess what? I even made you some of that cappuccino you and Rhoda like so much. I figured you and her and Pee Wee would want some this mornin'."

"Thanks, Muh'Dear. I'll call up Pee Wee, and he can help me drink it." My mother fanned her face, complained about having to go to work, and then excused herself. I pulled my knees up to my chest and stayed that way until I heard Muh'Dear leave the house.

The first few days were the hardest. Every time our phone rang I jumped, praying that it was not Rhoda. There was nothing she could say that would change my feelings. The burden of knowing her crimes had become too much of a cross for me to bear. As I expected, everybody asked me when she was returning or when I was going to Florida to visit her. My excuses were vague. She's going to Jamaica for a while to spend some time with her husband's family, she's having marital problems and it's better if I keep my distance, I lied.

"Marital problems? Oh is Rhoda's husband foolin' around with another woman?" Muh'Dear asked with wide hungry eyes and a half smile.

"No, Ma'am."

"Well is Rhoda foolin' around with another man?"

"No, Ma'am. They're just having the usual marital problems. How to raise the kids. How to spend the money. Things like that."

"*Is that all?*"

"Yes, Ma'am."

"Damn." Muh'Dear sighed. She was visibly disappointed. I could tell she had hoped that Rhoda's marital problems were something really juicy. Something juicy enough to discuss with her gossipmonger friends. "Well, that's what she get for marryin' a foreigner. She should have married one of them Hawkins boys. They let they wives do anythin' they want." Muh'Dear paused long enough to catch her breath. "Like I told Mr. King—why you lookin' so sad, girl?" Muh'Dear felt my forehead and frowned. "I'm goin' to give you a dose of castor oil in a minute."

"I'm fine, Muh'Dear."

"Well, you sure don't look fine. Lookit all them dark circles around your eyes and look how slack your jaws is. I know constipation when I see it." The dreaded castor oil only made me sicker. I threw it all up as soon as Muh'Dear left for work.

Florence returned the following Thursday.

"I'm so glad to see you again," I told her as soon as she entered our living room. It was just me and her. "Where are your boys?"

Florence had gained about thirty pounds, and she had more gray hair than me and Pee Wee put together. She had on a pair of dark glasses and walked with a white cane.

"The boys are resting. Larry had to go back to work today," she told me. I led her to the couch, where we both sat down.

"I hear you're doing well," I told her after we hugged.

"I'm blessed. God shuts one door, but He opens another. I don't have my sight anymore, but I've still got so much to be thankful for."

Florence was completely blind, but she was still smiling.

"I'm sorry about your sight."

There was an awkward moment of silence.

"Oh, I've adjusted to it quite well. I'm getting a seeing-eye dog next week." Florence grabbed my hand and squeezed. "Did you get my letters? My cards?"

"Oh yeah . . . I kept meaning to respond. But . . ."

"It's not important. I didn't expect to hear from you."

"I'm sorry," I said, squeezing her hand. I felt truly bad.

"Oh it's nothing! You're not the first person to ignore me." She sucked in her breath. "How's Rhoda? Pee Wee told me you communicated with her regularly." There was not a hint of sarcasm in Florence's voice.

"Uh . . . I won't be communicating with her anymore."

More awkward silence. Florence nodded and let out a strange chuckle.

"That's too bad. She had a lot of influence over you."

"Yeah she did," I admitted.

"And so did that old Mr. Boatwright . . . even more so. Now that was one miserable old man! He used to talk about me like a dog. I could hear him in the kitchen talking about me every time I hung clothes on the line in the yard."

"Yeah he was a mess, that old . . . goat." I couldn't acknowledge the bad Mr. Boatwright had done without acknowledging the good. "He . . . taught me how to ride a bike and . . . he was a damn good cook," I said. "And the extra money he contributed sure did help me and Muh'Dear out a lot . . ."

"Uh . . . huh," Florence said thoughtfully, tapping her cane against the floor.

I never told her, but I was convinced she knew what Mr. Boatwright had done to me.

"That stepdaddy and those two foster fathers I told you about, they were a lot like Mr. Boatwright . . ."

"What . . . what do you mean?"

"*Nasty.* I couldn't see him, but I could sense when somebody was nasty. And he was, wasn't he?"

"Yeah . . ." I said slowly. I released Florence's hand because mine had started to shake. I jumped up from the couch. "Let's go make some tea."

As days went by, people asked me more and more about Rhoda. I finally had to tell everybody something more final. I told them that Rhoda's husband, who never liked me, pressured her into choosing: him or me. Like any good wife, she chose her man. I just prayed that nobody would approach her parents and find out any different. The undertaker and his wife were still as unapproachable as they had always been to the people around me. I had not talked to either of Rhoda's parents since my return. When I left our house, I usually left through our back door so that I would not risk running into them coming or going.

"Want to go to a boxin' match in Cleveland this Saturday?" Pee Wee invited the week before Christmas. He continued to come to the house and sit with me in the living room in the evenings and on weekends when he was not working. "It'll be my Christmas present to you."

I wanted to spend more time with Florence and her boys, but she was too busy planning her wedding. We talked on the phone every chance we got. Pee Wee and I even double-dated with her and her husband-to-be.

I hated all sports events and would rather get a whupping than sit through one, but I accepted Pee Wee's invitation. "Yes. I would like to go," I told him with a smile. It was hard to look across the street at the Nelsons' house without tears forming in my eyes. I was sorry that I didn't get a chance to tell Rhoda what Aunt Berneice had told me about my daddy and the rest of my family in Florida. I still had not told Muh'Dear or anybody else and didn't know when I would.

Pee Wee had made a lot of new friends over the last few years and they soon became my friends. My phone rang off the hook now, when before I moved to Erie, Pee Wee, Florence, and Rhoda were the only ones who ever called me. Most of Pee Wee's new friends were the same people who had tormented us both in school.

I see Lena Cundiff, my former nemesis, all the time. The first time I bumped into her at the shopping center, she ran up to me and gave me a hug and introduced me to her two sons and daughter. After we chatted for a few moments, I apologized for knocking out her four front teeth at the prom, and we both laughed about it.

"My new bridgework looks a lot better than my real teeth ever did anyway," she told me.

I was disappointed that she didn't apologize for all the torment she had caused me for so many years in school, but in my heart I knew she was sorry. I think that we all came to realize that life was too short. I missed Rhoda enormously, and I knew I would, but she and Mr. Boatwright were the two chapters in my story I would never read again.

One night, two months after my return, after Pee Wee had made love to me in my new bed, we got up and went to the front window in my bedroom and saw a big moving van in front of the Nelsons' house. Movers were hauling boxes and furniture out left and right. Nobody knew why or where Rhoda's parents, Lola, and Uncle Johnny had moved to.

A month later, we had the worst snowstorm we had had in thirty years. Some businesses and all the schools had to close. Muh'Dear was unable to leave Mr. King's house because the roads were too bad. She stayed over with him often, so her staying over this night was not unusual. Pee Wee was with me, and, for the first time, he spent the whole night. Sirens woke us up in the middle of the night, but we were too exhausted from hours of lovemaking to get up to investigate. We found out the next morning that the Nelsons' house had mysteriously burned to the ground.

"I heard that Antonosanti had somethin' to do with that fire. He was so angry with Brother Nelson for not payin' off all that money Johnny borrowed," Scary Mary told me and Pee Wee the next morning. Knee-high snow had not prevented her from leaving her house and coming over for coffee. "Another story I heard from Caleb is that Brother Nelson paid somebody to set that house ablaze so he could collect the insurance money."

We never found out what really happened, and whatever it was I didn't really want to know. To me, the fire destroying the Nelsons' house was symbolic. It was the last connection I had to Rhoda. For reasons I can't explain, one beer-filled night a week after the fire, I dialed her number in Florida. A recorded message informed me that the number had been changed and was now unlisted. Just like Mr. Boatwright, there was nothing left to indicate that she had ever existed.

I was living on the rest of Mr. Boatwright's insurance money and money I have saved up from my job in Erie, but Mr. King promised I could start working as a hostess or a waitress at the Buttercup whenever I was ready. It was a long way from the corporate environment I used to believe I wanted when I was younger.

Like Muh'Dear taught me, God'll come through when the time is right. He did for her. After so many years, Muh'Dear felt it was the "right time" for her to take her dream trip. She *finally* made it to the Bahamas, and, in a roundabout way, she got her own restaurant; Mr. King married her. He took her to the Bahamas for a two-week honeymoon.

Even though she didn't have to work anymore unless she wanted to, she continued to cook and clean for Judge Lawson because he wanted her to.

"You can rest now, Muh'Dear. You've worked long and hard enough," I told her. Just thinking about the fact that she had been breaking her back to cater to other people even before I was born reduced me to tears.

"I ain't about to go back on my word to old Judge Lawson. He been good to us, and the least I can do is stay on with him in his last days," Muh'Dear told me, adding, "I got a feelin' Judge Lawson goin to outlive all of us." She laughed.

I wanted her to retire, but I also wanted her to honor the judge's request. I don't know what would have become of us without him and people like Scary Mary, who were forever pulling us out of a hole. Mr. Boatwright's abuse was by then nothing more than a memory to me and one of several ugly secrets I'd carry with me to my grave.

I have the house on Reed Street all to myself now and Judge Lawson said I can stay in it for the rest of my life if I want to. He even encouraged me to rent out two of the three bedrooms and to keep the money for myself. But I'd had enough of boarders a long time ago with Mr. Boatwright and his mess.

I moved into the room that used to be Muh'Dear's, and I turned mine into a guestroom. I had not been inside Mr. Boatwright's old room since the day I returned from Erie and every time I passed it, I shuddered. As far as I was concerned, that room no longer existed.

A week after Muh'Dear and Mr. King returned from their honeymoon, the day after Easter, I started waiting tables at the Buttercup. In mid-December, Mr. King decided to have the inside of the restaurant painted so he closed it for two weeks. It couldn't have happened at a better time. I had a lot of Christmas shopping to do and several parties to attend. Even with all that on my plate, I constantly thought about all the things that had happened to me. Having Mr. King as my new daddy made me think about my real daddy every day and what my aunt in New Jersey had told me about him. It had been a while since my last conversation with Aunt Berneice. New Year's Day seemed like a good time to give her a call.

"Happy New Year, Aunt Berneice," I hollered.

"Girl, I'm gwine to pray that 1980 be better to you than all the rest of your years been," she cried as soon as she heard my voice.

"It will be," I assured her. "Now, give me my daddy's phone number, please."

I used to wonder what I would look like if I had been born white. Now I know.

The white woman standing on the steps of the wraparound porch of the shabby clapboard house could have been my twin. As far as I could tell, sandy-blond hair and a narrow nose were the only things she had that I didn't have. I had to repress a gasp. I had to remind myself that this woman and I shared the same amount of blood from the same man. Black blood.

Throughout my plane ride from Richland, Ohio, to Miami, where I'd originally come from, with the help of several glasses of strong wine, I had composed and rehearsed several speeches. I had no idea what the appropriate things were to say to a father who had deserted me when I was a toddler, more than thirty years ago. What I wanted to say was not what I planned to say. It would have been too much, too soon. *Good to see you again, Daddy. By the way, because of you, I had to spend ten years of my childhood living under the same roof with my rapist. But don't worry, my playmate killed him for me and we didn't get caught.* I had promised myself that I would say something simple and painless. But now my head was spinning like a loose wheel and I felt like I was losing control of my senses. I didn't know what was going to slide out of my mouth.

Confronting my daddy was going to be painful enough. But having to deal with him and a *white* woman who looked like me at the same time was going to be another story. Especially since I'd hated my looks for so many years.

I sat in the cab parked in front of the house on Mooney Street that steamy afternoon in August, looking out the window at that ghostly woman standing on her front porch, looking at me. The makeup that had taken me half an hour to apply was now melting and slowly sliding, like thick mud, down the sides of my burning face. I had licked off most of my plum-colored lipstick during the cab ride from the airport. Warm sweat had almost saturated my new silk blouse, making it stick to my flesh like a second layer of skin.

When the impatient cabdriver cleared his throat to get my attention, I paid him, tipped him ten percent, and tumbled out of the cab, snagging the knee of my L'eggs pantyhose with the corner of my suitcase.

As soon as my feet hit the ground, I looked around with great caution, because this was Liberty City, the belly of one of Miami's roughest, predominately Black areas. I had hidden all of my cash in a cloth coin purse and pinned it to my girdle, but I still clutched my shoulder bag and looked around some more. I would have been just as cautious if I'd just landed in Beverly Hills. As far as I was concerned, the world was full of sharks; no place was safe for a female on her own. Especially one who attracted as much turmoil as I did.

It appeared to be a nice enough neighborhood, despite its reputation. The lawns were neat and the few Black people I saw seemed to be going on about their business like they didn't have a care in the world. In front of the house to my left, a man in overalls was watering his grass with a hose, while a gospel singer wailed from a radio on the ground next to his feet. The man smiled and greeted me with a casual wave. I smiled and waved back.

An elderly woman, looking bitterly sad and walking with a cane, shuffled pass me. "How you doin' this afternoon, sister?" she asked me in a raspy voice, hawking a gob of brown spit on the cracked sidewalk, missing my foot by a few inches.

"I'm fine, thank you," I replied, hopping out of the way as the old woman dropped another load of spit. "Sister," I added as an afterthought, even though the old woman didn't hear me. It was a word I had to get used to now. Especially because of the *sister* with the blond hair on the porch looking in my direction.

The glare from the blazing sun made the woman on the porch squint. Then she shaded her eyes with a thick hand that displayed rings on every finger, including her thumb. She stared at me with her mouth hanging open. She seemed just as stunned as I was by our matching features. I was glad that she was the one to break the awkward silence. "Honeychile, come on up here so I can hug you! I been waitin' a long time for this day."

For a few moments, I just stood in the same spot, looking toward the porch, blinking hard to hold back my tears. Words danced around in my head, but I still didn't know which ones to release.

A limp, plaid bathrobe that looked more like a patchwork quilt covered the woman from the neck on down to her wide, dusty bare feet. It pleased me to see that blood wasn't the only thing we shared. Judging from her size, she enjoyed food as much as I did. I couldn't tell where her waistline was, but the belt to her bathrobe had been tied into a neat knot below her massive chest. Her body looked as much like an oil drum as mine did. I had been wearing a size twenty-four for the past ten years. I couldn't lose a single pound no matter what I did. To me, diets were a rip-off and exercise was too dangerous for people in my shape. An obese woman from my church had had a heart attack and died while trying to do sit-ups. Therefore, I ate everything I wanted to. I figured that since we all had to die eventually anyway, I might as well enjoy myself along the way.

I had been stout every day of my life. My mother said I'd been such a butterball of a baby, she had to diaper me with pillowcases. I was finally comfortable with being large, but it was more important that I was now comfortable with just being myself. With me, comfort and strength were one and the same. It had enabled me to do a lot of things that I had been afraid to do for years. Like tracking down the daddy I hadn't seen since I was three years old. Unlike some of the other abandoned children I knew, I had refused to write my daddy off until I got some answers. I wanted to see him again and I wanted him to see me.

At least one more time.